My Scot, My Surrender

LORDS OF ESSEX

My Scot, My Surrender

LORDS OF ESSEX

AMALIE HOWARD
&
ANGIE MORGAN

This book is a work of fiction. Names, characters, places, and incidents are the product of the author's imagination or are used fictitiously. Any resemblance to actual events, locales, or persons, living or dead, is coincidental.

Copyright © 2018 by Angie Frazier and Amalie Howard. All rights reserved, including the right to reproduce, distribute, or transmit in any form or by any means. For information regarding subsidiary rights, please contact the Publisher.

Entangled Publishing, LLC
2614 South Timberline Road
Suite 105, PMB 159
Fort Collins, CO 80525
Visit our website at www.entangledpublishing.com.

Amara is an imprint of Entangled Publishing, LLC.

Edited by Alethea Spiridon
Cover design by Erin Dameron-Hill
Cover art from Hot Damn Designs

Manufactured in the United States of America

First Edition January 2018

For our daughters.
May they always be fighters.

Chapter One

Selkirk, Scotland, 1819

It had to be a miracle.

Brandt Montgomery Pierce, connoisseur of horseflesh and stable master to one of the most venerated stables in England, stared in stunned silence at the glossy gray Scottish thoroughbred tethered in the auction paddock. *This* was the very horse he had traveled to Scotland for.

Lochland Toss was by far the finest animal Brandt had set eyes upon, and ever since he'd first seen the Scot-bred stallion, two years ago at the races in Kelso, he'd wanted him. The horse hadn't been racing and never would; he wasn't sleek or fast enough for that. No, Lochland Toss had been bred into the Duke of Dunrannoch's legendary line of horses for incomparable brawn, endurance, and extraordinary stamina.

Reverently, he reached for the aristocratic beast and, starting at the withers, ran his fingers down his velvety back to his hindquarters, feeling along his strong legs and examining his joints for any abnormalities. There were none, of course.

Dunrannoch wouldn't have brought anything less than perfection to the common lands auction. Brandt had met the Scottish laird at Kelso and had made an offer for the two-year-old on the spot. He'd been turned down that day with a firm *no*, and then twice more since. The horse wasn't for sale, he'd been told. And yet now, here it stood, in the auction ring.

It was a stroke of blind luck. Brandt had been stopping at the common lands festival only to purchase a mare for the already well-stocked Bradburne stables before traveling north to Maclaren, Dunrannoch's home, where he'd planned to make yet another offer for the horse in question. Beg, if necessary.

Rising from his crouched position, Brandt signaled the auctioneer. He'd waited long enough to make a bid on the stallion, and he'd pay whatever coin Dunrannoch wanted in order to take him off the auction block. He wanted, and needed, the stallion to begin a new, unparalleled breed. Something bred to win.

The auctioneer came over, tipping the short brim of his hat. "My lord?"

Brandt wasn't a lord, but he didn't correct the man. "What is the opening bid?"

"For *this* horse?" the man said, his eyes turning toward Lochland Toss. "Apologies, my lord, but 'tis no' up for auction."

A stone of disappointment dropped into the pit of his stomach. Bloody hell. *Not again.*

"Then what is it doing here?" he bit out.

The auctioneer cocked his head. "He's with the Maclarens, o' course. Fine animal, he is. Owner's o'er there."

Brandt followed the man's eyes and turned to view an exhibition match in a nearby paddock. Two men—one monstrous and the other a youth half his size—covered in thick padding and wearing metal helms, dueled with heavy claymores. The bigger one had to be the Maclaren in question. He would easily seat Lochland Toss, and if the steady thrashing he was giving the smaller man were any indication, he could handle him as well. Brandt admired the skill and pluck of the youth, but the outcome was not in his favor.

He revised his prediction as the youth spun and vaulted into a flying leap to bring the flat of his blade behind the man's knees. His opponent crumpled like a sack of bricks. The onlooking crowd went nearly quiet in shock. Brandt laughed. The sound drew the attention of the victor, who chose that same moment to pull off his helm. A long, inky braid tumbled from its hold, and a blazing blue gaze met his, knocking the breath from his lungs.

The fighter wasn't a young man, but a woman. A heavily scarred woman, with three parallel welts running diagonally across her face from mid-brow to right cheek. Her hair was combed away from her crown, declaring to all that she didn't give a whip what anyone thought of her ruined face. A lesser mortal would have hidden behind a fringe or a veil, but with her proud mien and broadsword lifted in triumph, she was Athena incarnate.

Brandt stared at her as the crowd began to cheer, a few people chanting something that sounded like "beast," though he couldn't be sure. With a hard twist of her lips, she turned away to collect her winnings. In that moment, she had weighed, measured, and dismissed him as nobody of consequence. He supposed she was right. He was a poor, inconsequential stable master, charged only with the welfare of the Duke of Bradburne's stables.

Though neither of those were entirely true. He also *owned* one of the finest breeding stables in England. And he wasn't poor. Far from it. He had more wealth than he knew what to do with, thanks to certain well-timed investments and the advice of his longtime friend, Archer Croft, the Duke of Bradburne.

His eyes drifted back to the clearing paddock as the crowd dispersed, opening up his view. Brandt couldn't help but take in the details of Athena's appearance, from her proud cheekbones to a hard, expressive mouth that seemed bent on ferocity. Though she'd been a head shorter than her opponent, she was nearly as tall as some of the men surrounding her, and her arms, bound in supple leather, were limber with muscle. They'd have to be strong to wield a broadsword with such confidence and ease.

She was a Highlander through and through. As hale and spirited as Lochland Toss, shifting restlessly beneath his touch. Which reminded him, he had business to conduct. Brandt gave the beautiful animal another once-over and shifted his attention to the felled Maclaren giant. Once the man had soothed his wounds and his pride, Brandt intended to make him an offer he could not refuse.

He turned back to the auctioneer and gestured toward the spotted mare he'd been looking over earlier. They'd already reached an agreement on that horse, and now, after making the arrangements for delivery to Essex, Brandt gave one last pat of appreciation to the gray stallion and headed back to where his own mount was stabled. Archer would be pleased with the mare, he knew. The beautiful horse would be a fitting gift for his wife, who loved horses almost as much as Brandt did.

Having been raised at the Duke of Bradburne's estate, and as the son of the previous stable master, he'd been surrounded by the animals all his life. They had always soothed him, giving him comfort as a boy and then as a man whenever his mind betrayed him by turning to things he'd rather not dwell upon anymore.

Like his cold-blooded Scottish mother.

Brandt loosed a shallow breath. He hadn't lived up past Hadrian's Wall since he was an infant, and he certainly had no memories of it. He had no memories of *her*, either, and if the reluctance his father, Monty, had always shown in speaking of his birth mother told Brandt anything at all, it was probably best he didn't know. Shaking off his maudlin, unwelcome thoughts, he signaled for his horse.

His mount, Ares, was brought forward quickly, and he motioned the horse toward the road when a female bellow and sounds of a scuffle reached his ears. Brandt closed his eyes and released a sigh. These Scots were always getting into barneys over something or the other. It wasn't his fight, but even he could not ignore the sound of a woman in distress.

The crowd cleared for the big horse, and what Brandt saw made him gape. Five men of varying sizes wearing yellow and brown kilts surrounded the swordswoman from earlier in the exhibition paddock. She didn't look afraid at all, despite the trickle of blood running from a shallow cut near the trio of scars that traversed one half of her face. The bloody trail, combined with the lurid marks, should have made for a daunting picture, but instead, she reminded him even more of a warrior goddess.

Utterly fearless.

"You lost fair and square, Craig," she snarled, her fists high. Brandt was struck by her proper English speech, underscored by a lilting brogue, though it was nowhere as thickly accented as some of the Scots he was used to bartering with at these festivals.

Craig, the large man she'd been fighting earlier, scowled. "'Twas no' a fight for a woman."

"Though you got beaten by one."

Her opponent's face darkened with rage as he swung out a hamlike fist, which she deftly dodged. "Ye cheated, Sorcha Maclaren!"

Brandt sat straighter in his saddle. Sorcha *Maclaren*?

"Take that back, ye goat-faced lout!" She rushed him headfirst. It was an error on her part; she was soon hidden by the crush of Craig's four friends.

Brandt couldn't fault her courage. But courage or not, one woman against five men was not a fair fight. Apparently, he was the only spectator to think so. He dismounted and pushed past the cheering mob to the edge of the circle before jumping into the fray. Plucking one man up by the scruff of the neck, Brandt tossed him to the side as the familiar rush of mad strength filled his blood. It'd been ages since he'd been in a good tussle.

Warming to the task, he sent a second body flying into the crowd and rammed his fist into the face of a third to the satisfying crunch of bone. He wasn't even breathing heavily by the time he got to the female pinned to the ground beneath the man she'd mocked, her arms banded to her sides. Struggling fiercely, she sank her teeth into his cheek, and Craig howled, wrenching back a fist aimed at her face. Brandt didn't waste a breath before delivering a heavy kick into his side, forcing the man to suck in wind and roll out of reach. He lunged to dispatch the brute properly when he was shoved from behind.

By the time he'd knocked his attacker to the ground with one punch and turned back around, the woman was on her feet, her tunic ripped during the fracas, exposing the lacy edge of her chemise. The unexpected sight of such delicate embroidery made Brandt halt for a startled second just as she executed a well-placed kick to Craig's nether regions.

"Ye're a right bastard, Craig Dunbar!" she swore as he keened loudly and crawled away from her on all fours. Clearly overcome by emotion, her brogue had eclipsed her earlier proper English speech. "Aye, ye're lucky my brothers were no' here, ye ken? Next time I see ye, I'll slit yer throat."

She turned on the crowd next, holding her torn shirt together. "As for the rest of ye, go find something else to gawp at!"

Brandt watched as most of the crowd dispersed, though some remained, as if to see what she would do next. Dusting the dirt off his jacket, he smoothed a hand through the locks of hair that had fallen into his face. He wasn't fully prepared for the moment she faced him. Arrested, Brandt's jaw slackened. Not because of her scars, but because of her eyes. Across a distance, they had blazed. At close range, the fire in them was near unbearable.

They were a startlingly deep blue, reminiscent of the Ettrick Water flowing through the village, and they held his with unswerving tenacity, her head thrown back and one hand on her hips. Seconds, or an eternity, went by. Brandt was aware of nothing beyond this woman and her bold, incisive stare. He saw intelligence glimmering in her eyes, and humor, too, as her gaze scoured his.

"You're a Maclaren," he said.

"I am," she answered.

And she'd called the other man Dunbar. Which meant he wasn't the owner of Lochland Toss. *She* was.

Brandt cleared his throat as something assessing flickered in the blue depths of her eyes. He had no time to ponder it before she released his stare and smiled, drawing his attention to her lips. Her mouth had seemed sullen from a distance, though now, it was…not. The generous curve of her bottom lip looked silky and inviting. His heart galloping slightly, Brandt's gaze focused on the blood crusting on her cheek. He lifted a hand, and she shied away, her smile fading.

"You've been hurt," he murmured.

"You're Sassenach," she said, her eyes narrowing, a different light coming into them. Calculating, almost.

"Scottish-born, though raised in Essex."

"Essex." The sound of that word on those lips made

a knot of pure lust tighten in his belly. Brandt sucked in a stiff breath, growing warm as her eyes appraised him with a practiced sweep as if he were prime horseflesh on display for auction. "Do you know the Marquess of Malvern?"

Brandt frowned at the strange, abrupt question. The marquess she spoke of was a man many people in England had heard of, mostly because of his notoriously savage wartime exploits on the Continent. A cousin to the Countess of Sutherland, he was also known for his open approval of the brutal Clearances employed by the countess and the Marquess of Stafford. Still, he was a man of some influence with allies in both England and Scotland.

"I know of him," Brandt replied carefully.

She pursed those sulky lips, drawing his attention there again. A shout that sounded vaguely like her name resonated from somewhere behind them. The lady's gaze slid to the remaining audience with something like guilt and resignation warring in her eyes. Another shout of her name echoed, this time closer.

"Someone is calling for you," he said.

"I should thank you," she whispered in a husky voice that made warmth rush to his groin. "For your help."

"You don't need to thank—"

But Brandt's words were cut off as she grasped the lapels of his jacket and hauled herself against him. The soft hints of feminine sweat and a touch of lavender invaded his nostrils before the barest pressure of her lips grazed over the corner of his mouth.

Brandt didn't think…he only reacted.

Chapter Two

She shouldn't have kissed him.

Regret was followed by a dizzying sensation at the surprising warmth of his lips. That austere mouth of his was sleeker than Sorcha expected, the spice and leather scent of him a double-edged assault. It was enough to throw her practical thoughts into disarray. And bring on a fair amount of alarm.

God above, his sheer size and strength took her breath away.

Before she could pull back, strong arms lashed around her, the corded sinews she'd admired earlier holding her flush against him. Every bold, bracingly hard inch of him.

Sorcha gasped, and the stranger took full advantage, his mouth breaching her lips for a sultry flick of his tongue. A shock of pure sensation rioted through her. Everything went soft…every muscle, every thought in her brain, every bone in her body, *everything.*

With fumbling inexperience, she mimicked his teasing stroke, licking lightly. A strangled sound echoed between them—hers, his, she didn't know—and the kiss took a dangerous turn. Growling low in his throat, the gentleman's mouth angled persuasively over hers, coaxing it to open wider before he delved deep, and heaven help her, she gave in, parting her wicked lips wide for his pleasure. Glutton that she was, she wanted more. More of the pulsations skittering over her skin. More of his clever mouth, more of his hands. More of *him*.

Sorcha was dimly aware of the murmurs from the dwindling crowd, but that had been her plan. She'd hoped to provoke gossip with the scandalous embrace. The fact that her quarry was well-appointed in expensive tailored clothing that hugged his broad frame to perfection, and the fact that he was remarkably handsome, had made her decision only slightly less deranged.

In the moments before she'd lost hold of her senses, she'd taken in the deep, reddish bronze tones of his hair. He had a square jaw, a nose that looked like it had been broken a time or two, and a stern but sensuous mouth that seemed like it smiled more than it scolded. His hazel eyes had been hypnotic, changing color like a crystal when held to the light.

The idea to kiss him had come to her like a bolt of demented lightning. He was clearly an English nobleman visiting Selkirk for the common lands festival, and once he rode off, she would likely never see him again. She'd only been desperate…desperate enough to try what she imagined any young woman in her situation would do to escape an unwanted betrothal—cause a scandal. And getting caught in the arms of another man seemed the best way to do it.

Not that she was entirely adroit at seducing strange men. The Beast of Maclaren was far better suited to swinging a sword than kissing.

She'd intended the kiss to be brief and chaste…not whatever *this* was.

Chaste would be the last word she'd have used to describe the sublime onslaught of his lips, teeth, and tongue. It made her want things she'd never dreamed of wanting... like his body, stripped of all its clothes, and his mouth on other smoldering, aching parts of her. *Diah*, Lord knew only a loose woman would have such lewd thoughts.

His mouth left hers to travel down her neck, and desire spiked, making her weak-kneed. Moaning incoherently, her hands fisted in the fine fabric of his coat as she fought to stay upright. His hands moved, one rounding over the indent of her waist, while the other skimmed over the torn fabric of her tunic. Gentle fingers brushed against the lace of her chemise and across the swell of one breast.

Pressed to an entire length of aroused male, his heated mouth and hands touching her so intimately, her dependable, sensible mind went gloriously blank. Sorcha couldn't think. Her breath, along with what was left of her brain, fizzled and died.

"What the bloody hell are ye doing, ye rotten knave?"

Slowly, Sorcha became aware of angry shouts as rough hands separated them.

"Explain yerself before I castrate ye," her brother, Finlay, yelled. "Ye've ruined our sister."

She blinked as her other brother, Evan, yanked the stranger by the arm, though, unlike the man's earlier savagery with Craig and his friends, he did not fight back. Instead, his hot stare met hers, dark and intent. The greenish-brown irises flecked with gold seemed stormier now than they had before, when they'd reflected the clear afternoon sunlight. His lips were swollen. She'd bitten and sucked them like a brazen hussy. Flushing, her gaze fell away.

"It's not what you think, Finlay," she muttered in a hoarse voice, clenching her hands. "I competed with the sword in the ring, and then Craig and his cousins started a fight when he lost, and this man beat them all—"

"I dunnae care who Craig fights," Finlay snarled. "This bounder had his bloody hands on ye...on yer *chest*. Kissing ye in the middle of the street like some doxy. Our sister, a lady of Maclaren," he said, advancing on the man. "Ye've brought dishonor to her and our clan."

"Her tunic is ripped," Evan hissed. "Ye right bastard."

Sorcha glanced down, absurdly grateful that it was the right side, and not the left, that had been exposed. Not that she wished to be exposed at all, but the left side of her body would incite quite the opposite of desire. Revulsion, in fact.

Feeling the stranger's eyes on her, she snatched the torn ends together. "He didn't rip it. Craig did, during the fight."

"He was fondling ye, ye daft lass," Finley said. "In the middle of bloody Selkirk. What will the marquess think? He'll cry off, and then where will ye be?"

Yes.

Sorcha couldn't help the tiny burst of triumph that flared inside. Perhaps success was within her grasp, after all.

"There's naught to be said for it; they'll have to be married at once," a new voice proclaimed.

To Sorcha's horror, she noticed that their cousin Gavin, the one who had spoken, and a vicar of all things, was standing behind Evan and Finlay. The look on his face was one of devout determination. Her stomach sank.

No, no, no. This was not what she intended at all. She could see her fate stretching before her like a hangman's noose...wedlock to a complete stranger.

Surely Gavin couldn't be serious?

But a new expression was overtaking Finlay's face, one she'd seen time and time again, especially when he and Evan dueled, and he was already scenting victory.

"What if the bounder's already married?" Evan asked, glaring at him. "Are ye?"

The surge of relief Sorcha felt at the notion that he could be married slipped away as the gentleman shook his head and squared his wide shoulders. With a quick shake, he shrugged out of Evan's grip and straightened his cuffs. His face was oddly serene, but it sent a frisson of dread through Sorcha.

This was a man of uncommon restraint…reminding her of the kinds of predators that sat in wait for prey to get dangerously close. He had not been flustered when he'd fought off Craig and his cousins. Even now, he did not seem agitated. His stoicism in the wake of her brother's anger worried her more than if he'd decided to rail and scream.

"No, I am not married," he said finally, and with a pointed glance at Sorcha, added, "nor do I intend to be."

Three pairs of matching gazes swiveled toward him. "Ye've ruined our sister, a lady," Finlay said again. Contrary to his tone before, now he spoke slowly and loudly as though making a proclamation to the remaining crowd, and the hint of melodrama made Sorcha frown. She'd half expected Finlay to decapitate the man in blind rage, but he suddenly seemed rapt with Gavin's sanctimonious idea of marriage. "Ye'll do right by her, ye ken?"

Christ's swinging bagpipes, was this truly happening? Sorcha felt faint.

A muscle leaped in the man's jaw. "Your sister kissed *me*."

"Ye lying sack of—" Evan looked ready to murder him with his bare hands, but he was saved from that end as the local constable approached with two burly men in tow. The situation was quickly explained, and Sorcha panicked when she saw the constable nodding in unison with her brothers and cousin, who still insisted the only solution was a wedding.

Why in the blazes was the fool agreeing? She had to do something.

"No," she said, shoving her way to the constable. "I kissed

him. It was my doing."

"Nae, Cousin," Gavin said, also a hair too loud and dramatic. "The Sassenach kens better. Ye're naught but a lass, and he's a grown man. He took undue advantage when he just as well could have pushed ye away."

"He did not take anything that wasn't willingly given," she said, flushing hard.

Her brothers scowled at her, but neither of them relented. They exchanged glances as Finlay set his jaw. "He will marry ye, and that's the end of it."

Sorcha made one last effort, her voice laced with panic. "Are the three of ye cracked? Cannae ye see he doesnae want to?"

"Perhaps some time in a cell will change his mind," Evan suggested with a dark look. The constable nodded and stepped forward.

The stranger did nothing as a pair of irons were clamped around his wrists, though she felt the weight of his inscrutable gaze the entire time until he was led away. A massive brute of a horse with a patchwork of scars along its flanks clopped along after him. No wonder the man hadn't flinched at her scars, if he kept a horse like that.

Guilt leached through her. An innocent man was in shackles because of her…one who had come to her aid in a brawl. And one who hadn't looked at her as if she were the victim of a killing gone wrong. Instead, he'd responded to her kiss as if she were any other woman, unscarred and desirable.

Sorcha pressed a finger to her still throbbing lips, a plan once again forming in her head as she faced her brother. "I need to go to the seamstress—"

"Dunnae even start, Sorcha," Finlay muttered. "Ye've done enough."

"It's for Mama," she said, the lie burning her tongue. "Fabric for dresses. The shop is just over yonder. You will see me the whole time."

He narrowed his eyes at her as if he knew she was lying, but nodded with thinned lips. "To the shop and back. I'll wait here." He placed a hand on her shoulder. "Sorcha, five minutes or I come after ye."

"It will take more than five minutes to sort through Mama's order, Finlay," she said in a patient tone, hoping that her underlying desperation would be hidden. "'Twill be at least ten."

When he agreed with a scowl, she hurried away, toward the lane of shops that cut through the village, feeling his eyes on her until the door to the seamstress's swung shut behind her. Greeting the sewing girls who had seen Sorcha many times before, and ignoring the way their eyes always flared at the sight of her marred face, she hastened through the shop to the back door, and then turned toward the village prison. Evan, Gavin, the constable, and his two men were in deep conversation outside, arguing about the best course of action. She slipped inside and released a pent-up breath, relieved there was no one in the entrance hall. Sorcha glanced at the thick processing ledger resting on a nearby desk.

Mr. Brandt Montgomery Pierce of Worthington Abbey, Essex, England.

He had a distinguished name. He wasn't a titled lord, but he was evidently a man of some means. The fit of his clothing had been tailored for his powerful shoulders and those long, muscular legs. She'd gotten enough of an eyeful of his bunching muscles when he'd thrown Craig's cousin arse over heels. Sorcha pocketed the iron keys that lay on a hook near the desk and made her way down the narrow, darkened hallway.

The first two cells were empty.

"Come to gloat?" a low voice drawled.

Sorcha whirled and peered into the third cell, obscured

with shadow. She pressed closer to the bars, her hands going around the rough iron, and gasped as long, ungloved fingers captured hers with leashed masculine force. An unexpected thrill shot up her arms, along with unwanted impressions of those lean-fingered hands roaming all over her body.

"Release me," she whispered, cheeks scalding.

At first, it seemed as if he wasn't going to, and she looked down; his shins were close enough for a swift kick through the bars. But then his grip went slack, and she stepped away, catching her breath. Sorcha wanted to run from the accusatory press of his eyes.

"I am sorry," she said quietly. "I didn't mean for any of this to happen."

"And yet it did, Lady Maclaren."

"I can explain."

"I am glad to hear as much," he replied. Then after a beat, "I'm waiting, my lady."

But in the moment of truth, words failed her. How could she explain that she had temporarily lost her mind and initiated the scandalous kiss to get out of marriage to another man? She'd *used* him. It had been dishonorable and desperate. Sorcha knew he deserved an honest answer. Haltingly, she explained, and when she was done, silence reigned.

As the next minute ticked by, Sorcha flicked a worried glance down the hallway. Her ten minutes were almost up.

"Are you…angry?" she asked, uncertain as to what the man might do if she unlocked the cell door. She checked the head of the corridor again, impatient to free him already and be gone.

"You are betrothed to the Marquess of Malvern?" he asked, instead of answering her question.

She nodded miserably. "The betrothal was part of a settlement to Lord Malvern from King George. We thought the marquess had forgotten about the betrothal, but he has sent a missive that he will arrive for me in a sennight." She fisted her hands into her skirt. "Stupidly, I thought he wouldn't want me..." Sorcha trailed off, embarrassed to call attention to her disfigurement. "Because of my scarring. But I misjudged his greed."

"How did you come by them?" he asked. "Those markings?"

Sorcha saw no reason to lie. Mr. Pierce would soon be gone, back to England where he belonged, and most everyone had already heard the tale of the Beast of Maclaren. "When I was nine, I found a wolf den in a hillside cave. The cubs were friendly, though their mother did not take kindly to an intruder. I barely escaped."

His eyes glinted with surprise. "You fought off a wolf and lived? At nine years old?"

"It was foolish, I know, but I often wandered into the glens, looking for mischief. I was a headstrong girl."

A rumble of impressed laughter filled the space between them that did absurd things to her senses. "No wonder you weren't afraid of five paltry men."

"Craig had it coming." Sorcha inhaled a determined breath and unlocked the metal door. "Let's get you out of here while we can, Mr. Pierce. You don't need to be saddled for a lifetime with the likes of me just for falling for some clot-heided scheme." She blushed at the recollection of her boldness.

He watched her where she stood, neither of them moving for a long moment. He approached her past the cell's open gate. His hand rose to graze her scarred cheek, and this time she did not shy away. "You have blood just here."

Sorcha swallowed, flinching at the tenderness of his touch. "Is that all you see?"

"Yes."

Embarrassingly, she felt the sting of tears. No man had

ever touched her scars before. No man had ever *not* noticed them. When she'd met the Marquess of Malvern for the first time, she'd overheard the marquess's men making cruel remarks that her intended would have to put a sack over her head to bed her. Her own betrothed had laughed and said his solution for a satisfactory bedding would be to flip her over and bury her face into the pillows. She'd fled the hall, her face burning with shame.

The memory of Mr. Pierce's scorching kiss flitted through her mind, heating her blood. He'd seen her as a woman, not as a monster.

"You need to go," she whispered. "There's a door at the end of the hallway past the privy." She turned on her heel and made to stride down the hallway, but a hand on her arm stalled her.

"Lady Sorcha."

The sound of her name on his lips, not the tether of his fingers, made her feet grind to a painful halt. Did he want to punish her for the way she'd used him after all? Take his pound of flesh for what he'd suffered? Slowly, she turned back to him. He hadn't moved from where he stood. Once more, she had the impression of ruthlessly guarded control.

The sound of voices echoed toward them, and Sorcha tugged his arm. "Mr. Pierce—"

"I'd say we are well beyond formality at this point," he murmured. "Brandt will do."

She didn't care what his name was, she wanted him to leave. But Brandt's stare met hers across the narrow space between them and captured it, driving the breath from her lungs. He still hadn't released her arm, and the heat of his palm sank through the soft wool of her plaid. His eyes were unfathomable as they bore into hers. Sorcha had never felt so vulnerable…so exposed.

"The gray in the auction paddock, Lochland Toss," he

said after a long pause. "He belongs to you?"

She blinked her surprise. "Lockie?"

"How much do you want for him?"

"He's not for sale."

His gaze narrowed. "Everything has a price, my lady. Including me. And that horse is my price to free you from the consequences of your unfortunate advances."

"*My* unfortunate advances?" she spluttered in shock. The man was daft. She was giving him a chance to escape unscathed, and he wanted to purchase her *horse*? Her eyes snapped to his in sudden understanding. "Are you saying you want the horse or you won't go?"

Brandt pulled her closer to him, his fingers firm, though not hurtful. One corner of his mouth tilted upward. "We are in a predicament. You need a groom to escape your unwanted betrothal. And I have desired that particular stallion for my stables for some time."

He released her and with a slow forming smile, stuck out his hand. His changeling eyes remained cool. "Do we have an agreement, my lady?"

Sorcha frowned, backing up a step as the voices of the constable and her brothers grew louder. What kind of man would offer his name and a lifetime of wedlock in exchange for a horse? Even one as magnificent as Lockie. She loved him and had resisted offers of purchase for years—the stallion's value was immeasurable, both in coin and sentiment. Then again, no one had ever offered this price…a way to escape Malvern. She should say no. The man was clearly dicked in the nob. But apparently, she was even more so.

"To be clear, you're offering marriage for my horse," she said. "Not anything else."

He raked a hand through his bronzed hair, his eyes flicking to her mouth, a sliver of hesitation flashing for the barest instant before it was squashed. "Yes, the marriage will be in name only and annulled as soon as possible."

In name only. Annulled.

Her limbs went soft with relief.

A way out, simply for the price of her most cherished possession. Her heart ached at the thought of turning Lockie over to another, but the sadness would pass. Eventually.

A marriage to Malvern would last forever.

Sorcha nodded and took his proffered hand with numb fingers.

"Aye, Mr. Pierce, we have an agreement."

Chapter Three

The wedding was immediate and brief. Brandt's future brothers-in-law served as grim-faced witnesses while Gavin Maclaren, thin-lipped vicar and cousin of the bride, performed the ceremony. It was a small church wedding, instead of the usual anvil wedding at the local blacksmith's. Which might have been preferable, considering he and Lady Sorcha Maclaren were declaring fictitious intentions and exchanging false vows.

Well, at least he was getting something out of all this madness. Lochland Toss was a worthy prize. Or so he'd told himself at least a dozen times since he'd made the asinine offer.

He clenched his jaw tight as he retrieved the only ring he had in his possession from a cord around his neck—a woman's ring his father had given him, with a green and gold crest emblazoned upon it. It had belonged to Brandt's mother. Why Monty had kept it, and why Brandt had worn it all these years, was something he didn't want to think about right then. As he slipped it on the third finger of his wife's hand, he supposed it no longer mattered why. It was Sorcha's now.

His wedded oath.

Hell.

All for a horse. An *invaluable* horse. One he'd wanted for years. Lochland Toss would finally be his. What was Brandt's name worth anyway? With luck, the marriage would be annulled within a week, once her betrothed was thwarted, and Brandt would be free to resume his life and his plans.

As would she.

The unbidden image of a brave, dark-haired little girl fighting off a ferocious wolf filled his mind. A woman of her courage would not have sunk to such drastic measures if she hadn't been desperate. And to be fair, *she* hadn't suggested marriage…her brothers and cousin had. She'd initiated a kiss only to cause enough gossip for someone to cry off.

And he knew why. The Marquess of Malvern was rumored to have a streak of brutality running through him that would make grown men cast up their accounts. The thought of this woman being possessed by such a man left him cold. The marquess would take pleasure in breaking her bold spirit until no spark remained in those vibrant blue eyes.

No, even though Sorcha had been a stranger up until that morning, Brandt could not have stood by and done nothing, knowing what he did about Malvern. Just as he could not have stood by when he'd found Ares, trapped as a foal in barbed wire and being stoned by a few ragtag hooligans.

She is not a horse, an inner voice whispered.

Nor was she a child.

A vision of delicate blond lace over a swelling bosom arose. Indeed, she was neither. But she had been in danger just the same, and Brandt's *acute sense of empathy*, as Archer had often called it while rolling his eyes, had not allowed him to walk away.

Then again, his empathy had little to do with taking advantage of the perfect bargaining chip to finally lay claim to Lochland Toss. The opportunity had fallen into his lap, and while helping the lady would have been noble, Brandt was no altruist.

He was more than happy to let her brothers believe they had forced them to the altar. In all fairness, they *could* have hunted him down and threatened to beat him to mash, but no one could have strong-armed Brandt into marriage. Not even two thickly built Highlanders foaming at the mouth to defend their sister's ruination. A ruination *she* had completely fabricated.

Though it wasn't as if *he* hadn't enthusiastically participated.

He'd wanted his mouth on hers the moment he'd seen it shape the word "Essex." The sultry sound of it had prompted a number of lascivious thoughts, and that was *before* she'd kissed him. When she had, her lips had been sinfully sweet, the taste of her burning through him like a dram of the finest whiskey. That had been the only cause for hesitation in the Selkirk jail. Clearly, he was attracted to her, but he would not let lust deter him from his prize.

Lochland Toss had no equal.

Once his bride was free of Malvern, he would ensure that the marriage was annulled, and he and his new mount would travel south, back to Essex. It would all be a neat, tidy transaction. He'd be a stallion richer, his stables set up for immeasurable prosperity, and she would be rid of her unwanted fiancé.

As for the wedding night, self-restraint would not be a problem. Brandt had never allowed any woman to hold such sway over him, and he wasn't about to start now—not even for one who kissed as well as Lady Sorcha Maclaren.

Brandt glanced at his new wife standing beside him,

recalling the passionate cling of her mouth and the feel of her lithe, graceful body beneath his hands. She had fit perfectly in his arms, her hips cradling his in a snug fashion that was both intimate and arousing. A sudden sweep of lust shot through him, making him question his earlier conviction of sexual self-restraint.

"God bless ye," the vicar said, "and yer marriage."

Blessings that should have been hollow and meaningless, considering his and Sorcha's agreement, now seemed ominous. Sorcha's blue eyes were shadowed as Brandt led her from the church. Though she put on a brave countenance, he could feel her slender fingers trembling within his.

"What is it?" he murmured.

"Nothing." She gnawed on a corner of her lower lip, her scars dark against her ashen face. Cold understanding of their new, if temporary, bonds of wedlock must have been settling in. Or perhaps she was upset only about losing her prized mount in the deal. Brandt felt a stab of satisfaction. *Play with fire and you should be ready for the burn.*

"Where are ye staying?" Finlay, the larger of her brothers, asked. "At Pollock's?"

It was the only decent inn in Selkirk. Brandt nodded.

"Good, we'll have yer wedding feast there." Finlay shot him a hard look. "Then ye'll do yer duty as husband with the bedding."

Sorcha's body pulled taut at his side at the blunt command. Brandt bristled as well, disgusted by the ease in which her brother called for the end of her virginity. Brandt squeezed her hand, but said nothing. He would tell her of his plan when they were alone and observing eyes and listening ears were no longer attuned to them. For now, she needed to eat something to put some color back into her cheeks.

However, it seemed he'd underestimated her. Moments before they entered the inn, Sorcha squared her shoulders and smoothed the red and navy Maclaren plaid pinned to her dress. The waxen anxiety disappeared from her face and a stoic, icy calm replaced it.

The transformation was astonishing. This was the fearless woman he'd seen in the paddock. Her confidence then had been innate, part and parcel of her skill with a sword. Now, this poise was all an act, and she wore it like armor. Her palm remained shaky and sweaty, clasped in his, but her chin angled upward as she followed her brothers into the boisterous eating room.

"Congratulations!" someone shouted drunkenly, "on yer blessed nuptials!"

"More like cursed," another voice muttered. It belonged to Craig Dunbar, the man his bride had neatly dispatched earlier.

The former chant was taken up until the noise was deafening. Some patrons eyed him with curiosity, others with suspicion, but it was clear the inn got its fair share of anvil weddings. Brandt noticed a table of Scots looking at Sorcha with unmasked grimaces. They nudged one another, and only after looking their fill at Sorcha's face did they glance at Brandt. Their expressions shifted, changing from horror to pity, as if to say they knew he'd been shackled to her by way of some scandal. They shook their heads. One man even had the ballocks to murmur, "Poor lad."

The renewed tension in Sorcha's body told Brandt that she'd heard. He hauled her up against him, his gaze hard until the men at that table averted their pitying eyes.

"You don't have to do that," she said.

Brandt eyed her. "Do what?"

"Defend me. I'm used to it. The stares, the comments, the whispers. People have been doing it my whole life. They're not going to stop now that some Sassenach was fool enough to wed the Beast of Maclaren."

Beast of Maclaren? Was that what they called her? It was absurd. The scars gave her a wild, nearly savage look, but she was far from a beast.

"Perhaps those worried looks were for you," Brandt said in a light tone, even though he knew it wasn't true.

She shot him a look. "For *me*?"

"You did marry a poor English stable master, after all. Perhaps all these pitying glances are on your behalf, not mine. We English tend to be dry and humorless, stingy with our coin, and predisposed to rampant cases of gout."

Sorcha slowed as they made their way toward a table at the back, near a low, peaty hearth blaze. Her gaze raked him from head to toe, a faint blush coloring her cheeks as her eyes met his once more. She strained against a smile. "Your claims of gout would serve you better if you had a paunch or jowls to your credit." Her lips finally curved slightly, a sparkle blooming in those blue eyes. "Furthermore, a man without a sense of humor does not marry a woman on a whim, Mr. Pierce. Even for a horse of unequaled value."

"Brandt," he murmured. "And humor has nothing to do with it. I'm making out in spades with this arrangement, *wife*."

The smile froze and faded from her lips. He cursed himself, recalling her brother's coarse command minutes ago about Brandt claiming his husbandly rights. He might have been in this for the horse, but he wasn't a complete scapegrace.

"That isn't what I meant," he said, but she'd looked away from him, her expression only more frigid. They'd agreed on an annulment, and that would only be possible if he didn't bed her. He'd assumed that was obvious. But perhaps not.

Brandt abandoned the idea of explaining, given the dozen pairs of ears in such close proximity hanging on to their every word.

Following Evan and Finlay, they took their places at a large table at one end of the room. Within minutes, it was covered in freshly baked breads, fruit, trenchers of thick mutton stew, an entire roasted pig, and foam-topped goblets of ale. They were joined by Gavin shortly thereafter, who had remained in the chapel to prepare the necessary documentation of their marriage vows.

Brandt was in no mind for food, but he forced himself to consume some of the meat and bread. The raunchy comments from the crowd did nothing to stimulate his waning appetite. A silent Sorcha picked at her plate.

"Pierce," Evan said, folding his thick arms across his chest and glaring daggers at him after he'd drained his third mug of ale. "What do ye do in Essex?"

"Shouldn't you have asked that before dragging me to the altar?" Brandt replied smoothly. "What if I were a beggar? Or a poor farmer or smithy, unable to properly care for your sister?"

Evan smiled. "The tack on yer horse costs more than a blacksmith earns in a year."

"Perhaps it belongs to my employer."

"Are the clothes on yer back his, too?" Finlay asked with a sneer.

"Finlay!" Sorcha said, her elbow shooting out to catch her brother in the ribs. "Don't be foul."

Palming his side, he shot her a glare. "I'm no' being foul, Sorcha, and ye ken that Ronan will be far worse once he gets wind of yer wedded state, especially with the marquess on the way to Maclaren."

"You sent word to Ronan?" she asked.

Brandt sat back in his chair, a tankard of ale in his hand. "Who is Ronan?"

Sorcha straightened her shoulders, that cool mask of indifference slipping over her features once again. "Our eldest brother," she answered, her gaze stuck on her plate.

"Christ, how many brothers do you have?" Brandt asked, to which Evan and Finlay both chuckled, each of them eating heartily of the feast laid out before them.

"Four brothers and two sisters. And our father is—"

"Angus Maclaren, the Duke of Dunrannoch, chieftain and laird of Clan Maclaren," Evan interjected. Brandt took a swig from his tankard, not mentioning that he'd already known as much. He'd heard the duke had a parcel of children in addition to his stable of fine horses, but Brandt had been more interested in the latter than the former. Perhaps he should have paid better attention. His head throbbed with the beginnings of a headache.

Sorcha glared at her brother. "You know I hate it when you interrupt me, Evan."

"Ye've no right to complain today, sister. Once our father hears tell of what ye've done, ye won't be able to sit down for a week."

Brandt crashed his tankard onto the wooden table, shaking the plates and cutlery. A cloud of silence rose up over the long table, the half-dozen Maclaren men looking up from their meals and ale to stare at him. Brandt leaned forward and speared Evan with a thunderous look.

"What *she's* done? As I recall, it was you and your brother who insisted on marriage."

And if the Duke of Dunrannoch dared lay one finger on his daughter in punishment, Brandt would happily snap it in half.

Finlay slammed his own tankard onto the table. "Only when ye dishonored her in public."

Of all the idiotic notions, this was the one that irritated Brandt the most. "And what sense does it make, I wonder, to force your sister to marry the stranger you're so certain was accosting her?"

Glowering, Finlay shot up from his seat, knocking the

chair over backward. Brandt lounged back in his and arched a lazy eyebrow.

"Enough," Sorcha said, standing up from her own chair, her gaze cutting between them. "I'm finished eating," she announced, even though she'd barely touched her food.

"You should try to eat a little more," Brandt said, indicating the half-eaten plate.

"I don't require a man to tell me when my belly is full and when it isn't," she shot back, twin pricks of color rising high on her cheeks. "I said I've finished."

The blasted woman was as thickheaded as her brothers. Brandt pushed his chair back and stood, drawing himself to his full height. He couldn't recall the last time he'd lost his temper. He never let his emotions boil to the surface. But now he wanted to shout. He wanted to rail at something, anything, just to release the pent-up agitation that had been simmering all day, ever since he'd made the damned offer of his name for a horse. His choice, certainly, but he was beginning to regret it.

Instead, he lowered his voice and said evenly, "Then I suppose it's time we retire and make this marriage true."

Sorcha's eyes flared. The color in her cheeks spread like a stain of wine, drenching her, running up to the shells of her ears. She held his stare, though, her stubborn pride—or perhaps it was only her ability to act—unflinching.

Behind her, Finlay sat down in his chair again. The scowl was still fixed upon his lips.

"Ye dunnae have to like him, aye," Brandt thought he heard Gavin murmur under his breath to Evan, but he could not be sure.

Brandt frowned but stepped away from the table, taking his tankard with him. He headed for the stairs, a set of bare board steps that led to a platform overlooking the inn's main room. From there, a turn in the stairwell would take them out of sight. As Sorcha rose to follow him, whistles and hoots rained through the room, making it almost impossible for Brandt to hear the innkeeper as he met them at the base of the steps.

"Second room on the right!" the old man shouted, and with a nod, Brandt took up his wife's hand. It was no longer sweaty, but like a block of ice. He closed his hand around it and pulled her along behind him, raising his tankard to the jeering crowd below. He had to at least give them a show of excitement at taking his bride to bed, otherwise, he wouldn't put it past the drunkards and heathens to follow them up and listen at the door.

Once they'd entered the upstairs corridor and fallen from view, Brandt could have released her palm. He didn't, though. His hands were warm and dry, and he already felt her skin beginning to thaw. She stayed quiet and didn't tug her hand free.

Their chamber was spare but clean. His belongings had been moved from the smaller room he'd taken for lodgings two days before, along with a portmanteau of clothes he suspected belonged to his new bride. As he'd requested for himself the prior nights, a tub full of steaming water had been filled and placed behind a screen at one end. He eyed the floor and a lumpy armchair by the bed. Either would do for the night.

Sorcha followed with none of the bravery she'd been able to manifest downstairs during the feast. He closed the door as soon as she entered and threw the lock. Her shoulders jumped at the sound, and she spun around on her heel to face him. What he saw nearly stopped his heart. She wasn't just hesitant, she was frightened. Of him.

The faster this ended, the better.

Brandt took a step toward her. "Is there any place you'll be safe from Malvern?"

Sorcha's lips pulled into a frown. "What?"

"Here in Scotland, or even England, is there a place where Malvern won't be able to touch you?"

She shot him a mystified look but nodded. "My sister is a Brodie and her husband will protect us if need be."

"Why didn't you go to her before?"

"I would have, but my father would have pursued me to fulfill the betrothal contract." Uncertainty swam in her eyes. "But Lord Malvern *can't* touch me now. Don't you have a home in England? Essex or someaught?" she asked, her voice rising on a rattled note.

"Until I bed you, the marriage can still be annulled. Malvern can see to it. And if you were promised to him, there's the possibility he won't give up his claim so easily."

In England, broken marriage contracts were call for serious reparation. He doubted it was any different in Scotland. If anything, the consequences were even more dire. But as he'd said to Sorcha earlier, all men had a price—and he was willing to bet Malvern had one, too.

Brandt crossed to the other side of the small room in four fast strides and pulled the drape in front of the window, blocking the unfettered view of the lush rolling fields surrounding Selkirk and the tents that had been erected for the common lands festival.

"Yes, well…I believe that is why we are here. In this room. At this…uh, time," she replied, her voice tripping over the words. She cleared her throat, and when he turned back to her, saw the blush riding high on her cheeks. It had spread down the creamy column of her neck to the pillowy décolletage her dress plumped up into view. He wondered idly how deep the rose-tinted flush descended, whether it bloomed over the neat curves of her breasts to that nipped-in waist as well.

Damn it all to hell.

He had to act before he lost whatever was left of his reason—and his will. Brandt drained his tankard of ale, set it down, then crouched to pull his hunting dirk from the sheath he kept inside his boot.

Sorcha retreated. "What are you doing with that?"

Brandt stood, rolled up his sleeve, and with a fast, firm motion, sliced open the top of his forearm.

"Stop!" she gasped, lurching forward, as if she meant to take the blade from his hand.

"I don't think you really want me to stop," he replied as the shallow slice welled with enough blood to drip down the curve of his arm. "Pull back the bedsheets," he ordered.

"What? Why?"

"Just do it," he bit out, losing his patience. Hell, the day had started out perfectly well, and yet now here he stood in a rural Scottish inn saddled with a wife and a bleeding arm. The only bright spot was the coveted stallion waiting for him at the end of this very frustrating road, and even that was fast losing its appeal.

Sorcha held back what would have surely been a tart reply and yanked the coarse woolen blanket back to the plain linen sheet below. Brandt held his arm over the center of the bed a moment and allowed the blood to drip freely.

"Six or seven drops should be enough to convince them," he muttered, though he wasn't entirely certain. The few women he'd taken to bed had never been virgins. He'd made sure of it. He'd never contributed to any maiden's ruination, and yet, here he was, caught in the very trap he'd always prided himself on avoiding.

When he retracted his arm and met Sorcha's eyes again, her shocked stare had changed. She was no longer confused at his intention, but instead of the relief he'd imagined he'd find, he saw something unexpected. The barest flicker of injury. She quickly blinked and pulled down that mask of composure. Hiking her chin, she crossed her arms. "I see."

But she didn't see. The hurt he'd glimpsed for a moment was testament to that. Brandt sighed. "We agreed this marriage was for show, didn't we?" He searched for something to staunch the trickle of blood and, finding a cloth near the washbasin, did so. "I intend to take you to your sister's, where you'll be safe from Malvern. We'll have the marriage annulled, and you can stay there for as long as it takes for him to forget the wrong done to him."

"And you?"

"I will return to Essex, of course." He gave her a pointed look. "With my new horse."

Sorcha's mouth tightened, her eyes sparking. "I'm glad it's so easy for you."

Brandt shrugged out of his coat. "If you think bartering my name is easy, my lady, then perhaps you don't appreciate my sacrifice."

"Sacrifice?" she snapped. "In a few weeks, you'll walk away with a stallion worth its weight in cairngorm crystals, while I…I…"

"While you eschew marriage to a marquess." He stared coolly at her. "Isn't that what you wanted?"

Sorcha's mouth opened and closed, her eyes like pieces of blue flint, though her fingers curled into trembling fists at her sides. Her face paled as resignation settled upon it. Brandt sighed, throttling his anger. She was only a girl, after all, one who, despite her own machinations, had found herself wedded and nearly bedded within the space of an hour.

He glanced at the wooden tub, his tone gentling. "You should bathe before the water gets cold. I'll wash after you do." His gaze shifted to the bed. "And you needn't worry that I'll lose control of my desires with you. I'll sleep on the floor."

Sorcha's hands wound into her skirts as her eyes slid to the bed, and the smear of red at its center. She swallowed and nodded stiffly. "Thank you."

He took a moment to reply. Perhaps he should be thanking her as well. She wouldn't have parted with Lochland Toss—or *Lockie*, as she'd called him—if she hadn't backed Brandt into this corner. But he didn't feel like gloating. He was too damned tired.

"You're safe with me, Sorcha," he said instead.

"Am I?" Her reply was near inaudible.

"Your sudden skepticism offends, my lady," he said quietly. "Weren't you the one who decided I was a far step safer than Malvern in the first place?"

She flinched as if he'd struck her but did not snap back with a sharp-tongued answer. Uncomfortable with the tightening sensation of guilt-speckled fury in his chest, Brandt walked to the window, his arms clasped behind his back. He had nothing to feel guilty for. He'd played his part and, when all was said and done, he would claim the reward he deserved.

No more, no less.

Chapter Four

Sorcha's eyes cracked open to a slim golden beam of sunshine cutting the darkened room in half. It was coming from a window, its coverings drawn and blocking most of the daylight. Stretching her arms wide across the bed, she recognized the dated, peeling decor of Pollock's. It wasn't the first night she'd spent in the inn, and it wouldn't be the last. She'd probably drunk too much, and one of her brothers had thought it best if she slept it off.

She blinked, her eyesight adjusting over the lone spear of light in the room, and froze. A man slumbered in the armchair near the window. Swallowing a scream, she sat up abruptly, the previous night's happenings coming back to her in a brutal rush—a kiss, her brothers, the chapel, a ceremony, dinner—and the indisputable fact that the man asleep in the chair was her husband.

Lifting her fingers, she stared at the antique ring with the green, blue, and gold crest he'd given her in the chapel after pledging his vows. She squinted at it. The blend of colors looked familiar, but all the Scottish family crests tended to blur after a while. He could be a Lowlander for all she knew. Then again, she did not care about his last name, so long as it was not Malvern.

Christ in a tartan, she was bloody married.

She was no longer Lady Sorcha Maclaren; she was Lady Sorcha *Pierce*.

Well, she wasn't his wife in truth. Shifting her hips quietly, she stared down at the brownish-red markings on the white linen and clutched the blankets to her chest. She would be lying if she didn't admit she was grateful he hadn't seen the whole of her. No one had in years, not even her maids, who drew baths for her but knew their lady preferred to see to her own ablutions. With the drapes drawn. *Always* with the drapes drawn.

Sorcha had learned that painful lesson and would never repeat it. She closed her eyes against the memory, though it echoed no matter how she tried to banish it. Her bedchamber at the Maclaren keep. The sound of gasps and horrified whispers as she had risen from a bath. Her maid, rushing the open arched window and telling someone to shoo.

Three boys, Sorcha learned the next day, when her father had leveled a punishment of horsewhipping for their spying. She had been fourteen, the boys all a year or two older, and one, Aric Ferguson, she'd admired for ages. The son of a neighboring laird, Aric was the only boy who ever looked at her twice, and she'd quickly learned why.

He'd found her later, forced to apologize by his father and hers, but his apology had been naught but a twisted, sullen insult. *I'm sorry we peeked on ye. 'Twas a dare, ye ken.* He'd lowered his voice then, so their fathers, standing nearby, could not hear. *Ye have my promise—I'll no' look at such a beast again.* And with a grimace as his eyes drifted over her newly blossomed chest, Aric had walked away.

He never looked her in the eye again. Nor did the others.

Though soon after, Sorcha had started hearing the word *beast* in passing. And eventually, *Beast of Maclaren*. The painful nickname had gutted her at first. Then she'd gotten her revenge a year later at a clan fair when she'd trounced Aric soundly in the ring, dressed in her brother Evan's old clothes.

"How does it feel to be beaten by the Beast?" she'd spat.

The dumbstruck look on his face when she'd revealed herself had been priceless, almost worth the cost of his cruelty. Her gratification, however, couldn't erase what he'd said, or the years of loneliness that followed.

Aric had been the first, but she vowed he would be the last. No man in his right mind would want—let alone want to *see*—what lay under her shift, and she would never subject herself to such scorn again. Sorcha had long given up hope that any man would truly desire her. Except for Malvern, who had wanted her dowry, not her body.

Though she'd consented to the agreement of marriage in name only, she hadn't been certain if her new husband would expect to carry out his conjugal rights. He was a man, after all, and after their kiss and the way he'd touched her…she'd started to think he might want what was owed to him.

Only he hadn't.

Sorcha closed her eyes on a silent sigh, her heart pinching slightly with thwarted longing. Had she *wanted* him to bed her? She'd been promised to Malvern for so long that she'd never even thought of other men. And certainly not a prime specimen like *him*.

Turning carefully, Sorcha sneaked a glance to where he slumbered. Brandt Pierce was a tall man, and the armchair looked far too small to contain his lanky frame. He was not as broad as her brothers, but his lean physique was deceptive. She had seen his strength with her own two eyes when he'd walloped Craig and his cousins. His chest, a swath of tanned skin visible through the loose lawn shirt he wore, rose and fell with deep, even breaths. A lock of bronzed hair hung over his brow, and his mouth was parted in repose.

Beneath that tumbling curl, she could recall the color of his eyes in minute detail—they were the earthy, changeable hues of the Highlands in the throes of autumn. But now, thick russet eyelashes rested against his cheeks, hiding them from view. Fine grooves bracketed that stern but sensuous mouth. It was, without a doubt, a mouth molded for pleasure. One she'd experienced firsthand. With a tiny sigh, Sorcha remembered the feel of those wide male lips on hers and the clever, silken glide of his tongue. A rush of heat swamped her limbs, and she pressed her suddenly slack legs together.

Brandt grunted softly in sleep and twisted his long body in the chair. It could not be comfortable, sleeping in such a cramped position, and yet he had kept his promise that he would not lose control of his desires. Her brain tripped over the memory of his words. His *desires*. She hadn't known what to make of it then, and still didn't. Had he been expressing sarcasm, the idea of feeling desire for her ridiculous? Or had he been genuine, honestly saying that he would fight the urge to give in to his body's craving for her?

The thought was a dangerous one, making the blood in her veins start to simmer. Restlessly, Brandt shifted again. He stretched out his long legs in front of him, hooking one ankle over the other and causing the edges of his shirt to ride up against his muscular torso. The night before, she had averted her eyes while he undressed and bathed not two lengths away. Now, though, her gaze took greedy inventory, and Sorcha found it suddenly hard to swallow. Or breathe. Or do anything of use at all.

Christ's holy baubles.

She shouldn't swear, but her breath fair fizzled in her throat at the tantalizing display of chiseled abdomen and hard male flesh descending to the noticeable rise of his trousers at the juncture of his trim hips. For a moment, she wondered whether the thin line of bronzed hair arrowing beneath his waistband would continue on to that riveting swell, and then, Sorcha's breath well and truly abandoned her.

It wasn't that she'd never seen a shirtless man before—she'd seen plenty of them on the Maclaren training fields. But none of them had ever had such a heathen effect on her. Her nipples had contracted to hot points beneath her night rail, the wool deliciously abrading her too-sensitive skin. She wanted him to kiss her again. She wanted to feel every inch of that lean male frame plastered against hers, bracing her body into the mattress.

God's teeth, she was shameless! Closing her eyes, consumed by the arousing tableau her imagination conjured, a tiny moan escaped her lips as she knotted her fingers into the bedsheets. Sorcha flipped over and groaned into the feathered pillows.

"Sleep well?" The warm voice slid across her overheated senses, and every muscle in her body tensed in frenzied awareness. Her husband was awake.

"Yes," she replied into her pillow. "Thank you."

More sunlight flared into the chamber as Brandt parted the drapes. Feigning sleepiness, she stretched and turned to face him. His grin and notched eyebrow made her abandon the pretense. "It didn't look that way. You seemed to be moaning and groaning. Night terrors?"

Sorcha narrowed her gaze at him. The amusement in his voice hinted at knowledge...knowledge of her shameless perusal. The blasted bounder had been awake and hadn't made a sound! She blushed to the tips of her ears and wished that she could pull the sheets over her head.

"That was probably it," she said as blandly as she was able.

"Tell me about them," he said, walking over to the washbasin to splash some water on his face and clean his teeth with a square of linen and tooth powder.

Sorcha stopped herself just in time from sticking her tongue out at his back as his hazel eyes caught hers in a sphere of mirrored glass on the wall. "I dreamed I went to a country festival and married a complete stranger."

"That sounds frightful."

"It was," she said. "Terrifying."

"Was this stranger you married a dreadful ogre?"

"Of the most monstrous ilk." She sat up and shifted her legs over the edge of the bed, the sheet falling away. Brandt's eyes met hers in the mirror again, his hand stalling in midair as his hot gaze dropped to a spot below her chin. Sorcha glanced down and resisted the urge to grab for the discarded sheet. The worn woolen fabric of her nightgown was snug against the curves of her body, and at his stare, her nipples, which had not ceased tingling, tightened even more. Flushing, she crossed her arms over the offending points and glared at him. "Worse than you can imagine," she added sourly.

He laughed, and the deep rumble made her pause. She couldn't help noticing how his laughter lit his eyes in the most fascinating way. "Did your monstrous ogre threaten to boil your flesh and suck the marrow from your bones?"

It should have been awful what he was suggesting, but the teasing words shot bolts of exquisite heat down her spine. The combination of *flesh* and *suck* together with her earlier fantasies made her face feel as if it were on fire.

"No," she gritted out and hurried behind the privacy screen. "I kicked him in the head."

The thought of using the chamber pot with him so close by made her cringe, but she managed it quickly when she heard him walk to the opposite end of the room to get dressed.

Her husband's reply floated over the barrier. "Poor ogre.

Sounds like he got the raw end of the deal."

"Why is that?" she couldn't help asking.

"Because ogres need love, too."

A ripple of laughter bubbled in her chest, and Sorcha poked her head around the barrier. Except for her little brother Niall, banter did not come this easily with other people, especially with a lout who was using her plight to get his hands on her horse. Though, to be fair, she was using him, too.

"Tell me more," Brandt said as he deftly fastened the buttons of his waistcoat. "Was he a strapping young blighter?"

Strapping. Handsome. Irritatingly attractive.

Once more, Sorcha flushed and cursed her body's idiotic response. Undressing swiftly, she tied her stockings and garters, then pulled a chemise and clean dress over her head. "He was a bit of a runt, actually," she said, her voice muffled by the layers of cotton and wool.

"A runt? I think not," Brandt said in an affronted voice that seemed suddenly loud. Sorcha realized why as she settled the dress into place. She almost screeched. He was standing right in front of her, *behind* the screen. "Let me," he said, turning her shoulders around before she could form a tart reply. "This one looks to have fasteners up the back."

She felt the deft tug and pull of the fabric as he buttoned her dress. At home, Kira, her maid, would often help with buttons and sometimes dress her hair. But no man had ever attended to her like this. Was this what husbands did for their wives? Surely, Malvern would never have offered such a thing. Sorcha closed her eyes as Brandt finished. She had to stop worrying about the marquess. She was out of his reach now. And, most of all, she needed to stop making a martyr of her pretend husband who had traded marriage vows for horseflesh.

"Playing the servant comes easily to you," she said in a

cool tone, peering over her shoulder. "Well done."

Fathomless gold-flecked green eyes met hers. "My lady's wish is my command."

"Until you get your hands on my stallion."

"Until then, of course."

She watched him, interest sparking. "Why do you want Lockie so badly anyway?"

"I hope to breed him with one of my mares," he said. "His brawn with her speed should make for spectacular foals."

It was the first bit of true excitement she'd seen from him…outside of their kiss. Sorcha fought back a shiver. Then, he'd been as enthusiastic as she.

"You breed horses?" When he nodded, she went on. "I confess, I'm not as horse-mad as my father, but I've raised Lockie from a colt myself. He's special—" She broke off, the *to me* sticking in her throat as a rush of guilt swamped her. "He'll make a great sire."

"That is my hope."

His hands fell away from her dress, but Sorcha continued to feel the heat from his body. He remained behind the screen with her, the small space growing warmer. She turned, thinking to slip past him, but was caught by the flat of his palm as it gently gripped her elbow. Brandt peered at her, one brow propped high.

"When you're angry, you sound like your brothers, but otherwise…you sound English. Why?"

Sorcha frowned at him. It was true. She lost control of her accent whenever her temper flared, and it was something her mother endlessly chastised her about. No English lord would want a wife who spoke with such a provincial, rustic brogue, her mother had always claimed. She would need to be as cultured and elegant as any of the fine English ladies she would undoubtedly encounter in London or Edinburgh when she became Lady Malvern. *Any daughter of mine will bring honor to Clan Maclaren*, her mother had intoned so often that it popped into Sorcha's mind without warning whenever she lost her temper *and* the pretty manners and rounded vowels she'd been bred to possess.

"My mother is from Cumbria," she replied, noticing with growing unease that Brandt's strong hand was still on her arm. "She insisted her daughters break from the Scots tongue whenever we went to London, but, since I was the one chosen for an English marquess, she concentrated her efforts on me."

Brandt's fingers tightened around her elbow. "They chose you for Malvern, not your sisters. Why was that?"

The question brought with it the same slow, gouging sensation of some invisible injury that Sorcha had suffered for years. Annis and Makenna were beauties, and as such, they were the Maclaren daughters who could secure those important alliances with the Brodies and the Campbells. Malvern was not an alliance. He was an unfortunate and unavoidable attachment. Her father would have never considered giving Annis or Makenna to him.

"My sisters had their own matches already."

Brandt's eyes narrowed by a fraction. It was enough to indicate that he didn't believe her. She wriggled her elbow, wanting freedom from the closed-up space behind the dressing screen and from his knowing stare. Brandt held on firmly.

"And neither of them feigned scandal in order to avoid those matches?" he asked, a muscle in his jaw twitching. Ever since waking up in that lumpy chair, he'd been conversing easily with her. Joking even. Sorcha had started to hope that perhaps he was no longer furious, that his plan to leave her at the Brodie keep and then return to his home with one of the most valuable horses in the Highlands as payment would be a balm. But here his anger was, yet again, bubbling to the surface. Hers notched in response.

She pressed her lips together and twisted her arm more forcibly. "Graeme Brodie and Malcolm Campbell are fine men. My sisters didn't need to worry about marrying *them*."

Finally, Sorcha successfully pried her elbow from Brandt's grip. She pushed past him, into the open part of the room, and took a deep breath. The air was no longer filled with his scent, a heady mix of sun-warmed leather, spice, and clean soap, and her body instantly felt steadier, her mind, sharper. She found her boots and sat upon the edge of the bed to pull them on, ignoring the press of Brandt's eyes. She didn't have to look up to know he was watching her slide the snug leather over each foot.

"Will your sister's husband agree to keep you on Brodie lands?"

Her hands slowed, and her heart pumped out an extra few beats. Well, why shouldn't he already be thinking about possible obstacles for his plan to leave her there?

"I am kin."

"Yes, and so far, what has your kin done for you? Other than throw you into a betrothal you wanted no part of, and then force you down the aisle to wed a complete stranger."

Sorcha finished with her boots, yanking indignantly on each lace, and shot to her feet. "You *chose* to marry me, in case you've already forgotten. And you don't know anything about my family."

Except that they were brutes. And intolerably rude. And tied down by harsh tradition and loyalty. All these things her brothers had laid bare to Brandt yesterday, and clearly, his Sassenach mind held it all in contempt.

He came to stand within inches of her, so close her breasts would have brushed against his chest had she taken a deep breath right then.

"I know enough to understand we have two very different

views of what good kin is," he replied.

"Don't insult my family."

"You'd defend them, even after how they've treated you?" Brandt asked, his brows furrowing in confusion. The expression cut small lines around his eyes. It was skin that had seen sunshine and wind, harsh elements and a rugged life. It was stunning how clear and perceptive his eyes were.

"Of course I do. They're…they're my brothers," she said, her throat constricted. They were untamed jackanapes most of the time, but they were still her blood. They defended her as much as they bullied her. They teased her as much as they protected her feelings. But with Malvern, they'd had no choice. Neither had her father. A part of her hoped, at least, that Finlay and Evan had been relieved to find her kissing a stranger at the festival, if only because it allowed them to order her to marry someone other than Malvern.

She heard the riot of clomping footsteps in the upstairs corridor and twisted away from Brandt's judgmental glare as a heavy fist came down on the locked door to their room.

"Mr. Pierce!"

It was Gavin, and by the loud voices joining his in the background, she assumed her brothers had come to fetch them as well. Someone pounded again, and then the doorknob jiggled.

"Open the door," Evan said.

Brandt rolled each of his shoulders as he opened it and stood within the frame. Evan and Finlay looked ready to push inside, while Gavin stayed in the center of the corridor. But Brandt didn't give an inch. He wouldn't let them pass.

"Is it done?" Finlay bellowed. It took Sorcha a moment to understand what exactly he was asking, and then a blush rushed to her cheeks.

Brandt said nothing, but turned, and with his mouth set in a grim slash, went to the bed and pulled the bottom sheet from the mattress. He balled up the linen and lobbed it at Finlay. Her brother caught the sheet, and Sorcha watched with mounting humiliation as he and Gavin inspected it for the telltale sign of her innocence lost. She thought she might be ill, not just because it was brash and barbaric, but because it was yet another lie.

Finlay lowered the sheet and dropped it onto the floor. He entered the room and picked up her portmanteau. "We leave for Maclaren immediately."

And with that, Sorcha's brothers and her cousin departed. She and Brandt stood, motionless, for a few seconds. The room seemed to deflate around them. Their ruse had worked. She had the notion she should have felt more relieved than she did.

"Are you ready?" he asked, without looking at her.

She nodded and followed Brandt out of the room, trying not to look at the bundled-up sheet on the floor. Her brother had accepted Brandt's blood as her own. If they knew the truth, what would they do? Force him to commit coitus? While standing over them with forbidding glares and sharpened claymores?

Sorcha bit back a crazed giggle at the image.

Those intense hazel eyes met hers, tinder to her ribald thoughts, and the laughter died on her lips. Neither she nor Brandt spoke a word as they descended into the inn's main room, where a handful of revelers were still drinking and dozing. The conscious ones raised their tankards in acknowledgment and made sputtering comments that Sorcha pretended not to hear or understand as Brandt stopped to speak to the innkeeper. He asked for pen and paper, and after jotting something down quickly, folded the parchment and handed it to the innkeeper with hushed directions. Sorcha strained to hear, but couldn't make anything out under the sudden and off-tune rendition of "Johnnie Scot" now making its way around the room. Brandt then took her by the arm and led the way outside, to the inn's stables.

Her brothers and their men were busy saddling their mounts. They loaded the wagons with the goods they'd purchased and traded for at the festival, including a few fat hogs, several bolts of woven wool, cotton, and linen, a crate of pipe tobacco, small casks of gunpowder, and several more of barreled mead.

Sorcha had ridden to Selkirk on Lockie, and as she approached her beloved gray stallion standing beside a Maclaren groom, she saw he'd been saddled and readied for her. With a stroke of sorrow, she reached for him, her eyes skipping to the enormous, scarred horse closed into the next stall over.

With its ragged coat of scar-torn midnight jet, the animal looked like a beast born of nightmares. Brandt went to him, clicking softly and whispering words Sorcha could not decipher. The animal nickered a brief hello to its master, its great nostrils expelling misty clouds into the cool spring morning air.

"Rest well, Ares?" he murmured to the horse, taking an admiring, and entirely too possessive, glance at Lockie. "Make a friend?"

Sorcha's chest constricted, but there was nothing to be done for it. Lockie was now his as well. "Ares?" she asked, running a hand up Lockie's velvet snout and scratching him behind the ear. "He certainly looks like a warrior."

She wondered how he'd come by his scars.

"He is," Brandt said as he saddled him. "Brave enough to carry my backside into any manner of hellish situations, at least."

Like the one he'd found himself in the day before. She was certain it was what he was thinking, too.

"I'm sure he and Lockie will get along fine," she said,

drawing him to the stable entrance and feeling another pang of regret.

"He's magnificent," Brandt replied, taking the time to look at Lockie and even run his hands along the gray's flanks and neck. "Even though he's young, he seems rather good tempered. Easy to command." He slid his gaze to Sorcha and with a salty grin, added, "Nothing at all like his mistress."

She parted her lips to let loose with a biting retort when a shrill whistle parted the inn's stable yard.

"Finlay!" one of the Maclaren men, Bogan, shouted as he entered the yard, mud splattered up his ankles and onto the hem of his tartan. "'Tis Malvern."

The ground beneath Sorcha's feet turned to sand. She gripped Lockie's traces and felt the horse stiffen with alarm, reflecting her own sudden panic.

"Malvern?" she repeated, her throat closing. "He's here?"

Bogan continued to address Finlay. "He arrived last night, and must've heard news of the wedding. He's coming with his men now."

"Shite," Evan growled as he and Finlay went to their horses and swung up into the saddles. Gavin crossed himself and closed his eyes, muttering a prayer before doing the same. The tension in the stable yard snapped tight as the rest of the men mounted, fast.

Behind her, Sorcha felt the ground tremble with Ares's hoof falls. Brandt appeared beside her, his shoulder brushing hers.

"Stay close to me," he said, his tone composed. She wanted to feel the same level of quiet dignity, but her body rebelled. What was bloody wrong with her? Hadn't she bested Craig in a sword fight the day before? And he certainly hadn't curbed his blows. When it came to battle, Sorcha was skilled and able, though the impotent rage she felt now was debilitating. Malvern held the power and the means to destroy her family, and his despicable man, Coxley, was more than happy to carry out his orders.

At that moment, a handful of armed men on horseback turned into the stable yard. They were dressed for war, it seemed. Sorcha held her breath as Lord Malvern turned in, pushing through his men and coming to the fore. He had not changed since the last she'd seen him, months ago.

The marquess was straight-backed and tall, thickly built, and fox-faced. His mouth was constantly drawn, as though perpetually disappointed in something, as it was right then. Malvern's glare cut around the stable yard until it landed upon Sorcha. His watery blue eyes froze her with a pointed look of ownership that made her flesh crawl. His thin nostrils flared and then his eyes shot to the man standing at her side. Brandt was unnaturally quiet as every last sound in the courtyard perished. None of the Maclaren men moved. Not one horse nickered.

Until the marquess drew his sword from a saddle sheath and pointed it straight at Brandt. "I demand satisfaction. Raise your sword, upstart, and prepare to pay for your presumptuous mistake."

Chapter Five

A ripple of agitation shivered through Ares, and Brandt hushed him with a soft sound. His horse could sense the threat hanging in the air just as keenly as every other man and animal present.

And woman.

Beside him, he could feel Sorcha bristling, her jaw fused shut and her eyes sparking with frustration. Lord Malvern was not a man to be taken lightly, not with several of his men surrounding him and a dozen more out front of the inn. They outnumbered the Maclaren men two to one, and there was something else present. Some sense of forced obeisance surrounding not just Sorcha, but her brothers as well. Malvern commanded this stable yard and all those within it. That much was clear.

Even as he struggled to understand why her dauntless brothers would bow down to someone like Malvern, Brandt stepped forward, Ares's reins still in hand. "You'll have to seek satisfaction elsewhere, Lord Malvern, for I've made no mistake, and I've no wish to fight," he said to him.

Malvern's eyes narrowed. "You know me."

"I know *of* you."

He could read men the same way he could horses, and Brandt had known from the first time he'd encountered Malvern in London at White's, years back, that he was a master of deceit. A man like Malvern didn't play fair at anything, and he wouldn't fight fair, either.

The marquess shifted his sword, pointing it at Sorcha. The fact that he would ever align the tip of his sword with a woman infuriated Brandt. That it was Sorcha he'd taken aim at, enraged him.

"Then perhaps you do not know that this woman is to be *my* wife, as dictated by the king himself."

"You'll do well to lower your sword," Brandt said, reining in a flash of irritation. "And she is no longer a maiden, but a married woman."

"Aye, Lord Malvern, 'tis so," Gavin said from his saddle, his hand clasped around the cross resting against his chest. "Lady Pierce's reputation was at stake. 'Twas nothing to be done but see them wed."

The somber words hung thickly in the air between them like a cloud.

"Lady *Pierce*?" An animalistic growl ripped from Malvern's throat as he sliced the sword through the air before returning it to its sheath. "You inbred fools. Do you have any idea what punishment Maclaren will suffer for such a betrayal?"

Sorcha sucked in an audible breath and lurched forward. "It wasn't his fault—"

"Silence!" the marquess seethed. "I will not listen to the words of a maimed harlot."

Sorcha drew back, as if she'd been slapped, and the desire to tear Malvern limb from limb shook Brandt to his core. Finlay and Evan directed their horses between him and

Malvern before Brandt could charge forward.

"Calm yerself, Malvern," Finlay said in a bizarrely placating voice. "Ye'll be compensated, I vow it."

To this, Finlay received a contemptuous scoff from the marquess. "Compensation," he repeated. "What I *want* is the alliance I was bequeathed by the bloody King of England, you cock-brained idiot."

A collective hush fell over the stable yard. Maclaren men eyed one another as Sorcha's brother tightened his posture in his saddle. Brandt expected him to reach for his sword and swing at Malvern's head for the insult. But, other than the slight hitch of his blocky chin, Finlay remained motionless. He said nothing in his own defense, though his jaw clenched tight with anger and his fingers whitened against the reins. Brandt frowned as a peculiar sense of dread trickled into him.

"The marriage will be annulled," Malvern announced. "Immediately. Coxley, fetch the magistrate."

A hulking soldier behind Malvern turned to follow the order. *Coxley.* A chime of recognition strummed at the back of Brandt's mind. Coxley had been Malvern's colonel during the war, and his deeds on the battlefield had chilled Brandt to the bone when he'd first heard of them. Coxley had slain many a soldier, but it was his penchant for disemboweling his enemies with perverse fervor that other Englishmen had remembered.

Brandt pushed the sickening images away. He would not be intimidated by Malvern's man. Nor would he pay attention to the unnatural cowardice the Maclaren men were displaying.

"An annulment is no longer an option."

Coxley stopped his horse, and Malvern's livid glare came back to rest on Brandt.

"Well then, Pierce, as you've already done your duty as

husband, I will take pleasure in making my future bride a *widow*." He paused, a slick grin thinning his lips, and then he repeated what he'd ordered earlier. "Take up a weapon."

The man was tenacious, Brandt would give him that.

"Lord Malvern!" Gavin shouted from his saddle. "There will be no bloodshed upon sacred ground."

Malvern's men eyed one another, then roared with laughter.

"It's an inn, not a church," one of them shouted back.

Gavin extended his arm, an adamant finger pointing to the gray stone exterior of the building that flanked the other side of the stable yard. Brandt felt like clapping Gavin on the shoulder. "*That* is a house of the Lord, sir, and ye're standing upon consecrated ground," Sorcha's cousin said, while Brandt's eyes shot to the narrow opening between the stables and the corner of the church.

Quickly, while Malvern's men shouted foul objections to Gavin's claim, Brandt determined the layout of Selkirk's village, its proximity to the nearest copse of trees, and the forested hills beyond. He had a brace of pistols, his boot dirk, and a sword sheathed in the harness of his saddle along with a quiver and two dozen arrows.

He could stay and fight Malvern, but his senses warned that there was absolutely no way for him to win, not here. Not on Malvern's terms. If Brandt knew anything, it was to trust his instincts.

"You heathen bastards wouldn't know God if he kicked you in the arse," Malvern muttered, but he turned up his nose at Gavin's pious claims and speared Brandt with a venomous glare. "Follow me to the paddock opposite the smithy." His eyes flicked to Sorcha. "Leave the Beast here."

Brandt held Malvern's stare another moment and nearly gave in to the desire to ignore instinct, and stay and fight. He wanted to break every single tooth inside the man's arrogant mouth. The marquess and his men turned and rode out of the stable yard. No doubt he was currently instructing his soldiers to circle the village to cut Brandt off should he cower and run.

Sorcha gripped Brandt's elbow, and he could feel the tremor in her hand. Glancing back at her, he saw her eyes had rounded into alarmed orbs. Before, she had merely appeared paralyzed by frustration and disgust for Malvern, but now she suddenly seemed wary and afraid.

For me, Brandt realized.

"What are you going to do?" she said. "You can't mean to duel him."

He shook his head. No, he didn't plan on being so agreeable. He wouldn't be surprised if one of Malvern's men loosed an arrow straight to the middle of his back. His gaze slipped to the muscled gray stallion at her side. And he didn't plan on losing his hard-won gains, either. He needed a way out of this stable yard—and he needed to take Sorcha and Lockie with him.

"Get on your horse," he said as softly as possible. "Be ready."

Obeying his command, Sorcha climbed into her saddle and wrapped her fists around the reins. He pulled himself up onto Ares's back and met Sorcha's wide, intense eyes.

"I need you to trust me, Sorcha," he said, but before he could explain, Finlay rode to his side. Evan was busy riding between the other men, giving terse orders.

"He willnae let ye live, Pierce, ye ken," Finlay said. "He'll cheat ye."

"I know."

Finlay jerked his chin at Sorcha. "The lass will stay with me."

"Like hell." Brandt wrapped his hands around one of Sorcha's reins. "I don't know what Malvern did to crush your ballocks and your spine, but it's clear he owns you. She stays with me."

Finlay grit his teeth, his jaw muscles jumping, but Brandt didn't have time to argue. "I'll ride for the northern woods. If you want to keep your sister safe, we'll need a distraction. A big one. *Now*."

Brandt tugged on Sorcha's reins and dug his heels into Ares's ribs. His horse leaped in response, and with a yelp of surprise from Sorcha, they rode toward the narrow opening between the stables and the church. Once they cleared it, Brandt saw the side street was packed with market vendors for the festival. Ares and Lockie weren't the only horses in the crowd, but they both stood out. Ares especially.

"What are we doing?" Sorcha asked, her voice rising.

Brandt hushed her before he darted his eyes up and down the street, searching for Malvern's armed men. The paddock Malvern had indicated wasn't far on the western side of the village, and well within view of the copse of trees into which Brandt was aiming to escape.

As they picked their way up the street toward a knoll of green grass and beyond that, a thick cluster of whitebeams, Sorcha tugged the rein he still had in his grip. "I can direct my own mount."

"He's mine, remember?" he replied with a sideways curl of his lips that made Sorcha growl under her breath.

"Yes, of course I remember," she snapped. "We're both your property now."

"I'm a man who always protects his investments."

Her eyes snapped with affront and turned the hue of a thundercloud. But he was saved from the bite of her tongue as a sharp whistle sounded from behind them, followed by a bellow of alarm. Brandt didn't look back.

"Ride, Sorcha!" he shouted, pushing Ares into a full gallop. Lockie came along, fast and powerful, and Brandt forced Ares to slow until the gray had surpassed him, Sorcha leaning forward over his mane. Clods of dirt and grass kicked up in their wake as they drove toward the knoll, Brandt's heart thudding, wind screaming in his ears. Behind them, a commotion began to break out.

And then a heavy explosion swallowed it whole.

Brandt twisted in his saddle to see a black cloud billowing into the air above the village, with shrieks and cries echoing from the streets. The smoke cloud appeared to be just above the inn.

"What was that?" Sorcha shouted as they crested the knoll and kept on, toward the forested hills a few leagues away.

"I suspect it was the distraction I had hoped for," he said with an unreasonable surge of affection for her stubborn brothers. It lasted for a handful of moments as they kept on toward the trees, Brandt checking over his shoulder every few seconds. There was another explosion, followed by a resurgence of screams and the tolling of a bell, but so far as Brandt could see, they weren't being followed.

The cool spring morning air dropped in temperature as they entered the woods. There was no path, no trail, but Lockie took a gallant and decisive lead onward, through the trees and up the incline. With Ares chomping at the bit, they traveled deeper into the wood. Rocks and scrub brush littered the forest floor, and Brandt worried for the integrity of their mounts' strides. But then they came upon a thin trail, likely used by goats or sheep, and he and Sorcha picked up speed.

Within the hour, the distant drumbeats from the festival could no longer be heard, and Brandt, now certain Malvern and his men had not followed, slowed Ares. The forest had opened into valleys in spots and then closed again into hilly woodland, and when looking south, toward Selkirk, he had not seen riders on their trail.

Neither he nor Sorcha spoke when they stopped to fill

their waterskins and let their mounts drink from passing streams. They didn't speak when Sorcha dismounted Lockie and dipped into the woods to relieve herself, nor when Brandt did the same. They didn't speak when they heard the hollow bells of a herd of sheep as they crossed another verdant valley and the sound of a shepherd lounging somewhere in the tall grasses, singing a ballad.

The noon hour came and went, and still Sorcha didn't utter a word. A part of him didn't care. And yet, her silence gnawed at him. He could suss out what a man or horse was feeling without trying, but this woman…he couldn't make heads nor tails of her. She'd fought Craig like a banshee, yet she had seemed rattled when faced with the marquess, much like her brothers had. Brandt wondered at the unusual sway the man held over the Maclarens.

When they finally saw a small stone cottage tucked in the bowl of one valley, he cleared his throat. "It looks deserted."

She granted an, "Aye," and directed her horse in the cottage's direction.

It was more a ruin than a home, but their horses needed rest, and Brandt didn't want to push them too far. They closed Ares and Lockie in the dilapidated paddock attached to one side, with water from a nearby crick and some grass for grazing. Once they were settled, Brandt took Sorcha by the elbow and swiveled her to finally look at him.

"Your brothers were cowards with Malvern." Sorcha set her jaw and began to pull away, but Brandt held her firmly. "They forced the man they found kissing you into marriage, but another man insults you and they let him walk away, still breathing. What kind of kin are they?"

"They don't have a choice," she said, her arm writhing for freedom. The tumble of her dark hair, unkempt from the hard ride into the country, made her appear ferocious. Inexplicably, it made his blood thunder in his veins.

"Explain," he snapped, irked at his body's carnal response to her.

Fury glinted in her eyes at the order for a scant second before it was dulled by resigned submission. He much preferred the fire of the former, but for now, he wanted her to speak.

"The Maclarens are oath bound not to raise arms against Malvern," she replied in a wooden voice. "It was part of the terms of the king's settlement upon his father. When he received Maclaren lands because of my uncle's deception with the Jacobites, he became the English lord of Tarben Castle and was charged with keeping an eye on the rest of the Maclarens. My father retained his title and his portion of the holdings, and when Malvern's father died, he petitioned the English crown for the lands to be returned. Malvern refused. He lied, claiming that he was fearful for his life in a keep that was full of clan Maclaren rebels, and my father was sworn never to bring arms against him or any effort to reclaim my uncle's lands."

She kept attempting to break free of his grip, and not wanting to bruise her skin, Brandt released her arm. He frowned. Though her explanation made logical sense, it did not explain why Malvern was allowed such insulting freedom. "And yet they broke another oath to him. The one that said you were to be his bride." He took a step away from the moss-covered paddock rails and raked a hand through his hair. "Malvern was right about one thing: your brothers are fools."

Sorcha struck him square in the chest with such alacrity and force, Brandt nearly stumbled backward. "My brothers are not fools! Malvern is wrong, and *ye're* wrong!" she cried, lashing out at him again. This time he caught her fists and wrapped his hands around her slim wrists. "They'd murder Malvern if it didnae mean the dozens of Maclarens living on Tarben Castle lands would pay in blood for it!"

He dragged her against him as she continued to struggle, and with her hands restrained, she resorted to kicking. She connected with his shin before he swept her legs out from under her and took her to the ground, bracing her back with his arms to cushion her fall.

"Ye ken nothing of my family or of me!" she yelled as he pinned her hands above her head and held himself aside of her thrashing legs. "Get off me, ye dunderheid!"

"Stop, Sorcha. Stop," he said, her knees coming up, her hips wriggling. Finally, he pressed the full weight of his body against hers and flattened her to the ground. She writhed once more and then, with a frustrated grunt, lay motionless. Brandt knew he'd made a mistake the second he felt the press of her breasts against his chest, her hips flush against his, and the wisps of her hot breath on his neck. Her body was soft, but he could still feel toned muscle beneath her curves. *Jesus.* He was already getting hard.

As if sensing his hesitation, her hips bucked up off the grass in an attempt to lever him off her, and Brandt's instinct took control—he ground his lower half into hers in response. Sorcha made a half-desperate sound in her throat, and hell if it didn't sound like a moan.

"Enough," he muttered, though not to her. Not entirely. No, *he* was the one who had to stop. He had to get control of himself.

She shifted and took small breaths, each pant a shot tormenting his growing erection. There was something entirely dangerous in knowing he had every right in the eyes of both the law *and* God to push up Sorcha's skirts and bury himself in her. But he'd promised her, and himself, that she'd still be a virgin when he left her on Brodie lands. Giving in to his lust would only create more problems.

As if they weren't already swimming in them.

"My brothers protected us," she said. "Those were the

gunpowder casks they blew to distract Malvern and his men."

"The least they could do," he muttered.

"Malvern's retaliation will be swift," she said. "And bloody. My family will pay for what you asked of them."

Something in her tone made Brandt lift himself, releasing her and sitting back on his heels. "You'll defend them no matter what I say, won't you?" he asked. The woman was a stubborn mule.

Sorcha sat up, pushing her tangled hair out of her flushed face.

A provocative, stubborn mule.

"Don't you have brothers? Sisters?" she asked, her temper receding. He could tell by the way her brogue had lessened.

Brandt stood up and held out his hand, but she ignored it and got to her feet on her own. Monty had married Brandt's stepmother, Anne, when Brandt was two years old, but they'd never given him any siblings. It hadn't been a loss for Brandt, really. He'd had Archer growing up.

"Bradburne is the closest thing I have to a brother," he replied.

"Your employer?" she asked, her quizzical expression giving away her surprise.

He nodded, supposing it was a bit odd for a duke to count his stable master among his closest friends, but Archer had never been typical in anything.

Sorcha's raised brow settled. "Well then, wouldn't you defend him no matter what?"

A smile lit upon his mouth. "I would take a bullet for him."

She blinked, clearly not ready for such a declaration. "You would?"

"Actually, I already have," he said with a short laugh. "So I suppose it's his turn to take a bullet for me now."

He hadn't felt any tenderness in his thigh lately where

a bullet had ripped through four years before. Brandt had saved Archer's life during his stint as the notorious Masked Marauder, a gentlemanly highwayman who stole from the *ton* and gave, anonymously, to the poor. The fact that Brandt had both warned him that particular heist would be perilous, and had been the one to be arrested *after* being shot, had provided plenty of opportunities for Brandt to tease Archer—and guilt him enough to cover more than a few tabs at the village tavern.

"*You've* been shot?" Sorcha asked, her eyes going round with disbelief, and Brandt fought back a laugh at her reluctantly impressed expression.

"Ages ago, a superficial wound," he replied, patting his thigh. "Don't worry, it wasn't a permanent maiming."

She lowered her lashes and bit her lips, and Brandt wondered what he'd said to dim the light from her eyes. Then it hit him: *I will not listen to a maimed harlot.* Malvern's words, vicious and cruel. He felt the renewed urge to pulverize the man's face. He opened his mouth and closed it. Sorcha wouldn't want his pity, and he shouldn't be feeling any inclination to offer it in the first place. Letting himself care would be a slippery slope.

She shrugged. "So then you know, in a way, what it is to love a sibling."

He supposed she had a point.

Sorcha moved past Brandt toward the cottage. He took a breath and looked up, away from the sway of her hips as she walked. He was reminded of her lightness of step in the paddock with Craig and the ease with which she'd moved, though that fighting spirit seemed diminished by the shadows in her eyes.

Brandt loosed a breath as they climbed the rickety stairs to the rotting stoop. It was little more than a shack, but the skies to the south had clouded and would bring rain. The sorry thatched roof topping the cottage would not offer much, but it would have to do.

"I do understand," he finally answered her. Capitulating to her felt easier than he thought it would, and the brief smile she flashed at him over her shoulder made him want to agree with her again. About anything.

Idiot.

He moved in front of her, stopping her hand before she could open the door. No one was likely inside, but he didn't want Sorcha entering first. Just in case. The chit had the audacity to roll her eyes at him, before throwing one arm wide and sketching a sarcastic bow.

He pushed it wide, and the musty, dank air of an unused hovel was the only thing to greet him. Dirt floors, a blackened hearth, and foggy glass windows…what was left of them, that was. But for some empty barrels, there wasn't a scrap of furniture.

"I'll start a fire," Sorcha said, immediately setting for the hearth. There were some sticks and some old, charred logs. Brandt found more kindling in a box beside the cottage, and soon, they'd worked to build a small flame in the grate. They sipped from their waterskins as the first drops of rain pattered the ground outside.

"Do you think Malvern and Coxley will track us?"

Her voice was calm. Too calm. She had heard the marquess's threats about making her a widow, and the man was well known for his reputation in battle. Coxley, too. They were both military men of sadistic persuasions—a dangerous combination. Brandt couldn't tell her not to worry, that Malvern couldn't find them or would abandon the hunt. She was far too intelligent to believe such rubbish.

"He'll try," Brandt answered. "We won't stay here long. We'll go north."

"We're not going to Maclaren," she stated, understanding

lighting her eyes.

Brandt shook his head. "Too risky. We'll head straight to your sister. And Malvern might also expect us to head south to England. I've sent word to Bradburne just in case."

Before going to the stable yard that morning he'd tasked the innkeeper with sending a hastily written note to Hadley Gardens in London, where Archer and Briannon and their young daughters were currently spending the season.

Going to Brodie would also mean not having the chance to face the Duke of Dunrannoch at Maclaren and inform him that he'd not only obtained the steed he'd been refused time and time again, but that he'd also taken his precious daughter to wed. Brandt couldn't say it didn't give him a bit of gratification. Dunrannoch was an irascible old man who deserved the title of beast more than his daughter.

"You're not afraid of Malvern," Sorcha said, crouching to warm her hands over the meager flames. Again, it was a statement rather than a question.

"Are you?"

"I'm wary of him," she said. "There's a difference. He's a terrible person to have as an enemy."

"Yes," he agreed. "He is not one to be underestimated. He has a ruthless reputation, particularly with Coxley at his beck and call."

Brandt stooped beside her in an effort to generate more warmth between them. "Why does Malvern want you so badly?"

She pursed her lips. "My dowry. Land rich in cairngorm topaz. My father offered to give it to him and release me from the betrothal, but Malvern wants to make sure no one else lays claim to the land. An heir would guarantee that." Sorcha shuddered as if the thought was an unbearable one.

"Your brothers seem fearful of him," Brandt said quietly. "Why?"

"It's not fear. Any one of us would kill him if we could, but he has the ear and favor of the king." Her throat worked convulsively, and for a moment it seemed as if she wasn't going to continue. Sorcha's fingers curled into fists as she looked up at him, pain blooming in her blue eyes. "Finlay is a hothead," she began. "Evan, too."

Brandt didn't dispute the statement. He'd experienced it firsthand.

"They were young, and wanted our lands back and the threat of an English lord gone. Malvern hadn't shown an interest in Maclaren after the death of his own father, and Finlay hoped to make him stay away for good. He set fire to one of the unattended fields, but the winds were fierce that day and the fire spread." She drew a ragged breath. "It was contained, but not before it destroyed part of the keep, and Malvern's steward was badly burned. Malvern somehow found out it was a plot by Finlay and Evan and demanded recompense." She swallowed, her lip trembling. "In flesh."

Brandt's frown deepened. "Flesh?"

"For his wounded steward. The man lived, but lost the use of his arm. As payment, Malvern took Niall's hand."

"Niall?"

"My brother," she whispered. "The youngest and most innocent of us all. He was only ten. The king gave Malvern carte blanche to take his pound of flesh as he saw fit. My father pleaded, begged to give his own limb instead, but Malvern did not bend. The blackhearted bastard had Coxley do it in the courtyard with all of Maclaren present to bear witness. He smiled the entire time." A guttural sob escaped her lips. "Niall was so brave, so courageous. He fainted from the pain before he let himself utter a sound. Malvern swore that the next time we lifted arms against him, he would take his life."

Brandt reached out a hand, but she shied away from him, the suppressed fury in her eyes like a demented living thing.

"*Och*, I should not have brought you into this madness," she said. "Who knows what he will do to you as punishment. He is a powerful man with powerful friends."

Brandt set his jaw. "I have powerful friends, too."

"You don't know what he's capable of," she said.

He felt something unfamiliar in his chest clench—the desire to safeguard any woman was new to him, but the fear in her eyes was real. Fear for herself. Fear for her family. She had used him with her plot to thwart Malvern, but he sensed no deceit in her now. "Why did you choose me that day, Sorcha? You could have kissed a hundred men in the square. Why me?"

Defiance flashed in her eyes, and she ducked her head briefly. "Because of the way you looked at me…as though you *saw* me." She gestured at her face. "Like you saw beyond what everyone else usually does…the dreadful Beast of Maclaren."

Her answer was halting, but Brandt knew what she meant—she wanted to be seen beyond her disfiguring scars.

"No one had ever looked at me like that. I felt a flicker of what it was to be truly desired." She faltered, her cheeks aflame. "It was foolish, but I'd meant it to be only a kiss."

A kiss that had sealed their fates.

Embarrassed, Sorcha kept her eyes averted, and Brandt lifted his fingers to graze her rosy cheek. His thumb stroked gently. She was so guarded that it was hard to tell if she was playing coy or whether she was truly *that* innocent. Despite her blush, her soft skin was cold in the paltry heat. Her body shivered.

"You need to get warm," he said. "We should get you out of this damp dress before you catch a chill."

She gaped at him. "That isn't proper."

"We're married, remember? And we have the sheet to prove it."

Sorcha's lips formed a wry smirk at his attempt to lighten the moment. "How's your wound?" she asked, her eyes glancing to his forearm.

His mouth twitched with mischief. "I think my arm might be with child."

A shocked laugh broke from her as she turned around to let him loosen the fasteners. "On the first try?" she asked.

"It takes only one time, you know," he said from behind her. "And I have it on good authority that I'm a very virile man."

"Is that so? Then you and your forearm should be very happy." Sorcha eyed him over her shoulder, eyes crinkling with amusement, and Brandt had the sudden desire to enfold her in his arms and kiss that saucy mouth. He balked at the thought. She would not welcome it, nor should he even be encouraging such a thing.

But then he pulled the gown over her head, leaving her standing in only her stays and chemise, and any rational thought deserted him. His breath stuck in his throat as the flames from the fire outlined the silhouette of her long, slender legs. All amusement disappeared in a trice, replaced by a brutish ache in his loins. *Christ.*

Mumbling a hasty excuse, he stepped outside to retrieve his cloak from his saddlebags and gulped in the chilly night air before making sure that Ares and Lockie were dry in the stable. The brisk air did nothing to calm the fire racing through his blood, though by the time he returned to place the woolen cloak over Sorcha, he was shivering, too. Brandt rubbed his hands briskly together.

"What about you?" she asked. "Won't you be cold?"

"I'm accustomed to the cold," he lied.

"In Essex?" She arched a dark eyebrow, a smile playing about her lips. Her eyes were warm, glowing with gratitude, amusement, and approval. His pulse resumed an unsteady cadence. Brandt did not want or need her approval, and he most certainly did not expect to *like* how it made him feel.

Focus on the goal, you idiot. Get her to her sister, claim the horse, go home.

His future did not include a wife. Wives would eventually want children, and he had no interest in being a father. His misbegotten, sorry line would die with him. Just as his heartless mother had intended when she'd tossed him out with the slop.

"It can get quite cold during the winters there," he said, keeping the rise of bitterness at bay and his tone neutral. "Nothing like your Highland winters, but I'm fine, trust me."

"Suit yourself."

Sorcha reached back to adjust the thick cloak around her shoulders, and her shift stretched tight over the rise of a pair of pert, round breasts. She was not buxom, but her curves were more than enough to catch his attention. *Damnation*. Brandt cast his eyes up, away from her charms, and pretended to inspect the condition of the sagging thatched roof.

"Tell me about Maclaren," he said in a strained voice. "And your brothers, especially Finlay and Evan."

Sorcha shot him a doubtful look, but Brandt nodded enthusiastically. He let out a pent-up breath when she began. Stories about Finlay and Evan were the perfect solution—a solid metaphorical kick to the ballocks. Irritation was far preferable to half a cockstand in a deserted cottage with his baggage of a wife wearing nothing but a snug chemise and a smile that could melt the strongest inhibitions.

He would keep his distance if it killed him.

Even if it meant listening to the head-splitting tales of Evan and Finlay Maclaren.

Chapter Six

It had been a long while since Sorcha had thought about all the trouble Finlay and Evan had wreaked upon Maclaren lands when they'd been younger, but over the next few hours, she recounted a number of stories to Brandt.

Like the time they had set all the horses loose and a few of their father's valuable foals had gone missing for days, or the time they had dared her to climb the tallest tree in the glen and then left her up there until the duke found her hours later, nearly frozen from cold. They were barely a year apart and egged each other on abominably. When Sorcha was old enough to want to prove herself as capable as they were, they became the bane of her existence…and the source of most of her near-death scrapes.

Her sisters, Makenna and Annis, had been older by five and seven years, and they'd never so much as gone against the grain, so her stories revolved mostly around Finlay and Evan, and their father's meager attempts to take them in hand. Ronan and Niall were the end caps of her siblings. Ronan had always been serious, the weight of being laird one day resting on his shoulders from the time he drew his first breath. And Niall was the baby, though he was by no means spoiled or coddled.

Sorcha had a sneaking suspicion Brandt was trying to distract her, but she was grateful for the attempt. "Niall turned fifteen last winter," she said. "Of all my siblings, he and I are the closest. He likes to play tricks, especially on Evan and Finlay. He sewed all the cuffs of their shirts closed once."

"With one hand?"

"You'd be amazed at the things that boy can do." Sorcha smiled softly. "He never ceases to amaze me."

Brandt stoked the fire, listening as she spoke, his eyes tracking the play of the flames in the hearth. He smiled and shook his head at all the right moments, and every now and again, glanced her way to see if she'd stopped shivering. She could see the concern in his eyes before averting his gaze again. It was because of how she was dressed, she knew. Or rather, her lack of dress.

Sorcha had seen the brief, but definite, burn of arousal in his eyes when she'd been standing before him in nothing but her shift. His lips had gone soft with surprise in the moments before he'd stalked out of the decaying cottage, gotten his cloak, and covered her with it. Now every time he looked to see if she was still cold, a shot of heat lit through her. He'd distracted her from their situation, not only by asking her to tell him stories about her home and family, but simply by being there, seated on the worn floor, across from her.

Though being this close to him—to any man—was foolish.

Even if he was her husband.

Sorcha sighed. Once they parted ways, it was unlikely she would ever marry again, even if her maidenhead remained intact. Too many men feared the look of her or feared her father and brothers. The arrangement with Malvern had been a matter of duty, until she'd seen the disgust in his eyes when he'd come face-to-face with her years ago. *A maimed harlot* was his latest insult, but she'd heard them all. She was unfit to be anyone's wife. Simply looking in a mirror while unclothed told her that. Aric had had the right of it. She bit down on the inside of her cheek, his voice invading her mind. *I'll no' look at such a beast again.*

The rain had tapered, though the leaky roof still dripped in multiple spots around the one-room cottage. Dusk had settled over the valley, and as Sorcha finished with another tale, this one about Evan wrapping their cousin Gavin in bedsheets and hanging him out one of the castle windows until Gavin apologized for calling him a hell-bound heathen, she fell quiet.

Brandt held his hands to the flames, which he'd built time and again with more wood scavenged from around the property. She'd dried out and warmed up long before, and now her limbs had that satiated, loose feeling that reminded her of lazy summer afternoons in the fields near home. Or after hours of rugged training with her sword and bow and arrow. She drew his cloak closer around her and inhaled, yet again, the oddly comforting combination of soap, leather, and horses.

"Thank you," she murmured.

Brandt allowed his eyes to meet hers. "What for?"

"For calming me," she answered. "My brothers infuriate me to no end, but they also remind me of home."

It was a place where she knew she would not be able to return anytime soon, and it saddened her. She prayed if she stayed away, it would also keep Malvern away. It was a foolish hope, though, and she knew it.

"What if he goes to Maclaren?" she asked.

Brandt didn't need to ask to whom she referred.

"He won't kill Niall," he said. "Your father, your brothers

and people...they won't stand for it."

Sorcha didn't believe they would, either, but she'd seen how intimidated they were by Malvern. People called her the Beast of Maclaren, and she had spent years honing her skill with a sword and bow, determined to live up to the name in a way no one had ever intended. But how could she have possibly found anything but pain and degradation as Malvern's wife? He loathed her, saw her as little more than an animal. The wolf had stolen more than her flesh; it had stolen her dignity.

"We could go there," Sorcha heard herself saying, her stomach tight with the same burden of ugly shame she'd borne for much of her life. "To Maclaren. We could warn them that Malvern has been wronged—"

"No. It's too much of a risk."

"But I can't leave them to—"

"Your presence won't save anyone. They can fend for themselves, Sorcha. Your father is a chieftain and your brothers are trained Highland warriors. They'll protect their own. You're *my* responsibility now, and I'm bringing you north to your sister." Brandt stood and dusted off the seat of his trousers. "I'm going to take Ares and retrace our last few miles, make sure no one has discovered our tracks."

But just as he rose, the sound of hoofbeats—a small army of them—rent through the air. Sorcha jumped to her feet, her heart hammering as she tugged her dry dress over her head. Without Brandt's help to redo the fastenings, she looped his cloak around her shoulders, and hurried to where he stood peering out through the dirty window into the darkness.

"Who is it?" she asked. "Can you see?"

"They haven't yet come over the rise, but it will prove difficult to see anything without moonlight. The clouds are still thick."

Sorcha tried to push past him to get a clearer look, but

he restrained her with a rigid, powerful arm. She'd forgotten how deceptively lean he was. The man was as strong as an ox.

"Stay put," he told her, crouching to douse the flames with ash. "And stay out of sight. Whoever it is may ride straight past."

Or come banging on the door.

Anyone heading out this way to an old goat herder's hut wasn't going to be riding past, especially when they scented woodsmoke on the air. And if it was Malvern's men, she wanted to be prepared, not cowering without a weapon in hand. She ducked out of his reach and grabbed hold of one of his pistols that he'd brought in from his saddlebag. There was no way she was going down without a hell of a fight.

Pressing a finger to his lips, Brandt met her eyes and nodded. She'd expected him to demand the weapon back and tell her to go hide in a corner, but he only palmed the second pistol and gripped his sword hilt in its scabbard. Sorcha wished she had her own sword, but she had left it behind in the wagon in Selkirk. She hefted the gun.

"Do you know how to use that?" Brandt asked in a low voice.

Sorcha set her jaw grimly. "Yes."

She was an excellent shot. Ever since she'd been betrothed to the man who had cruelly maimed her brother, she'd practiced with single-minded purpose. For so many years, she'd bided her time, training herself. If the chance arose to kill Malvern in a way that would not implicate the Maclarens, she would take it without hesitation.

"I always hoped one day Malvern would be vulnerable, and I planned to be there with a weapon in hand."

"You're a bloodthirsty lass."

She grinned, pleased at the compliment.

The pounding of the hooves drew closer. The noise was thunderous, and Sorcha's heart banged in time with the rhythmic sounds as she and Brandt took up places behind a large overturned barrel. His face was calm, but his body seemed bunched and ready. It struck her again that her taciturn husband was far more than he seemed. The look on his face was one that she had seen many a time on the faces of Maclaren soldiers—the look of a man not afraid of death.

"How good of a shot are you?" she whispered.

"Decent."

"Then if it's Malvern, let me take it," she said. "I'm better than decent."

His sudden smile was unexpected. Breathtaking. It made his hazel eyes gleam and a shallow dimple appear in his left cheek. He looked almost boyishly handsome. Pinpricks of awareness flickered all over her skin, and the rest of her words seized on her tongue.

"Humble, aren't we?"

Sorcha colored. "I know my skill."

"I don't doubt your skill in the least," he said. "But the minute you fire, you will be a target for his men, and I've made you a promise to see you to safety. I'll deal with Malvern."

"How? You're going to *talk* him to death? He won't listen."

"Trust in me, Sorcha. I'm not a complete imbecile."

"I didn't—"

But the rest of her words were snatched from her lips as the door slammed open. The breath left her lungs with a terrified exhale as a massive hulking form filled the doorway. And as recognition set in, a different kind of dread took hold of her body.

Not him.

Her heart sank. She was relieved it wasn't Malvern, but she would have preferred nearly anyone else to the man who stood before them: her eldest brother, Ronan. Nearly ten years her senior, she'd always viewed her unsmiling giant of a brother as an extension of their father, and he was. He was relentless and commanding and everything a great Scottish laird would have to be.

Sorcha had always been a little in awe of her oldest brother, though he had only ever been gentle with her on the occasions that their paths did intersect. Now his lips were a hard, flat line, and every muscle in his body was braced for a fight. With a quelling glance to the silent man at her side, she rose.

"Ronan," she began as his glacial blue gaze swept the darkened room. Sorcha felt it flick over her and then rest for a hard moment on Brandt. A torch was brought into the room by one of his men, and the small dusty space was instantly illuminated.

"What have ye done?" her brother bellowed. "Ye were spoken for, Sorcha. Ye've broken the terms of the alliance *and* insulted the marquess."

She felt Brandt stiffen at her side at Ronan's gruff tone, and she hastened forward, despite her quailing heart. Ronan would never hurt her, but she'd seen grown men piss their pants in the face of his anger. "I know how it looks, but I can explain. He, I—"

How could she explain that she'd seduced a stranger in an attempt to save her own skin? That she'd run from her duty to marry Malvern like a frightened hare? That she'd betrayed Maclaren for the sum of a horse? She swallowed hard.

But before she could speak, her husband was moving to her side. Her brother's eyes narrowed at his advance. Though Brandt was of a height, Ronan was twice as wide and twice as fierce.

She put out a hand to stop Brandt's approach, but he clasped her numb fingers within his and laced them together. A show of solidarity, she assumed with a jolt of surprise. His skin was warm, engulfing her cold fingers with heat and strength. Ronan's gaze dipped to their joined hands, and his hard lips flattened.

"Don't speak to her like that," Brandt said. "Insult me if you must."

Ronan folded his massive arms across his chest. "She's promised to another."

Brandt stepped forward until they were nearly nose to nose. "That's too damned bad. She belongs to me now."

Though Sorcha knew his possessive words were an act—he was more likely thinking of the horse that had been promised to him—she still felt something small and delicate unfold in the pit of her stomach.

But then, her eyes flicked to the shadowed yard beyond his wide shoulders, and she swallowed a nervous gasp. A dozen of his best Maclaren men were armed and grim-faced. They stood silent, deadly and dangerous, waiting for their leader's command. She felt the blood drain from her face.

Did they mean to drag her back to Maclaren? To *Malvern*? Make her a widow? Could Ronan be that cruel? Her brother was not prone to displays of emotion. He'd been there in the courtyard when Niall's hand had been severed, but he had not reacted as violently as his siblings. His face had been devoid of anything, his eyes dead and cold. Much like they were now.

"Are ye prepared to die, Sassenach?"

Sorcha gasped. "Ronan!"

"Stay out of it." The ominous rasp of steel against leather broke the silence. "Are ye prepared to pay the price for defiling my sister? For scorning an agreement signed in blood?"

Brandt smiled, though it was not like the one earlier. This one was no more than a stretching of lips over his teeth. "If you truly cared about your sister, you would want for her happiness. And safety. What the hell do you think Malvern will do to her now, if you do manage to hand her over? Which you won't."

Ronan's face hardened, something glinting precariously in his eye. A muscle flexed in his cheek. When he spoke, her brother's voice was little more than a snarl. "And ye think ye can provide safety for her, *Sassenach*?"

Brandt did not react to the underlying threat. "A damn sight better than you can. And the name is Pierce. It would serve you well to remember it."

The growl came from deep within her brother's chest, and from the corner of her eye, she saw his gathered men draw closer. Sorcha moved to throw herself between the two of them, but quickly found herself restrained by Duncan, Ronan's first man, who had been standing beside Ronan. He was two heads shorter than her brother, but no less lethal. Brandt dropped a murderous look to Duncan's hands on her arm and clenched his jaw.

"Cat got yer tongue, *Sassenach*?" Duncan laughed.

Sorcha could have sworn she didn't see Brandt move, but suddenly she was in his arms, and his pistol was pointed at Duncan's temple. Shouts filled the room as every man outside rushed the doorway, and only Ronan's raised fist stopped the ensuing melee.

"The fact that you're still alive is your warning, *Scot*," Brandt hissed to Duncan. "Put your hands on her again, and she will be the last thing you ever touch."

"Stand back," Ronan said to his men, keeping an alert gaze on Brandt.

The man had surprised her brother, which was nearly impossible to do. Hell, Brandt had surprised *her*. She didn't know anyone could move so quickly. Clearly, neither Ronan nor Duncan had expected it either. They both studied him with a measure of grudging respect. Duncan seemed undaunted by a muzzle in his face, but then again, he'd faced death and won more times than he could count.

Brandt moved her gently but firmly behind him, keeping the pistol cocked and ready. Did he mean to protect her from her own brother? From Duncan? She'd known the man since she was in swaddling; he would never lay a finger on her without say-so from Ronan. But Brandt didn't know that. Her heart felt encased in butterflies' wings, and her chest suddenly shrunk two sizes.

Good God, you ninny, get ahold of your wits, she told herself sternly. *All this is for the blasted horse, not you.*

She *knew* it was all a bloody act for her brother's sake… Brandt was protecting his investment, as he'd said. But for the space of an indulgent breath, she let herself wonder what it would be like to be cared for by a man such as Brandt. One would never have to fear for anything.

A wretched tremor shook her. If she were fit, perhaps such a dream could be possible. But men like him deserved women who were sound in body. And she was not.

Furious with her stupidity, she shoved past Brandt and glared viciously at Duncan. "Get out."

He obeyed after a look from his commander.

"Enough, Ronan," she said through her teeth. "I was the one to marry Mr. Pierce at Finlay's and Gavin's insistence. What's done is done, and either ye deal with that or ye take yer men and trot back to Maclaren. Blustering yer weight about is no' going to help anyone." Her voice broke, her tongue shortening vowels and falling back to her brogue. "I didnae want to marry Malvern, and Mr. Pierce agreed to help me."

To her everlasting surprise, Ronan's scowl relaxed slightly. His stare panned to Brandt. "Why are ye doing this? Ye don't owe her anything. Ye don't even ken anything about her."

Sorcha's gaze shot to Brandt as well. Would he expose

what was truly motivating him? That he was doing all this for Lockie?

"Because she sought my help."

"And ye give it, just like that, even if yer own neck is on the end of the rope?"

Brandt nodded. "It was the way I was raised."

Sorcha stifled a snort. The way he was raised, her arse. He was an enterprising horse breeder who had taken advantage of a windfall. Now that Ronan was here, Brandt could take Lockie and go without a backward glance. Technically, she was safe. And *safely* married. An annulment could come later. The tug of disappointment took her by surprise.

"Strange ways for the English." Ronan's tone was disparaging. "They care naught for anyone. No' even their own."

"I'm not English."

Ronan grinned and cuffed him on the shoulder. "Ye sound like one."

Sorcha could feel Brandt relax at her side and knew the worst had passed. Something had changed between the two men—an acceptance, an understanding, perhaps. The tension disappeared like a receding wave. Ronan hadn't given any signal, but suddenly the men in the yard were unpacking and preparing to settle down for the night, without any bloodshed.

"Who's yer clan, then?" Ronan asked.

A muscle rippled along his jaw. "My Scottish mother abandoned me at birth, so your guess is as good as mine."

Sorcha flinched at the stony, sharp-edged coldness of the words. It was clear he held his mother in little esteem, and rightly so. Any woman who would abandon her own baby suffered from a complete lack of moral decency.

"I'm sorry."

His gaze pivoted to her. "You needn't be. She means nothing to me."

Though he sounded indifferent, Sorcha saw a spark of anger in his eyes before he turned away. Or was it pain?

It doesn't matter anyhow, she reminded herself and was relieved when her brother signaled to one of the men who then brought in a sack containing bread, cheese, and a whole roasted chicken. Sorcha's stomach rumbled. The last time she'd eaten a full meal had been supper the night before, and only an apple earlier that morning. They used a standing barrel in one corner and divided the food between them.

"The marquess will no' be far behind," Ronan said, after chewing and taking a long draught from a flask. He offered it to Brandt who took a deep swallow. "We were riding to meet Finlay and Evan on their way back to Maclaren when we intercepted one of their men, traveling fast with a message for Dunrannoch. We shifted direction to find ye. Malvern is rabid with bloodlust, Pierce. He willnae stop until ye're dead and he's taken the lass to wife."

Brandt handed the flask to Sorcha next, and she felt a hollow thrill at the fact that her lips had touched the exact spot his had. Brandt's eyes met hers as if he could see right through her, and Sorcha choked on the mouthful of wine. She gulped, coughing until her eyes burned, as Ronan pounded her helpfully on the back. She didn't know which was worse—expiring of mortification by a lungful of wine or the pressure of her brother's fist.

"Why are ye heading up this way?" Ronan asked. "Ye should go back to England."

"We are going north to the Brodie," Sorcha said. "The keep is deep in the mountains. Malvern wouldn't dare attack there."

"'Tis a smart plan," Ronan said. "I will hold him off for as long as I can to buy ye enough time. Makenna and the Brodie will protect the both of ye."

Sorcha didn't see the need to add that Brandt's plan had

been to leave her there all along. Whether he left now or later made little difference. They were clearly unsuited. He belonged in England. She belonged in Scotland. He would never survive in the Highlands. She could never survive out of it. He wanted a quiet life with his horses. She had never been a quiet lass in her life. He did not want a wife. She did not want a husband.

Liar, a voice said.

She shook her head. Brandt had never been hers to begin with. Yes, he was clever and capable, he'd stood up to Malvern and Ronan, and his kisses were, in a word, sublime. But what she *wanted* and what she was able to offer in return were two different things.

Brandt's next question made her forget all about her inner debate. "Would you have let her marry Malvern?"

To her shock, Ronan shook his head. "Nae. I would have found a way." He smiled wryly. "'Tis truth I'd planned to fake her death and send her off to the Brodie in secret. It was near arranged already, but Malvern's arrival in Selkirk took me by surprise. Though it seems my brothers stumbled upon a solution of their own—with yer help, of course."

"What?" Sorcha fairly screeched as blood rushed to her ears. "Ye let me ken all this time that I would go to that slithering bastard?"

Ronan's voice was gentler than she'd ever heard it. "I would no' have let anyone hurt ye. Finlay or Evan wouldnae either. But I didnae want to give ye false hope until 'twas sorted."

Sorcha threw herself into her brother's arms, feeling them wrap around her to hold her close. She was not a crier, but several fat tears rolled down her cheek.

"'Twill be best if ye left at dawn," Ronan said gruffly when she managed to compose herself. "The rain washed away most of yer tracks, but that doesnae mean Malvern's men won't be able to track ye." He stood and patted her head, his large frame dominating the small room. His blue eyes swept from her to Brandt. "If any harm comes to her, I'll no' hesitate to tear ye limb from limb."

"You won't have to," Brandt said. "I won't be going north. She'll be safer with you."

Sorcha froze, her lungs tightening painfully. Here it was... the moment he would take his leave. A frown drew Ronan's brows together. "With *me*?"

"You have warriors aplenty to get her north to your sister."

"And where will ye go, Sassenach?" Ronan's tone had cooled.

"Back to England."

"But ye married her."

Brandt tented a slow eyebrow. "I offered her the use of my name to avoid marriage to Malvern, nothing more. She's welcome to it for as long as she needs, as I do not intend to marry again."

Gulping a breath, Sorcha met her brother's questing gaze. "'Tis all right, Ronan," she said. "What he says is true. The marriage was an agreement to protect me from Malvern." She hesitated to reveal all but did so anyway. "He wanted Lockie in exchange."

"*Lockie*?" Ronan asked incredulously, his face darkening as he glowered at the man he'd just broken bread with. "Ye took my sister's virtue for a damned horse?"

Disaster was about to strike if she didn't do something. "Ronan, please understand. I *kissed* him in the square. I was the one who dragged him into this. If someone should be blamed, 'tis me. He gave me his name, and the marriage had to be incontestable." She placed her hand placatingly on his arm. Ronan's eyes were still spitting fury and brimstone, but he was listening. "You said yourself you wanted a way out for me. Brandt—Mr. Pierce—offered it. Lockie is a small price to pay for my freedom. It was *my* choice, Ronan. Mine."

Ronan exhaled without looking at Brandt, who also stood rigid a foot away. He looked like he wanted to smash something with his big hands. Probably Brandt. Though she'd seen him fight, too, and he wasn't exactly a milksop. Sorcha held her breath, waiting.

"Fine. We leave at dawn for Brodie." Ronan stood and left the hut without another word.

She didn't dare look up at Brandt, though she felt the weight of his gaze. "I need some air," she said after a few scattered heartbeats and rushed from the shack.

Once she was alone and past her brother's soldiers, Sorcha slumped against a tree in a small clearing. She wasn't surprised that it had come to this. Brandt had been a means to an end, and now that Ronan was here, Brandt's part was over. He would leave for good. Glancing down, she twisted off the ring on her finger with its faded crest. She wanted to hurl it away, but instead she clutched it to her chest, cursing fate and the future she could never have.

Chapter Seven

The sky was a bruised purple when Brandt finally gave up his night's watch. Not against Malvern's men, but on the off chance Sorcha's brother would come into the derelict cottage seeking revenge for his sister's honor. Brandt had spent the hours reclined on the floor, his back against the crumbling wall of horsehair plaster and stone, his eyes fixed on Sorcha's sleeping figure.

She'd curled up before the hearth, his cloak thrown over her like a blanket, one arm propped under her head acting as a pillow. Every now and again, his eyelids would droop. The dreams that set in first, the kind that always felt more like hallucinations before deeper sleep could claim him, had shown a young, faceless boy with his arm on a chopping block, Malvern's twisted face maniacally laughing above him. He'd heard Sorcha's screams and seen her fighting off an attacker, one that transformed into the face of a massive, snarling wolf.

Brandt had forced himself awake countless times, getting up to stretch his legs, stoke the fire, and sober his exhausted mind. Soon he would be back in Essex where he belonged, and all the madness of the last two days would be in the past. Well and truly in the past, if he had his say.

He had overheard Duncan explaining to the men that Finlay and Evan had set a false trail south, toward Maclaren, hoping to draw Malvern and his men in that direction. The ploy would not last for long, though, and Ronan had instructed his men to rise at first light in order to move north. The men had nodded, and their wordless, unflinching loyalty to their future laird had been yet one more thing about Sorcha's eldest brother that Brandt had admired. In other circumstances, Ronan was a man Brandt could have easily called friend.

He was nothing like Finlay or Evan, who not only wore their pride, but flaunted it like a pair of peacocks. Ronan had the muted dignity his brothers lacked. Though Brandt knew that was a factor of age—the two men were barely one or two years older than Sorcha, whom he would put at no more than twenty. Whereas Ronan was a seasoned man. He knew his power and led with confidence, not bluster or emotion.

It also helped that Ronan had admitted to his plan to fake Sorcha's death in order to save her from marrying Malvern. As Brandt stood up and felt the blood begin to course back into his legs, he thought of how unfortunate it had been for Ronan to keep his plan a secret from Sorcha. Had she known to what lengths her brother would go in order to protect her, she would not have been tempted to take matters into her own hands as she'd done at the common lands festival.

He would not have kissed her.

He would not have struck a deal to marry her.

Malvern would not be on the rampage now for Brandt's blood and the wife from whom he'd been cheated.

In short, Ronan's plan had been shot to hell. It wasn't any one person's fault, but a collection of errors. They mattered little now, though. Brandt crouched before the hearth and glanced at Sorcha. Her pink lips were parted enough to emit her soft, rhythmic breathing. Her lashes, like the black wings of a raven, touched down on ivory cheeks, flushed from the fire he'd kept going all night. He took the opportunity to view her scars up close. The three stripes weren't thick or raised. Her brow and cheek had been neatly scored by the she-wolf's paw. It could have been far worse—the animal could have taken her eye or gouged out chunks of flesh.

"So fierce," he murmured. "Such singular beauty."

And Sorcha *was* beautiful, scars and all. Without them, she would not be her. They were part of her, like her tart humor and her brazen courage. She reminded him of a wild creature in a jungle somewhere…all sleek limbs and savage beauty. He could truly get close only when she was sleeping. Despite the doused flames in the hearth, Brandt's body grew warm as he stayed, crouched beside his wife. Without the shadows of worry in her eyes and the mask of fearlessness she wore during the day, she appeared so innocent.

Because she is.

He hadn't taken that from her, even though her brothers— and Malvern—believed the contrary. Even though the touch of her body, pressed against the length of his the afternoon before had woken him to just how warm and pleasurable she would be. More than pleasurable. She'd make love as she fought—with lust and passion.

Brandt expelled a ragged breath, allowing himself the dangerous thought. Because soon it would be good-bye. He would never see her again after today. A coil of her hair hung low, nearly covering her brow, and he gently pushed the strands back. She slept on, undisturbed by his touch. Good. She'd be rested for the day's hard ride north.

He brushed his fingers over her forehead again, then drew the tip of his index finger down her silken cheek and along her jaw. She'd yet to part her lashes when he followed the urge to drag the pad of his thumb over the plump curve of her lower lip. Her breath gusted over his skin. Brandt recalled the taste of her lips at the common lands festival and the brazen response of her tongue, as if she had been pulling him into her, wanting to possess him.

Or, he thought with an unwelcome dose of reality, as if wanting to trap him.

And she had. Though, in all honesty, he hadn't yet stopped to think about where he would have been right then had she not kissed him. Well on his way to Essex, he supposed. But thinking about anything other than claiming his due and departing would be unwise, especially if his mind kept circling back to his wife's exceptional lips or her long-limbed figure.

He jerked his hand back and stood quickly. He needed air. Cold air. And a place to empty his full bladder and restrain ravenous parts of his body that kept forming other ideas. Dawn was still a half hour or more away when he went outside, closing the door to the cottage quietly behind him.

Why he felt a prick of conscience as he walked farther from the cottage, into the deep blue remnants of night, he didn't wish to think about. Sorcha had agreed to his terms. She didn't expect him to stay, and he'd never promised any such thing.

As he relieved himself far from the cottage, he focused on what needed to be done before he took his leave. He'd need to refill his waterskins and find something to eat before beginning the long journey back with Ares and Lockie.

Brandt had just buttoned the fall of his trousers and turned to retrace his steps to the cottage when a boulder slammed into him. He landed, hard, on the grass, his brain catching up from the shock to relate that it wasn't a boulder at all. It was a man, and as a fist buried in Brandt's stomach, his instincts took over. It didn't matter that it was still dark. He intercepted his attacker's next fist and, swiftly calculating his height, jabbed out with his own. He heard the crunch of bone, and when Brandt ducked, anticipating his attacker's revenge jab, he angled his next blow for the kidney.

He heard the man grunt in pain, but the brute didn't go down—not until Brandt kicked his kneecaps. In the darkness, he could not discern the size of his attacker, though he was marginally faster, and as thoughts of who it could be—one of Malvern's men?—surged through his brain, he absorbed another fist to the chin and doled out two rapid jabs to the throat and temple.

"Who are you?" he shouted before his feet went out from underneath him. Again, he landed like a sack of bricks on the grass, and this time, a heavy arm pressed down across his chest. He grappled for the hilt of the knife he kept tucked in his boot.

"Who do you think, ye sack of pig shite?"

Damn. *Ronan.*

A spitting mad Ronan. Brandt rolled to his side and stumbled to his feet. He should have expected the attack. Brandt could see the dark stamp of Ronan's outline now that he wasn't frantically defending his life. He didn't want to hurt the man, but he wouldn't take a beating willingly, either. He felt brief satisfaction that Ronan was also breathing with difficulty.

"Is this how Scots settle their differences?" he asked. "Ambushing a man in the dark while taking a piss. Are you satisfied?"

"No' by a longshot." Ronan grunted. "What else did ye promise her, Sassenach? Sweet nothings while ye seduced an innocent, gentle-bred lass?"

"She told you, it was her choice," Brandt answered, his jaw smarting from where Ronan's knuckles had nearly taken off his head. "I offered nothing that wasn't accepted."

Silence reigned in the dark clearing; the only sound disturbing the peace was their discordant breaths. "And so that's it, ye'll just take yer prize and leave without nary a care for her at all?"

Brandt wasn't going to answer the question, but the accusatory tone in the man's words struck him. He didn't much care for it. "I do care. Your sister is brave and fearless and deserves better than either Malvern or I can give her."

"What if she's with child?"

Brandt didn't expect the notion to spear him with such force, though of course there was no possibility that she could be. Then again, Ronan didn't know that. "She's not."

"And her heart?"

"It was never part of the bargain," he said quietly. "I am not your enemy, Ronan. We both want the same thing—her safety from the marquess."

"No, ye just want her horse."

"I'm not that callous, but yes," he admitted. "That, too."

The silence stretched interminably between them, until Ronan shifted in the darkness. Brandt braced himself uneasily for a renewed attack, but it never came. Ronan cleared his throat, sighing heavily several times, and when he spoke, there was no anger in his voice.

"Next time, be more vigilant," he said. "Malvern has a habit of sending scouts forward. He doesnae care about how many men he loses, only that he wins. Before he inherited his father's title, he was like that on the battlefield in France, too. Putting his own men at risk to safeguard his worthless hide, ye ken. He's naught but a coward, and a ruthless one." Ronan spit out a mouthful of blood. "Christ, ye've got a decent throw. I think ye loosed a tooth."

Brandt didn't admit that one of his ribs felt painfully tender as they began walking back toward the cottage. A thin line of orange and purple now trimmed the horizon of trees.

"Thank ye for what ye did for Sorcha," Ronan said after they'd gone a few strides in silence, each of them nursing their aches.

The guilt sluicing through his veins was not unfamiliar. "Of course."

Ronan grunted fiercely. "Malvern's men will be on yer trail. Ye're welcome to travel with us until the crossroads south of Sinclair lands. 'Twill be safer than on yer own. About a day's ride west, then ye can journey on south from there."

"Thank you."

"I am in yer debt."

Brandt shook his head, uncertain if he wanted any lingering connections to the Maclarens. "The price for my help has already been agreed, as you know."

Grimly, Ronan met his eyes. "*My* debt, Pierce, no' my sister's. I will no' forget that ye saved her from that monster."

...

Sorcha glanced over her shoulder at the man following on horseback. Riding atop his scarred stallion, Brandt was deep in conversation with her brother. She squashed the burst of pleasure that flared through her at the sight of him. It was no use letting herself feel anything. He'd be gone in a day.

She was surprised that he hadn't departed south at dawn, but supposed it made sense for him to travel with the protection of Maclaren soldiers, especially in unfriendly territory. And she couldn't deny it had been an unexpected gift to be able to ride Lockie once more. Tomorrow, she'd have to turn him over into Brandt's hands and truly say goodbye. He'd take care of the stallion, at least. For all his hard edges, she knew Brandt would be gentle with any horse.

A vague memory of fingers caressing her face crossed her mind, and a man's voice telling her she was beautiful. Sorcha shook herself roughly. Dreams were impetuous, unruly things—giving voice to one's deepest, most hidden desires.

She was not beautiful in the least, and it would do her no good hoping to be so, even while she slept. And even if it *had been* him, she'd already spent half the night convincing herself that Brandt's departure would be for the best.

That morning, when they'd readied the horses, she couldn't help noticing the bruising Brandt had on his cheek or the fact that he'd clutched at his ribs a few times while saddling Ares. She'd also noticed that Ronan cradled a sore, equally bruised jaw. She frowned. They'd come to blows in the middle of the night, but neither of them was amenable to talking about it. At least not to her.

She urged Lockie into a faster run, pulling abreast of Duncan, who led the line of rapidly moving horses. She arched an eyebrow and hooked a thumb to the two men at the rear. "Ronan didn't have that mark on his chin yesterday. Neither did Brandt."

"'Twas a misunderstanding. They couldnae see each other in the dark, ye ken."

Sorcha frowned. "What were they doing out there in the middle of the night? Brawling?"

"Ask Ronan," Duncan replied gruffly. "He'll tell ye if ye ask nicely."

"And where are we heading?" she added. "Brodie's to the northeast."

Duncan shot her an aggrieved look.

Sorcha scowled. They'd been riding hard for a few hours through lush valleys speckled with fragrant heather, staying close to the tree line in case they needed to take cover. But there'd been no sign of pursuit or more than passing interest from any of the farming villages they'd come upon. "We just went through Dunbar lands to the west. Is he expecting trouble from the Sinclairs?"

"Lassie, ask yer brother." Duncan spurred his mount ahead, indicating that the conversation was over.

Sorcha slowed her pace, resuming her position at the middle of the small company. Ronan would tell her when he was ready, though she suspected that he was concerned about the Sinclairs. There was no love lost between the Maclarens and the Sinclairs, ever since Ronan had refused to marry the daughter of the laird for the sake of an alliance five years before. It wasn't that the girl wasn't comely. She was, but Lady Mairi had only feathers instead of brains in her head. Rumors of her ignorance reached far and wide. Her brother valued alliances, though clearly, he valued intelligence more.

They rode hard through the afternoon, after stopping to water the horses and eat a light meal of bread and cheese. They would hunt when they stopped for the night. Growing up in the Highlands, Sorcha was more than accustomed to hard riding. She kept glancing back at Brandt, but he seemed to be as comfortable in the saddle as he was on the ground. His beastly mount, too, showed no signs of tiring. Both horse and rider seemed as comfortable as hardened Scottish warriors.

Though she'd felt the weight of his gaze upon her from time to time, Sorcha preferred to keep her distance. It did not make sense to endear herself to the man, not when they intended to part in a few hours. It was the safest, *smartest* course of action, if only because of her own ungoverned reactions whenever he was near.

After a while, Ronan called out to his men, pulling his horse into a shaded glade at the foothills of a thickly forested mountain. "We rest here."

Sorcha reined in her mount beside his. A small stream ran through the trees at its base, and the thirsty horses took to the water eagerly.

"You should have married Mairi," she told her brother with a sour glance. "Then we could have had food, beds, and protection on the way to Brodie. And it would have been half the distance paying respects to the Sinclair instead of going around through the hill pass."

Ronan started to scowl, then schooled his features into a calmer mask. "'Twas a long time ago, and that's no' the reason we're no' going that way."

"Then what is it?"

He shot her a resigned look as if knowing she wouldn't let it go. "There's been some looting in the village. The Sinclairs feuding with the Buchanans."

Highland Scots were always feuding with other clans. It was the way of things.

She wrinkled her nose. "Isn't the Sinclair's son married to a Buchanan?"

"That's part of it," he said, unrolling a pallet from his saddle and handing it to her. "She's had a bairn, and the laird wants to introduce his grandson to the rest of the Buchanans."

She watched as Brandt settled Ares and gathered a bow from Duncan while a few of the men made camp and built a small fire. His stare touched on her, and then he nodded to Ronan before disappearing into the woods with two other men armed with bows and arrows.

"Ye like him, admit it," Ronan said, following her gaze with a thoughtful look.

"What happened last night?" she asked, bluntly ignoring the comment that seared a hole in her chest. "Did you pick a fight with him?"

"Nae, 'twas a misunderstanding. And yer lover has a powerful fist."

Sorcha went red and froze at her brother's teasing words. "He's not my anything. That should be clear, since he is leaving, with my horse I might add." She turned on her heel and grabbed the bow and quiver of arrows that was hooked on her pommel.

"We've enough hunters, Sorcha," Ronan goaded her with a knowing smile. "Unless ye're going into the woods for some other reason."

"Go to the devil, Ronan."

To prove her point that she was *not* following Brandt, she entered the woods at the opposite end of the copse. She could hear Ronan's laughter behind her and swore under her breath.

Sorcha stomped through the thick undergrowth, making no attempt to be silent so as not to scare away the game. She was too unnerved by the ragged direction of her thoughts. Brandt *wasn't* her lover, unless one counted a deflowered arm as such. But Ronan was right. She *did* like Brandt. She liked his sly humor and the way he looked at her. And she liked his touch. Too much.

It irritated her how much she wanted him to kiss her again. If she was being truthful, she craved even more than that. She craved his hands upon her in a way that was not ladylike in the least.

"Blast it," she muttered and nocked one of her arrows. She'd be lucky if she hadn't already frightened away all the game in the vicinity.

Sorcha continued on, this time creeping through the woods, following the bubbling brook that fattened to a wide pool and then narrowed again. The thick cloak of the forest swallowed the sounds around her, until she sensed rather than heard movement to her left. A small doe drank at the riverbank. Though she was not the only one who had set sights upon it. She watched quietly as Brandt took aim from across the river, his strong arm pulling back on the string. The fletching of the arrow caught against his cheekbone, and Sorcha inhaled with him, exhaling as he released his shot. The twanging sound reverberated through her body as if she were tethered to him.

The arrow caught the doe in the hind leg, and Sorcha was quick to release her own arrow before the deer took flight.

Her aim was true. She and Brandt reached the fallen animal at the same time. Her breath caught in her throat as they stooped together.

"Good shot," Brandt said.

"Yours brought it down." She felt like blushing and kicking herself in the same breath. She had shot dozens of deer, but the approving look in Brandt's eyes made it seem as if this was her first. All she wanted to do was bask in the warmth of his praise like an utter imbecile. She clenched her jaw instead. "Ronan will be pleased that the men will have fresh meat for sup."

Deftly, she gutted and cleaned the animal, burying the inedible entrails so as not to attract predators. Then she and Brandt carried the small doe back to the camp. The men were indeed pleased, as the other two had returned with only a rabbit and a rangy-looking fowl that would not have been enough to fill the bellies of a dozen robust Scotsmen. They set in, skinning the deer and then spitting it to roast above the fire.

It wouldn't be long before the meal was ready, so Sorcha gathered a cloth and scooped some soap from her saddlebag with the intent of making use of the pool she'd spotted before. Her skin felt gritty, and she wanted to wash the layers of dust from her body. Unlike while she was hunting, she knew Ronan would not let her bathe alone, not in open territory. As she searched through the men, Brandt met her eyes, but she looked away.

"Duncan," she said as she reached him. "I need you to accompany me to the river for a moment to stand watch."

Duncan's lips parted to reply, but then shut again as his eyes settled on something just beyond her.

She hadn't heard Brandt approach. "I will go."

"I wish for Duncan to go," she said.

"He is not your husband."

Duncan snorted a laugh before walking away. She shot Brandt a glare, her voice a cutting whisper. "Neither are you."

Irritated, Sorcha did not wait for him to follow. She glanced over her shoulder a few times as she stalked into the woods toward the pool. Brandt followed at a distance. When she finally reached the water, she turned to see he'd stopped some ways back. He stood, rooted to the spot, staring at her.

Men. They were so obtuse. Without bothering to shout at him to turn around, as Duncan would have already done, unbidden, she pulled her dress over her head and waded into the water in her shift, gasping at its biting chill on her bare legs. She soaked her cloth and wiped the grime from her face and arms before moving to her legs and torso. The brisk scrubbing and cold water were exactly what she'd needed.

Sorcha longed to go for a swim, but it would not be wise to tarry with Ronan's men so close. She knew most of them and trusted them. However, she was not naive to their unscrupulous urges. She'd seen many a drunken Maclaren grasping the arses of the giggling serving girls at the keep, and she knew exactly what bedding entailed thanks to the loose lips of her maid, Kira, at Maclaren.

The air suddenly turned heavy with tension, and Sorcha knew Brandt had approached the pool. She felt his gaze settle on her back. Awareness, and not the cold, made chill bumps rise all over her body. She was grateful for her shift, though it clung damply to her skin. Horrified, she realized how revealing the drenched fabric would be. Would it show the hideous map of scars that traversed her body underneath? Would he gape in disgust?

She peered over her shoulder, but his gaze was politely averted.

"What did you mean when you said I wasn't your husband?" he asked as she hurriedly climbed the bank and shook out her clothing. She would have preferred something clean, but it could not be helped. There would be more grueling riding the next day. Keeping an eye on him, she stripped off the sodden shift and dragged her dress over her head too quickly, managing to get tangled in the yards of fabric. Thank God, she'd forgone stays. They were a nuisance on the road.

He stepped closer to her. "Sorcha?"

"I meant nothing," she said in a low voice as she lined up the openings and tugged her skirts into place. "You're leaving, so what does it matter?"

"We both knew I would. You're safe now. With Ronan."

She fastened the front-facing hooks just as he turned to look at her. "So why are you still here pretending?"

"It's not all a pretense."

"Isn't it?"

"No." His gaze swept her, and the desire burning in his eyes made her weak. Made her bold. She stepped forward until her breasts almost grazed his chest.

"Sorcha," he began as if to stall her approach, but she silenced him with her fingers, holding them against his lips. Perhaps it was the fact that he was leaving, but she couldn't help herself. She needed more to remember him by. She craved his touch, his *kiss*, one more time.

Boldly, she explored the contours of his mouth with her fingertips. Brandt's eyes widened, and he opened his mouth to speak, most likely to protest. Before he could utter a word, she rose to her toes and pressed her lips to his. His entire body went ramrod still, but she did not let that stop her. Bravely, foolishly, desperately, she traced his mouth with hers...delighting in the smooth feel and the heady scent of him. When she darted out her tongue to taste him more fully, with a defeated sound, he gathered her into his arms.

The tentative kiss exploded as Brandt parted her lips with his, his fingers sinking into her hair to cup her nape.

Sorcha couldn't string two thoughts together when his tongue found hers, licking the insides of her lips and exploring all she offered. Greedily, he devoured her, and Sorcha gave no quarter…biting and sucking and stroking.

She was lost in a furor of lust, her entire body made of heat and flame, stoked by his mouth and his hands. Her limbs were useless, but she was braced so tightly to him that she knew she wouldn't fall. The kiss gentled as he brushed her bruised lips with soothing grazes, sending feathery ripples of sensation down through to the tips of her breasts and between her thighs.

Sorcha sighed as Brandt's lips traced a hot, wet path down her jaw to her throat. He bit gently at her flesh, and heaven above, she almost swooned at the erotic pressure of his teeth. She clutched at him, pressing her full length against his, and feeling his arousal grind against her hips in the most thrilling way…the most scandalous way. Moaning, she closed her eyes and was startled when he detached his mouth from her skin and set her firmly away from him. His eyes, splashed with green and gold, were the vibrant color of the forest around them, his lips delicious and swollen.

"Enough, Sorcha, I cannot do this."

It was as if he'd dunked her in the icy river water.

She blinked and sucked in a harsh breath. Hurt pushed through the layers of passion still clouding her senses. His gaze was unreadable, and Sorcha couldn't stop herself. "Why do you not want me? Is it because of the scarring?"

The pathetic words echoed between them, making her cringe and wish she could take them back. Brandt opened his mouth and closed it, his face growing pinched. Mortified, she spun on her heel and ran back toward the camp. She didn't look over her shoulder this time to see if he followed.

She couldn't imagine meeting his eyes ever again.

Chapter Eight

Brandt's body woke like clockwork as dawn was breaking across a pinkening sky, just visible from beyond the seam of the tent. It'd been late when he'd finally joined Sorcha the night before, and she had already been fast asleep. As he had planned.

It was still dark, but he never failed to wake at the same time each morning. Not surprisingly, his entire body ached, though it was not just from being in the saddle for hours on end. His limbs felt restless and coiled with tension. Tight. His body was painfully erect. He adjusted himself on the hard ground and then registered the delectably warm female body beside him. Sometime during the night, she had tucked herself into the crook of his arm and shoulder.

He froze, mid-motion. Now he understood his body's stiff, frustrated condition. The soft press of breasts against his ribs and legs twined with his would tempt a monk. He'd never been a man led by physical impulses. No woman had ever driven him to such an ungoverned state. And yet, she seemed to do so without any effort whatsoever.

She was the most dangerous female he'd ever encountered, and he'd met a few.

Sorcha shifted against him in sleep, one long arm reaching out over the expanse of his chest. Brandt's breath seized. The smell of lavender and heather from her wash in the river would forever be imprinted on his brain, as would the sinuous outline of her body he'd glimpsed under her damp shift.

If it were even possible, he grew harder, his mind gripped by coarse thoughts of burying himself to the hilt into her slick, wet depths. Brandt groaned. He was so sodding hard it was painful. In the privacy and solitude of his own home, he would have found no shame in a few quick strokes to relieve his engorged discomfort, but here, the very thought seemed vulgar. Barbaric.

Hell.

Swiftly, he shifted out of her half embrace and rolled into a crouch. The sooner he put some distance between them, the better. He started to pack up his belongings. Though his body was lost to lust, his mind was clear, reminding him of what women like her were capable of—highborn women who took what they wanted when they wanted. As she had done in that Selkirk square.

Granted, he'd gotten something out of the deal, but even the prize of Lockie couldn't erase the fact that he had been manipulated from the start. Perhaps he was unfairly holding on to ancient hurts, but he could never completely trust a woman, not even one who seemed as guileless as Sorcha.

She *wasn't* guileless, he reminded himself harshly. No woman was. A man could be made a fool only if he allowed himself to be one. And while Brandt could accept that Sorcha had had desperate intentions with her kiss, trust was something he guarded fiercely.

It had started with his mother, he knew.

In all his life, he had trusted only two people: Monty and Archer. And only Archer remained alive and well. Even with the two of them, Brandt had never opened himself fully. He had never let them see his true heart or the self-doubt he kept at bay on a daily basis. The fact that he belonged nowhere.

Brandt had given up on the idea of ever finding his mother. A jeweler in London had told him that the ring he possessed appeared to be the colors of one of several possible Scottish Highland clans, but given the faded crest of the ring, it had been impossible to narrow it down further. He could not summon the enthusiasm to travel to the Highlands in search of family that hadn't wanted him in the first place. After Monty died and he became the head stable master at Worthington Abbey, life had taken on a pleasant and consistent turn. He'd been content, his existence peaceful and predictable.

Until that kiss.

And now his own body conspired against him. Sorcha made him feel things that he did not want to feel...made him have thoughts that awakened the voices within him that clamored he was nothing, could never offer anything of worth to anyone.

For that reason alone, he was glad this whole marriage was a ruse.

Only at times like these, it didn't feel like one.

His gaze swept his wife, who had awakened and followed his lead to stand in silence, wrapping herself in a Maclaren plaid. Sorcha did not meet his eyes, her face inscrutable. The glimpse of vulnerability he'd seen the night before was gone. Now, the warrior stood in her place. When she left the tent to see to her needs after a guarded look at him, Brandt expelled a pained breath. Though part of him recognized her innocence, he had never been able to tell with women.

The courtesans in London he'd encountered with Archer

in their wilder years had been masters in the art of seduction and manipulation. He'd even fancied himself in love with one who had convinced him of her undying devotion. That devotion had disintegrated the moment she'd learned he wasn't a titled lord like his friend, the Duke of Bradburne. She—a glorified prostitute for all intents and purposes—had laughed at his true vocation.

It had only compounded the little he knew of women. That they weren't to be trusted. Ever since, he'd barricaded his unwanted heart and relieved himself from time to time with women of a lower persuasion. Not like Sorcha...the daughter of a duke.

He was a bastard with nothing to offer her. If their marriage were real, the scandal it would cause in drawing rooms across Scotland and London combined would be unavoidable. The daughter of a duke marrying a lowborn man of uncertain origins? She'd be shunned from society. Even Malvern was a better choice than him...at least she would have been a marchioness.

"Marrying her was a sodding mistake," he growled.

Brandt swore coarsely and heard a gasp from behind him. He turned to see Sorcha had returned. Her eyes were wide. Agonized. Hurt swam in them, before a practiced expressionless look consumed her features. He opened his mouth, but then shut it. Better for her to think the worst of him than to glorify a few kisses and a shameless bid to win a horse into something more than it could ever be.

A shout from outside had them both pushing past the tent flaps. Ronan's men were gathering their belongings in haste as they broke camp. Brandt searched for the big man, but he was nowhere in sight. His gaze landed on Duncan who was directing two of the younger men.

"Where is Ronan?" he asked. "What's happening?"

"Malvern," Duncan growled, his mouth a hard line. "His

trackers followed us from Doncaster, even when we rode through the river fer four miles and cut through the hills. Ronan knows these lands like the back of his hand. It should have been impossible to find us so quickly."

Brandt frowned as something occurred to him, but Sorcha beat him to it. "Who was it? The traitor?"

"Ye brother's questioning the lad now."

"Was he a Maclaren?" Sorcha snarled.

Duncan shook his head. "Nae, a Cleland. Make haste, lass, our scouts report that there's a contingent of Malvern's men that rode through the night and are nearly upon us. Quickly now, arm yerselves."

He nodded at Brandt before marching off toward where one of the men was dismantling their tent from the night before. Sorcha stood rigid, her arms flexing at her sides. She'd abandoned her dress in favor of riding trousers today, he noticed, though she wore the Maclaren plaid draped above it for modesty. Brandt tried not to notice how well the breeches framed her hips through the pleated folds of the navy and red plaid, nor the way the white linen shirt accentuated her chest.

Her glare was frosty enough to freeze a loch. "Why are ye just standing there staring, ye lummox?" she hissed. "Move!"

Those terse words spoken in a lilting brogue gave away her anger, if in fact the look in her eyes and the rigid set of her shoulders already had not.

Ares had already been fed, and Brandt saddled him quickly just as Ronan thundered into the clearing. He was covered in blood, his sword raised high. His battle roar made every man take up arms. "They're upon us, lads!" He directed the horse toward Brandt, his eyes darting to where Sorcha stood. "I know ye're set upon leaving, but I need ye, Pierce. I need ye to protect my sister with yer life."

She scowled her displeasure. "I don't need protecting."

Brandt ignored her, drawing himself atop Ares. "How

many?"

"Two dozen, maybe more," Ronan said.

"And the turncoat?"

The Scot's mouth twisted in distaste. "Slit his own throat. I should have known when he kept asking about the clans in these parts."

"How did he do it?" Sorcha asked.

"Left behind bits of Maclaren plaid," he said, whirling his horse around. "Breadcrumbs that led them right to us."

"Will you break your oath not to raise arms against Malvern?" Brandt asked.

Ronan's steely blue gaze met his. "If our lives are threatened, we have no choice but to defend ourselves."

He didn't seem to be too worried about the oncoming attack. One Highland warrior was the equivalent of ten English ones, but Brandt knew Malvern. The man was deviously clever. He'd earned his dubious rank in the British army by trickery and misdirection. And Coxley was a hundred times worse. He opened his mouth to warn Ronan when shouting and the sounds of battle distracted him.

Loud noises of steel crashing upon steel reached them from the other side of the clearing, when suddenly a band of armed men broke through the tree line behind them.

"They're attacking from both sides!" Duncan rushed toward them, his sword raised, followed by three other men. They were quickly surrounded and outnumbered, but lived up to their fierce reputation. The first wave of men was easily dealt with, but more kept coming.

"Take her into the forest," Ronan shouted to Brandt before delving into the fray.

Brandt gritted his teeth. He did not want to run from the fight, but at the moment, Sorcha's safety was his only concern. "Come," he said to her. "You heard what he said."

Angry flames flared in her blue eyes. "Are ye insane?

And leave my brother to die? Ye're ape-drunk if ye think I'm leaving, Sassenach. We Scots never run from a fight."

He ignored the bite of her address. "Ronan is a trained soldier."

"And I, too, am a Maclaren." Her ferocious gaze flashed daggers at him as if daring him to contradict her. "Ye may run if ye like, but I am staying."

Brandt did not have time to argue as two men on horseback burst through the forest, riding hard toward them with guns raised. He didn't think. Bracing his thighs on Ares's flanks, he pulled the pistols from their holsters and fired. Both men toppled off their horses, but they weren't out of danger yet. More men followed, and Brandt drew his sword at the same moment that Sorcha reached for the bow tied to her saddle.

Instinct took over as he swung and parried, cleaving another man clean off his horse and disarming another with a ferocious upward swipe. Blood spattered onto his clothing, but he was too busy trying to locate Sorcha to notice. Wheeling Ares around, he searched through the dueling bodies. With relief, he found her at the edge of the glade. She was standing in the stirrups, her arrows departing her bow with lethal precision. Enemies fell one by one, and Brandt felt an odd sense of pride in her skill. When she ran out of arrows, she leaped off Lockie and swung her sword with as much finesse as he'd seen that first time in the Selkirk paddock.

Fearless and savage, she was indeed every inch the Maclaren warrior she'd claimed to be. For a charged moment, her blue gaze met his across the clearing, and she scowled, her lips pulling back from her teeth as if he were to be her next target. God, she was magnificent. Exhilaration churned in his blood, and Brandt realized with a start that he was half aroused. He almost laughed. Only one woman could provoke him so indecently in the midst of a turbulent battle.

Kicking Ares into a canter, he ran through two more of

Malvern's men, and intent on reaching her side, he did not see the horse charging toward him from the back. He did see the warning shout freeze on Sorcha's face as he tumbled face forward over Ares's neck. The fall knocked the wind out of him, though he had crashed into another soldier who had cushioned his landing.

The man who had knocked him off his horse was a brute almost as large as Ronan, his face beneath the dented helm, scarred and ugly.

"Mr. Pierce," he greeted him in a guttural voice. "'Twill be my pleasure to deliver your head to his lordship and collect the reward of one hundred guineas."

"That's all?" Brandt scoffed, retrieving a fallen sword from a dead soldier. "My good man, I'll have you know I'm worth much more than that. You've been cheated."

"No matter, the marquess will pay in gold, and you will pay in blood."

Brandt swung the sword in a slow circle as the man wheeled his mount around to charge him again. Though it agonized him to do it, at the last minute he fell to his knees and swung the blade backward and upward into the rump of the horse. It was not a killing stroke, but enough for the animal to rear up wildly and toss the rider from his back. For a man of his size, the soldier vaulted into a fighting stance with unusual grace.

He and Goliath circled each other. Out of the corner of his eye, he saw Sorcha slashing her way toward him. He wanted to shout for her to stay away. She would only be a distraction, and he sensed he would need all his wits to not be killed at the hands of this monster. The man was not hired muscle like most of the corpses littering the glade, but a trained assassin. It was evident in the way he moved, in the glint of his eye. Here was a man who had delivered death, lived in rivers of blood, and would not hesitate to split him in two, if he was distracted even for a moment.

Brandt drew a breath and lifted his sword. He danced out of the way of Goliath's strikes and fended off a third that reverberated down the length of his arms. Sparks flew from the edges of the steel as they met again. The man was strong and skilled, and it took all of Brandt's concentration to read his body language. It was the only way he could stay ahead of him.

Suddenly, a feminine shout diverted his attention, and the next thing he knew a fist hit him square in the chest and he was flying through the air. He crashed down to the ground in a tangle of arms and legs, his brain rattling around in his skull at the impact. It took him two seconds to collect himself before the giant was upon him. He rolled out of the way as the sword came down in a glinting silver arc. Brandt didn't care. His attention was behind the man, on Sorcha.

Driven only by instinct, Brandt sidestepped Goliath's blows, weaving and ducking as fast as he was able. He managed to get in a few strikes and drew blood at the man's torso, back, and legs. It wasn't enough. The behemoth kept coming like an angry bull. Brandt needed to change his strategy.

"I told you I was worth more than a hundred quid," he said.

"Your head is still going to be at the edge of my sword." The man's eyes flashed in anger, and he rushed forward. It was the opening Brandt needed. He, too, charged forward, but at the last minute, he threw his body flat and jerked up with his blade. Blood fountained over him as Goliath teetered and spun around, his eyes wide. Then he clutched at his stomach and stared at the bright gaping swatch of red that blossomed on the waistband of his breeches, spilling out his innards. With a disbelieving groan, he staggered to his knees and fell face-first into the dirt.

Another strangled scream rent the air, and Brandt felt all the breath leave his lungs in a whoosh at the sight of Sorcha being dragged toward a horse by her hair. He had no time to savor his victory, and hopping over the fallen giant, he ran toward his bride. Covered in blood, he was like a berserker streaking across the field of battle, his only objective to reach her. He got there at the same time that Ronan did—and right as Sorcha drew a dagger from her boot and plunged it into the man's neck. She kicked him for good measure.

"Ye need to get to safety," Ronan said, breathless. He, too, was drenched in blood, and from the easy way he was moving, Brandt guessed that most of it wasn't his. "Malvern sent an army from the south and from the north. At least a hundred men."

They glanced around at the bodies strewn on the field, noticing the plaids of some of the dead men. "Aye, and some of them are Scots." Ronan spat in disgust to the blood-soaked ground. "Craven, gutless traitors bought by a pouch of gold."

"How many men did we lose?" Sorcha asked, her chest heaving.

"Seven," Ronan replied. "Five left, including Duncan and me. There are more of them hiding in the woods. We can take them, but ye need to run."

Sorcha's brows slammed together, her voice low and angry. "I won't leave you, Ronan."

"Ye dunnae have a choice, lass," he said gently. "It's ye Malvern wants, and the death of yer husband. He intends to make ye a widow." He turned to Brandt and grasped him by the forearm. "I'll hold him off for as long as I can. Get my sister to the Brodie, 'tis the only place she'll be safe. Ye fought well. Take care of her, ye ken?"

"You have my word."

As Ronan mounted his horse and rode back the way he'd come, Brandt wondered if he'd see him again. He could see the same thoughts reflected in Sorcha's face and in the sadness that shimmered in her eyes. She bit her lip hard, her nostrils flaring. Brandt wanted to comfort her, but he sensed it would not be welcomed. Not after how he'd left things between them in the tent. Perhaps it was for the best. Distance would serve them better than any kind of familiarity.

He watched as she retrieved Lockie, and then whistled for Ares who trotted up within moments. Leading their horses together with weapons drawn, they melted quietly into the woods toward the river, until the noise started to fade in the distance behind them. Brandt was relieved to see both stallions seemed no worse for wear and suffered no fresh wounds. Ares, particularly. Every new scar made him ache for the brave beast. Ares had endured more than his share of pain over the years, and the horse's loyalty was enough to rival most men's.

Sorcha groaned and leaned against Lockie after leading him to water, where he drank thirstily. Brandt frowned. "You're hurt," he said, noticing the strip of red across the side of her shirt beneath the plaid.

"It's nothing, a flesh wound."

"Let me see," he said and lifted the edges.

She snatched at the plaid, but Brandt had already caught sight of the weeping incision that traversed the span of two lower ribs. It was a shallow cut, though it seemed to be bleeding profusely, making the scarlet-hued linen stick to her flesh. Sorcha grimaced as his fingers snagged on the cloth. "We should clean it."

"I'll be fine, I told ye!"

"Not if you invite infection. Don't be stubborn, Sorcha."

The look she sent him spoke volumes. "*Stubborn*," she hissed. "Perhaps ye should have considered that before ye stayed and took me to wife, instead of running like I told ye to. Then you wouldnae have the burden of regret on yer shoulders."

Brandt did not respond to the anger in her voice, if only because of the sheen of tears in her eyes. "I'll regret if you die on my watch when I've just given my word to your brother to keep you safe. Now let me see that wound."

Grudgingly, she let him examine her, and though he was gentle, she still flinched away from his touch. He took a piece of linen from his saddlebags and soaked it in the icy river before applying it to her split skin. Sorcha winced but bore the pain in silence as he cleaned the wound and bandaged it with another wide strip of clean linen.

She eyed him quietly the whole time, not saying a word until he had finished the wrapping. Brandt couldn't help noticing she kept both forearms banded tightly over her breasts, allowing him only a limited view of her torso. Not that she had need to worry—open, ragged wounds had a way of deterring carnal urges.

"There," he said. "Good as new."

"Shouldn't you be on your way to England by now?"

Her brogue was gone, he realized. Brandt met her blazing blue gaze. "That can wait," he said. "We need to leave before we're discovered. We aren't far enough away for my liking."

"Why do you even care?" she asked. "It's exceedingly obvious you don't wish to be saddled with a wife…or me. You should leave while you can. I can look after myself."

"I don't doubt that, but I gave your brother my vow."

"You seem to hand out vows rather easily, Mr. Pierce." Her nostrils flared. "Your word is not worth the breath that expelled it."

"Sorcha—"

She spun on her heel and moved toward the grazing horses, but froze at a crashing sound from the nearby bushes.

"She went this way, I tell you," a man's voice said. "I saw her and the Englishman with that gray horse of hers."

"Are you sure, Coxley?"

Brandt frowned. *Damn.* Malvern's dog...the twisted, belly-slitting ex-colonel who had been at his liege's side in the Selkirk stable yard. If Coxley was here, it meant Malvern was close. Brandt met Sorcha's eyes and placed a finger to his lips, wishing that the horses were closer and not at the river's edge. But it was too late to make a run for it, or to whistle for Ares. The approaching sounds grew closer, and then Coxley and his guard emerged from the other side of a large tree, his expression triumphant as it fell on the two of them.

"Well, well, what have we here," he crowed, pointing two pistols right at them.

Chapter Nine

Sorcha couldn't breathe. She couldn't move. They were standing in the wide open, with nowhere to hide. Nowhere to run. And blast it all to hell, she'd left her sword and bow with her horse!

Brandt had planted himself directly in front of her, obscuring her view of Malvern's two men a split second after each of them aimed their pistols right at Brandt. A spike of fear took hold inside of her, a lick of fire racing up the back of her neck and sending out a frenzied beat of panic.

"Send the Beast over here," Coxley said, beckoning with his free hand. The words did not bother her, but the sight of the man, as always, made her feel nauseated. She loathed Malvern, but Coxley made Malvern seem like an angel in comparison. "We've instructions to deliver her unharmed."

"She isn't going anywhere with you," Brandt replied, his tone flat and obstinate and so bloody certain. Was the man addled? He sounded far too confident, as if there weren't a brace of pistols a crack away from ending his life.

"You're not very bright, are you?" Coxley's man asked

with a bark of mean laughter.

"I just have a better view," Brandt replied.

Sorcha peered up at her husband's profile, trying to understand his words, when a shot rang out. She startled and yelped as the man beside Coxley crumpled to the ground, gunpowder smoke clouding the air directly behind him. With a war cry, Ronan leaped from the woods the two men had just come through and collided with Coxley, taking the man to the ground.

"Go!" her brother roared to them as he used his spent weapon to crack the man across the temple.

Sorcha felt a hand wrench her arm and then she was being dragged back, toward the dense forest, Brandt shouting at her to run.

"Ronan!" she cried, half turning as they stumbled toward the woods to view her brother facing off against Coxley, who'd somehow found his feet. The brutish soldier attacked Ronan with a fist to the ribs, but she didn't get to see what happened next. Her feet tripped over themselves and she spun forward, nearly falling on the uneven ground. Ronan could handle himself, but she'd seen Coxley's cruelty before, when the marquess had visited Maclaren. He'd pummeled one of his own men bloody just for looking at a wench he'd been lusting after. The man fought dirty, and without any shred of honor.

"Faster, Sorcha!" Brandt ordered, wringing her arm practically from its socket to keep her from falling. But she couldn't. Her legs were jelly, her heartbeat thrashing. Her brother was the most powerful and capable warrior she knew, but he had just come through battle and was tired. What if he faltered? What if he *lost*?

Her eyes stung, and the tree trunks and thick canopy were blurred as she and Brandt entered on foot, their horses left behind at the river's edge.

"We must go back, we must help him!" she said as they

veered around a giant boulder, Brandt still gripping her arm and pulling her, as if he knew she would stop and turn back otherwise. And he was right, she would have. She *should*. What had she done? Seven of Ronan's men had died that morning. *Seven.* And now her brother... She squeezed her lids shut to clear the haze of tears. No. Ronan would not fall. He was the future laird of Maclaren, and he would survive.

But those other men. Their blood had been spilled, their lives extinguished, because of her and her foolish and selfish desire to avoid marriage to Malvern. Her feet turned to lead.

Brandt stopped running then and stooped to wrap his arms around her waist. With an easy toss, he flipped her over his shoulder and took off again, running through the forest's undergrowth. Her furious shriek snagged in her throat, the blood swamping her head at the ungainly position.

"Put me down, ye wretched *amadan*!"

"You're too slow," he huffed, "and too damned mulish."

Sorcha pounded him on the back, insisting he let her down, that she could run just as fast as him. But with every pounding step he took, she felt the sharp press from the shallow slice in her ribs. The tip of an enemy sword had sliced into her during the several moments of pure terror she'd spent distracted by the sight of Brandt being tossed from his horse and set upon by that hulking warrior. She'd quickly skewered the man who'd injured her, but the cut hurt like the devil, and now, folded over her husband's shoulder, she felt the brunt of it.

"Brandt," she protested again, "put me down!"

She wasn't by any means light, what with her long legs and the muscle she'd built over years spent in the keep's training grounds. And yet here this lunatic was, running with her with as much ease as if she'd been a sack of feathers instead of a full-grown woman. His strength astounded her. If she weren't so fuming angry and worried, she might have appreciated his brawn and determination. She might have even spent more time viewing the hard, muscled backside and powerful legs that were fully in her view. Even upside down, she felt her pulse quicken.

Diah, she was more of an *amadan* than he was. Sorcha hissed through clenched teeth. She'd call herself a fool in Gaelic, English, and every other language if she had to. She was no damsel to be rescued, to be scooped into a man's arms—no matter how sinewy they were—and whisked to safety. She could bloody well take care of herself. Ignoring the burn in her side, she resumed her pounding.

"How dare ye manhandle me! Who do ye think ye are!"

The chill air coming off the river hit her back, and she knew they had come to a crossing. Brandt splashed through the shallow fjord.

"Your husband."

She wriggled, flinching at the sting in her ribs. "Husband or no', ye don't have the right!"

"Oh, I do," he replied huffing. "Even in this Godforsaken place there is law, and by law you are my property. I can do with you as I like."

Brandt emerged from the river, the splashes of water having soaked Sorcha's hair, tumbling down over her face. He kept moving, holding her firm even as she struggled for release. How *dare* he? She was *no one's* property!

"Ye brute!"

"Give up," he grunted.

"Never!"

Blood rushed into her head and through her ears, but within a few minutes the noises surrounding them suddenly muffled. The bright dappled sunlight darkened. And when Brandt finally crouched and slid Sorcha from the prison of his shoulder, she realized he'd taken them into the shelter of a rocky outcropping. Her vision spun from the sudden shift of blood flow, draining now from her head, and Sorcha stumbled.

Brandt's arms came up and locked her in a steadying embrace. He was breathing heavily from exertion, his skin ruddy and misted with sweat from carrying her. Perspiration had dampened the curls of his hair, turning them to burnt copper as they clung to his brow.

She shoved at him, even with her head feeling faint and black speckles swimming in her vision. "Ronan's my family, and ye made me run like a coward!"

"You'd have been nothing but a distraction, and you likely would've gotten him killed!"

A spear of guilt lanced through her chest. *Like the others.* She'd gotten the other men killed. Good men. Husbands and sons. Brothers and fathers. Back home at Maclaren their families would mourn them, and they would know...they would know their loved one had died trying to protect a selfish woman.

She felt her body sag, the anger swirling inside of her snuffing out like a doused wick.

"Sorcha," Brandt murmured, trying to gather her close. She wanted to let him wrap her in an embrace. Wanted to drink in the comfort his arms and strong body offered. But she shook her head and pulled away. This time, Brandt released her.

"Don't," he said as she turned from the mouth of the outcropping and sank into a crouch.

"Don't what?" she asked.

"Don't blame yourself." She stiffened, uncertain if she liked, or was annoyed, by the fact that he could read her so well.

"Easy for you to say," she said.

"It isn't easy." The stone cavern reverberated his voice, making it seem louder. Closer. "A part of me is angry with you. Furious even, that I am here, caught in this mess and running for my life. Even to gain a horse I've wanted for years—that's now likely lost for good—it's more than any sane man should be expected to bear. That part of me longs to cast blame on you."

Sorcha hadn't expected such a brutally honest reply. It made her twist and stare up at him. And there was no denying that it gutted her.

She exhaled a ragged breath. "Then why shouldn't I blame myself? If you do?"

"I said I longed to, but Sorcha…I can't."

Brandt dropped into a crouch, too, coming face to face with her. The gold-flecked, autumn-colored eyes that held hers glowed in the muted light. A bevy of emotion—sorrow, compassion, understanding—chased through them. Her chest hollowed with a sudden sharp ache, one that left her confused.

"If for some reason I woke up and found myself back at the festival that day, I'd let you kiss me all over again."

More heat saturated her, but this time it wasn't guilt or temper. It swam low in her stomach and snaked out to her thighs. She stared at him, her lips parting in surprise. "Why?"

"Because no woman should ever be made to marry a man such as Malvern. Because I want you to fight," he answered, his hand reaching for her face. His fingers, the ones that made her skin tingle and flare with every random touch, tenderly stroked her cheek. "Because you wouldn't be the woman your brothers know you to be, the woman I'm beginning to know, if you'd just lain down and given up."

She watched his lips moving and heard the words falling through her ears, into her aching, needy soul. They filled her and immediately pushed the tears she'd been holding at bay over the rims of her eyes. He swiped the first few teardrops as they fell, before tugging her close. Sorcha didn't fight him.

She was tired of resisting, and his hands weren't the enemy. This time, she let him fold her in his arms, both of them sitting on the hard-packed dirt of the cavern.

"I don't like crying." She sniffled into his shirt and felt a rumble of laughter echo in his chest.

"And I don't like losing my temper," he said. "So we're both at sixes and sevens."

She peered up at him with a wry look, slanting her brows. "You wouldn't know what a temper is, Sassenach. Trust me, with brothers like mine, I'm an expert."

He matched her expression with one of his own. "I'm learning. My father, Monty, was quite even-keeled."

"He was English, wasn't he?"

"No. Scottish."

"A Scot?" she replied. "If your birth mother was Scot as well as your father, then that makes you—"

"A bastard. They weren't married, Sorcha. And considering I was raised in England, I don't consider myself Scottish. I have no ties here. No family that I know of, nor that I want to know of. I know where I belong."

She sealed her lips, swallowing a ready reply about a person needing to know where they come from. *Who* they come from. Blood ties mattered, even if a man was born on the wrong side of the blanket.

A pained look shuttered his features, tugging at her insides. Sorcha knew she should pull away. The harsh way he'd admitted his regret about marrying her that morning had hurt something fierce. But resting against him now, sensing his vulnerability and hearing the steady, soothing rhythm of his heartbeat, made everything outside the cavern seem to disappear. It almost made her want to forget what he'd said, but words could scar just as deeply as a pair of claws. Or a sword. She shifted slightly and winced.

"Your wound?" he asked.

"A scratch," she said, eyeing the grimy linen. "I'll have to clean it properly and find some packing herbs to ward off infection." She grunted, feeling a renewed wave of self-disgust. "I was careless."

"Without you, Sorcha, more men would have died," Brandt said quietly. "You acted bravely, and you're one hell of a warrior."

"You're a competent fighter, yourself," she said.

It felt like a truce. Like they were starting afresh. She offered him a slight smile.

"Only competent?" he asked, amusement lightening his tone and drawing up the corner of his mouth.

"For a stable master."

"I have my skills," he said.

Indeed, he did. Her gaze dropped to his sensuous mouth and darted away. Unconsciously, she shivered, recalling one of his skills in particular in devastating detail. Their eyes met, and she fought to conceal her thoughts from him. It was a losing battle. That stare of his could unmask the secrets of a saint, let alone her too transparent desires. Her cheeks flamed, and she licked her lips. His eyes fastened to her mouth, and the inadvertent motion of her tongue wiped the humor from both his face and hers.

It had to be the shortest-lived truce in existence.

"Sorcha," he began and, knowing what he was going to say, she wriggled from his grasp.

"There's no need to speak of it," she said. "It was a mistake, like you said."

Sorcha knew he'd growled the declaration to what he'd believed to be an empty tent. His conscience, perhaps, had been his only intended audience. Which made it even more painfully honest and impossible to ignore. When this was over, she would gladly give him Lockie and a dozen of her father's horses for his trouble. It was the least he deserved.

Brandt scrubbed a palm over his face. "I was upset at the situation. And I was…frustrated."

"Why?"

A sudden smile made his eyes crinkle. "Waking up in the arms of a half-naked woman can do that to a man."

"Oh. *Oh*." Her mouth went dry. He meant sexual frustration. Every nerve in her body came scorchingly alive. Sorcha couldn't think, couldn't formulate any response that required more than one syllable.

"Clearly, I've shocked the speech from you." He made it sound like he'd won a badge of honor.

Bristling, Sorcha opened her mouth, closed it, and opened it again when a noise outside the cavern startled them both. *Thank God*, was her first thought, and then, *Oh God, Ronan*!

Brandt rocked to his feet, a hand in the air to signal her to wait. She heard the distinct sound of horse tack and an irritated nicker, probably ten yards away, closer to the river. Had Coxley followed them? Found them. Sorcha's stomach collapsed. Brandt moved slowly to the cavern entrance…and then the tension along his shoulders fell away.

He gave a short, sharp whistle and a few moments later, Ares and Lockie appeared through the short ridge of trees. Sorcha got up on wobbly feet, gaping at the horses.

"How—" she started to say.

"Ares," Brandt answered, taking his horse by the traces and rubbing his nose. "He can always find me."

And he'd brought Lockie along on the hunt, she figured, smiling with no small amount of relief as she stepped out from under the outcropping and reached for her mount's intact saddlebags. Inside she found one of several tins and glass vials, all of which contained salves and ointments, herbs and tinctures. Exclaiming her delight, she pulled a thin tube from the satchel.

Brandt eyed her. "What is that?"

"It's a salve my mother made. She's a healer. I've picked up a few of her skills here and there, though I'm no means as good as she is. This liniment will accelerate the healing."

Gathering more supplies, she sat on the ledge and drew a deep breath. She tucked the hem of her shirt high, exposing a pale swatch of her torso. She didn't miss the way Brandt's gaze scoured the display of skin before he angled his head away. Blushing, she stifled the burst of modesty. She was careful not to raise the hem too high, to keep the grotesque web of scars above it hidden from view. She'd sooner die than let anyone, much less *him*, see her ugliest secret.

Gingerly, she unwrapped the dirty bandage, recoiling at the sting as the dried, hardened linen tore at her exposed flesh. It was not a bad cut, but she knew more than anyone how injuries could fester if not properly cared for; one speck of dirt left in a wound could undo everything. The reason the ones on her face hadn't succumbed to infection and left ugly, puckered scarring was because of this very balm. The ones on her body, sadly, had become septic, and though the salve had been applied, the mangled skin, even after the stitches had been removed, had left behind a grisly patchwork.

Brandt watched her as she poured some clear liquid from another bottle onto a cloth and gently dabbed at the incision. She bit her lip hard and tasted blood. It stung, but pain now meant less of it later.

"Let me," Brandt said, crouching and taking the cloth from her.

She didn't protest, but as before when he'd first cleaned the wound, she gripped her forearms tightly over her breasts. He skimmed softly along the cut, and she winced again. He bent to blow gently on it, his breath feathering against her skin. The unexpected combination of his warm exhalation and the icy sting of the liquid made her gasp. But it was when he gripped her right hip to steady her that a different kind of sensation radiated through her veins—a crude, frantic sort of sensation that both thrilled and terrified.

Sweet Saint Andrew.

The press of his fingers left a scorching imprint upon her flesh, burning through her clothes and making infernal urges take flight as desire spun into a storm inside of her. She'd never been more acutely aware of a man in her life… his big hand clutching her, his mouth gusting on her exposed stomach. Every feminine part of her throbbed.

Sorcha nearly levered her body upward, if only to make contact with the parted lips that hung inches away from her skin, expelling that stream of cool air. She wanted him to press his lips to her skin. To kiss her everywhere, scars and fears be damned. The span of his hot palm together with the sight of his head bent over her torso caused her inner muscles to clench almost violently. Christ, if he did put his lips on her, she might very well faint from the pleasure.

Her body alternated between acute pain and intense arousal as he ministered to her wound, and by the time he was finished, Sorcha was strung as tightly as a bow. Brandt lifted his palm, and she could swear that the shape of his hand remained imprinted on her hip. Blushing fiercely, she reached for the salve but was too slow.

"Do I just swipe it on like this?" he asked, smearing some ointment onto the pad of his finger. His voice was husky, his eyes heavy-lidded, which made her feel like she had not been the only one affected.

Incapable of speech, she nodded.

And nearly died when his hot fingertip grazed her skin. Gooseflesh erupted everywhere. On her ribs, her torso, her breasts. With infinite care, he rubbed in the balm while Sorcha clung to reason by a slim thread, unraveling by the second, as every greedy inch of her burned and begged for more. One more stroke and she would splinter into a thousand pieces right there and then. *God.* It was torture. Exquisite, hideous, *excruciating* torture.

His thumb grazed the linen gathered beneath her forearm covering the underside of her breast, and she stifled a shriek. A desperate sound born of longing and a healthy fear of discovery.

"That's enough," she gasped, rising and tugging her shirt down.

Putting a few healthy steps between them, she drew a ragged breath at the sting from the balm and fetched some more strips of linen from her bags. Without looking at him, she deftly wrapped the bandage and tucked the shirt into her trousers before rewrapping her plaid. His eyes met her, smoldered across the space, and Sorcha resisted the urge to strip herself bare and leap at him.

Gulping a lungful of air, she backed farther away and added another thing to her list of dislikes. She hated feeling trapped. She hated crying. And she bloody well hated this brain-melting, wit-consuming, goddamned *wanting.* It had even somehow been powerful enough to steal away the sensation of pain. Surely, that wasn't natural.

"We should go," Brandt said, his voice huskier than normal. "Put some space between us and Malvern's men."

"Yes," she agreed.

A hell-for-leather, bracing ride on Lockie wouldn't be unwelcome, either, to put herself to rights. She was truly shameless. Her brother could be dead, and all she could think about was dragging the man standing two feet away to the ground and having her wicked way with him.

Sorcha hesitated, guilt returning in force as she thought of Ronan. Brandt eyed her, correctly interpreting her expression. "Your brother's only wish was for your safety, Sorcha. Even before you met me, he planned to get you away.

Don't let whatever you hope to do by going back there get in the way of what he wanted." His words flowed over her like the salve on her skin. Calming. Soothing. "Ronan will find you."

If he isn't dead.

"He's not, Sorcha," Brandt said, reading her. "He would move mountains to see you safe. Death is a paltry enemy for a warrior like him."

Huffing a shallow breath, Sorcha stared at the stranger she had married, at the conviction on his face. No man, outside of her father and brothers, had ever been so mindful. He had no reason to be here but for a promise made to her brother to see her safe. He'd already won Lockie. There was nothing in it for him to comfort her, though he did it anyway.

Once more, the slightest intuition of danger settled over her, as if she were standing in the shallows of a loch and about to step into precariously deep waters. It wasn't because of Coxley or Ronan. It wasn't because they were alone in the woods on the run from a mad marquess. Or because she'd sustained an injury.

It was because of *this* man.

Brandt was more dangerous to her than any of them combined.

Chapter Ten

Brandt scanned the surroundings as their horses carefully picked their way along the rough gravel path of the mountain pass. They had ridden through the night, stopping to sleep for a scant hour before heading deeper into the hills once dawn crested. The pass was far too dangerous to ride by night, and a challenge even during daylight.

Sorcha rode ahead of him, and he could see her also alertly looking around, every so often throwing a glance over her shoulder to him. He liked their unspoken communication—a nod here and there to make sure each of them was faring well as they covered more and more ground. Sorcha was leading the way given her familiarity with the terrain, although the gentleman in him did not like the idea of her being so open to any oncoming attacks.

She had scoffed, of course, at his concern. Brandt smiled at the memory of her indignant expression, as if he had called her very honor into question by suggesting she ride behind him.

"I'm a Highlander," she'd said, affronted. "How do you

think 'twould appear if anyone were to see me riding behind a Sassenach? I'd never hear the end of it."

Brandt had resorted to logic. "How would anyone know who you are?"

She jabbed at her face with a finger. "Don't forget, everyone knows of the Beast of Maclaren, even old Coxley back there."

"I don't like that name."

Sorcha had stared at him then. "Why?"

"It's cruel, it's untrue, and it's no name for someone like you."

Her eyes had sparked with affront. "Someone like *me*?"

"A lady."

She had clamped her lips together as if to stop herself from saying something she would regret before turning her back and galloping off. It was true. She was the furthest thing from a beast, and Brandt disliked the cruel moniker. He couldn't imagine her without her scars…her beauty and strength were interwoven with them. But even so, she was still the daughter of a duke, and a highborn lady.

In London, he'd encountered his share of well-bred English society ladies. A vision of Sorcha's savage expression as she stood like an avenging warrior goddess upon her horse in that thicket came to him. She was so much more viscerally appealing than any of those women. Now, Brandt could see why none of them had ever caught his fancy. It was like comparing a gentle sun-shower to a lightning storm.

"We'll stop soon," she called over her shoulder. "There's a valley around this bend where we might find water and a cool place to rest. From what I recall, it's below this rise, and there's a village nearby." She squinted. "We should be entering Dunwoody lands. We're not feuding with them."

"That sounds like a good idea. Ares is tiring."

The horse wasn't really tired. He was bred of sturdy

Arabian stock and could go on for miles, but every so often, Brandt noticed the drooping slope of Sorcha's shoulders and the rigid tension in her left side. Her wound had to be paining her, and yet she soldiered on. The rocky ground did not make it easier, and even with his full physical strength, Brandt found it difficult to keep his balance at the brutal pace they were maintaining.

The vegetation—and cover—was sparse, unlike the rest of the Highlands they'd traveled through with Ronan. At the thought of the Maclaren heir, he sobered. He'd said what he had to in order to convince Sorcha to stay the path and not go back. Though he had seen and heard enough of Ronan's skill to know that he was more than capable in a fight, in a one-on-one match against Coxley, it would likely take a miracle to bring him down.

Brandt shook his head furiously. Malvern was bad enough, but thinking of Sorcha anywhere in the same space with someone like Coxley made his stomach sour. If the man ever got his hands on her, she would not make it back to Maclaren unviolated. His tone when he'd called her *the Beast* suggested his intentions as such. No, no one, especially not Coxley, would put their filthy hands on her. Not while Brandt drew an ounce of breath.

His anger returning in smoldering force, Brandt gritted his teeth as he followed Sorcha down the hill. Ares whinnied, as if sensing his master's ire, and Brandt gave his mount's sweaty flank a reassuring pat, forcing himself to calm. Ares had always been aware of his moods.

There was a reason he didn't want anyone to touch Sorcha. Envy, he was beginning to realize, was a terrible companion. He was even envious of Lockie, and how Sorcha's slender thighs were wrapped so lovingly around the horse's sides. Her body rocked rhythmically in the saddle, the provocative flare of her hips the precursor to a punishing erection on his part.

It couldn't possibly be healthy to remain in such an engorged state for hours on end.

Jesus.

Brandt swore under his breath. Fury and fear, tangled with unrelieved sexual frustration, tended to make a man slightly insane. He wanted her with a desire that made him breathless. She wanted him, too. He remembered her excited breaths as he'd soothed her wound in the cave.

It had taken all of his control to not press his lips to her dewy skin, to push those trousers down and seek out the delectable heaven he knew the taste of her would be. He'd been hard as Scottish steel the entire time. Brandt had felt her thighs quiver, seen the seam of her legs press together, and only the sobering sight of her torn flesh had saved him from tearing her clothes off and thrusting into her.

Brandt expelled a sigh. This journey would be the sodding death of him.

He dragged his eyes away from Sorcha's delicious rump and focused on the sheep dotting the rolling hills in the distance. In his childhood, he used to count them to put himself to sleep. Perhaps now he could count them to deflate the brute in his pants.

Some two hundred sheep later, the gravel turned to grass beneath Ares's hooves as they left the path, and sprigs of purple heather brightened the landscape. They rode past more sheep grazing in the lush meadows, but Brandt had no more need of them, at least for the moment.

Now that there was more space, Sorcha slowed her mount to ride beside him. The hills were open enough to see if anyone was in pursuit, and the slackened pace gave the horses a chance to cool down after the grueling trek in the mountains.

"How's your wound?" he asked her.

"The dressing needs to be changed, but it's bearable."

From her wan face, he could see that she was minimizing the pain. "There's a farmhouse over yonder that may spare us some food and water for the horses."

"Fine."

She eyed him sideways, her expression hidden behind a bland but clearly false facade. "Why did you say you didn't like that name? The Beast of Maclaren?"

"Because you're not a beast."

Sorcha shrugged. "I used to hate it. Cried myself to sleep when the children in the keep sang it to my face and ran away hiding. Finlay and Evan used to beat them silly on my behalf, until I learned how to defend myself." She pursed her lips. "After that, it became like armor. Like it was a badge. People knew who I was."

"It's not a name for a lady," Brandt said staunchly. "For a duke's daughter."

"I never wanted to be a lady."

He sent her a look. "What we want and who we are sometimes do not coincide. Life is funny like that." He paused, his heart giving a painful kick. "You deserve the life you were meant to lead, to marry a man of influence."

"A man like Malvern? I'd rather drown in manure."

Brandt shook his head. "No, not like Malvern, but a titled man. One who can offer you your rightful place in society."

Not someone like me.

"But what if that's not what I want?" she shot back. "I can't fathom wearing dresses and primping and playing coy all day, having tea, singing and playing the pianoforte or any other infernal instrument. Wasn't there something you wished to be? More? Less? Just not what you were?"

To have a mother. To know who I truly am.

"No."

Brandt stopped his horse so suddenly that Sorcha had to pull sharply on Lockie's reins to see what had stopped him. Her face grew alarmed when she took in the horrified expression on his. "Lady Sorcha Maclaren, did I just hear you confess that you don't sing or play any instrument? Nor primp or flirt? And what, pray tell, do you have against tea? *Sacrilege* to the English."

She compressed twitching lips. "You're not English."

"Honestly, what kind of pagan have I married?" She was valiantly attempting to swallow her snickers by that point. He rolled his eyes skyward, clapping a dramatic hand to his chest. "What, dear Lord, did I do to deserve such an abominable punishment?"

Laughing out loud, she punched him in the arm. "It's Lady Pierce, I'll have you know."

Something inside of him warmed, but Brandt squashed it brutally. He'd jested only to turn the conversation away from his empty childhood wishes and the cruel voices she'd inadvertently awakened. The ones that clamored that he was undeserving of her smile or any part of her. His amusement evaporated. He needed to quash this, and he needed to quash it now.

"You're a Maclaren," he said. "Trust me, you wouldn't want to be a Pierce anyway. We're a tedious, pissant lot." He kept his gaze straight ahead, his tone even. "An annulment is for the best. No reason for you to be the wife of a bastard when you can be a lady with the life you were born for."

The humor drained from her lovely blue eyes, hurt shining there for a minute before it was replaced by sparks of anger. "You're an arse, Brandt *Pierce*. You and your precious name."

"Precious as dirt."

"I've changed my mind. *Amadan* is too good for you. Haven't ye heard a word I've said? I never wanted to be a lady."

"And I never wanted to be a bastard!"

The words slipped out from some hollow, cavernously painful space within him, and the minute he said them, he regretted it. He regretted being so vulnerable. And he hated the sudden pitying look in her eyes. His temper boiled and exploded.

"You're not the only one who ever wanted another life. You're not the only one who wished on every star and every ha'penny to be someone else. But we've all had to grow up and smell the horseshit. So stop whining about not wanting your life of privilege, when many are born to far less."

Sorcha recoiled at the last few words, and as his rage receded, Brandt felt a pang of bitter remorse. Angry, hurt tears shone in her eyes. Once more, he'd lost control of his temper.

"I'm sorry." He reached for her, but she flinched away. Shaking, she opened her mouth and closed it. And then kicked Lockie into a wild gallop.

Bloody hell.

Brandt stared at her disappearing shape and nudged Ares into a canter. By the time he got to a rambling cottage in the direction she'd ridden, Lockie was tied in the nearby stable, munching happily on a bucket of oats.

A small boy who looked to be no more than ten standing beside Lockie gave him a friendly wave. "*Och*, the lass said ye'd be along soon." His brogue was thick as he eyed Ares. "Wha' happened to yer horse?"

"He got tangled into some wire."

The boy's eyes widened to huge round orbs. "Are ye Sassenach?"

"No, but I was raised in England."

"Ye talk funny."

Brandt shrugged. "I suppose I do." He leaned conspiratorially down to the boy. "What does *amadan* mean?"

The lad gave him a delighted grin. "It means idiot."

Indeed, he was that and more. Brandt gave Ares a brief rubdown and settled the horse beside Lockie. Running his fingers along the horse's gray flanks, he stroked down its nose. The horse nickered and turned its head into his shoulder.

"At least I'll have you," he murmured. "Even if I can't have her. No matter what your mistress thinks, she deserves better than me."

Sorcha was nowhere in sight, but he expected she was already inside. He thanked the boy and made his way to the cottage. It was a tiny, well-kept place, though he could see that recent repairs had been made to the wooden planking. He knocked on the front door, and it was opened by a pleasant, plump-cheeked lady who all but dragged him to the kitchen where his wife was face-deep into a bowl of stew.

"Yer man is a fine-looking one," she remarked, pointing out a chair for him. Sorcha scowled into her stew. Cherub-faced children peeped at him from behind a nearby door and scampered back when they saw him staring. They had the look of the boy from the barn.

"I'm Mrs. Maxwell," she said and placed a hearty bowl of stew on the table. "Sit and eat up, lad, afore it gets cold."

He offered her a clipped bow and took the seat. "Thank you, madam."

"*Och*, lad, so proper," she said, fanning herself. "We dunnae get many visitors around here. Yer wife said ye were travelin' through to Inverness. That's where Mr. Maxwell is, ye ken. For the wool." She bustled around the small but cheery space, shooing two children from underfoot. "If ye're lookin' fer a place to bed doon, ye can sleep in the barn, but 'tis no' any place fer a lord and his lady. Sorry that we've no' go' the room." She grew embarrassed. "The nearest monastery's a full day's ride west."

Brandt had no desire to put this kind family in any danger,

and the shorter the amount of time they tarried here, the better it would be for all concerned, especially with Coxley on their heels. No, they would camp in the woods.

"We'll be on our way. You've been very generous, Mrs. Maxwell," he said as he tucked into the savory stew. After eating nothing but venison, salted meat, and beechnuts during the endless journey north, it was delicious. "Thank you for your kindness and the wonderful meal."

She blushed. "Dunnae fash yerself, lad. 'Tis a right pleasure."

Sorcha said something in Gaelic that had the children bursting into laughter. Brandt knew it was likely about him, though he was grateful he hadn't heard the word *amadan* thrown in there. Clearly, she was still furious; she wouldn't even look at him.

Her cold silence continued until long after they'd eaten and been packed up with vittles for the road. Brandt noticed the odd looks Mrs. Maxwell was giving them, and she pulled him aside at the door when they were leaving.

"A bit icy lately, aye, lad?" she whispered. "Yer lass is wantin' fer yer affection. Dunnae wait too long, ye ken."

She winked, her meaning evident, and Brandt found himself flushing dully. Good God, since when did he require advice on sexual congress from a sheep farmer's wife? Was the tension between Sorcha and him that obvious? To his consternation, Mrs. Maxwell gave him a hearty pat on his behind and winked again. "Get the wee lassie with a bairn, and she'll settle right doon."

For the briefest of seconds Sorcha met his eyes, as if she had heard what Mrs. Maxwell had whispered in parting, and the ensuing image of Sorcha pregnant with his child stole every rational thought from his head. She would be radiant. But Brandt knew it would snow in hell before he'd let that happen, no matter how much he desired her. He had no intention of spreading his bastard seed about, not for all the horses in Scotland.

Heading west in the direction of the monastery, they did not speak for the first few hours. Brandt busied himself with the counting of sheep again, then cattle, and then boulders. In all that time, Sorcha had not so much as glanced in his direction. He was beginning to long for Malvern's men to come along so he, at least, would have a diversion. Soon, he grew weary of his own company and pretending to be a human abacus.

It was an odd turn of affairs. Normally he was a man who loved his solitude. Valued it, even. Now, the abundance of it was driving him mad.

Kicking Ares into a canter, he pulled alongside Sorcha. Her face was stony. "You know, most men would long for a wife who doesn't speak," he began conversationally.

"Ye don't want a wife. Ye've made that abundantly clear."

Success! The first words that had left her mouth in hours. "I'm becoming quite partial to the way you fall back into your Scots brogue when you're angry."

She looked like she wanted to jump from her horse and pummel him into the ground. Her lips flattened into a line as she increased Lockie's pace. Ares kept up easily. "Can't *you* see I wish to be alone?" she snapped.

Her emphasis on *you* and her rounded vowels were not lost on him. Brandt smiled. He preferred her temper to the cold silence she'd subjected him to for the better part of the day, and he couldn't help goading her. "Young ladies tend not to know their own minds."

He could practically see the flames coming out of her ears. "Ye...*you*...conceited, arrogant—" She broke off in suffocated rage. "I very well ken my own mind."

"Ken means know, correct?"

She snarled at him, and Brandt laughed. Her face turned

the color of a ripe apple, but he did not heed the warning. The sight of her impassioned, ferocious glower made him ache all over, particularly in his nether regions as he succumbed to the most erotic arousal of his life. Brandt reached for her reins and her eyes widened. He pulled them to a stop, and before she could make a sound, he set his mouth to hers.

Their lips met in a tangle of lust and heat and simmering mutual hunger. Her tongue circled his, drawing it into her mouth. He gave it to her, and she sucked it deep, eliciting a strained groan from his throat. Sorcha tasted like honeyed ale and sunlight, fire and ice, and everything in between. She made him see entire constellations and feel like his body was no longer his own. Brandt clutched her closer, losing himself in the heady sensation. Without breaking their kiss, he plucked her from the saddle into his lap.

Her pliant thighs—the sight of which he'd gorged himself on for days—pressed delectably against his stiff groin. Sorcha moaned into his mouth, her hips wriggling as if she, too, sought the satisfaction that only the merging of those two parts could bring. She experienced pleasure in the same way she expelled anger—with unabashed fervor. Panting softly, her lips parted wider as they sipped and stole from each other. Brandt wanted her mouth, her heart, her soul.

His hand cupped her breast, and his greedy fingers sought her taut nipple beneath the linen of her shirt. God, he loved the shape of her...the soft round weight of her in his palm. Plucking the ruched tip between his fingers, she arched hungrily into him. He needed that pebbling peak in his mouth, but he did not want to release the sweet cling of her lips or the marauding, bold tongue of hers that set him aflame.

Lockie whinnied softly, and reason pierced through his lust.

"Sorcha," he gasped, pulling apart. "We must stop."

"Who says?" she asked, banked blue flames simmering in her eyes.

Her mouth was so deliciously pink that he had to kiss her again. It was a mistake; it only made him want more. With reluctance, he dragged his mouth away. "We can't. We shouldn't."

"You want this as much as I do." She wriggled her bottom atop his jutting length, making his head spin. "It's just kissing, Brandt."

Her words made him want things. Impossible things. Things that were out of reach for someone like him. With her, it could never be *just* kissing. He understood that as well as he knew his horses. She was as lethal as opium…one taste, and he would be lost. Willingly and forever.

And he would drag her down with him.

Brandt reached for the restraint that had never failed him until lately. "I know," he said hoarsely, "but I also know where this leads, and we have to do what's best for you."

"What's best for me or what's best for you?"

"They're the same thing." He drew a shuddering breath. "And not just so you can have the chance to marry a man of your station. I'm not the man for you."

Sorcha's body went still. "Why?"

He did not speak for a prolonged minute, the demons of his past choking him. "I shouldn't have kissed you. I'm…not worthy of you."

"Because you're illegitimate?"

He went still, though he was unsurprised by her candor. He'd come to learn that she was not a woman who played word games. "That's the least of it. I never wanted a wife. I'm not fit for marriage, Sorcha. Not a *true* marriage."

"And there is nothing true about any of this?" There was no hurt in her question, simply quiet curiosity.

"Our deal was real," he said, avoiding her question. "You

had something I wanted."

"Lockie."

Brandt nodded. "Yes. At the time, I thought it an acceptable trade."

A shallow breath lifted her shoulders. "And now?"

Now it was dangerous. More than dangerous.

In the beginning, it had been a neat, quick transaction—a name for a horse. The spark between them had been there from the start. Stupidly, he'd hoped to throttle his desires as he'd done countless times in the past with other females, but then, he'd never met a woman quite like her. Even now, his body's tension against her soft thighs hadn't abated in the least. Passion had a way of blinding people to reality. And the reality was he should never have married her.

"Now, everything has changed," he replied softly.

Something indecipherable flickered in her expression before she hid it. "You told me earlier that what we want and who we are sometimes do not coincide. But sometimes they do. Sometimes things make sense." She put a hand on his arm, and his pulse leaped beneath it. "What I feel now makes more sense than anything has in days. And I know you feel it, too."

"That's lust, nothing more." He felt her flinch at the vulgarity of his words, but he closed his eyes, knowing she would not let the matter rest. "This is not what you're imagining it to be, Sorcha," he said. "I am not your savior, and the emotions you're feeling are...misleading, brought upon by recent events. Trust me, your gratitude and your misplaced esteem will fade."

Sorcha didn't answer for a long time, only sat pondering him in deep thought. Without a word, she slid from his lap to the ground. "I may not be as worldly as some of the women you have known, Mr. Pierce, but I think your life has jaded you to the point that simple things have become unrecognizable.

What two people feel for each other can be more than the sum of its parts."

He watched as she led Lockie to a clearing and started to set up a place to camp for the night. Every time he thought he'd gained the measure of her, he realized how much he didn't know. She continued to surprise him at every turn, whether it was with her courage or her wit or her intelligence.

Brandt knew he should say something, but words seemed to have deserted him. Perhaps she was right. Maybe he truly was that jaded. It did not matter. She—and no other woman—could not change who he was.

After a while, he descended from his saddle. "I'll keep watch."

Chapter Eleven

By the following afternoon, Sorcha's wound had finally ceased hurting. Though the dried blood on the bandage had clung to the incision that morning when she'd changed it again, this time without Brandt's help, the sharp pain was gone, replaced by a bruised ache. She had no complaints over small aches, and had learned in the past not to voice them.

After seeing Niall's hand taken, and the pain he'd endured, even after the bandaged stump had slowly healed, Sorcha had known she would never again complain about cuts, scratches, or any sort of ailment. His wrist and arm, he'd explained, would light up in pain every now and again, as if reliving the brutal separation of his hand. The agonizing sensations had finally gone away, though it had taken well over a year.

Sorcha pictured Niall now, a strong, capable Maclaren warrior. If Malvern sent a contingency of his men from Tarben Castle to the Maclaren keep with orders for retribution, Niall was powerful enough to fight this time. He and the rest of the Maclaren men and women would put up with only so much oppression. Once they learned Malvern had attacked and killed Maclaren men, they would raise arms.

She closed her eyes against the images of her home being attacked. Of her people fighting for their lives. *Stop whining about not wanting your life of privilege, when many are born to far less.* Brandt's admonishment the day before kept coming back to haunt her, and each time it did, what felt like a piece of her soul ripped apart. Her healing wound was nothing in comparison, and no salve like the one she'd been applying to heal and keep out infection would ever be able to extinguish it. He was right. She'd been more than selfish.

The afternoon sun had risen through the canopy of trees, which had been starting to spread out, making it a bit easier for her to direct Lockie through the mossy and rocky undergrowth. It would be several days' journey to Brodie, and stopping at the monastery would be a welcome respite after their punishing pace. She heard Ares moving close behind her, his low huffs and snorts more noise than Brandt himself had been making all morning. He'd said more than enough yesterday, after he'd pulled her into his lap and kissed her with unmistakable longing. He'd wanted her. Badly.

I'm not worthy of you.

As much as she shunned being a lady, Sorcha wasn't naive. She knew what her rank demanded. She was the daughter of a duke and would be expected to make marriage alliances as her sisters had for the good of the clan. She would be required to marry according to her station, as Brandt had said. But if marrying a nobleman meant marrying someone like Malvern, she'd rather elope with the pauper son of a pig farmer. She'd come close, though Brandt wasn't a pauper and he raised horses. The fact that he was illegitimate had no bearing on his worth as a man, but Sorcha knew many others, including her father, might not see it that way.

What Brandt felt and why was an old injury, one as old

as the scars the she-wolf left upon Sorcha's body, and just as deeply rooted. It had to do with his mother and the callous way she'd abandoned him, Sorcha supposed. He did not trust easily, and for good reason.

If only Brandt knew the truth, that she did not intend to marry, either. There was no man she trusted enough to get that close. What she did want, however, was to experience what it would be like to be thoroughly seduced by a man. What woman wouldn't? Just because people called her the *Beast of Maclaren* didn't mean she didn't dream of having someone look at her the way Brandt did. With thirst and desire in his eyes.

Lust, he'd called it.

She blushed, her insides clenching. Sorcha knew exactly what he expected their kissing would lead to. *Copulation.* Consummation of their false marriage vows. But what he didn't know was that she'd gladly surrender her precious virtue for one night with him. One night of unstoppable pleasure. Lord knew she'd never have it with anyone else.

Sorcha shifted in the saddle and winced at the pull of her healing skin. Her mother's balm had indeed done its job. The cut was no longer weeping and had lost its angry red color. It had been a stroke of luck—no, a miracle—that Lockie had turned up, saddlebags intact, with Ares.

When she'd asked Brandt if that was normal behavior, he had smiled.

"Horses are like humans. Ares and Lockie respect and like each other."

"But they're both males."

He chuckled. "Not all relationships are about mating." It had taken every ounce of her self-control not to blush at his matter-of-fact statement, though she had failed miserably.

"I only meant," she said, thankful that he was busy murmuring to Ares and not looking at her, "that as a pair of males, I expected them to butt heads the way most men do."

Brandt smiled. "Like your brothers?" Sorcha answered with a roll of her eyes. "No. Like humans, horses just seek connection. Some do it by color, by breed, by instinct."

Fascinated by the unexpected change in his demeanor at the turn of the conversation, Sorcha had gestured for him to go on.

"Different groups gravitate toward each other. Certain breeds like to be with other equines of a similar temperament. They eat together and graze together. A gentle mare can find it quite stressful to be with a high-strung stallion." His expression had grown fond when he'd stroked his horse lovingly from mane to hindquarters, and the envy she'd felt had been surprising. What would it be like to have such devotion directed at her? "Horses have a wonderful ability to bond. They're amazing creatures. We can learn a lot from them."

When he'd spoken about his beloved horses, Brandt's face had relaxed, along with every corded muscle in his body, and his chameleon eyes had warmed several notches. His voice had warmed, too, making her skin tighten and her body achingly attuned to his every word. Crooning to Ares and stroking the stallion's withers, Brandt's voice had taken on dulcet tones that made *her* want to rub against his palm.

It had been puzzling, such an indecent reaction to his whisperings. She was *not* a horse. Though she had not been able to help imagining how it would feel to have those large, callused palms running the entire unclothed length of her body.

"Enough, Sorcha," she murmured, focusing on the widening path.

She eased a breath into tight lungs as the edge of the forest thinned, a stretch of heather-topped field on the horizon, and grew anxious. With every change in the landscape, it reminded her that they drew closer and closer to their destination. And when they arrived, it would be the end. None of this would matter…not her unfulfilled desires, nor his. Brandt would leave, and she would stay.

She came through the trees and into a field and, moments later, spotted the spire of a monastery. Just like Mrs. Maxwell had said. Her chest throbbed, her ribs feeling constricted. It wasn't the wound, but another ache. One of blessed relief shot through with deep-reaching desolation.

God's teeth, she felt as if she were being sundered in two.

They were nearly upon the ancient stone monastery, and she did not want Brandt to see her transparent feelings when they stopped to dismount and he finally looked at her. Not one to miss a thing as they drew near, his eyes narrowed on her face and dipped to her ribs.

"What is it? Are you well? Is it your wound?"

She shook her head, her body humming at his nearness. "It's fine and healing."

Sorcha steeled herself as Brandt continued to regard her with a doubtful look. She pushed a smile to her lips to reassure him, but it only made him frown. "You Scots like to insist you're not in pain when you are."

"I am not in any pain."

Brandt went on as if she hadn't spoken. "And while that is admirable for some, I know from experience that ignoring signs of pain can lead to greater injury."

She scowled. "I am not one of your animals, Brandt."

"You misunderstand," he said mildly. "Monty broke his ankle when he fell from a horse. Instead of tending to the break, he ignored it. The break worsened, and he ended up walking with a limp for the rest of his life."

"It's a cut, not a break."

His gaze swept her. "And yes, you are most certainly not an animal."

Something in his eyes and the faintly suggestive tenor of his words made her temperature spike. The knowledge that men at their basest *were* animals crept into her brain. Sweet Lord above, her entire body went molten at the prurient thought of their bodies entwined in the most primitive and bestial of mating rituals. Their gazes collided, and sensation upon sensation scoured every hot inch of her.

"I am well," she croaked. "I promise you."

Diah, the man had an unholy way of making her lose her wits. Last night, she'd barely been able to sleep for the way she'd longed for him to abandon his post guarding their camp and come ravish her where she lay on the mossy ground.

And earlier that morning, when she'd woken to find her waterskin filled and a pile of beechnuts he'd gathered for her on the ground at her side, together with the remaining leftovers from Mrs. Maxwell's basket, she'd sighed at the unexpected thoughtfulness. How many times had he put her own comfort and safety before his own?

Her body and her mind were equally susceptible to the force that was Brandt Pierce.

She would have to be especially careful with her heart.

Banishing her thoughts, she dragged her eyes away from him and, instead, focused on the monastery itself. Paddocks surrounded the monastery's collection of small stone buildings, enclosing sheep, pigs, and a few cows. The main structure, with its moss-covered, crumbling stone architecture, looked much like an abandoned monastery bordering Maclaren and Kincannon lands, where she often used to go as a child to pray to a very busy God to take her scars. He'd never answered her frantic pleas, and eventually, Sorcha had stopped asking.

A quintet of matching curved archways dotted the stone on the lower levels, rising to a square upper story with a pointed stone-slate turret. This monastery seemed to be in good repair. Sorcha wondered blasphemously if the God who resided here was as deaf as the one near Maclaren. Though, in hindsight, she'd since come to terms with her scars, which was perhaps what He had intended all along. She'd give Him the benefit of the doubt.

Chickens wandered helter-skelter, and as they cantered toward the main chapel, a man in plain brown robes carrying buckets of water upon a shoulder yoke stopped to greet them.

"*Madainn mhath*," he called, showing no fear at all at the two armed strangers riding up to his place of worship. But why should he, Sorcha reasoned. Being hunted by Malvern, with a savage such as Coxley on their heels, seemed to have colored her own perception. This was a man of the cloth, who believed in the inherent good of people. She had, too, once upon a time.

Until the devil had showed his face at Maclaren.

"*Madainn mhath,*" she replied in Gaelic, and then with a glance at Brandt, "good morning."

"Good day," Brandt said as he reined in Ares beside Lockie. Sorcha kept her eyes on the Franciscan monk, who had stooped to remove the shoulder yoke. "I'm Brandt Pierce of Essex, England, and this is my wife, Lady Pierce of Maclaren. We're journeying north, toward Brodie lands, but our provisions are low. Could we implore for your aid?"

The monk brought his palms together before his chest, showing no surprise at Brandt's clipped English. "We will aid any traveler in need of it. Please, come. Let us see to yer horses."

They thanked the monk and dismounted, Sorcha sliding from her saddle and landing on her feet with less steadiness than she usually would have. Despite her avowals to the contrary, her wound and the hours she'd spent in the saddle over the last handful of days had taken their toll. It was not her shameless thirst for her husband's hands and mouth leaving her lightheaded. She wouldn't *let* it be.

The monk took her hand, bowing over it and pressing his lips lightly to her knuckles. "Lady Pierce of Maclaren. I am Abbot Lewis. Ye're the daughter of Lord Dunrannoch?"

She expelled a breath before nodding. What she'd told Brandt was indeed the truth. It didn't matter how far they traveled in any direction in Scotland, her facial scars were all that were needed to announce who she was.

"He will thank you for your kindness," she replied. The abbot started to straighten, but paused. She saw his eyes were fastened to the ring she wore. The one Brandt had slipped onto her finger what seemed like ages ago.

After a few beats of silence, the abbot stood and showed them into the monastery. The modest chapel at Maclaren keep had always soothed her, even though she had never paid much heed to the vicar when he would drone on and on. Instead, Sorcha would look at the stained glass windows and try to piece together the meaning in the depicted scenes of holy bloodshed, grace, and beauty. She would imagine stories for them all, only half listening to the sermons. But the chapel was a place of peace, she knew, and she felt it settle over her as she and Brandt were led through a series of cloisters.

They entered a large room where the abbot directed them to a circular stone basin, water bubbling down from a small fountain in the center. A few other monks appeared and left folded lengths of toweling upon the stone rim. Sorcha and Brandt washed their hands and faces and necks in silence while the abbot directed the monks to prepare some food for their guests.

"Come," the abbot said after, "the refectory is this way. Ye must be hungry and weary, if ye have traveled from Maclaren lands."

They followed the abbot through another cloister and into a high-ceilinged dining room.

"We travel from Selkirk," Brandt said before taking a seat at a long table. The room was cold, and the bench lining the table, hard. But as Sorcha sat across from Brandt, she felt her legs throb with relief.

"Selkirk?" The monk's eyes widened. "'Tis more than three days' ride from here, and two days more from Maclaren. Ye have been traveling some time, then?"

"Yes," Sorcha said. She was well aware of the distance, and how much ground they'd covered. She'd learned to ride a horse before she could walk, and Scottish horses were bred for their endurance and distance, but even she was bone weary from being saddle bound.

"We're being followed by a band of men belonging to the Marquess of Malvern," Brandt said. The abbot's calm expression pinched.

"I see," the abbot said, pouring cups of wine from a jug in the center of the table. His hand shook and, though it could have been from his age, she thought it more likely the palsy was due to knowledge of Malvern. "And yer destination is *Brodie* lands?"

The emphasis he made on "Brodie" made Sorcha pause before she could sip from her cup.

"Yes," she answered. "Is there any reason you know of why we should not travel there?"

Had there been a conflict? If the Brodie had taken up arms against another clan, she and Brandt could be riding into hostile lands.

The abbot poured himself a cup of wine before answering. "I only wonder why ye shouldnae travel to Montgomery lands instead. They are much closer."

Across the table, Sorcha saw Brandt's eyes snap to the abbot. He swallowed his gulp of wine and slowly lowered the cup, his jaw tensing.

"Montgomery?" he asked.

The name had come up during her time with Brandt. His father, she remembered. *Monty.* Short for Montgomery. And Brandt's middle name as well, she recalled from the register at the Selkirk village jail.

"Aye," the abbot replied, his hand gesturing toward Sorcha's own, currently wrapped around the simple wooden mug. "Yer ring's crest. 'Tis the Clan Montgomery's coat of arms."

Sorcha looked to her ring and the faded colors of the crest. Brandt's utter stillness was not lost on her, and when he finally spoke, his voice was hard as iron and flint. "Are you certain?"

The abbot opened his palm in a silent plea for Sorcha's hand, and when she slipped her fingers into his waiting palm, he nodded. "Aye, quite. I assumed ye wore it because of yer relation to the Montgomerys."

She turned her eyes to Brandt again, her hand still resting in the abbot's grip.

"It belonged to my mother," he said, his eyes not on her or the ring, but some spot on the table. His mind was miles away, sinking into a past she knew haunted him.

The abbot released Sorcha's hand. "Then ye are a Montgomery," he said, as if it were the simplest reckoning in the world. But by the untethered expression upon Brandt's face, it was no such thing. From his earlier admissions, he had grown up with absolutely no knowledge of his mother or the circumstances of his birth. And now…with this abbot's confident statement, he had learned.

Brandt's gaze again shot to the abbot, the distance his mind had traveled having closed within seconds. "Where are Montgomery lands?" he asked, biting off each word as if it were poison in his mouth.

The abbot blinked, surprised at the leashed violence of the question. Sorcha felt the chill of it and understood the place of pain from whence it had come. Her heart ached for Brandt, but she knew he would not welcome her concern. Or her pity.

She had come to know his private thoughts only by chance because of goading him, not because he had trusted her enough to confide in her. He would not appreciate any outreach. Instead, Sorcha schooled her features into a blank mask.

"West," the monk answered. "Perhaps one or two day's ride, depending on yer haste."

Her sister and brother-in-law were to the north, many more days than that. And Coxley would not be far behind. Sorcha had heard of the Montgomerys, one of the oldest Scottish clans, though the Maclarens did not have many dealings with them. They were not one of her clan's enemies, but what she did not know was whether they were friend or foe to Malvern. The man had his fingers embedded in every part of Scotland. She thought back to the men who had attacked Ronan…their plaids had been varied. Mostly Lowlanders, but a few Highlanders, too. Trust was a luxury that neither of them could afford, at least until they got to Brodie.

"We are going to the Brodie," she hissed to Brandt through clenched teeth. He considered her for a moment. That was all. The blasted man. What was going through his mind?

"We will take the closest sanctuary from Malvern we can find," he replied. "And that is Montgomery."

"And are you so certain they will offer it?" she asked softly, even as her thumb touched the underside of the gold band on her finger. Even if he presented the ring and said it had been his mother's, there would be no proof he was telling the truth. The ring could have been got in any number of ways—sold, pawned, stolen. Scottish heirlooms and antiques were traded and sold like common goods to keep families fed, thanks to the Clearances. But if it was indeed his mother's and he was a Montgomery, then the woman who'd birthed him and hadn't wanted him could deny him now, as well.

He already harbored enough hurt. Sorcha didn't want to see him rejected again.

Brandt didn't answer her question before a few more monks entered the refectory with plates of food for them.

"Eat yer fill," the abbot said, "and then we will show ye to yer room."

Brandt shook his head tightly. "It isn't safe. Your monastery is unprotected."

"We are protected by the Lord's light and love."

"I prefer stone walls, a moat, and plenty of steel," Brandt replied. "Besides, I don't want to put your monks here in danger. We'll rest for a while, but will ride before sunset and make camp again."

Sorcha was secretly grateful Brandt did not want to stay. When the abbot had mentioned a room, she had thought of the small one at the inn where they had shared their wedding night. Too much had happened between them since then, and sharing the intimacy and luxury of a real bed would have been untenable.

The abbot bowed. "Then I insist ye take what ye need from our kitchen and cellarium. Whatever supplies ye require are yers to sustain ye."

It was a generous offer, but as Brandt thanked him, Sorcha imagined the abbot would have parted with a week's worth of provisions if only to avoid a skirmish at his monastery involving Malvern's men. She had not missed his look of relief when Brandt had said they would be leaving. She clenched her jaw. Malvern was a monster who needed to be stopped. His reputation for brutality via Coxley's hands ran far and wide. It was no surprise that the monks here feared his name. Sorcha had no idea why the king would condone Malvern's actions, but perhaps he simply did not know his man was committing such atrocities in his name.

They finished eating their simple meal of venison, turnips, and bread, made all the more palatable by the ewers of wine brought to replenish their cups. Brandt spoke little, his mind no doubt tumbling over the revelation the abbot had laid down before him. She longed to ask him what he was thinking. Longed to touch his cheek and force him to look her in the eye. But the abbot's presence didn't allow it. Nor did her own sense of self-preservation. It was both a blessing and a curse, for if she touched him as she wanted to do, the desire to touch him more would catch fire inside of her.

It would not surprise her if he was a Montgomery. Though he spoke and dressed like an Englishman, he had the heart and courage of a Highlander. But in truth, it would not have mattered if he were a blue-blooded, English-bred Sassenach…she would have come to respect him anyway.

But Sorcha also understood that what she felt could be exaggerated because of their circumstances. After all, people thrown together in impossible situations came to depend on one another out of necessity. Brandt had said as much, too.

This is not what you're imagining it to be.

Perhaps he was right. She was confusing fondness for respect. Or her physical desires for something more. And there was no denying her attraction—she'd begun to vibrate like a tuning fork whenever he was near. After the last few days, she couldn't deny the way he made her feel…as if she could take on Malvern with him at her side.

For a moment, Sorcha wondered if it were possible to keep one's heart completely detached from the demands of one's body. She could, she supposed, with effort, though it wasn't just his kisses she craved…she delighted in his spare smiles and his sly repartee. His wit and intelligence. The mellow voice that resonated through her worries, calming her in an instant.

Diah. A small sigh departed her lips. None of it mattered anyway. He was incapable of ever truly trusting anyone, and she had her own demons. Real ones that had carved their marks upon her flesh. Best to keep them covered—both her scars *and* her utterly unwelcome feelings.

Chapter Twelve

When they left the monastery, the afternoon sky had been crisp and clear, but by sunset they were riding into the odd pale light of a brewing storm. It was far too late to turn back and retrace their steps to the monastery. They would just have to endure the storm when it hit. *If* it hit. Weather in the Highlands was more capricious than he'd expected. Sunny one moment, and stormy the next.

Much like how Brandt's life had been the past few days.

Brief breaks in the thunderous sky above showed a fiery setting sun, intermittently glazing the vibrant green grass with golden light before the slate clouds shut them out again. They rode west, toward the blocked sunset, squinting when the rays pierced through. Though even then, Brandt felt cold and empty, and yet also filled to the brim with restless energy.

Odd, how he found he had nothing to say to Sorcha, who kept Lockie only a few paces in front of Ares. No, that wasn't entirely true. He had plenty to say, including an admission that she had every right to be angry with him, considering he'd deviated from their plan. However, the looks she kept sending his way were not ones of anger, but of concern.

Perhaps it was his silence that worried her. Ever since the abbot had spoken the name Montgomery, it had felt like one stone after another piling onto his chest. Until he felt grounded, but breathless. He couldn't seem to open his mouth to utter one bloody word.

His mother's ring. His father's name.

It could not be a coincidence. Brandt's mother was a Montgomery. *He* was a Montgomery.

He had no idea what to expect as they rode westward, the feeble protection of the monastery sliding behind the hills and valleys in their wake, and uncertainty over whether they would find welcome and shelter with the Montgomerys weighing heavy. But Brandt could not have continued north, not only because Brodie lands were still days away, and there was the risk of Malvern having already predicted it was their destination. Nor because Sorcha's wound needed more time to heal while she was inside stone walls that had warriors on guard instead of monks with wooden crosses. No, he could not have continued north because of the unassailable driving need to grasp the one vision his mind had clung to for nearly all of his life.

He wanted to find her...his *mother*. He wanted to show her what he had become. And then he wanted to leave her with the knowledge that he would never think of her again.

Perhaps it was selfish. Brandt didn't care.

It was too close. A few days ride, and he would have the answers he'd sought for so long. Answers his father had never been able to truly explain. He'd had an affair with a married woman, but had he loved her? Had he asked her to run away with him, and had she dismissed him without care, as she had clearly dismissed her own infant?

One night, during one of the rare times Monty had been in his cups, Brandt had made the mistake of questioning him and had gotten answers that had cut him to the bone. Loosened by drink, Monty had sobbed, bits and pieces of truth spilling out in incoherent parts. That Brandt's birth mother had been a Scottish highborn lady. That Monty and Brandt had both been sent away from the clan and begged never to return.

When Monty sobered, Brandt had confronted him with his ramblings, but he had resumed his staunch refusal to talk about the land of his birth or his clan. Only to say that Brandt's mother hadn't wanted either of them to come back, and that Brandt had been a mistake she could never recover from.

A *mistake*.

The knowledge had ruined him.

After that day, Brandt had stopped asking. He'd finally accepted that Monty would never part with the whole truth, and that perhaps, it was for the best. But Anne, even with all the things his stepmother had done to care for him and Monty until she'd died, had still not been Brandt's *mother*. He hadn't seen the same love and adoration in her eyes the way he would when the Duchess of Bradburne would look upon Archer. She hadn't hugged Brandt, or kissed him good night. She had provided. She had made Monty smile from time to time. And she had never raised her voice, or her hand, to Brandt, but there had always been something missing.

It had settled inside of him, that vacancy. He knew meeting his birth mother would not fill it, but the need to lay eyes upon her was undeniable. Especially now that he knew she was so close. Or at least, her clan. *His* clan, if the vicar was right. The yearning he'd experienced as a child seemed to return in full force. It boiled down to one thing after all these years; he wanted to know *why*. He wanted answers. How could any mother abandon her own child?

On his own deathbed, Monty had confessed again. His

body had been frail with fever, his eyes rheumy, but he'd beckoned Brandt close. "Sorry, lad," he'd wheezed. "I never... got chance...tell...truth." A violent spasm of coughing had rocked through him. "Ye're...*cough, cough*...ye must ken... *cough, cough*...yer mother..."

"All is well, Father," he'd said, tears falling down his cheeks. "I know what she did. I won't go looking, I promise."

"Nae...forgive...I'm no', no'..."

But words had failed Monty then. Words and then breath. And as the light left his eyes, Brandt didn't care about what he'd been trying to say. Consumed with sadness, he'd simply wept at the loss of the only family he'd ever known.

Brandt felt a dull stinging in his eyes as streaks of lightning brightened the sky over some distant hills. He blinked, and they were gone. He hadn't thought of the night he'd lost his father for a long time. Until now. A few moments later, a rumble of thunder made Lockie whinny and rear wildly. Sorcha reached forward to stroke his mane and neck, trying to calm him with some whispered words, but the gray kept tossing his head.

Still without a word, Brandt rode to her side. Having Ares canter beside Lockie seemed to calm the gray, and the two mounts rode in time, ignoring another flicker of lightning and the answering toll of the heavens.

"We should find shelter," Sorcha said when another jagged fork cleaved the sky in two, the white light tearing long fingers into the rapidly condensing fog. Ares reared up onto his hind legs, which was uncharacteristic for him. Brandt frowned, calming the animal with a soothing click of his tongue, but ignored what should have been a clear warning and urged Ares forward. He scanned his surroundings.

They seemed to have ridden into a rocky valley, with two mountainous hills rising on either side. The misty clouds had dropped to obscure the tops of the hills, as well as smoke trailing up from any nearby homesteads, and the Highland fog was already starting to thicken. Monty used to tell him stories of men who had gotten lost in the mists over the moors with only a few misplaced steps. Soon, they would not be able to see two lengths in front of them. Brandt did not want to put Sorcha in danger, but a different furor kept driving him forward.

"A bit farther," he managed to say, kicking up his speed. Ares shot forward, with Lockie staying close on his heels.

"We aren't going to get there tonight!" she shouted.

She meant Montgomery lands. Of course she would know what was consuming his thoughts.

Brandt kept riding, determined to reach the end of this narrow crevasse between the two sharply angled slopes. There had to be something ahead, some barn or ruin, a place for them to spend the night. And by the look of the sky and the thunder and lightning crawling ever closer, it would likely be a long, wet, and dangerous night.

Spitting rain flecked Brandt's cheeks and forehead, and then within seconds, it seemed, the drops fattened, striking his eyes as he rode straight into a wall of rain. It soaked them almost immediately, their mounts galloping at full speed through the quickly muddying ground as more thunder shook the earth. The sound of it echoed off the hills surrounding them, reverberating in Brandt's ears, and was made even more ominous by the suffocating mist that wrapped them in thick, heavy bands. The wind had picked up, too, howling a mournful sound like an animal lost in the wilderness. It made the hackles on the back of his neck rise and Ares toss unsteadily beneath his seat.

They needed shelter. *Now.* Finally, a curve in the terrain opened up to show a stretch of valley, the mists moving low over the grassland.

"There!" Sorcha shouted, and when Brandt followed the

direction of her pointed finger, he saw what looked to be a small hut ahead. It was a squat stone lean-to, likely built for sheep or goats wanting shelter from either sun or wind or rain. It would have to do, at least until the worst had passed and the fog had cleared.

He and Sorcha rode pell-mell for the shack. He could barely see three feet in front of him by the time they dismounted. The shed was not empty. Two drenched and forlorn-looking sheep stood huddled in one corner, bleating their terror at each cracking peal of thunder. Brandt led Ares and Lockie next to them, and he and Sorcha took up refuge in the opposite corner. The hut provided more protection from the rain and wind than he'd expected. The fourth side was not fully open, and though it let in some wind, for the most part, it kept the rain out.

Brandt stood, his head nearly touching the stone slab of the roof, and inhaled his relief. He nearly gagged. The stench was unbearable, and not just because of the wet sheep. It stank to high heaven of fermented animal excrement. His eyes met Sorcha's and she wrinkled her nose with a light shrug.

"It's not that bad," she said. "You get used to it."

"You are the strangest female I've ever known." He arched an eyebrow, surprised at her nonchalant response, though he did not know why. He had known that Sorcha was unlike any other woman of his acquaintance. Any other lady would have shrieked or swooned, but not his fierce Highland bride.

A plucky grin rose to her lips, her face illuminated by a bright slash of lightning. Her face was ghostly in the strange gloom left behind from the flash and the undulating mists. Brandt couldn't help thinking that she looked like a woodland fairy with her wild hair and shimmering eyes.

"When we were children, my mama always used to say no weeping for shed milk." She shrugged. "We're here and we have to make the best of it. It could be worse. We could be out there in that, unable to see our heads from our arses."

Brandt laughed. Somehow, he could not imagine ever losing sight of that particular asset belonging to her. He'd practically memorized it on the way to the monastery. "Speak for yourself, lassie. I have eyes in the back of my head."

"Bold words for an Englishman."

His humor faded. Not English. Scottish. *Montgomery* Scottish.

Sorcha must have seen the expression falter on his face in the eerie pale gloom, because she busied herself with feeding the horses some mash from the abbey. Once they were settled, she moved back to the corner with two extra plaids from her saddlebags wrapped over one arm and a bundle of sticks in the other.

"Where did you get those?" Brandt asked, eyeing the sticks.

"I learned the hard way when I was hunting with my brothers to always keep a stack of firewood wrapped in oilskin with my tack. The rain and the mists can roll in quicker than you can blink, and without heat, the Highlands are a frigid mistress. We can probably start a small fire in that corner," she said pointing to the unoccupied space. "It's out of the rain and cold. But we're both going to have to get out of our wet clothes or risk the chill setting in."

Amazed at her foresight and calm, he nodded, and a few moments later, Brandt could hear Sorcha undressing behind him as he set himself to task with the fire. He tried not to pay attention to the intimate rustling sounds or imagine the glow of her pale skin by storm light. She would look like a pagan Celtic goddess. It took every ounce of willpower he possessed not to turn around and see for himself. When she moved to settle in beside him, bundled in one of the Maclaren plaids, he saw that she had hooked her damp dress and underthings to a nail that jutted out on the wall.

"I've left a plaid for you there," she said and turned her face away.

Brandt noticed the rosy tinge of her cheeks—clearly, she was as potently aware of him as he was of her. And for good reason. She was stark naked beneath that covering. Gritting his teeth, he ignored the dangerous knowledge that made lust simmer to life within him.

He removed his own clothes swiftly and found other nails on which to hang them. By the time he was finished, Brandt was shivering, but the warm woven plaid felt like heaven as he squatted beside Sorcha.

"How long do you think the storm will last?"

"Hard to tell with squalls like these. Sometimes they can last for minutes, other times for hours." She peered through the door opening. "This one looks like it means to stay a while."

"We should get some rest, then," Brandt said. He rose and went over to the horses, where he unrolled the pallet he had saved from Ronan and spread it on the hard, filthy ground behind them. He was grateful for it, mostly for Sorcha's sake. She might have been accustomed to rough conditions, but that didn't mean she wouldn't appreciate the small comfort. He also grabbed two apples and handed her one.

"Thank you."

Sitting together, they ate the fruit in silence, watching the small flames that fought valiantly against the occasional burst of wind that slivered through the entryway. They threw the two cores to the horses. It had become only marginally warmer, even with the body heat of four animals and two humans, as well as the meager heat from the fire, and Brandt noticed that Sorcha was still shivering. He drew her toward him.

"What are you doing?" she asked, her eyes going wide.

"Warming you," he said. "And me."

Even through the layers of two plaids, her body was like a slab of ice. Her damp hair had already started to dry in tangled curls, but it seemed that the chill had already sunk into her bones.

"You're so warm," she breathed, wriggling closer.

"I spent many cold nights in the stables as a lad. I suppose my body got used to it."

Brandt tried not to react to her closeness and the faint lavender scent of her—vastly preferable to the other smells surrounding them. She sighed contentedly, snuggling against him. The loose plaid pressed between them was not much of a deterrent to his stiffening body, but Brandt steeled himself. He wasn't a beast, driven by rutting. She needed warmth, and he was simply providing it so she wouldn't catch a chill.

Or so he told himself.

"What do you know of the Montgomerys?" he asked, his tone gruffer than he'd intended.

Sorcha went slightly rigid beneath his arm. "Not much. My father used to know the prior Duke of Glenross quite well. Ronan said the old duke used to visit Maclaren on occasion before I was born when he was a lad. But when the new duke—his brother—took his place, things changed. The Montgomerys keep to themselves." She shrugged, her shoulder pushing into his rib cage. "Much like many other Highland clans, even Brodie. It's normal...only..."

She glanced up at him, something warring in her expression.

"Only what?" he asked.

"They don't like strangers."

His eyes narrowed. "How do you mean?"

Sorcha chewed her bottom lip and sighed quietly. "Well, I suppose you should hear it if they are indeed your kin. There were rumors surrounding the death of the old laird, the Duke of Glenross. He died in a suspicious accident. He was thrown by his horse and fell to his death in the quarry on Montgomery lands, and the one to find him was his younger brother, Rodric." Brandt stared at her, and she rushed to continue. "Ronan said he heard from Papa that it was near an old mining trench that they used to play in as children. Robert, the old duke, knew that land like the back of his hand. He knew all the traps and the dangerous parts, and yet he fell into a sinkhole."

"Was it murder?"

"It was never proven, but it was strange that Rodric inherited the title *and* went on to marry his brother's widow." Her voice went quiet. "He's known throughout the Highlands as the Mad Montgomery because of his rages. Ronan used to tease Finlay, Evan, and me when we were little that the Mad Montgomery was going to come and steal us away in the night." She shuddered slightly. "I do not know that we will be welcome there, Brandt, even if they are your kin."

"You will be safe, Sorcha, I promise you," he said. "Don't be afraid."

She drew a slow breath. "I'm not afraid, but I do fear that you won't find the answers you seek."

Brandt wasn't sure he would, either. But it was closer than he'd ever gotten to the truth of who he was. He owed it to himself, and to Monty, to pay his respects. And if he wasn't welcome, then he would leave.

After a while, they fell into silence, and as her weight slumped into his side, Brandt realized that she had fallen asleep. Gently, he lowered her to the pallet and tucked the plaid around her body. The small fire had already burned out to red embers, so he lay back next to her. Seeking his warmth with a soft sigh, Sorcha turned to fling one arm over him, and his entire body went taut as her forearm draped over the prominent bulge at his groin. He'd sported an inconvenient erection the minute she'd undressed, and now, at her unknowing touch, it swelled further. *Christ.* Even in sleep, she was going to be the death of him.

He loosed a shaky breath, and angled his hips a quarter turn so that her hand was no longer resting on top of him. And damned if he didn't miss the slight, innocent pressure of it. God, he was bitterly depraved if that was what he had sunk to. Moving quietly, he shifted his body so that he was resting on his side away from her. Instinctively, Sorcha followed the movement—and the source of heat—snuggling into his back and tightening her hold against his abdomen.

Brandt closed his eyes and tried to ignore the press of a luscious pair of breasts against his back and the spooning cradle of warm female thighs against his buttocks. He groaned as his groin tightened to the point of pain.

It was going to be a bloody long night.

Brandt moaned softly, awakening to warm wet lips nibbling on his chin…and to the sound of low laughter. Opening his eyes, he blinked, and a very large horse's head came into view as Ares tried to swallow his nose. He pushed the horse away and propped himself up. Sorcha had already risen and dressed and was grinning at him while munching on an apple, her gaze bright with amusement. "Nice dreams?"

"They were quite pleasant until a minute ago, thank you."

Brandt pressed the heels of his palms into his eyes and stretched, the plaid falling to his waist. Sorcha's gaze riveted on his bare chest and stomach before she turned hurriedly away toward Lockie. He half wondered what she would have done had he risen upright. His lower half was in no way relieved from the tortures of the night.

"He's hungry," she said, and Brandt blinked twice before

realizing she was talking about Ares. "But I didn't want to let him graze without checking with you first. Seems he had the same idea."

"By eating my face?"

"He was simply bidding you good morning with a kiss," she said with an irrepressible wink over her shoulder.

He'd have vastly preferred a kiss from *her* in the vicinity of his lap.

Smirking at the bawdy thought, Brandt grabbed the tartan and stood, making no move to disguise the conspicuous tent at his hips. He was rewarded with a smothered gasp as he strode from the shack. *Take that, Highland sprite.*

Outside, dawn was breaking across the cloudless skies in bright, pinkening touches. The storm had left everything washed and gleaming. Even the grass seemed greener and the patches of heather more purple. Tucking the plaid around his waist and throwing one end over his shoulder in a loose imitation of what he'd seen on Ronan, Brandt inhaled deeply and moved around to the back of the hut to take care of his morning needs.

"The plaid suits you," Sorcha said when he returned. Her voice had taken on a husky quality, no doubt from the eyeful she'd gotten.

"It's a bit too free for me," he said, grinning and arching an amused eyebrow. It had the intended effect. Her cheeks went scandalously pink as she caught his meaning that he was bare-arsed beneath the fabric.

"Most civilized men wear undergarments," she said primly. "And shirts."

"Do they?" he said, jutting his hips forward slightly.

Her face flamed. "This is unseemly conversation, *sir*, even for me."

"We are married, Sorcha. We have slept together, multiple times." He eyed her, enjoying her embarrassment.

"Surely, you're not going to turn into a proper, prissy maiden on me now?"

She scowled. "I'll have you know that I was brought up to be a lady."

"Sheathe your claws, wife." He chuckled and ducked inside to find his clothing. "'Twas only a bit of teasing. I wouldn't change one wild hair on your head for all the well-behaved ladies in London." Laughing, he ducked as her apple core came sailing at his head.

After a light meal of oats and grass for the horses and fruit for him, they mounted their steeds and headed west. The night's rest had done them all a world of good, and their pace was swift. With any luck, even with the delay from the rain, they would make Montgomery lands by the next morning. Sorcha cantered ahead of him, her back straight, her long hair braided into a neat, thick plait. He grinned. Undoubtedly, his comment regarding her "wild" hair had inspired her to be contrary. He had never enjoyed goading a woman more...and provoking the wit and fire of her response.

Suddenly, something whizzed by Brandt's cheek, tickling the tip of his ear. He glanced at Sorcha, expecting another apple core to come his way, but her back was to him. An arrow lodged itself into the dirt at Ares's hooves. Blinking, he looked over his shoulder to see two men in pursuit. They were mounted on two horses and dressed in brown striped plaids. Highlanders, then. They couldn't be Montgomery men—they wore the wrong colors for that. Who were they? Another arrow passed perilously close.

"Sorcha!" he yelled, drawing his sword.

But she had already turned, her own bow nocked. One of the men fell out of his saddle as her shot landed true. The second man released another arrow, and Brandt felt Ares rear up beneath him with a pained whinny. He jumped off the saddle, but there was no sign of an arrow in the horse's hide. With a furious shout, he ran toward the man, lifting his sword high above his head and swinging into the man's thigh as he rode past. His attacker toppled to the ground, clutching at his bleeding leg.

Brandt stuck the tip of his sword into the man's grimy neck. "Who sent you?"

The Scot scowled, his eyes going mutinous.

"It will give me great pleasure to carve your worthless head from your body," Brandt said softly. "Don't make me ask again."

The man paled as the point of the sword drew a drop of blood. "The Marquess of Malvern."

"*Malvern?*" Sorcha gasped, dismounting. "How? We've been on the road for days. They couldn't have followed us so quickly."

"How?" Brandt prodded the man.

"There's a bounty on yer head, dead fer ye, alive fer the lass."

Brandt stared at Sorcha. "He must have put the word out the minute we left Selkirk. These men will do anything for coin. We must make haste."

"What about him?" she asked.

Brandt felt loath to kill the man, even though he had most definitely intended to carry out Malvern's orders and kill *him*. He looked to be more desperate than he appeared to be a killer, though. His plaid was ratty and threadbare.

"Remove whatever weapons you're wearing," he ordered. The man quickly threw down a blade from his waist and one from an ankle sheath. Brandt then reached into the pouch tied at his hip for a few coins and offered them to the man, with the hope that the obviously desperate Scot would take the money and abandon any notion to come after them again. His eyes widened at the sight of the gold. "Go with your life, and remember the kindness I showed you."

The man took off, limping on foot, since both horses had disappeared.

"That was a generous thing you did," Sorcha said. "Though foolish. If there's a price on our heads, more will come. Scots like that one have likely lost their lands and homes, and Malvern's gold will be an easy lure."

"We've only half a day's ride to Montgomery," he said, but as he walked toward Ares, the horse shied away. His eyes rolled in his head and a pained sound emerged from his mouth. A streak of worry speared Brandt. He scanned the animal carefully, noticing the way Ares was favoring his foreleg.

"He's been hurt," he said, crouching to examine the leg with care. "There's a shallow cut here. One of the arrows must have nicked him." He sat back on his haunches and looked behind him to make sure the man was gone. They were in a field with little cover, exposed on all sides. "Damn it!"

"Can he walk?" Sorcha asked, also alert. "I spotted a thatch of trees a mile or so back near a stream. I could tend to it there."

But Brandt did not want to go back, not knowing if the man had more friends. "Where did you see the stream?" She hooked a thumb to the east, and Brandt pointed to a thatch of trees to the northeast. "We go that way and hope to intersect it. I'll walk him."

Ares did not complain, but after a short stretch, it was obvious that the animal was in pain. "I'll have to bandage it until I can clean it properly," Sorcha said. "Or it will only get worse."

Brandt kept watch with Sorcha's bow at the ready as she tended to the animal. At first, Ares nickered and tried to take a bite out of her shoulder, but the horse calmed at a quiet, though firm, word from her. Sorcha dug in her pack for a few bottles and then proceeded to mix together a hodgepodge of ingredients—moss, lichens, and bark—to make a poultice for the injury. She worked quietly and quickly, and Brandt couldn't help but be impressed at her knowledge.

"What is all that?" he asked as he traced a citrus-like scent.

"Lovage root and bog myrtle," she said, her lower lip caught between her teeth in concentration. "I cannot use my mother's salve until the wound has been washed. It heals so quickly that one speck of dirt can cause sepsis. These herbs will ward away the pain and help with the swelling."

"Have you always been a healer?"

Brilliant blue eyes met his, startling him for a moment, before they flicked back to their task. "I'm not a healer. I've learned bits and pieces over the years, that's all. My mother's the true healer."

She was being modest. The deft way she had tended to her own wound and the care that she was taking with Ares was remarkable. Brandt was surprised that the horse stood so quietly. Ares was a dependable animal, but his reaction to any type of laceration was to bite and kick. It was perhaps due to the weals he'd sustained as a colt. Horses had long memories.

"There," Sorcha said, tying a linen strip. "That should hold until we get to the stream. I'll ride ahead to make sure."

He watched as she rode away, and followed gingerly with Ares, who seemed more confident with each halting step. Though Brandt worried for Sorcha's safety, he knew she could defend herself. He didn't like *how* it felt to watch her leave, as if a part of his own body was riding away upon Lockie. He scowled. Where had *that* thought come from? That wasn't it. Her safety was his priority, that was all. And who knew if other bandits would be in hiding, waiting to ambush them?

It wasn't long, though it felt like an eternity, until she came back over the rise, her expression triumphant. "It's not far," she said. "Just over this hill."

The stream, more of a river now as it turned out, was enough for Sorcha to clean the wound and apply her mother's salve. Once more, Ares stood patiently, even rubbing his nose into her face at one point. Jesus. The horse was in danger of turning into as much of a ninny as he was.

"We should let him rest," she said, coming toward him. "Montgomery's not far."

"It's dangerous out in the open."

A level gaze met his. "Ares is your family. We'll keep watch. By the morrow, he'll be well enough to ride."

Her quiet words shocked him into silence. She knew how much Ares meant to him. Not many did. Ares was a horse… but he *was* the closest thing to family that Brandt had.

"Thank you," he said hoarsely.

Her slim hand found his, slipping around his palm and squeezing. "I'm sorry Ares is hurt, Brandt," she whispered. "This is my fault. I'm so sorry."

Overcome with emotion, he could only grip back. Brandt knew what she was sorry for, that she felt all of this was on her because of Malvern, but deep down, he felt like a fraud to accept her apology. He'd gone into it with his eyes wide open. It had started with wanting her horse, but over the last few tumultuous days, it had become so much more.

He wanted to help her.

And he also wanted to know who he was.

The problem was, he didn't know if he could do both.

Chapter Thirteen

The night had been long and cold, though Sorcha was thankful that it had, at least, not been storming. She and Brandt had tucked themselves into a small copse of trees near the river and lit a small fire, the rush and gurgle of the water the only noise throughout the night.

She'd barely slept, fearing both another attack from ruthless bounty hunters and an infection settling into Ares's injury. She'd washed the wound the first chance she'd had, applied her mother's salve liberally, and then bandaged it up. None of it, though, was a promise against infection. They needed Ares. *Brandt* needed him, and not just to transport him from place to place.

Ares was Brandt's companion. If something were to befall the horse, it would hurt him deeply. It would also be yet one more bad consequence of her scheming back in Selkirk. She didn't want to think of how Brandt might blame her, so instead, she'd looked up at the stars most of the night, the sky clear enough to show off every last twinkling constellation. She'd traced Orion and Gemini with her eyes, the Plough, and the Seven Sisters. It had been some while before she realized Brandt was not sleeping, either. His breathing was too quiet, his limbs restless as they stirred under his plaid. He might not have been keeping watch outside their encampment, but he remained alert. Alert and a few arm's lengths away from her own bedroll.

As dawn lit the fields, Sorcha had found her husband already at Ares's side, inspecting the animal's leg, the bandage off.

"It looks well," she said. The wound had started to heal instead of fester.

"Because of you," he replied, discarding the old strip of linen bandage into the meager flames of the fire. Sorcha tried not to flush at his praise, but her mind was relentless in the way it sought the pleasure such a thing brought.

She got to her feet and stretched, then went to her pack for the salve.

"Because he is a strong animal," she rejoined before moving toward Ares and reapplying a new layer. Brandt then bandaged him again.

"He'll be fine until we reach Montgomery," he said with a gentle caress of his palm over his mount's knee. "Once there, he can rest in more comfort until he recovers."

Sorcha bit her lip against the instant reply springing to her tongue. *What if the Montgomerys aren't welcoming?*

Saying as much would only cast a shadow over what was, so far, a fine, blue-sky Highland morning. The air was crisp, but with the sun and the rare lack of wind, it would soon warm. It might even get hot.

Self-consciously, she took stock of herself. They'd washed up at the monastery, but drenching rains and a night spent in a muck-filled field hut had made her feel as if she hadn't bathed in days. Before leaving the monks, she and Brandt had been welcomed to fill their packs with supplies for both themselves and their horses. Among the piles of stores found in the cellarium, there had been a crate of charity clothing and fabric. She'd found a simple green dress with few marks and mendings, a threadbare but clean linen shift, and a shawl that had but one spot of well-done darning.

Showing up at the Montgomery keep in her current grime-covered clothing was out of the question. She would already have to withstand the stares and whispers about her face; she would not give them anything else to gossip about.

"I'm going down to the river," she announced as she took the dress and shawl from her pack. As her hand reached, she saw how dirty it was. A small amount of her lavender soap remained in her saddlebags, and she palmed the jar now along with a square of linen.

Brandt gave her a small nod. "I'll keep watch."

Of course he would, she thought with a smile as she walked out of the trees, toward the wide, languid river. It wasn't as loud as it had been the night before. Sunlight did that; it muted things. Sounds, sensations, fears. Though as she stopped at the river's edge, placing her clothes and soap on a flat-topped rock jutting halfway into the clear water, she thought of how little it muted her longing for her husband. At night, yes, it was more pointed, but even now as she pictured him at the camp tending to their mounts and stomping out the fire, she longed for him. It was silly really, how thirty or so yards felt like miles upon miles.

Sorcha shook her head and undressed to her shift. The icy river water bit at her feet as she entered, but she knew the longer she took to get in, the worse the cold would be. So instead, she gripped her jar of soap and went straight into the shallows. The riverbed dropped into a pool, the rocks at her feet worn smooth, and the bracing cold sent a rash of gooseflesh all over her skin as she submerged nearly to her shoulders. Sorcha couldn't stop the little yelp of surprise, then a jittery burst of laughter.

Quickly, she lathered her body with soap, scrubbing at the streaks of dirt on her arms and hands, scouring her neck and chest and legs, concentrating hard on the rims of her nails. She took a breath and dunked her head, the cold water stabbing her cheeks and nose. She pushed back to the surface, another bubble of laughter at the cold releasing.

Her hair! It was a mess of knots, and as she lathered it with soap, tried to untangle each one. But it would take far too long, and already she was starting to feel numb from the knees down, her jaw beginning to chatter. The sun would warm her quickly once she was out, and then she could sit on the rock and comb out the tangles. So she gave up, simply dunking her head once more to rinse before turning to go back to shore.

Sorcha stopped, a pulse of shock skittering through her at the sight of Brandt, standing on the flat-topped rock next to her pile of discarded clothes. He held a length of clean plaid, one side of his mouth bowed into a mischievous grin. Sorcha felt another shiver through her body, though this one was unrelated to the cold. Instead, a spike of pure heat shot through her, centering low in her abdomen.

"How long have you been standing there?" she asked.

The grin intensified, encompassing his whole, beautifully formed lips. "Long enough to think you need to pay better attention to your surroundings."

"I was distracted," she said, the excuse and the cold making her voice high. "The water is freezing."

Brandt's eyes dropped to the twin slopes of her breasts beneath the wet shift just cresting the surface of the water, and Sorcha felt the graze of his stare to her shaking bones. The river water was clear, and she knew that despite the slight distortion the surface may provide, the outline of her body in her sodden garment was plain for him to see.

Though her nipples had tightened into hard, pebbled tips from the cold, her breasts still managed to suddenly feel heavy and full. And warm. This man. He was a flame, and she craved his heat. She wanted to throw herself in the very center of it and burn to willful destruction.

"I brought you this," he said, holding up the length of plaid. "To dry off."

He set it on the rock, by her clothes, and straightened to leave.

"Wait." Sorcha's feet moved over the smooth riverbed rocks, and her breasts cleared the surface of the water. She didn't know what had made her do it, only that she hadn't wanted him to turn and take his flame away from her. Or maybe because this was the last time they would truly be alone.

Brandt came to a halt, his smile fading as he took in the sight of her. Emboldened by the sudden smoldering press of his gaze, Sorcha took another step, the water sluicing down the clinging linen to her waist. She hesitated, her lips numb as well as her feet, and yet every inch of her somehow sparking with life. The drenched shift would leave precious little to the imagination, but it did cover her scars, and that made her bold.

That, and the blatant desire flaring in his eyes.

She stepped upward again on the angled riverbed and took a shivery breath. The rippling surface dropped drastically, to her hips, exposing the tops of her thighs to his view. Though she was chilled, a blush heated the underside of her skin. Brandt took a visibly sharp breath, his chest expanding as he gazed at her, drinking in every newly bared inch of her. Another step, and his stare hitched on her legs, a muscle beating in his cheek.

With a stab of shyness, she paused, torn between flinging herself back into the freezing depths of the river and making a mad dash for the plaid that lay on the rocks between them.

"Don't stop now," Brandt said in a low, husky voice.

Sorcha felt the familiar stirring of thrill she had every time someone challenged her. Only this time, there was something different about the thrill. It wasn't about winning the challenge. It was about sharing it, reveling in it.

She kept toward the shore, unable to stop, knowing that she could not. She didn't want to. Brandt's expression revealed more than simple lust. He looked dazzled, utterly fixated, as water droplets coursed from her hem down her bare knees, then her calves, and finally all the way to her ankles. No man had ever looked at her the way he did...like she was the sun and the moon and everything in between. She wanted more of it. Brandt took up the plaid again, his eyes slamming back into hers as she stepped up onto the rock and let him wrap her shivering body in the length of fabric.

And then his mouth took hers, his lips searing hot against her tingling ones. He held her close, his arms folding her against his body, her bare feet treading on his toes. He didn't need to coax her lips to part; she opened for him, seeking the warm thrust of his tongue. Needing it more than air. With swift, sweet licks he gave her what she wanted, one hand falling to her plaid-encased hip, and another raking up through her damp hair. His fingers caught on a tangle, and the pain only made Sorcha kiss him harder. She nipped his lower lip, and Brandt growled, fisting a handful of the quickly warming plaid at her hips.

"You are exquisite," he murmured as he rounded his free hand over her backside and filled his palm.

"No one has ever seen me like you do," she said, her voice cracking over the soft admission. Whether from cold or emotion, she wasn't sure. She knew she didn't want Brandt's hands to pull away, to stop touching her. How could she ever grow tired of his hands or his mouth? Just the weight of his gaze as she'd emerged from the river had made the deepest, most intimate part of her burn for his touch.

He pulled her closer, skimming his fingers up and down her back while his teeth found the lobe of her ear and suckled. The combination of his searching fingers and mouth, together with the open air against her lower limbs and the hot sun beating down on them, made Sorcha light-headed. She arched into him as his lips traced the shell of her ear. If possible, more gooseflesh prickled over her arms, and she sighed in pleasure.

Brandt's beautiful mouth went still, as did his hands… and for a moment she feared his untimely sense of duty had once more caught up to his rampaging desires and had finally convinced him to stop. She opened her mouth to protest, but then he gave a frustrated grunt and swept her straight off her feet, lowering her to the warmed, river-smoothed stone. With a sound of satisfaction, he covered her body with his, his arms caging her as he kissed her lips, then her chin, and dragged his tongue down the column of her throat.

He paused with a sharp exhale at the rounded slope of her right shoulder, and Sorcha knew he'd seen some of the minor scarring there. It wasn't as bad as the ones lower down, but ugly nonetheless. She didn't want to hear him gasp in shock, or pull back his hands in horror. She clutched at the fabric, not wanting anything to ruin the moment.

"Brandt, no. Please."

"Every part of you is magnificent," he replied fiercely, staring down at her. "These"—his knuckles brushed the scars on her clavicle and moved to the ones on her cheek—"and these."

His changeling eyes met hers as his lips feathered along the rough, reddened gouges. Sorcha shivered at the tenderness of his touch, but she wasn't ready to expose herself fully. She didn't know if she would ever be, but for now she wanted to enjoy every sensual jolt without feeling unworthy. If only for a moment.

"Please," she whispered. "Leave the shift."

"As you wish." He nodded, his gaze clouded with desire. "This is madness. I can't seem to stop myself from thinking about you…from thinking about touching you. What have you done to me, Sorcha?"

"No more than you've done to me," she whispered.

His mouth descended to graze her jaw. "Why can't I resist you?"

"Because I'm nearly unclothed?"

A chuckle broke from his finely molded lips, making her want them on her skin again. "There is that."

"I've heard the women at Maclaren say men can become so inflamed by their desires at the sight of a woman en déshabillé that they can't see reason…that they think with other…parts of their anatomy."

Brandt's eyes sparkled with mischief and humor. "Is that so?"

"Is it working?"

He laughed then, a deep-throated sound that made a lightness overtake her chest. "You're in a shift, and I'm at your mercy, so I'd be hard-pressed to say no."

"At my mercy?"

"Your devoted slave."

God, she loved their banter. It was as stimulating as the feel of his powerful body on hers. She wriggled her hips slightly, the motion making her gasp as his lean hips pressed her to the warm stone at her back. She went mute, as did he, their levity transforming into something deeper and darker.

The sunlight made golden flecks appear in his eyes, while passion darkened the green to the color of a stormy loch. A lock of sun-bronzed hair curled into his forehead as he bent his head to her collarbone, nibbling along the edges of her shift. His wide palms roamed her sides and skipped past each rib. His mouth and fingers met at her breasts and he filled his hands with her linen-clad flesh, kneading and caressing. A moan escaped her as his lips closed over the taut peak of one breast through the fabric.

"Brandt," she whispered, tugging at his hair, wanting to push him away and grasp him to her at the same time.

"So beautiful," he murmured.

His lips scorched her as he drew its rigid tip into his mouth, dampening the linen to wet, near transparency once more. His tongue raked over her nipple before he took it between his teeth with just enough pressure to make her arch her back. Crying out in mindless pleasure, Sorcha gripped his shoulders and tipped back her head, pushing her chest closer to him, only wanting more. The sight of him feasting on her body nearly made her faint.

"This is indecent."

He lifted his head to grin at her. "The only indecent thing is the depth of my hunger for you. I want to kiss every inch of these"—his voice was a rough rasp as he dropped a kiss to the peaks of both aching nipples protruding through her shift—"and touch every last inch of this beautiful body until you scream with bliss." He watched her, the devil in his slumberous eyes, as his erotic words seduced her as effectively as his mouth did. "And you're going to let me."

"Am I?" she gasped.

"Yes, you are. I'm your devoted slave, remember?" He flicked her taut, aching nipple with his tongue, the coarse graze of it beneath the dampened linen making her senses dilate. "The question is, what do *you* want, my lady?"

"I want…I want…" She wanted his kisses where it ached the most. She trailed off, biting her lip in mortification. "I can't."

He bit gently on the underside of her breast, his fingers

pinching its tip. "Yes, you can. Tell me what it is you want."

Damp heat gathered between her thighs at the unconscionable images flooding her brain. What she wanted was this man, body and soul. She wanted all the pleasure that was in his power to give her. She wanted him to soothe where the fires blazed the hottest. The heart of her throbbed almost violently as he held her eyes, waiting.

Sorcha wanted nothing more than to be honest with him. To be honest with herself, bugger propriety and modesty. Blushing furiously, she gave him her answer. "I want you to kiss me everywhere."

Brandt grinned and licked his lips like a man about to sit down for a banquet. "Now *that* I can do."

And it *was* a banquet. He gorged himself on her, leaving every part of her stroked, bitten, and suckled as he inched his way down her quivering abdomen. Sorcha felt like a river nymph, lying there in the sun, with her own adoring paramour serving her every need.

"May I?" he asked, his fingers reaching down to bunch around the hem of her shift. His knuckles grazed the bare skin of her thigh, and she couldn't breathe. She nodded, her throat tight. What she needed covered was above, not below.

Slowly Brandt pulled upward, and she felt the fabric slide until cool air chased through the curls at the junction of her thighs. His tongue dipped into the hollow of her navel, and she nearly came off the rock at the lush feel of his mouth on her bare skin. It almost made her want to tear off her shift, fears be damned. But then she forgot her thoughts as he circled the shallow indent and trailed lower, sending bolts of shivery warmth panning out wide. Reaching for his hard shoulders and tugging his shirt upward, she kneaded his muscles, splaying her hands over the hard, masculine planes of him.

Brandt shifted out of the reach of her greedy hands, and

she held her breath as his knuckles drifted over her hips, gently brushing the raven thatch between them. His touch was sinful. Divine. Some tangle between the two.

"You're so beautiful, Sorcha," he whispered, his hand grazing her again. This time, lower. A wild gasp left her mouth. Her world spun into blinding sensation at the fire his fingers left in their wake, stroking and seeking entry.

"Easy," he murmured when she clenched her thighs together. "You're safe with me."

Sorcha knew it was true, and slowly, let the rigidity out of her legs. Without hesitation, his fingers slid to the burning heat of her. She made a soft sound of protest, embarrassed to feel how damp she was there, but Brandt only murmured his satisfaction.

"You're perfect," he said, watching her intently as she felt the exquisite pressure of his finger glide into her. Her body felt like it was being pulled in different directions as wild currents coursed through her, centering at that one pulsing place where all her nerve endings seemed to gather. Instinctively, Sorcha curled her hips upward, wanting more, needing to be closer to him.

With every push of his finger, he stroked deeper into her, his thumb grazing over the small, sensitive pearl at her entrance. The pressure grew deliciously as another finger joined the first, stretching her, making her moan, but then he moved away, taking his clever fingers with him, and Sorcha whimpered her frustration.

"Brandt."

He laughed quietly, his breath tickling her skin. "Patience, my fierce lass."

Levering himself over her body again, his mouth moved down her overheated legs, finding sensitive spots behind her bared knee and inside the arch of her ankle. The pleasure he had stoked earlier seemed to turn into something more languid as he took his time crawling back up her legs, kissing every inch of her skin.

Basking in the sun, she gloried in it. Reveled in the sensation of being thoroughly ravished. But when Brandt's fingers slid between her wantonly spread thighs, his wicked tongue traveling in their wake, it made all the lethargy instantly depart her limbs. A burst of intense fervor built as he again parted the sensitive, slick folds of her body.

"You're so hot, so wet for me, Sorcha."

A deep flush suffused her at the raw need in his voice, and then she lost all capability for thought as he set his mouth to her with a strangled growl.

"Wait, what are you doing?" she gasped, pushing up onto her elbows. The lushly erotic vision of him kneeling between her legs was too much. She closed her eyes weakly. "Brandt, that can't be...decent."

He drew back, though just far enough to speak. "I believe I told you every last inch. You're not going to deny me, are you?" He lifted her ankles to his shoulders and Sorcha nearly expired on the spot when he bit her inner thigh. "And any shred of decency I possessed left me the moment I saw you splashing in this river like a naughty sprite." He grinned, his eyes turning mischievous. "Suffice it to say, I am thoroughly *inflamed* at this glorious, luscious display of skin, and as your devoted slave, I endeavor only to please my mistress."

Their teasing banter from earlier...come back to deliciously torment her.

Eyes glittering with purpose, Brandt's mouth descended, and Sorcha fell backward with a soft cry as sensation after sensation tore through her. The feel of his fingers had been divine; the feel of his mouth was positively sinful. Intolerably aroused, she writhed on the stone as his tongue lapped at her with swift strokes, and she clutched at his hair when it swirled, lashing against her swollen flesh without mercy.

Pleasure ran through her, low and deep. He wrung it from her like Poseidon wielding dominion over the sea. One finger slid deep into her aching passage, joined by another, and she arched into the velvet intrusion, her breaths turning into shattered gasps.

"More," she bit out on a sob. "Brandt, now."

With a triumphant sound, he gave it to her, swirling, nibbling, devouring with his mouth and tongue, while his busy fingers retreated and plunged until her last ounce of control disintegrated. She felt suspended. Untethered. *Alive.* Sorcha cried out as the paroxysm crashed over her, wave after wave of pleasure rolling and convulsing until she could barely breathe. Brandt crept up her limp, sated body, kissing her skin as if he couldn't get enough, even while little tremors continued to crest inside of her.

"You taste like heaven and heather," he whispered, his voice caressing her drugged senses. Her fingers curled around his back as he gathered her close, his warm skin sealing to hers. "Like sunshine in the middle of a summer storm."

As her world righted itself, Sorcha shifted her body. She froze as Brandt hissed, his jaw clenching. "What's wrong?" she asked.

"Nothing," he groaned. "Just...try not to move."

Oh. The hardness of him pressed into the warm, quivering crux of her...the place he'd so efficiently pleasured. Her body throbbed. Sorcha wriggled again as the fabric of his trousers rubbed against her over-sensitized body, making the brand of his engorged length settle between her thighs. She rocked upward, and he gasped. Pleasure stabbed through her core.

"Sorcha, stop, you'll undo me."

She caught his eyes and gave him a wicked smile. "I want to undo you."

"You don't know..." But he lost his words as she tilted her hips up and wrapped her legs around his. He obviously liked the friction, because his body started to grind against hers. A tortured groan left his mouth, and his eyes clouded with desire as he quickened his motions. Sorcha's fingers found his face, stroking over his sharp cheekbones and bristled jaw. She wanted to remember him like this, lost in the throes of passion.

She dragged his lips down to hers, even as he mimicked the act of lovemaking with his hips. The soft fabric rasped rhythmically against her core, and Sorcha moaned into his mouth. The second climax caught her unawares, dragging her down into its blissful depths. Her release incited his, and a shout tore from his lips as he collapsed against her, his hot breath fanning her temple.

In the midst of so much pleasure, Sorcha felt a tear trickle from the corner of her eye. Brandt looked up, his lovely eyes concerned. "What is it? Am I hurting you?"

"No, it was better than I ever imagined." She faltered for the words to explain the unexpected hollowness that had descended upon her. It'd been beautiful and ferocious, but strangely empty. A parody of the real thing. "I just...want more."

"I can't give you more, Sorcha." He raked a hand through his tousled hair, regret creeping into his eyes and dousing Sorcha's insides with ice. "Hell, I shouldn't have allowed it to go this far. I can't seem to think straight when I'm with you."

"That makes two of us."

Brandt swallowed with an embittered expression and reached for his discarded shirt. "This is my fault. I shouldn't be doing this with you."

Sorcha stared at him, her heart thudding painfully, adolescent fears rising from the dead to taunt her. "Because I'm a duke's daughter? Because you're illegitimate? Or do you think you're not good enough? Or I'm not good enough? Which is it this time, Brandt?"

Brilliant gold-flecked green eyes bored into hers, shimmering from warmth to impenetrable frigidity in the space of seconds. "All of the above."

Sorcha exhaled. It was suddenly hard to take in air...to breathe at all.

"Those are all true, but you left out the most important bit," he went on in a carefully detached tone. "This agreement was a means to an end. I have but one desire and that is to take possession of your horse." His words were as dead as his eyes...eyes that had been so full of heat and life only moments before. "What just happened between us was a moment of weakness."

Anger and shame exploded within her. "*Weakness*? You deceive yourself, and you know it. We both wanted this, and if you can't admit that, then you're more of a coward than I thought."

His furious gaze met hers. The coldness there made her shiver. "I am not a coward, but you're right. It wasn't weakness, it was pure idiocy." She flinched. His expression gentled somewhat, though the damage had been done. "Regardless of motivation, this cannot happen again. Once you are on Brodie lands, my part will be over."

"Your *part*?"

"My role as your husband."

His role. What they'd just shared had been nothing more than an *act*. Something fractured within her. Her body felt numb and empty, much like the state of her mind. Once more, she'd been a sublime fool when it came to understanding him. Or understanding men in general.

He was no better than any of them. Once he'd gotten what he wanted, his tune had changed. At least Malvern hadn't hidden the fact that he loathed the sight of her, and bedding her would be a nightmare. There'd been no risk of falling for his kisses or wanting more.

She was the groveling fool here, no one else.

"So what was this, then?" she asked, her voice shaking with an awful combination of misery and fury. "A scene in some sordid play you felt compelled to enact?"

"This was pleasure."

If that were true, pleasure seemed like a hollow and lonely place.

Sorcha grabbed for her plaid, pulling it around her like a shield. "Ye're nothing but a clot-heided bastard, Brandt Pierce."

"I know," he said as he started to turn away toward the riverbank. "And for what it's worth, I am sorry."

She wanted to stand, but her legs, still limp from his efforts, and now trembling with frustration, wouldn't hold her. "Ye can take yer bloody apologies straight to hell."

Chapter Fourteen

The ride to Montgomery was quiet and strained. Brandt did not want to put additional weight on Ares's injured foot, so they had agreed to share Sorcha's horse. The agreement had been stiff and unfriendly, given the circumstances, but it could not be helped. On foot, they would be even more vulnerable and would lose valuable time. Sharing Lockie was a matter of logic and safety.

Logical decisions aside, it had been worse than purgatory from the second he climbed up behind Sorcha. The feel of her strong, svelte body made him think of things he had no business fantasizing about, especially after his brutal words. He knew he'd hurt her, but he'd had no choice. Here in the wilderness, the pretense between them as husband and wife was not the same as it would be once she returned to society.

A few of her family members had encouraged the marriage, but for the wrong reasons. And with too much haste. She would most likely be shunned by her people for marrying someone so below her in status and rejected by any influential English society. It wasn't something he'd considered when striking their original deal, given their marriage wasn't destined to last more than a fortnight, but should they remain married, his shame would become hers to bear. And he did not want that for her.

No, he'd done the right thing. He knew from experience that a smaller injury now was better than a larger one later. And he also knew how easily esteem could be misconstrued the more time two people spent together.

The attraction between them was mutual, and one could easily confuse lust for love in the heat of passion.

But lust wasn't love.

He'd learned that the hard way with his faithless courtesan. Sorcha didn't have to.

Sorcha's spine braced forward as they climbed a small hill. It was evident that she was as aware of him as he was of her. Brandt could tell in the rigid way she held herself, as if to refrain from touching him at all, though it was unavoidable given the rolling gait of the horse. His hands clasped her hips loosely, and all he could think about was the feel of those same silken curves writhing beneath her shift. The scent of her skin. The glorious expanse of creamy limbs that had been velvet to the touch. And her taste had been indescribable.

Images of her lying on that rock, giving in to the demands of her body with so much passion, filled his mind. He'd wanted her fiercely, with a savage need he'd hardly recognized. And then what she'd done, cradling him between her thighs, taking the rough thrusts of his hips...it had excited him more than he'd ever dreamed possible. Brandt couldn't imagine what truly being inside her would be like. Heaven. Hell. Somewhere in between.

"How much longer?" he asked hoarsely, furious with himself and willing his hardening body to subside.

"Soon," Sorcha said tightly over her shoulder. Her voice was clipped, her posture like a stone statue. "We entered

Montgomery lands a mile or so back. Word will have already reached the keep."

Sentries would have been posted near the borders, he knew, hidden within the hills. Though it spoke of the Montgomery men's stealthy skill, it left him slightly uneasy that he had not seen them or felt their presence as he and Sorcha had passed.

Brandt had noticed the huts dotting the hillside and the occasional farmer wearing plaids of colors he'd memorized while staring at his mother's ring as a child. He'd wished for hours on end to know what that striped design and bold blue, green, and gold colors signified. And now he did. They were Montgomery colors. He felt a strange tightness in his chest. Was it anticipation? Anxiety? He recognized an undercurrent of fear and grimaced. He would not allow himself to be afraid. Not of the truth.

Was the woman who had birthed him even still alive? There was a good chance she could be dead, like Monty. And it stood to reason that he would show up at his family's keep and find no answers. He didn't even know his mother's name.

As they climbed down a narrow pass into a lush valley protected by slanted, rocky crags on both sides, Brandt realized how well situated the immense stone keep was. It was tucked into the indent of the valley and protected, with only one point of ground entry. A giant loch shone at its back, a few fishing boats dotting its glistening surface. The loch itself was surrounded by tall mountain peaks, making a water approach difficult at best.

Brandt wondered if they would be granted asylum and protection from Malvern. Any attack from an approaching army would be easy to defend, but if the Montgomerys were allied with Malvern, the castle and its bolstered environs could become a trap. He didn't have time to ponder that as three men emerged from the rocky crags and rode toward them on horseback. Clearly warriors, they were large, armed, and grim-faced.

"Let me do the talking," Sorcha said quickly before the first man's steed was upon them in a cloud of dust.

"Who comes to visit the Montgomery?" the biggest of them, and the obvious leader, asked. He was as wide as he was tall, with scars nicking his face and an untidy mane of black and silver hair.

"*Madainn mhath*," she said crisply. "Sorcha of Maclaren."

The big man's eyes narrowed on her and then nodded as he took in her scars. "*Madainn mhath.* 'Tis a fair journey from Maclaren, lass. Who've ye go' with ye?"

Suspicious eyes roved over Brandt. They paused at his face and widened slightly, a beat of surprise breaking across his features before he schooled them back into a scowl. Brandt frowned. The man's surprise had been one of recognition or at least some familiarity. Was there a resemblance, then? The two other men behind him pulled to a sharp stop. Their reaction upon seeing his face was the same as their leader's.

"Och, he's the spit—"

"Enough, Seamus," the big man barked, cutting him off. Seamus obeyed and shut his mouth but kept his eyes glued to Brandt's face as if he were some kind of hideous oddity. Brandt did not like the feeling in the least. He resisted the inclination to put his fist in the man's eye.

"He's my husband," Sorcha said.

The big man's attention refocused on her. "I had no' heard ye'd taken vows, Lady Maclaren."

"It's Lady Pierce now," she said with a prim toss of her head as she straightened her shoulders. "It was a recent event. Will your laird offer the daughter of the Duke of Dunrannoch his hospitality?"

The man bowed and wheeled the horse around. "Aye, follow me."

Brandt noticed that the two brawny men with him did not release their grips on the hilts of their broadswords as they fell into line behind them. His body tensed at the sensation of them riding just beyond his peripheral vision, but there was nothing he could do. He could feel their curious attention on him as well. Perhaps he had the look of his mother. Lord knew he'd never favored Monty with his shock of carrot red hair and blue eyes. No, Brandt's coloring was more muted…his hair a deeper auburn than true red, and his eyes were hazel. Fey eyes, Monty used to call them because they changed color so much.

Children gathered as they rode past, their faces alight with interest and curiosity. They ran alongside the horses, hooting and hollering. At one point, Brandt heard "Beast of Maclaren" called out, but he couldn't be sure. Sorcha must have heard it as well because she stiffened, though she held her back upright and her chin at an imperious angle. His hand tightened on her hip in a reassuring motion.

"It's fine," she said shortly. "Haven't I told you? I am legend now."

He opened his mouth but quickly shut it when he saw the corner of Sorcha's mouth bow into a smirk. Perhaps she didn't mind the name so much after all, though he imagined it must have taken a number of years for her to settle with it. He saw the way the children widened their eyes in awe and even the grudging hesitation of the warriors leading them when they'd first learned her name. Her scars were legend because she was.

As they neared the gates leading up to the keep, the man in front raised his arm, and they slowly swung open. Men in the nearby training fields stopped their work to gawk. Sorcha made a soft exclamation of surprise.

"What is it?" he asked.

"There aren't many of them," she said in a hushed breath.

"Fighters. We have dozens more soldiers at Maclaren. My father used to say that the former Montgomery laird was a great warrior, and no one dared take up arms against him."

"Perhaps there are more than what we see here now. Besides, they aren't expecting trouble, and their lands are quite protected."

As they passed by the ragtag band of men, Brandt couldn't help noticing that, though Sorcha drew their attention with her scarred face, he was the one who kept it. Mouths dropped open in shock, and heads bent together to whisper. His fingers clenched again.

"I told ye, I am fine, Brandt."

He blinked at the reappearance of her brogue. "For once, I don't think they're talking about you, Sorcha. I think they're talking about me."

"Why would they be—" She cut off abruptly as they passed a group of women who dropped their washing as they saw him and crossed themselves.

"'Tis a ghost, surely," one of them mewled, her eyes wide with fear.

Brandt frowned. A *ghost*? Things could not have been stranger, but the feeling of uneasiness grew as they approached the massive stone steps of the keep. A huge man stood in the archway at the top. His face matched his guards—fierce and unsmiling—as he bent his head to listen to what his first man had to say. Brandt reckoned it had to be the Duke of Glenross, the laird of Montgomery. But as they drew near, his pulse started to pick up speed.

The man on the steps could have been his brother. A much older brother, perchance, but the resemblance was there in the wide slope of his forehead and the angular planes of his cheekbones. They had the same nose, though Brandt's had been broken once in a London boxing ring.

Sorcha noticed it, too. "You look like him," she

whispered. "Perhaps that is why they were all gawping at you. Your mother could be a relation to the laird."

Brandt did not answer. They dismounted and walked up the steps. The duke's hair was brown, not auburn, and though he was tall, he appeared to be a few inches shorter than Brandt.

"Lady Maclaren," the duke boomed. "I bid ye welcome. Ye and yer husband. I am Rodric, Duke of Glenross and Laird Montgomery."

Glacial blue eyes passed over him with the same interest as everyone else in this bloody clan, but there was a malevolence beneath it that Brandt felt to his bones. The duke was not a good-humored man. Something dark and ominous glinted in the pale depths of his eyes. Brandt remembered what Sorcha had said he was called—Mad Montgomery—and he made a vow to keep an eye on him.

"Though," the laird went on, "I was surprised to hear of yer nuptials. Were ye no' betrothed?"

Sorcha nodded, her face giving away nothing. "The betrothal was broken."

Rodric's frigid eyes cut to Brandt and assessed him as one would a piece of exotic horseflesh. "Ye've the look of a Montgomery," he commented. "Where are ye from?"

"England, Your Grace," Brandt said. "Essex."

The duke's eyes widened at his clipped English, and an odd expression broke across his face. "'Tis a verra long way, England. What brings ye here, Sassenach?"

"My father was kin to the Montgomery. He passed several years ago and bid me come pay my respects as his last dying wish."

He felt Sorcha tense next to him at the white lie, and the lack of mention of the ring. Something told him to keep the ring hidden from the duke. He did not trust the man. Neither did Ares, who whinnied a few feet away and seemed agitated.

Rodric noticed. "What's wrong with yer horse?"

"He's injured, Your Grace," Brandt said. "He would be happy for a good meal and a warm place to rest if you have room in your stables."

The duke raised his arm, and two stableboys hurried forward. Brandt watched as Ares and Lockie were led away. Brandt wasn't worried. The horses the warriors had ridden earlier had seemed in good health. They were treated well, and Lockie and Ares would be, too. He and Sorcha, on the other hand, were a different matter. The gazes from the clansmen had not abated in the least, and Sorcha was also getting her fair share of attention.

"Come, then, be welcome, daughter of Dunrannoch." Rodric frowned. "How is yer father faring these days? Heard he lost some land to an English marquess when his uncle was proven guilty of associating with the Jacobites."

"He's well, thank you, Your Grace."

She said nothing about her uncle or about Malvern, and after a moment, Rodric continued. "And yer mother? She was a bonny lass for a Sassenach."

Something in the way he said it was insulting. His gaze scoured Sorcha, his mouth curling in a leer as they rested on her scars. A flush suffused Sorcha's face, but she did not drop her chin even when his eyes lowered to her breasts in the borrowed green gown. The man was coarse and seemed adept at playing games. Brandt shifted his footing and brought himself closer to her side, the act earning him a sideways glare.

"She's well, too," Sorcha said sweetly. "And my brothers and my sisters, and all my cousins. They are all well."

If the duke sensed the underlying irritation in Sorcha's sugary tones, he did not remark upon it. They followed the laird into the keep. Surprisingly, the great hall was pleasantly kept with fresh rushes before the fireplaces and beautiful tapestries adorning the stone walls. Nothing about it was familiar, though he felt a strange kinship with the stones of this place. Had he been born here? In the castle or in one of the cottages that had dotted the rambling hillside? If he was indeed the son of one of the duke's relations, was she still alive? Brandt's mind roiled with question after question.

The keep was bustling with people, though the expressions were the same—morose and stern. Other than the laughing children, Brandt had not noticed a single smile on any of the adults. The happiness of a lord's people said a lot. Though Archer was a stern man, his tenants in Essex and his other estates respected and loved him. They had always nodded and called out a pleasant greeting whenever he and Archer had ridden through while inspecting the farms and properties. And Archer would often stop and chat with all of them. The solemnness of these people made Brandt uneasy. All was not well here.

"Morag will show ye to yer chambers," Rodric said before leaving the keep again. "We sup at eight."

A slight figure hurried forward and bobbed before her laird, then turned to them. Morag was an older woman with a shock of cinnamon hair and a lined face. Kindly blue eyes shone and widened when they took in Sorcha's scars. Her mouth fell open when she looked at Brandt.

Morag didn't speak until she'd led them into a large chamber at the end of the hall. It held a grand bed, a pair of throne-like wooden chairs set before a hearth, and a table and mirror, though a thin layer of dust had gathered upon the furnishings. Their packs and belongings had been removed from the horses and set on the floor in the middle of the room.

"The laird and lady were no' expecting guests," she said apologetically. "The chambermaids will see that 'tis cleaned while ye're at sup."

"Lady?" Sorcha asked.

"Lady Glenross," Morag said. "The duchess is in the village to tend a birth."

Brandt was surprised. "She's a midwife?"

"Nae, but she has a gift for handling difficult births. Our people say that Lady Glenross has the touch o' the fairies."

She trailed off into silence as her gaze fell upon him once more. Disbelief and confusion warred in her eyes as she drank in his features. Unlike the other women, she did not make the sign of the cross, but she did look as if she'd seen a ghost.

Since her eyes were the first warm pair he had met upon arriving at Montgomery, Brandt shot her a wry smile. "I look like your laird."

Morag shook her head. "Nae, lad, ye've the look of the laird's *brother*, Robert." Her hand flew to her mouth in horror as if something had occurred to her. "Her ladyship will no' be expecting it...to see the verra image of her husband back from the grave."

Brandt frowned, wondering whether the old woman could be of use. Morag was certainly old enough to have been around for a long time. "Does the laird have any sisters or female cousins?" he asked.

"Two sisters, and many cousins," she replied, squinting at the odd question and opening the door to admit some servants with water to fill the washbasin. They, too, gawked at them before Morag shooed them from the room. "Tongues will be waggin' all o'er Montgomery today. A ghost and the Beast—" She broke off in horror, her aggrieved gaze darting to Sorcha. "Beggin' yer pardon, milady. I didnae mean any insult."

"None taken, Morag." Sorcha smiled kindly at the woman's aghast face. "It's truth I am a beast. Ask any of my brothers and they'll swear to it."

Morag shook her head. "Ye were such a bonny lass."

Sorcha's eyes widened. "Did you know me?"

"Ye father brought ye here as a wee lass one summer. I wept when I heard the news of the wolf attack." Morag had tears shining in her eyes. "But 'twas no' as bad as I expected. Ye're still bonny, ye ken." Her gaze slid to where Brandt stood. "And ye're married to this strapping man."

Sorcha opened her mouth, as if to contradict the statement, and then closed it. Regardless of his opinion on the matter or what had happened between them, in the eyes of the clan and everyone else, they *were* wedded.

Morag looked like she wanted to reminisce more, but she straightened and made for the doorway as though suddenly frightened. She stopped at the door. "Be on ye way as soon as ye can," she whispered. "'Tis no' safe here. The devil roams these lands."

The door slammed shut behind her before either of them could respond, but her ominous words remained in the air like a warning. Brandt exchanged a glance with Sorcha, but she looked as bemused as he felt.

"That was odd," he said.

"Highland folk believe in their legends." She moved toward the washbasin. "It's said that when the old duke died, a curse fell upon the land. Perhaps that is the devil she speaks of." Sorcha glanced at him over her shoulder, and when their eyes met, hurt and resolve passed over hers. "I wish to wash in private."

Brandt frowned. His wife's voice had taken on the same chilling reserve from earlier that morning when they'd broken camp by the river. He missed their easy camaraderie, but he'd hurt her with his dispassionate remarks about what had happened at the river. Eventually, she would appreciate the sense of his actions, but for now, the more space between them the better. He nodded and left the chamber.

Brandt had half expected to see a guard posted outside

his door, but there was no one there. The occasional maid scurried by as he passed several closed doors that he assumed led into other bedchambers. He walked down a long hallway until he came to a large gallery. Immense portraits hung on the walls, spanning from floor to ceiling. His breath caught as he saw the similarities in some of the older paintings, but it was certainly nothing to lose one's accounts over.

He strode deeper into the room, hoping that perhaps there would be a painting of the laird's sisters. Deep down, Brandt felt that he would *know* his mother. But other than a few paintings of some older women and one painting of a family with two girls and two boys, one of which Brandt wagered was the laird at a young age, there was nothing that gave him any hope at all.

Frustrated, he'd turned on his heel and headed back down the gallery, when his gaze fell on a curtained portrait in an alcove at the end of the hall. Black silk hung over its surface, as if someone had wanted to banish the person in the portrait from the others. Brandt held his breath as he lifted one edge of the silk. His heart sank as his gaze took in a pair of strong male legs encased in boots and a kilt. It was not a woman.

He tugged harder on the silk, and to his dismay, the delicate fabric tore into ragged pieces and floated to the ground at his feet. But the portrait was fully exposed. It showed a man on a horse. A warrior in a Montgomery tartan with a broadsword held high and a proud look on his face. Brandt staggered back, suddenly understanding what all the clansmen had been whispering about.

Laird Robert Montgomery was Brandt in the flesh. From the deeply bronzed red of his hair to his stern features and long brawny stature. The only difference was the eyes—they were the same wintry blue of his brother's. Brandt drew his fingers along the edges of the man's plaid.

Had this been his uncle? Had he been the one to send Monty away with the newborn babe he'd fathered with one of the duke's sisters? Had it been some form of revenge? Punishment? Brandt's heart ached for his father, who'd been banished so callously from his clan for falling in love with a woman he could not have. Sisters of dukes did not marry stable masters.

And neither did daughters of dukes.

Suddenly, Brandt couldn't care less about his parentage. His heart ached for the woman he'd left in his chambers. The one he'd cut down so callously, before she'd had the chance to offer him her misguided affection. He had nothing to offer her in return, though, and if he accepted or encouraged her esteem, she would pay the price for her foolish choices.

Just as Monty had.

Chapter Fifteen

To Sorcha's surprise, there was a knock on the door and men waiting at Morag's side with a wooden tub. She had just splashed her face with the cool, refreshing water in the basin, and, though she'd been grateful for the chance to wash away the half-day's worth of travel dust, she longed for a bath. No sooner had she thought it than the knock had come. The servants emptied pails of steaming water into the tub until it was full. Some of them stared openly at her, and Sorcha resisted the urge to duck her head.

"Will ye need help, lass?" Morag asked. Sorcha shook her head, and the old woman curtsied, shutting the door behind her.

Stripping bare with a delicious sigh, she sank into the warm water, scented with rose petals and lavender. God, she missed baths. She loved riding and hunting, but being on the road took its toll. It made her long for the simple luxuries of home. After scrubbing her entire body from top to toe, she wrapped herself in a long length of toweling and sat before the fire to dry and comb her hair. She heard the chamber door open and close, but it was only Morag with a gown in hand. Still, she crossed her arms over her chest.

"Yers was filthy, so I brought ye another one." Morag studied the pale blue muslin she held with a critical eye. "Ye're a tall lass, but it should fit."

"Thank you," Sorcha said with a grateful smile as the maid curtsied and left.

She'd brought no other suitable gowns with her, and all of the clothing in her pack needed washing or mending. She hadn't wanted to go to dinner in the laird's hall looking like a pauper with borrowed threads from charity, but she didn't have any other choice. At least now she would not bring shame to Maclaren. Or her husband.

Not that he would care if she appeared clothed in rags.

Sorcha blinked. She hadn't allowed herself to think of Brandt since they departed for Montgomery. After what had happened between them at the river, she'd wanted to kick herself in the teeth. Repeatedly.

The bluntness of his response had burned through to her bared heart like hot embers upon an open wound. Even now, the memory scalded. What had she expected? That he would fall to his knees and confess his devotion? In truth, a small part of her had hoped he would. But his cruel words had shattered her girlish fantasies.

He did not want marriage. Nor did he want *her*.

Oh, he wanted her body. She'd felt his arousal on the way to the keep. But Brandt appeared to view any intimacy between them as weakness. Or *idiocy*. It seemed he was far more adept than she was at keeping his desires separate from everything else. Perhaps all men were built that way, able to take pleasure and only pleasure when it was given, without the inconvenient entanglement of feelings.

Well, no matter. Soon, they would be at Brodie, and she could put Brandt Pierce behind her for good, as he clearly wanted.

The chamber door opened and closed again, and she did not look up, thinking it was only Morag. But after a moment of strange silence, she did glance up. It wasn't Morag. Brandt stood watching her, his face pale as if he'd seen a ghost himself. Sorcha did not want to care, but she couldn't curb her tongue…or her sudden burst of concern.

"What is it?" she asked.

A muscle jumped in his stubbled jaw as he scraped his fingers through the bristle. "I saw a portrait of the old laird," he said. "The clansmen were right to stare. I look like him." He drew a slow breath. "Exactly like him."

Brandt walked toward the bed and sat on the edge, one hand raking through his hair. Sorcha clutched the toweling tighter as she stood, setting the comb down on the chair.

"What is it you're thinking?" she asked, her mind searching for possible explanations. The resemblance to Rodric was strong, and the stares of the Montgomery people had been too pointed to ignore. "That your mother is one of the duke's sisters?"

She walked toward him, her bare feet cold upon the stone floor. Brandt had asked Rodric earlier about other siblings, and she had suspected that was the reason why.

"Perhaps, and she must have had a tryst with Monty," he answered, his hand falling from the crop of hair he'd been clutching in frustration and landing upon his thigh. Without thinking, Sorcha reached for it, curling her fingers over his with a soft squeeze. He needed comfort, and she couldn't be so cruel as to withhold it. No matter if she still wanted to throw an overflowing chamber pot at his head.

"If she's married, she may not be here, then," she said, thinking of her own sisters, sent far away to other lands when they'd wed.

Brandt nodded, his fingers shifting to wind around hers.

"I know. My father told me my mother had already been married when I was born, but perhaps she had been staying here at the keep only for a time. I don't know."

It could have been the long shadows of the fading light outside and the flickering flames from the fire, but for the first time Sorcha noticed circles under his eyes. He'd been sleeping lightly in order to keep watch over their encampments every night for days on end. He had to be exhausted.

"I'll dress, and you can bathe," she said, attempting to pry her fingers from his. "We are eating soon."

He held on, though, his thumb rubbing the heel of her palm in slow strokes.

"It wasn't an act," he whispered, looking up into her eyes. "It wasn't just a role."

He was speaking of that morning.

"We needn't discuss it again," she said, dropping her eyes and twisting her hand to free her fingers from his. He stared down at his hand, looking torn, like he wanted to say more. After a protracted moment, Sorcha expelled a slow breath. Regardless of the hurt she suffered, she knew he would need her for what was surely to come at supper, and like her touch, she would not withhold it. "I'm here for you, Brandt. With the Montgomerys."

His eyes met hers. "How can you be so kind after I've been such a beast?"

Kindness was the least of her worries. She wanted to shake him until his teeth rattled. She wanted to run from this dank, ugly place with its maudlin ghosts. She wanted him to let go of the past that haunted him. Sorcha shook her head and formed the brightest smile she could manage. "The only beast here is me, and don't you forget it. Now bathe, or we shall be late."

She kept the toweling around her as she took up the blue muslin dress Morag had left for her and moved toward a wood paneled privacy screen. She dressed and braided her hair while Brant washed. After a decent amount of time had gone by without splashing noises, a furtive peek through a thin gap in the screen showed he had finished and had dressed himself in a pair of clean buckskins and a linen shirt. Which was well and good, for if she had to look upon his sleek, muscled limbs again, the keen ache she already felt for him would have sharpened into something unbearable.

Once she'd wound her braid into a loose knot and secured it with a few of her own pins and combs, she and Brandt walked together toward the great hall. They had both agreed that it would be wise to leave her wedding ring tucked away in Brandt's pocket. At least for the moment.

Sorcha expected to hear a boisterous cacophony of voices and laughter, along with the clink and crash of cutlery and glass as they entered the hall, but instead, she found a muted din. There were two long tables with benches set up in the hall, each one filled with Montgomery clansmen. Sorcha's feet faltered as she and Brandt walked toward the dais at the end of the cavernous room upon which the laird's table stood. Though there was a fire within a giant hearth, candles on every table, and a number of guttering wall torches, the room was still cloaked in shadows.

Eyes turned toward them as they approached the laird. Stares were nothing new to Sorcha, but what Brandt had whispered earlier was unmistakably true: these stares were not solely aimed at her and her scars. These were fastened on Brandt.

There were five open seats at the laird's table—the one to Rodric's right, and four more placed farther down the table, two on the side closest to them and two next to two younger men. Each man stood, their resemblance to the duke clear, though one was fairer than the other. The dark-haired one, to the right of the duke, speared Brandt with a narrow-browed stare and an unmasked grimace.

"Welcome, my honored guests," Rodric boomed, banging his tankard down on the table so that the entire hall went silent. Sorcha was certain she didn't miss the sarcastic emphasis on honored, as if it was some kind of well-intentioned slight. Or maybe it was the way the laird enunciated each syllable with such cold, courteous precision. It felt like she was caught in a Shakespearean production she'd seen once in London with her mother.

"Thank you, Your Grace," she heard Brandt say.

"These are my sons," Rodric said, a loose hand gesturing toward the two men. "Patrick," he said, and the dark-haired man nodded once, "and Callan."

Patrick looked to be Brandt's age, perhaps a few years younger, and Callan, the lighter-haired one, closer to Sorcha's own age. He pulled out the chair beside him, and Brandt took it. Sorcha started to sit beside Brandt, but the duke cleared his throat. "Ye are to sit over there, Lady Pierce," he said, indicating an empty seat on the other side of the table.

Surprised, Sorcha paused, but she kept her back straight and her shoulders pressed down, and moved toward the three open seats on the other side. She had always been welcome to sit wherever she liked at her father's own table, and when visiting other keeps, she would sit beside one of her brothers. It was also customary at Maclaren, and with most other clans, for wives and husbands of the laird's family to sit beside each other. She would have liked to have been able to sit beside Brandt as his wife, if only for the familiar comfort of the only face she knew within the room. But as she took the seat farthest to the left, directly opposite from Brandt, she refused to show her unease.

Tankards were filled with ale and goblets with wine, but the food had yet to be served. Sorcha was starving, and yet she knew she wouldn't feel like eating a bite of anything the maids would be whisking in on large platters soon. Across the table, she met Brandt's eyes. They were hard and watchful. He didn't like this place any more than she did, and she had no doubt the endless looks being thrown his way every few moments were frustrating him. She understood how wearying it could be.

Patrick and Callan got to their feet as a young woman entered the great hall, her strides swift and sure as she approached the tables. She appeared to be no more than sixteen, with sparkling brown eyes set in a heart-shaped face. Her long, fair hair matched that of Callan's and had been woven into one thick plait down the center of her back. Brandt stood as well, though Sorcha noted Rodric did not.

"Father," the young woman said, stopping at the head of the table to bob a curtsy to Rodric.

"Mr. Pierce, Lady Pierce, this is my daughter, Aisla," Rodric announced, and when Aisla turned to bob a curtsy to Brandt, she did not falter or stare as the others had. Perhaps she had already heard about his resemblance, and she was too well-bred to make any open notice of it. Aisla then turned to take her seat on the left-hand side, and Sorcha prepared herself. It was instinct, really, the steeling of her spine before meeting a person for the first time. But again, the girl only smiled and murmured a soft, pleasant greeting. Her eyes stayed firmly hitched to Sorcha's own, without roving over her scars.

"Welcome to Montgomery," she said, leaving the chair directly next to Rodric open.

"Thank you," Sorcha replied. Just then, a few words rose above the subdued conversation in the room. "Face" and "worse than I heard" reached her ears before Aisla picked up her goblet of wine and asked her a question, loudly, as if trying to distract her.

"Where do ye and yer husband travel to, Lady Pierce?"

She took a sip of her wine and, looking into Sorcha's eyes, smiled. She was a pretty young woman, a few years younger than Sorcha. She had sharp, memorable features, with a wide mouth, pale hair, a sprinkling of freckles over the bridge of her nose, and a pair of eyes—not brown as Sorcha had first thought—almost the color of copper.

"West," she answered, thankful for Aisla's attempt to spare her from the gossiping tongues of the Montgomery men. It hadn't been necessary, and it made her feel only guiltier for lying about their destination. But she didn't like the bleak, tense air of this keep, or the pointed, appraising way Rodric looked at her and Brandt. If Malvern's men tracked them here, she didn't trust him or his people to guard the truth of their true destination.

Aisla, perhaps sensing her reticence, did not ask for anything more specific. Another kindness.

"Yer husband," Aisla said next, her attention flicking down the length of the laird's table. "He's Sassenach?"

Her eyes lingered on Brandt for a few moments.

"No," Sorcha answered. "Scottish born, with Montgomery kin."

Aisla turned back to her, her coppery eyes wide. "Montgomery?"

Sorcha didn't know if it was her place to give away her husband's father's name or not, but she sensed something within Aisla that she had in Morag—a willingness to help. Perhaps, also, the possession of answers. But Sorcha wasn't able to speak before the men in the hall rose, yet again. Looking toward the entrance to the hall, she saw another woman threading between the row of tables. Lady Glenross, she determined.

Though older, with fine lines near her temples and around her mouth, she was beautiful, like Aisla. Lady Glenross had given both Callan and Aisla their fair coloring, and as she approached the table, Sorcha noted the regal poise of her back and chin. She'd nearly reached the laird's table before her steps slowed, then stopped completely. Her attention seemed to be hinged on Brandt, who'd also stood in greeting. But the moment he lifted his gaze, hers floundered and fell away.

With every passing second, Lady Glenross's pale complexion grew more pallid. Her initial expression had been shocked, as if she had not been forewarned in advance of their visitor...or his uncanny resemblance to her dead husband.

Recalling Morag's words, Sorcha's gaze swung to the duke, who was watching his wife with narrowed, calculating eyes. Of course—he'd planned it this way. Rodric was relishing every moment of what had to be an awful shock for her. It was clear the lady still grieved the loss, and it was also abundantly clear that the current duke resented it. Something was at play here, something sinister. Sorcha didn't like it.

Aisla stood. "Mother?"

The woman faltered on her next step, and Callan's chair scraped against the stone floor as he pushed it aside. He reached Lady Glenross within seconds, but by then she was already shaking her head and apologizing.

"I am fine, perfectly fine. I was a little dizzy for only a moment," she said, Callan leading her to her chair anyway. Two bright spots of color had suffused her cheeks by the time she sat beside Rodric, and as she reached for her goblet of wine, Sorcha noticed her hand was trembling violently.

Rodric, who had also remained seated for his wife's entrance, let an uncomfortable—somewhat punishing—minute pass by before finally opening his mouth and introducing her. "Mr. Pierce and Lady Pierce, this is my wife, Catriona, the Duchess of Glenross."

"'Tis my pleasure."

Lady Glenross kept her eyes on the table, though no food had yet been delivered. She had not greeted Sorcha as warmly as Aisla had, but it wasn't due to blatant rudeness. No. Sorcha knew from the woman's dazed and distant expression that she was a thousand miles away in her own mind. The goblet rose to pale lips in an unsteady hand until the entire glass of wine was drained. It was just as quickly refilled by a waiting servant.

Sorcha glanced toward Brandt and found him sitting rigidly in his chair. His jaw was tight, his nostrils flaring. She cursed Rodric and his stringent rules separating the men and women at the laird's table. It wasn't normal asking an honored guest to sit apart from her husband, but nothing about this wretched hall was normal. Though the men conversed, it was in low, controlled tones, not the boisterous noise she was used to in her own keep, interspersed with the animated sounds of laughter and praise.

"Pierce," Rodric said as the first tide of serving maids entered the hall with large trenchers in their hands. The appearance of food distracted the Montgomery men, but not Sorcha. She cut her eyes to the duke. At last, perhaps his game would be made clear. "Ye've come all the way from England to pay respects to yer dead father's kin."

Brandt was still as stone in his chair when he answered, his voice tightly leashed, "Yes."

"'Tis a long way for such sentiment. His name?" Rodric asked.

Brandt seemed to pause, considering his reply and how much of the truth he should impart. "Montgomery Pierce," he answered, adding, "he worked in the stables."

Lady Glenross's glass lifted to her lips, but Sorcha was intent on the duke.

"I cannae recall him," Rodric said quickly, not having taken enough time to truly try to remember. He just as swiftly directed his attention to his left and met Sorcha's stare. "Though I do recall the name of the man ye were betrothed to, Lady Pierce. The Marquess of Malvern. The verra Englishman yer traitor uncle lost his lands to."

Though she had not set eyes upon him since Selkirk, the mere sound of Malvern's name was enough to sour and turn her stomach. "Yes. It was the marquess."

"And he released ye from the betrothal so ye could marry this Sassenach?"

A platter of roasted venison was set on the table before her, and she felt even more ill. "No," she answered. "We eloped."

The lie was like a mouthful of salt. So focused was she on not meeting Brandt's eyes that she did not realize that the duke was staring at her with his mouth set in a white line until she became aware of the eerie silence descending upon the table.

"Ye *eloped*? Ye've broken yer betrothal contract, ye foolish chit," he said in a low, yet strangely pleasant, voice. It made Sorcha's skin crawl, and every hair rose on the back of her neck. She'd always trusted her instincts, and right now they were signaling danger.

The Duke of Glenross was not an ally.

"If 'tis asylum from Malvern ye seek here, then I cannae help ye. It is ye who have wronged." His pale eyes flicked to Brandt as he went on in the same conversational tone. "Have ye no honor, ye coxcomb? She was given to another. A contract was signed. She was her father's property to do with as he wished, and 'twas his wish for her to marry the Marquess of Malvern, ye ken."

Sorcha felt her temper rise and fought to control it, but something inside of her snapped. Perhaps it was the combination of the subdued hall, the insult to Brandt, or the stricken look on Lady Glenross's face, but she couldn't curb the words that leaped to her tongue. "I am not property," she hissed, drawing the consternated eye of every man in the room. "Promised or not, would you marry your own daughter to a man such as Malvern? A man whose cruelty and greed touches every corner of Scotland?"

Waving his arm for chatter to resume, Rodric arched an eyebrow, impaling her with his reptilian stare. "Aye. Aisla will do her duty, even if 'twere my wish for her to wed a dog."

Sorcha saw the young woman stiffen beside her, but Aisla did not utter a word. Clearly, the man was a despot. "And if that dog bit and mauled her?"

The duke smiled. "'Tis a husband's right."

A man such as Rodric would not hesitate to put his hands on his wife if she disobeyed him. And even now, Lady Glenross remained silent, her gaze upon her plate. If Sorcha's father dared speak to her mother like that, said dishes would be flying. She felt sick to her stomach.

"Then any daughter of yours has my deepest condolences," Sorcha muttered, uncaring of what her words might provoke. *And also your wife*, she added with a look to the lady who had taken on the hue of a ghostly wraith.

"Why? Malvern is a marquess," Rodric said, his lip curling. "A powerful, wealthy English lord. Ye have betrayed yer family and forgone yer duty for what? A quick tumble in the woods? Perhaps that encounter with the wolf did more to ye than disfigure yer face."

"Rodric!" Lady Glenross gasped.

Once more, his words made the hall go quiet, his vile insinuation echoing in the silence...that she was little more than an animal herself. Flushing with shame, Sorcha opened her mouth, but Brandt shoved his chair back slowly and pushed to his feet.

"Do *not* insult my wife," he snapped through clenched teeth as the duke's sons both stood, ready and bristling. "I married her because *I* wanted her. If you wish to take offense with someone, do so with me. We have sought sanctuary here, but perhaps it's best if we leave."

The duke smiled and speared a piece of meat with the tip of his knife. "Rest easy, Mr. Pierce. Apologies to you and your lady if any insult was felt." The insincerity in his voice was clear, as was the fact that he hadn't truly apologized. "There are untold dangers roaming the fells at night. Be assured Montgomery is welcome to ye for as long as ye require."

Though Sorcha had the forbidding feeling they would be better off out there than in here, they had no choice. The journey to Brodie, in the remotest part of the Highlands, could not be made upon a lame horse. Brandt would not leave Ares behind, nor would she ask him to do so.

Two days, she thought. Three at the most. Perhaps by then, Brandt would be able to find the answers he sought and Ares would have had enough time to heal. She would just have to stay out of Rodric's way before she did something stupid and truly unforgivable, like sink her dirk into his blasted eye.

"'Tis all right, Brandt," she whispered, and then lifted her voice and her chin. "No insult taken, Your Grace, but you can be sure my father, the duke, will be pleased to learn of your kindness."

Rodric's pale eyes narrowed at the veiled threat, but Sorcha did not cower. She stared right back at him. Maclaren was a powerful clan, and he knew it. Insulting her father with his wide-reaching influence would not be wise, no matter how protected Montgomery lands were. She only hoped she hadn't lost her father's support. No use making threats that wouldn't come to fruition if Dunrannoch had disowned her.

Lady Glenross cleared her throat, breaking the silence and the tension, and lifted her goblet. "To new friends," she said.

Everyone, with the exception of the laird, lifted their glasses and echoed her toast. And as Sorcha sipped her wine, she couldn't help noticing Rodric and Brandt engaged in a silent battle of wills, the resemblance between them more marked than it had been earlier. Her skin grew chilled, as if touched by the spirit of whatever it was haunted these halls.

She suppressed a shiver. She recognized the expression on Rodric's face, having seen a similar one on Malvern. It was full of calculated malice. She realized then that Rodric had never inquired about the identity of Brandt's *mother*.

Sorcha was willing to bet anything it was because Rodric already knew exactly who she was.

Chapter Sixteen

Once the Duke of Glenross had finished his ducal posturing, the dinner conversation took on a lighter, more jovial, tone. As much as one could be jovial in such a suffocating atmosphere. Brandt was glad for it because he was two breaths short of tossing the duke on his privileged arse in front of all his men in his own keep, and teaching him a much-needed lesson.

He'd known men like Rodric before...men who believed women were meant to be seen, not heard. That they were little more than possessions. Men like him wielded their power—and cruelty—with equal ferocity. It was clear in the way he'd tried and failed to intimidate Brandt. In that respect, Rodric was very much like Malvern. It made him regret that he'd brought Sorcha here.

He spared her a glance. She was deep in conversation with Aisla, and the worry that had been written all over her before had disappeared. He had not told her how beautiful she looked in blue—the light color made her creamy skin luminous and her eyes glow like sapphires.

Brandt had been proud of how well she'd stood up to

Rodric's interrogation, but he hadn't been about to let the man insult her. It was only by a slim thread that he'd been able to stop himself from calling the duke out. Not that he doubted his own skill at twenty paces, but he'd made a promise to Sorcha to see her through to Brodie, and he couldn't do that if he were wounded or dead.

Still, Brandt wondered if anyone would miss the duke if he met an untimely end. His sons, perhaps. His wife and daughter, not as much, he'd wager. Other than having the blond coloring of her middle son and daughter, he hadn't taken much measure of Lady Glenross. Though she was tall, she seemed frail and delicate. Her features were fine-boned, much like her daughter's, and she had long elegant hands. Shadows slunk beneath her eyes, and like the rest of the women in the keep, she seemed beaten down. Brandt wondered if she would be amenable to questions about her sisters-in-law, their whereabouts, or any secret bastard children born out of wedlock.

Brandt's gaze tumbled to where Lady Glenross was moving the food around her plate. Other than her earlier toast, she hadn't spoken once. Neither had she looked up. The duchess's reaction upon seeing him had been expected, especially after he'd seen the portrait of the late duke in the gallery, though the depth of her surprise had been puzzling. The previous Duke of Glenross had been dead over a score of years. Brandt wondered at loving someone so deeply that no matter how long they had been gone, they never truly left you. His gaze flicked back to Sorcha, and he felt an unfamiliar sensation compress his lungs. He couldn't imagine ever forgetting her, not in a week, not in twenty years. Not in a lifetime.

Brandt gave his head a hard shake. He would have to.

He sighed and speared another mouthful of poached fish. The food, to his surprise, was delicious and flavorful.

The roasted fish was seasoned with herbs and cooked in a buttery wine sauce that hinted of French origins. The duke clearly did not spare the expense to employ a superb cook, which Brandt knew was uncommon for the Highlands. It was another thing about the man that rankled. He was a duke, and chieftain of Montgomery, but he acted like a king. A pampered, spoiled king.

Callan, the younger of the two brothers, cleared his throat, drawing Brandt out of his thoughts. "Whereabouts do ye hail from in England?"

"Essex," he replied, with a longer look at the lad sitting beside him. He seemed to be about twenty and wore a less constipated look than his elder brother.

"Have ye been to London?"

Brandt nodded. "Many times."

"White's?" Callan's brown eyes had grown more animated.

Brandt understood the allure. White's was the most famous gentleman's club in London. He'd, of course, been to it only with the Duke of Bradburne. But to any young man, White's was the exclusive, crowning glory of a gentleman's social life in London.

Before he could reply, the duke's voice interrupted. "White's is a members-only establishment, ye ken," he scoffed. "How would the pauper son of a stable master ever set foot in such a place?"

Brandt tented a slow eyebrow. "Perhaps by not being as poor as you've assumed." He turned his attention to Callan. "And yes, I can assure you I've been to White's."

"How is that possible?" Callan asked with a nervous glance to his father. "If ye're no' a lord, ye ken?"

"The Duke of Bradburne is like a brother to me."

Brandt was not a title-thrower, but he hoped his double entendre was clear. If anything should happen to him—

or his wife—no stone would be left unturned, not even in Scotland. Though Malvern was indeed a powerful marquess, Bradburne's sphere of influence was unrivaled. There weren't many men in England or the Continent who had not heard of Lord Archer Croft.

"Bradburne, aye?" the duke remarked.

Brandt smiled. "Indeed."

After a while, Rodric stood and moved to confer with one of his men who begged a word, the big older warrior who had met them on the road on the way in to Montgomery. They shifted out of sight of the great hall. At the duke's departure, Lady Glenross seemed interested in the conversation. In fact, for the first time since she had arrived, it seemed as if she could breathe. Yet again, Brandt frowned at the thrall Rodric Montgomery held over them all.

"Ye said yer father was a Montgomery," Patrick said.

It was the first time the Glenross heir had spoken directly to him. Brandt nodded. "As far as I understood it, yes."

"My father doesnae recall such a man."

Brandt inclined his head. "Perhaps it was before his time as laird."

Lady Glenross's head snapped up, though her eyes did not meet his. Patrick, too, seemed to notice his mother's unusual response. She did not look at Brandt, but her low-pitched musical voice was clear. "What did ye say his name was?"

Brandt noticed that Sorcha's attention had become focused on him. "Montgomery Pierce."

"We had a Pherson Montgomery once," she said softly. "A loyal lad who worked in the stables."

Brandt's frown deepened. Monty had been all of eighteen when Brandt had been born and he'd fled Scotland. It was conceivable that his name could have been Pherson. It wasn't that far from Pierce. Perhaps he had simply reversed the two for anonymity after he left the only home he'd known. Once more, Brandt felt a compelling need to determine the identity of his mother. For Monty's sake.

"I dunnae recall anyone of that name, either," Patrick said.

"Ye were no' even a glimmer in my eye yet, dear heart," Lady Glenross replied, smiling at her son. It was a smile that contained so much love that Brandt could feel its warm force like a wave cresting over him. She loved her children, that much was clear, even the stoic Patrick who seemed to be his father's man in the flesh. "'Twas a long time ago. Long before any of ye were even born, when I was but a young lass."

To Brandt's surprise, Patrick's eyes softened and, reaching for his mother's hand, he leaned over to place a kiss on her knuckles. "Ye never talk of yer childhood."

Lady Glenross stared affectionately at her son, her gaze falling to Callan and then to Aisla. "My life found renewed purpose and hope when ye were born. A wounded heart was restored."

Wounded from the death of her husband? The previous duke?

The duchess looked up then, her dark gaze catching Brandt's for the briefest of moments in the flickering light, and he was filled with the strangest feeling. He could see knowledge swirling in their glittering depths before she cast her gaze away. Lady Glenross knew more than she was letting on; he would stake his life upon it. He had to keep her talking before her husband came back.

Sorcha seemed to have the same idea because she was the one to ask the next question. "Who was he? Pherson Montgomery?"

A fond smile graced the duchess's lips. "A stableboy with the bravest heart a boy could have. He was my dearest friend."

It was an odd answer. Cryptic at best. He didn't understand why the laird's wife would have remembered Monty as brave, if indeed his father had been this Pherson she spoke of. Or even how he would have won the friendship of the lady of the keep to begin with. Had he impregnated the laird's sister? Had he been forced to leave Montgomery?

"What happened to him?" Brandt asked. "He never told me why he left."

But before she could answer, the laird came stalking back to his seat at the table, and the duchess stared once more into her plate. Brandt swallowed a curse at the lost opportunity. The duke did not sit.

Instead, Rodric hooked a hand toward Patrick. "Declan reports that there has been an incident at the mill. Come," he commanded brusquely before turning to Brandt and Sorcha. "My apologies for my absence. I'm sure ye understand."

"What kind of incident?" Patrick asked, but was quelled by the glacial look in his father's eyes. He rose and bowed. "I bid ye good night, mother. Mr. Pierce, Lady Pierce." Patrick nodded to his sister and brother, and followed his father out of the hall.

A dozen Montgomery men stood to fall in line with their laird, leaving the hall half empty. Callan called for more ale. Brandt was surprised he hadn't been allowed to accompany the laird, but perhaps it was the way things were done. The young man's sour face indicated that it wasn't the first time he'd been left behind.

"You wish to go with them?" Brandt asked.

"My father likes to keep us apart," Callan said, after a long draught on his mug. "Patrick is being groomed for the role of laird, and I am but a nuisance."

"Ye're not a nuisance," Aisla said loyally.

Callan grumbled but sent his sister a grateful glance. They were allies, then, Callan, Lady Glenross, and Aisla. Brandt could sense it in the easy way all three of them were acting together now that the laird, his heir, and half the men in the hall had gone, though he suspected Patrick cared deeply for his mother as well.

Catriona sipped her wine, relaxed again. In her husband's absence, it was as if another woman had taken her place...a vibrant hint of the woman she used to be. "I've no' met the Marquess of Malvern, but I've heard of him. I cannae blame ye for marrying another man, Lady Pierce. But pray tell, how did ye and Mr. Pierce meet? In England?"

She cast a curious look in Brandt's direction, but the moment he met her eyes, she glanced away again, concentrating instead on Sorcha. His wife had gone pink cheeked, her lips pressed tightly. Rodric had shamed her enough for eloping. Should the duke learn the truth that she'd coerced a man into marriage in exchange for a horse, too, his disgust would only be renewed.

"At the common lands festival in Selkirk," Brandt answered for her. The hell if he'd let one more thing humiliate her. "I caught sight of her as she was competing in a sword fight against a much bigger, much stronger man."

Sorcha's eyes widened, as if pleading with him to be quiet. He only smirked, his gaze trained on her. So much had passed between them since then...since that moment he'd first laid eyes on her, but Brandt would never forget the memory of her, ferocious and beautiful in equal measure. A virago in battle armor, flush with victory.

"And yet, she bested her opponent with her skill. I was watching from afar when she pulled off her helm and I realized she was a lady, not a boy as I'd assumed."

Aisla gasped and grinned, turning to stare at Sorcha with awe. Callan huffed an impressed laugh and drew from his tankard.

"I knew I had to meet her," Brandt went on, Sorcha's

alarm setting the tips of her ears afire. "And when I did, I knew…she wasn't just a swordswoman. She was a sorceress." Brandt raised his tankard to her. "Because I immediately fell under her spell."

Sorcha's tensed shoulders fell and, though her cheeks and ears stayed bright with color, she was breathing easier. Suddenly shy, she couldn't seem to hold his stare. It wasn't as though he'd strayed *that* far from the truth. He'd withheld only the specific terms of their agreement, but he had been mesmerized by her from the very start in that paddock.

Athena, he'd thought her.

Though now, as he had discovered, that comparison failed to come close to the reality.

"Love at first sight, ye ken." Aisla sat back in her chair with a sigh, a hand covering her heart and girlish stars in her eyes. "'Tis so lovely. So verra romantic."

Brandt saw Sorcha shake her head slightly, and he smiled. Their meeting had not been romantic in the least, despite his gawking, and he knew it was exactly what his wife was thinking.

What was romance anyway? A collection of words, maybe, said to another person. Promises made. Though words were forgotten, promises easily broken. It was action Brandt admired. Loyalty and resolve. Sorcha was a stubborn, unflinching, maddening woman, and yet she would not give up. She'd proven her mettle in the last handful of days as they'd traveled, fighting Coxley and Malvern's hired men at every turn.

Laying herself bare to him at the river—that had taken courage, too.

And he'd belittled her for it.

Aisla sighed again, though the sound had taken on an edge of despair. "Truly, I only wish I could meet a man as ye did. With my luck, I'll be married off to the Buchanans fer the sake of an alliance." She scowled and then laughed. "Or a dog. Though I ken I'd marry the dog over Dougal Buchanan. 'Twould smell heaps better."

Callan snorted with laughter. "Aye, dunnae fash yerself, Aisla. Patrick and I would toss the Buchanan into the loch before he put one finger upon ye."

She stuck her tongue out at her brother. "I'd elope with a handsome Sassenach over that lout."

"Hush, Aisla," Lady Glenross said with a nervous glance over her shoulder as if expecting her husband's return any moment.

"How did you and the duke meet?" Sorcha asked, and then clamped her hand over her mouth with an appalled look. It was well known how they had met, Brandt knew, and well rumored that the late duke's death had been fratricide.

However, the duchess did not seem troubled by the question. Brandt felt her gaze linger on him for a protracted moment before she answered.

"I was married to his brother, Robert," she said. "He died in a fall, and Rodric was there to share the burden of my grief. We married shortly after the mourning period had passed." She shrugged delicate shoulders. "'Twas the best thing for the clan."

Brandt grasped at the opening. "That must have been hard for you and the laird's sisters. Where are they?" he asked. "Did they grow up here at Montgomery? Were they of comfort to you as well?"

He didn't care if he sounded oddly inquisitive. He didn't plan to remain under Rodric's roof much longer, and he still wanted answers.

"Aye. 'Twas a difficult time, but Jean and Una had already married. They visited, of course, and mourned their brother's death, but they had their own lives. I was inconsolable, and Rodric was the only one there to pick up the pieces."

Brandt exhaled, his fingers clenching into fists on his lap. "Did Jean and Una have any children?"

Lady Glenross blinked at the question, her pale brows coming together in concern. "Several. Why do ye ask?"

"No reason."

And Brandt had none. None that would be acceptable. He had no way to ask outright if either of the Montgomery girls had been ruined by her friend, the stableboy, and given birth to a son some twenty-five years before. He wished that Monty had given him more to go on, a name even. But the names Jean and Una were not familiar. Brandt was certain Monty had never mentioned either of them.

"What was yer father like?" The soft question came from the duchess.

"Monty?" He smiled, noticing that Sorcha had also leaned forward in interest. Brandt didn't see any harm in talking about his father now that Rodric had left.

"He was a good man. Brave. Principled. Believed in the inherent goodness of men, and that one did not need to be born a nobleman to be noble. He managed the Duke of Bradburne's stables for years, and when he died, I took over." Nostalgia for the old codger crept over him. It had been a long while since he'd felt such a sharp yearning to see him again.

"Was he kind to ye?" The duchess was focused on her hands that were knotted tightly together on the table, but she waited intently for his reply.

"Yes, he was. Monty didn't have a malicious bone in his body."

"And yer mother?" she asked, her voice wobbling slightly. Her bloodless fingers weaved and cinched together as if in agitation, though her countenance remained rigidly composed. "Was she there with ye in Essex?"

"No," Brandt replied, not curbing his bitter tone. "My

mother remained in Scotland while my father raised me on his own. I was born a bastard."

Aisla gasped, as did Sorcha. Callan watched him with interest. But it was the duchess's response that stunned Brandt the most. Her shoulders curled backward as she gave a short bark of laughter, and then leaned across the table to meet his stare directly.

"Ye're *no'* a bastard."

The furious intensity of her reply hit him first, but Brandt couldn't breathe. All the oxygen was sucked out of the room the minute her eyes connected with his and held them. They weren't dark as he'd initially assumed.

They were hazel, flecked with gold and green. Fey eyes.

His eyes.

Everything tilted on its axis. The floor, the hall, his entire world. Brandt lifted narrowed eyes to the woman seated across from him. "Who are you?"

Lady Glenross's mouth opened and closed, but then she stood. Tears replaced her laughter and streamed down her cheeks as she rushed from the hall. Brandt's chest felt too small to contain his hammering heart. But if he had her eyes, and he looked like the dead duke, then that would mean…

Good God, it was impossible.

No. *Monty* was his father. His mother *had* to be the laird's sister. It was the only thing that made sense. Unless Monty had lied. The room spun in tune with his brain as Monty's broken parting words came back to haunt him.

I never told…you…truth. I'm no', no'…

His father. He'd been about to say *not your father.*

Chapter Seventeen

The torches had all been lit and the fire stoked by the time Sorcha and Brandt returned to their room. As she'd promised, Morag had sent a few maids in to clean and tidy during sup. Neatly tied sprigs of bog myrtle and thistle lay on the pillows, and Sorcha smelled freshly laundered sheets along with the soap she'd used during her bath, rather than the musty, closed-up air of the room as they'd first found it. Though she'd barely touched her food, she didn't feel hungry. Her stomach churned, but it was from unease, and the silence Brandt had wrapped himself up in ever since Lady Glenross had fled the great hall.

Their conversation had gone from pleasant and polite, to murky and barbed within moments, it had seemed. *Who are you?* Brandt's question had sent Rodric's wife running, with tears in her eyes. Aisla had excused herself to follow her mother, and soon after, Callan had also bid them a good night.

All the while, Morag's hushed and fervent advice to Sorcha and Brandt earlier, to leave as quickly as they could, that it wasn't safe here, and that devils roamed these lands, repeated in the back of her mind. There was something wrong with the Montgomery, and as Sorcha toed off her slippers and felt the shock of the cold stones against her feet, she wanted only to lock the door and stay safely tucked away in her room with Brandt.

He went to stand before the hearth, his jaw screwed tight just as it had been since the great hall. She watched the shadows play over his profile—the strong, sharp lines of his forehead and nose, the concerned furrow of his brow—and wished she could read his mind. She had her suspicions; all the talk about Monty had likely dredged up memories. Though before, when speaking of his father, there had been a softness to Brandt's expression. A softness that was not there now.

"Tell me," Sorcha whispered.

Brandt turned his ear to her, not bothering to soften his reply. "Tell you what?"

She flinched at the bleakness in his voice. "What was that with Lady Glenross?"

The duchess had been appalled at Brandt's confession that he'd been born a bastard. Affronted, even. The woman seemed to believe that he had not been born out of wedlock, which hinted to her knowing much more about Brandt than she'd led them to believe. But then she'd fled the hall like the very devils Morag had spoken of were at her heels.

Brandt didn't answer Sorcha's question, only giving an abrupt shake of his head. Clearly, he didn't wish to speak about it. And why should he confide in her? Her heart had swelled during sup, when Rodric had insulted her and he'd risen in her defense. But Sorcha also knew that had he stayed quiet, Brandt would have been pegged as a weakling. A man of no courage. Perhaps her husband had only stood in her defense to prove that he would not be trifled with.

The excuse hurt, and it also rung hollow. She wanted to believe he'd meant his words, and that his defense had been genuine. But he kept changing his mind, this obstinate man, and the moment Sorcha thought she knew what he was about, he seemed only to go and prove her wrong. One moment, he couldn't keep his hands off her. The next, he was walking away. She wanted him to at least talk to her, the way he had during their travels here. But most of all, she wanted to chase off the haunted look in his eyes.

Sorcha went to him, her feet padding across the floor, swept clean by the maids and covered in spots by rugs and animal pelts that had not been in place when Morag had first shown them the room. Brandt seemed to sense her approach, and she saw the muscles in his back and shoulders tense.

"You should get some sleep," he told her without turning around. "Take the bed, and I'll take the chairs here. It will be hours yet before I will be able to close my eyes."

Standing so close to him, she couldn't stop her hands from reaching for the knots of tension in his shoulders. He inhaled audibly when she touched him, her fingers pressing firmly into his bunched muscle.

"Don't be daft," she replied. "That bed is big enough for the two of us *and* our horses."

"I don't think Morag would appreciate that mess." She caught sight of his profile again as he tilted his chin, and saw his lips break into a smile. Sorcha massaged his shoulders some more, and his head lolled back, a soft groan expelling from his throat. Her thumbs dug into the muscled flesh beneath the soft linen of his shirt, kneading and rolling, until she felt the largest of the knots start to loosen.

"You have strong hands," he murmured.

"Sit," she told him, gently leading him into one of the cushioned chairs in front of the hearth.

"Sorcha—"

She pushed the heels of her palms into the tops of his shoulders. "Let me do this for you, *leannan*."

"What does that mean?"

Sorcha hadn't realized what she'd called him. She felt herself flush. "It's a silly Gaelic term of endearment; it means nothing."

Without giving him a chance to protest her touch or react to her stupid slip calling him *sweetheart*, Sorcha sank her fingers deep into the muscle tissue just above his clavicle, wringing a deep groan from him as she squeezed firmly. She kept the pressure on while following circular motions with her thumbs along his upper back. She worked for a few minutes in silence, punctuated only by the sounds of pleasure escaping his lips.

The small moans tugged at places deep inside her own body, but Sorcha kept herself focused on the task. She wasn't able to stifle a small gasp when she slipped her fingers inside the neckline of his shirt to palm his warm skin. She loved to touch him, the feel of his bare skin against hers. Any part of her. His muscles leaped reflexively beneath her touch, but she calmed them with wide stroking oscillations. She wanted to press her lips to the hollow where his neck met his shoulders, follow in the path of her fortunate fingers, and trail her lips along the length of his spine. Sorcha marveled at the texture of his skin. He was steel overlaid with silk, strength wrapped in tenderness.

Her fingers crept into his soft hair as she massaged his scalp, threading through the long burnished strands. Brandt sighed with pleasure again, and this time, her entire body responded. The more she touched him, the more she craved. Sorcha kept going, even after she'd felt the tension dissolve and his flesh became malleable. She was only torturing herself, she knew, but she was so drunk on the sensation of him that she couldn't stop if she tried.

"That feels incredible," he murmured.

"Good, I'm glad. You're as stiff as an old branch."

His chuckle was low and deep, striking a pleasant chord within her. "Stiffness seems to have become my Achilles' heel these past few weeks."

"Perhaps you need to stretch more," she suggested innocently.

Brandt made a choked sound and then forcibly cleared his throat. "Are you volunteering your services, my lady?"

A heated blush overtook her at the underlying innuendo, and she was grateful she was out of his range of sight. Their banter was most dangerous when combined with desire. She took the coward's way out. "Only my fingers."

"I give myself over to your leisure, then," he said softly.

Cheeks scorching, Sorcha returned to the muscles around his collarbone, thinking of how *his* fingers had pleasured her. How his tongue and mouth had done the same. Pleasing him now, giving him the same sensation of complete release as she massaged the worry and stress he'd built up inside over the last many days, made her feel powerful. In the moments when Brandt had brought her to ecstasy, there had been nothing in this world she wouldn't have done or given or said to be able to continue what she was feeling. In those moments, he'd held complete sway over her. He'd had the power.

Now, as his head relaxed against the back of the chair, and her fingers delved under the collar of his shirt, she knew she was the one who held sway. For a tantalizing moment, she wondered if she were to walk around the chair and climb into his lap whether he would continue to succumb. The scandalous thought made her dizzy.

The smooth feel of his bare skin was heaven and hell in equal measure. She wanted to lick his sleek neck. Bite into the corded muscle. Rub her breasts against his bare back in wicked abandon.

I want you, leannan. I want you.

Every rational bone in her body argued that she should move away, but she couldn't stop. He needed this. He needed *her*, even if he wouldn't admit it.

She moved from his neck to his shoulders once again, the breadth of them and the heavy muscle under her palms strumming a violent chord of want inside her. It throbbed along the insides of her ribs and cascaded down to her thighs in molten ribbons. Her senses were so heightened it wouldn't take much to push her over the edge…the same precipice he'd brought her to twice before. Sorcha squeezed her legs together, and her breath snagged.

Diah, what he did to her was beyond sinful.

Exhaling somewhat shakily, she concentrated on rubbing her thumbs into the base of his neck and working them in slow circular strokes. She aimed for safer ground with serious conversation. "Do you think your Monty could have been the man Lady Glenross spoke of? The one she knew as Pherson?"

A muscle jumped reflexively against her thumbs before settling down again.

"It's possible," he answered. She'd put him at ease enough to speak to her about it, at least.

"She spoke well of him," Sorcha added.

"Yes," Brandt replied, his voice hitching lower. "It did sound as if she'd been fond of him."

Sorcha heard the suspicion on his tone, and the knots in his neck suddenly became harder to massage. She lowered her lips to his ear. "Tell me something about him. A memory."

Anything to direct his mind along a different path.

He sighed, and she breathed in the warmed spice of his skin. This man drove her desire like nothing she'd ever imagined possible. Just the deeply masculine scent of him made her want to touch her tongue to his ear, press it against his neck, and feel his pulse leap. But she restrained herself.

He needed more than one kind of release; Brandt needed to talk.

"A memory," he repeated, again turning pliable beneath her constant ministrations. "I was young. Maybe eight, and my stepmother, Anne, had just passed," he started, his lashes having fluttered shut. "We didn't make it a habit to celebrate birthdays, but that year, Monty attempted to bake muffins. He burned them to crisps."

Brandt chuckled, the sound reverberating up through Sorcha's hands and into the small bones of her arms. "I managed to choke down two before he insisted we give the rest to the hogs. But even they refused to eat them, and hogs eat anything. He was a terrible cook."

She smiled at the lightness of his voice. "He sounds like he was a good man."

He opened his eyes, and from her vantage point, she thought she could see a flicker of doubt. But then he spoke, and the admiration he held for Montgomery Pierce, or Pherson Montgomery, was indisputable. "He cared for me, and I cared for him."

She stilled her hands. "Then why is it you sound so sad?"

Surely, he missed his father, but from what she recalled, it had been many years since his death. Sorcha also couldn't help noticing that he hadn't used the word *love*. Perhaps she wasn't the only one he was running from.

"Because he never told me the truth," he answered. "Though I think he might have tried. Near the end. I can't be sure, the words were muddled, and he never finished his sentence. At the time, I thought was trying to reassure me that being a bastard shouldn't matter. But now, after Lady Glenross insisted I wasn't bastard born…"

"What do you think he wanted to tell you?" she asked.

Brandt shrugged. "That I belonged somewhere. That I had a home with kin and people who shared my blood. But blood doesn't necessarily mean family." He paused as if thinking through his words. "Family is in the heart."

"Then why did you want to come here?"

He went quiet for a long time, though his body remained calm. He shifted, digging into his pocket to retrieve the ring he'd tucked in there earlier. They both stared at it, cupped in his palm. The Montgomery colors seemed to burn brighter, the thread of gold shimmering through the blue and green crest on its surface.

"You could show her, you know," Sorcha said softly. "Rings like these are heirlooms for a laird's family."

He twisted the ring in between his thumb and forefinger. "Which was why I thought it was one of the laird's sisters. But now I'm not so certain." His voice broke slightly upon his whispered confession. "We have the same eyes, Sorcha. Lady Glenross and I."

Sorcha stilled. She'd been sitting on the duchess's left and the woman had never once looked at her directly. Her mind tumbled over itself. There was little resemblance between them, if any at all. She was fair-haired and slight, while his looks and build favored the laird. What did he mean they had the *same* eyes? Did Brandt think he was her son? With Monty, or the late duke? If it were the latter, then that would make him...*Diah*...the Montgomery heir.

"Brandt, do you think the *duchess* is your mother?"

His entire body stiffened at the hushed incredulity in her tone. "I'm not entirely sure what to think."

A new rush of tension coiled underneath his skin, and Sorcha wanted only to soothe it away. Her attempts to get him to talk had worked, but besides the memory of those birthday muffins, thoughts of his father—or the identity of his mother—only seemed to make Brandt more upset. She wanted him to unwind, to bask in the soothing sensation of her fingers, as she always did his. Even now, she worshipped the feel of his body. She wanted more, though. More than just touch. And she wanted to give *him* more.

Blushing at what she was about to do, Sorcha forced her fears away. He was her husband...at least for this moment. She might not know much about marital accord, but she knew he wanted her. And want was a powerful motivator.

She leaned forward, over his shoulder, pushing her hands lower under his shirt, across his front. Her palms filled with his hard pectorals, his muscles leaping at her touch. Her fingertips brushed over each nipple, and she saw him shift his hips, readjusting his seat in the chair. His body went tense, but it was a different kind of tension. This one made his pulse speed up, his heartbeat quickening beneath her fingertips. Primal satisfaction curled through her.

"What are you doing?" His voice was a dark rasp that scraped along her senses.

"Touching you."

He inhaled sharply as her fingernails grazed gently over his nipples once more. "I don't think—"

"Then don't think. At least not right now," Sorcha whispered, her lips so close to Brandt's earlobe that she could not help but dart her tongue out to taste it. "How does this feel?"

He made a grating noise in his throat before clamping his hands down upon both of her wrists. "Dangerous," he said, his voice slightly hitched.

Brandt held her so firmly that she'd instinctively arched backward before she relaxed into him, letting her breasts come to rest against his shoulders as she'd craved doing earlier. The scent of his warmed skin wafted into her nostrils, and she inhaled deeply. Her mouth watered, and her nipples ached from under the confines of her bodice. Once more, she gave in to the inclination to taste him, scraping her teeth along the column of his throat beneath his ear. His body jerked as Sorcha lapped and nibbled her way down his neck, while her trapped fingertips scoured the shelved muscle of his torso. She wanted to taste every heated inch of him.

"We both seem to tempt danger," she whispered into his ear. "Don't we?"

"Why are you doing this?"

She tried to be as blasé and as self-possessed as he had been with her. "It's just pleasure, Brandt. Nothing more. Let me do this for you."

In response, he angled his chin upward and caught her lips with his. The kiss was dark and carnal, his hot mouth clinging to hers. A moan escaped her as his tongue delved deep in search of hers, finding it and coaxing it between his teeth until her knees felt like rubber. Her fingernails scraped gently against his taut chest, and the low fierce growl in his throat made her wild. Sorcha kissed him back just as fiercely. Just as possessively.

Still gripping her fingers, Brandt released her mouth and her hands and drew her around the side of the chair. The heavy-lidded look in his eyes made every drop of blood burn in Sorcha's veins and turn to liquid fire between her hips. God, one scorching glance from him was all it took to make her want to tear off her clothes and throw herself at his mercy.

"Sorcha, we both know where this road leads."

Brandt's words were at odds with his eyes and the thumb insistently stroking over her knuckles. He wanted her to resist him. As if she could do such a thing. She was hanging on to decency by the slimmest of threads, and she had no intention of walking away. Not from this. Not from him.

She licked her lips, and his eyes settled on her mouth. "Do we? Are you a savant now?"

"It is unwise," he murmured.

"Don't worry, *leannan*, your virtue will be quite safe, I promise."

Brandt chuckled as Sorcha made the decision for him and sat in his lap. He was aroused. Impressively so. He groaned as she wriggled against him, the rigid length of his erection settling in between the gap of her thighs. This time, slowly, teasingly, she leaned forward to catch his mouth with hers. His eyes darkened as her tongue slipped out, licking the inside of his upper lip before biting gently upon his full lower one.

Brandt's arms banded around her, pulling her flush to his chest, and he took her mouth with a ravenous, uncontrolled hunger. A pulse of worry wicked through her. Not worry exactly...more like breathless thrill. Excitement. She had never seen him like this. Brandt had always been so controlled, so in possession of all his impulses, but now he seemed almost feral, as if driven by dark desires he no longer wanted to keep at bay. Sorcha responded in kind, biting, sucking, licking deep. And when his mouth moved to her throat, she flung her head back in abandon. She wanted him to see exactly what he did to her. She could feel his arousal beneath her, growing harder by the breath.

Cradling his head, she gasped as he massaged her breasts over her bodice. And when his fingers closed around one of the aching peaks, pinching gently, she moaned her approval. His mouth moved to her neck, trailing down in wet nudges and bites that made her senseless. The day's growth of stubble abraded her skin deliciously as he laved and sucked her flesh. Sorcha couldn't wait. She wanted to feel him. Lifting her weight slightly, she slipped her hand beneath her legs to close around him.

Brandt tore his mouth from her skin, his stormy eyes darting to hers when her fingers gripped the thick length of him through his trousers. Without taking her eyes from his, she slipped off his lap and onto her knees, wedging herself between his parted legs.

"Sorcha..." he said in a hoarse voice, his hand falling on top of hers at his groin. The hard flesh beneath her hot fingertips jumped.

"Let me," she whispered.

After a searching look, Brandt lifted his hand. He was just as lost to passion as she was. Perhaps more so. And Sorcha wanted nothing more than for him to lose every bit of himself in pleasure. Briskly, she undid the fastenings to the fall of his buckskins. She'd felt him against her at the river, caressed him in her palm, but nothing prepared her for the proudly erect sight of him. He was beautiful and so devastatingly masculine, it took her breath away. Sorcha swallowed hard as her fingers cautiously encircled his girth. He was thick and warm and heavy in her grip, his body pulsing in hot, powerful surges.

"Bloody hell, Sorcha," Brandt swore, clutching the sides of the armchair with brute force.

Suddenly, she was gripped by a paralyzing anxiety. Brandt's face was contorted, his jaw clamped tightly and eyes screwed shut. In pleasure? In pain? Was she hurting him? She had no idea what she was doing. He'd liked her massage before. Perhaps it would be the same for this part of his body. With a tentative motion, she rolled her fingers along the shaft, pressing gently, trying to gauge his reaction. Brandt's eyes flew open, dilated, and a muscle hammered to life in his cheek.

"Do you like this?" she asked.

"Yes," he gasped, one hand reaching out to cover hers. He stroked hers up and down from base to tip, and then back again. "Like so."

She was an apt student. Once she got a rhythm going, his hand fell away, and indistinct sounds of pleasure left his lips. Emboldened by her success and his response, Sorcha dragged her thumb over the rounded blunt end of him, fascinated by the pearl of moisture she found there. His skin was boiling hot, so sleek and silky hard that she couldn't help herself. She leaned forward and pressed her lips to him.

Brandt almost bucked out of his seat as his entire body shuddered.

"You don't have to do that," he gritted out.

But she wanted it. Sorcha wanted to bring him the same bliss he'd given her. She opened her mouth and took him inside. Her husband's growl was primal and bestial. It made lust explode within her with the force of a thousand stars. She drew him deeper, teasing the ridge with her tongue, testing him, learning the shape of him. His spicy male scent made her dizzy, and his smooth, salted taste made her mouth water. She wanted to swallow every delectable inch of him.

Sorcha almost laughed. It was nigh impossible to fit all of him in her mouth, but she was determined to try. Using her hands and her mouth in unison, she delighted in the moans and coarse words that emerged from his lips as she continued her exploration…licking here and nibbling there. Watching to see how his body responded. Every muscle on his stomach clenched, his legs like stone on either side of her. She reveled in her power over him. Heat pooled between her legs as his breathing grew more ragged, his hips rolling upward into her mouth at a faster pace. She knew what it signaled from the last time he'd rocked frantically against her at the river. His release was close.

Clamping her damp thighs together, she felt something inside her own body tremble, and sensation rippled through her. It was nothing like the pleasure she'd experienced with him, but her entire body felt tied to his…tethered in some kind of sublime harmony.

With a guttural cry, Brandt gently disengaged her from him and moved one hand down to his groin. He drew her up with his free hand until she was splayed over him in his lap, rocking her wet, trembling core against his hard thigh and sobbing with her own unexpected release. A few frenzied strokes later and he thrust upward, spilling his seed between them with a deep groan of satisfaction.

Breathing harshly, Brandt rested his forehead against hers. Neither of them moved for several interminable moments. With a sound of contentment, he wrapped one arm about her, cradling her against his chest and nuzzling his face into the crook of her neck.

Sorcha craved the words that such intimacy brought. But she knew it was a hopeless wish. They would find pleasure in each other's arms, but not love.

She was ashamed to admit she would rather have that than nothing at all.

Chapter Eighteen

Brandt stretched his legs under the heavy sheets and blankets and turned his face away from the bright morning sunlight slanting through the mullioned window. He didn't want to wake up, even though the temptress he'd slept beside all night had been sliding her bare legs along his for the last quarter hour as she slowly rose out of her own dreams.

Despite most of the Montgomery keep's occupants being less than friendly, the bed that Sorcha had finally persuaded him to sleep in last evening had cradled his travel-weary back and limbs with all the tenderness of a pair of angel's wings. Having Sorcha tucked beside him, her rhythmic breath gusting against the hollow of his neck, had only added to the sensation of being transported to heaven.

Then again, the hard, pulsing tightness of his erection this morning had a distinct quality of hell.

Brandt was trapped between two desires as he lay there in bed, listening to the sounds of a castle rising for the day—chickens clucking, voices out in the courtyard, footsteps passing by their bedroom door. He wanted Sorcha on top of him, rubbing out his need with frantic thrusts of her hips, and he also wanted her away—so that he could stop wanting her so damn much.

She was passion incarnate, and she made him yearn with the same ravenous need. All he had to do was think about her, kneeling between his legs, her sweet velvet lips wrapped around his length, her tongue running in slick, endless strokes from root to tip, and another jolt of pressure filled his already straining erection. Damnation, if he didn't get up right now he'd lose whatever sanity had kept him from spreading her legs and doing the unthinkable.

In the light of morning, he wasn't quite sure how he'd kept his trousers on all night, the fall buttoned up. But when Sorcha had asked him to hold her as she slept, he hadn't been able to deny her. Not after the pure, raw pleasure she'd given him. And herself, he knew. She'd come apart in his lap, her center warm and wet through her drawers as she'd rocked against his thigh. It wouldn't have taken much to shift her to the side, drive himself into her, and find pleasure together, as one.

But then what? Brandt squeezed his eyes shut as he tried to force away the dull ache of his groin. Hell, they were less than a week away from Brodie lands. After one more day of rest for Ares, they could be on their way again. With the Brodie and her sister, Sorcha would be safe from Malvern, and his promise to Ronan would be met. Brandt would not leave her until he was confident in her brother-in-law's ability and promise to protect her. Only then would he be on his way back to Essex. Back to the life he'd led before he'd ever visited that damned fated common lands festival.

He tried to picture it in his mind. Worthington Abbey and the stables. Pierce Cottage, where he lived, quiet and content. And alone. Bits and pieces came to him, but they seemed to float through his mind, refusing to settle into place. Instead,

Sorcha's light lavender scent wafted into his senses, and the bright, clear picture of her riding Lockie, galloping in front of him, her long raven hair loose behind her, struck him. He heard her chiming laughter in his memory. Saw the bridge of her nose crinkling whenever she smiled.

A knock on their bedroom door brought him back to his senses. Brandt shifted himself up against the pillows as a maid swept into the room. It wasn't Morag, but another older woman, and she paid the two of them no mind at all as she went to the windows and pushed the drapes aside, letting in more light. Sorcha rolled over and stretched, her feet tickling Brandt's shins.

"The duchess is waiting for ye both in the great hall to break yer fast," the maid announced as she placed a fresh ewer of water and a new length of toweling near the washbasin.

"Thank you," Sorcha said, her eyes tracking the maid as the woman laid out Sorcha's own dresses, now laundered and mended, upon a bench at the base of the bed.

Brandt shifted himself away from Sorcha but didn't get up. It was bad enough his own wife was going to get an eyeful of his uncomfortable state. He didn't need this maid blushing as well.

As soon as the maid had closed the door behind her, Sorcha sat up, clutching the blankets to her breasts. She wasn't unclothed, but the shift she wore was of a fine cambric. When she'd climbed into bed, the torchlight doused and the fire in the hearth crackling low, he'd still been able to see the dusky points of her nipples.

His lips twitched in a half grin. "Need I remind you about the river?"

Her chin hitched as a playful scowl pinched her features. Sorcha dropped the blankets and swung her legs over the side of the massive bed. She strode to the bench, collected one of her dresses, and then, with a sly glance over one shoulder, replied, "I don't think we would arrive in time for breakfast if *I* reminded *you* of the river."

Brandt held his breath as she disappeared behind the privacy screen to dress. Sweet hell, she was going to drive him to madness. He needed no reminder to envision her, emerging drenched from the chilled water, her nipples taut, her hips swaying freely, every stunning inch of her figure outlined. While the sight of her in wet linen had been downright erotic, he'd still had no idea what she looked like fully naked. Brandt frowned, remembering her plea not to remove her shift. He'd forgotten, too caught up in the feel and taste of her to put much thought to it. Now, he wondered.

He got up, his erection barely constrained by the cut of his trousers, and quickly washed at the basin before throwing on his shirt and boots. By the time Sorcha emerged, dressed, his erection had ebbed, if only because of the frigid water in the ewer. He did not know if he could withstand another chaste night in that bed with her.

Hell, he'd never imagined avoiding his husbandly duties would be so excruciating.

The annulment was nonnegotiable. He needed to give his word, for her sake, to the Brodie laird, that she remained a virgin for her next husband.

His stomach clenched with a rush of something unpleasant. *Next husband.* It wasn't the first time he'd considered the true reason for leaving her a virgin, but it was the first time he felt like punching something hard because of it.

"Are you ready?" Sorcha said from behind him.

Brandt nodded and palmed the ring he'd given her on their wedding day, feeling oddly tight in the chest as he slipped it onto her third finger. "You should wear this. It's yours."

They both stared at their joined hands, though her expression was unreadable. The ring meant little...a hollow symbol of their agreement, but Brandt couldn't help the jolt he felt at seeing it there once more. Releasing her, they left their room, moving toward the great hall.

"You've gone quiet again," she whispered as they walked. "Are you reluctant to see Lady Glenross?"

Brandt shook his head, but again, couldn't speak. It wasn't reluctance to see Rodric's wife consuming him right then, but a different reluctance, one that shot spirals of unreasonable discontent through him.

You will *leave her with the Brodie*, he told himself.

He felt Sorcha's eyes on him as they entered the great hall but didn't acknowledge her glances. What had gotten into him? One night in a real bed with the woman he'd taken to wife only to see her to safety, and here he was second-guessing their plan. Though in truth, he knew it was more than just that. It was something that went deeper than even their attraction to each other. Though he couldn't articulate the words to describe it, he felt it clear to his marrow. She was in his blood and in his bones.

He was almost relieved to see Lady Glenross seated at the laird's table, her too-familiar eyes rising to meet his as he approached. She was perched in the same chair as the night before. Aisla was beside her, but the rest of the benches and tables in the hall were unoccupied.

"Please forgive the laird's absence," Lady Glenross rasped, as if her throat ached. Brandt noticed her red-rimmed eyes and determined the duchess had been weeping.

Sorcha stopped at the chair where Callan had been seated last night and gripped the back of it. Lady Glenross hitched her eyes on Sorcha's hands as she pulled out the chair, her pale brows narrowing into a frown. Aisla only smiled at Sorcha's defiance of Rodric's rule, and the duchess, though still frowning, did not comment. Brandt took the seat beside his wife.

"There is nothing to forgive," he replied, his tone clear. Rodric's absence, though rude, was not unwelcome. Besides that, he'd spent the night in a fitful state, distracting himself from his wife's glorious body curled up against his, by thinking of Lady Glenross and all she'd said during last evening's sup. Unless the duchess ran off in tears yet again, Brandt was determined to wring out some definitive answers from her today.

"His behavior last night," Lady Glenross began, "was unpardonable. He's a blunt man and doesnae take well to—"

"Forgive my interruption, Your Grace, but you needn't apologize for him. There is no one here who will judge you for his actions."

A new sheen of tears lit Lady Glenross's eyes as she nodded and attempted a smile. They broke their fast in peace, all the while Brandt noticing his wife's returned appetite. It gave him unexpected relief to see her eating. The last several days had been hard, their meals sparse, and last night she'd barely touched a morsel with Rodric breathing down her neck. When Sorcha sat back in her chair, the mountain of eggs, haggis, and oatmeal gone, Aisla laughed.

"Mrs. Hildreth will be happy to ken ye liked her cooking, Lady Pierce."

"Please, call me Sorcha. If she set another plate before me now, I'd kiss her on the cheek," Sorcha replied, also laughing. "And will likely need to be rolled from the hall."

Aisla pushed back her chair and stood. "Come. I'll take ye to the kitchens for a few oatcakes and then out for a walk."

Sorcha got to her feet. "I'd like to check in at the stables to see how Lockie and Ares are, if you don't mind."

She glanced down at Brandt, who nodded, appreciative that she'd thought of his mount. She cared for Ares, and that meant something to him.

After she and Aisla left the great hall, their arms linked,

Brandt turned back to the duchess. "We need to speak."

"The ring on Lady Pierce's finger," she said. "Where did ye get it?"

Her words surprised him with their force.

"It was my mother's," he answered.

Lady Glenross dragged in a shaky breath, the lines fanning out from her eyes glistening with tears. "Ye've kept it all this time?"

"It was all I had of her."

This answer seemed only to wring a suppressed sob from her, and she covered her mouth with her hand.

"You know who I am," Brandt hedged. "I'm related to the late duke. Aren't I?"

She nodded, the motion made choppy by emotion. "He was yer father."

A burning pain radiated out from his heart, through his chest, all the way into his soul. Monty was not his father. That was what he'd been confessing on his deathbed after all. Brandt's father was the dead Duke of Glenross. He lifted his eyes, which had fallen to his empty plate before him, back to Lady Glenross.

"And my mother?" he pressed.

But he knew. The way she gazed at him—those changeling fey eyes that were twin mirrors of his—with so much agony and guilt, gave away her answer before she'd even parted her lips. "I never dared hope I would see ye again," she whispered. "'Twas too painful. Too difficult to bear."

It *was* her.

Brandt stared into her eyes—his *mother's* eyes—and nearly drowned under the rush of the thousand questions he'd struggled with all his life. He drew a shattered breath to quiet the ragtag emotions clamoring for space in his head.

"You sent me away," he said, the most basic, most obvious statement tumbling out of his mouth first.

"Aye," she replied, her hand coming down flat upon the table, as if reaching for him. There were two chairs between them, though, and Brandt had the urge to stand up and fling them through the air.

"I thought he would kill ye," she said, blinking back tears. They continued to fall, streaking down her cheeks.

"My father?"

She shook her head sharply. "Nae. Robert adored ye. We both loved ye, Brandall, more than anything in this world, and ye hadn't even yet been born."

Brandall. What had she just called him? The answer to that could wait.

"Then why send me away?" he demanded, his jaw so tight it ached. "Who wanted to kill me?"

Again, Lady Glenross shook her head, shutting her eyes as if against a terrible memory. Her voice lowered to a whisper, though the great hall was empty, and on the dais they would have had a clear view of anyone approaching. "I was entering my confinement when Robert fell in the quarry. He had no business being there that day; he'd told me he and Rodric were riding out on a hunt. But Rodric said it wasnae so. He had men claim he'd been with them, but there were whispers, ye ken. And there had never been any love lost between Robert and his brother."

As she spoke, Brandt began to cobble answers together.

"He wanted to be laird, Rodric did, and Robert had often told me to be wary of his brother. To keep a keen eye on him."

"Sorcha told me about the rumors," he admitted.

Lady Glenross looked at him, her eyes tortured with the secrets she'd kept and the sorrow she'd borne all these years. "I thought he'd take another bride. A younger lass, perhaps. But Robert wasnae sooner in the ground than Rodric was telling me that we were to be wed. That he'd take on my bairn as his own." She paled, her chin quivering as she looked around the great hall, as if checking to be sure they were still alone. "But I dinnae trust him. Lad or lass, my bairn would be the true Montgomery heir, and Rodric would no' hesitate to cut down anyone who stood in his way. But it was that or leave Montgomery forever."

Brandt felt restless, his muscles kinking and begging for action. What he wouldn't give right then for Rodric to come walking into the room. To confront the man who had ruthlessly stolen a father, a future, and a family from him. He was not a violent man by nature, but he yearned for justice with a desire that frightened him with its intensity.

"So you sent me away with Monty," he said. Then corrected himself. "Pherson Montgomery."

"Pherson was my cousin, and there was no one else I trusted more. Rodric had everyone terrified; he made every clansman, down to the last child who could speak, all pledge our oaths of allegiance to him, and when one man—one who had been openly suspicious of Robert's death—refused, Rodric ran him through with his sword."

The vicious act reminded Brandt of Malvern. His mind leaped to Sorcha, and he fought the desire to stand up and go after her, to see her safe at his side. She was with Aisla and, though the young girl wouldn't be much when it came to protection, he knew his wife could protect herself. He also hoped that Rodric wouldn't be fool enough to lay one finger upon a Maclaren.

"You didn't have to stay," he told her. "You could have left."

"And go where? A pregnant woman on her own traveling through the Highlands? I wanted ye alive and healthy, and Montgomery was the only home I had with midwives I trusted." She smiled at him, a sad, pitiful grin misted by more tears. "And ye don't ken Rodric. Even if I had run, he would have hunted me down and killed us both. Nae. I could no' put ye in danger, my sweet boy. The moment ye were born, I had to say good-bye. For yer sake."

He looked away from her, unable to see her tears and not feel the answering tug at the base of his throat. He didn't want to feel sorry for her. He'd spent so many years hating her. Despising her for what she'd done. And yet within the space of a few minutes, everything he'd thought he'd known about his birth mother had started to crumble around him.

"The midwife and the lasses attending the birth vowed to protect ye. They spread word ye were weak and struggling to breathe. That ye had a strange rash and fever. They would no' let anyone into the birthing room, and no' a soul wished to enter, either." She bit her lower lip and looked to her lap, where her hands were twisting a cloth napkin. "A day after ye were born, the midwife announced ye had passed. They took a bundle from my room, wrapped in layers of muslin, and buried it. They said the laird didnae even bother to look upon the wrapped bundle."

Brandt frowned, his chest feeling as though a boulder had been dropped upon it. "What did they bury?"

Lady Glenross exhaled sadly. "Pherson had come to my room to fetch ye in the night. He brought with him a dead piglet. 'Twas similar in size." She lifted her shoulder in a helpless shrug and let it drop heavily.

He startled both her and himself with a harsh bark of laughter. "A piglet? You traded me for a piglet?"

Wounded eyes snapped to his. "I traded my heart. I would have done anything to protect ye, even if it meant losing ye."

His mouth flattened out again, the humor gone. In its place settled the weight of empathy. Damn it all, he'd never imagined he'd feel a shred of compassion for the woman who had given birth to him and sent him away. Why hadn't Monty *told* him? But as soon as the question formed, the answer did as well. Nothing would have stopped Brandt from riding, hell-bent on revenge, into the Highlands, straight to Montgomery lands. Monty had been protecting him.

He'd been doing exactly what Catriona, the Duchess of Glenross and his heartbroken mother, had trusted him to do.

Brandt tapped his fingers against the wooden grain of the table, uncertain what to say. He'd always had so many questions, but now they were all changing. He leaned back in his chair, numb fingers drumming the table, and perused the hall…the aged stones surrounding him that made up his home. A burst of anger shot through him at the childhood he'd lost. He would have grown up running barefoot in this hall, being read to by the hearth, eating at this very table with people who loved him.

Monty had loved him; he had no fault with that.

But he'd been cheated of the life that had been owed to him…that he had been born for. All those fears of not knowing who he was and where he belonged came back to haunt him. He was a Montgomery, which meant he belonged *here*. Or did he?

"You called me Brandall," he murmured.

She sniffled, and after a moment, cleared her throat. "'Tis yer name. Robert said ye would be christened Brandall if ye were a lad, and so I asked Pherson to change it slightly…just in case Rodric ever discovered my deceit and tried to hunt ye both down."

It was why, then, Monty had changed his own name as well. And fled to Essex. The new Duke of Glenross would have had a difficult time finding him there.

"Rodric never discovered it, though?" he asked. "Your ploy?"

Catriona—his *mother*—sighed. "Nae."

"And you married him."

"'Twas no' a choice," she whispered. "He didnae give me one. I would have met the same fate as Robert, and ye would have nae father or mother. I wanted to survive for ye, if one day ye came back. Pherson was supposed to tell ye all when the time was right."

"He tried," Brandt said. "He died before he could."

The great hall was silent, the echo of their hushed voices growing fainter by the moment. They were alone, but it wouldn't matter if everyone was still present and listening. Brandt wagered from Rodric's behavior that the duke already suspected who he was. And if he didn't, it would be only a matter of time. Which meant he and Sorcha would both be in danger. At the thought of Sorcha, Brandt's legs itched to stand.

"It has no' all been a nightmare," the duchess said, watching him with her heart in her haunted eyes. "I have Patrick, and Callan, and Aisla. They're naught like him."

Brandt held his tongue. Callan and Aisla, perhaps. But Patrick, though he'd appeared to soften for his mother, seemed the very image of his overbearing father. *His murderous father*, Brandt thought.

"But ye, my son," she said, even quieter now. "Ye are the true heir. Ye have every right to challenge the laird now. And look at ye." Her eyes shone with something unfamiliar to Brandt. An emotion he'd seen in the Duchess of Bradburne's eyes whenever she'd gazed upon Archer. He thought it might have been pride. "Ye're a grown man. Ye're strong and proud, and so verra much like yer father, *mo gràidh*. My beloved."

Brandt's mind automatically shot to Monty, the man he'd called father for twenty-five years. But it was not Monty she spoke of, it was Robert.

Robert Montgomery, the murdered Duke of Glenross.

His first thought should have been to avenge his father's name and his own stolen birthright, but instead Brandt's first thought went to his wife. She was not Lady Pierce...she would be Lady Glenross, a duchess and wife to a laird of a powerful clan. Though Brandt had given her a false name, he had sworn an oath to protect her, and that much was still true. But to do that, he would have to take back what was rightfully his.

He would have to take back Montgomery.

Chapter Nineteen

Tucked away in a cleft in the hulking cliffside, the sprawling Montgomery keep was situated on a ruggedly beautiful piece of the Highlands. The bright morning sun shone down upon the grass in the valley, gilding the coarse grasses with golden light and touching upon the fir trees that grew in thick groves on the hillside. Patches of purple heather popped up here and there, and brightly colored spring wildflowers flourished in the rich, arable soil. Though Sorcha was a Highlander through and through, and Maclaren was beautiful in its own way, there was something wild and untouched about these jutting crags and lush glens that seemed to be just beyond the reaches of human civilization. Its ungovernable nature reminded Sorcha of Brandt.

As she walked along with Aisla after checking on the horses—Ares was almost fully recovered and would be ready to travel with another day or so of rest—Sorcha couldn't help wonder what her husband was doing. She hoped that in speaking with the duchess, he would find the answers he'd been searching for. Now that he had mentioned it, that morning at breakfast Sorcha had been hard-pressed not to notice how similar their eyes were. Lady Glenross's were the same shimmering brownish-green hue, flecked with hints of gold.

In truth, they'd been identical to Brandt's.

And Sorcha would know. Those eyes of his had pierced her to her very soul the night before, when she'd sunk to her knees and done indecent things that would make a courtesan blush. But she had pleased him, that she knew. Brandt's eyes had been clouded with desire and passion, and he had splintered apart in her arms as she had in his. He had trusted her enough to let go, and that had been more satisfying than the release itself. Sorcha wrapped her arms around her middle with a sigh.

"Thinking about yer husband?" Aisla asked with a sly look as they ambled down a narrow path from the rear of the keep toward the loch that glittered in the distance.

Sorcha blinked. "No."

"Aye, I reckon ye were," the girl said with a wicked grin. "Ye get that faraway look in yer eye, and ye bite yer lip as if ye were thinking about him kissing ye."

Sorcha felt her face redden but kept her mouth shut. She couldn't very well insist she hadn't been thinking about kissing him when she *had* been…though not exactly in the place Aisla had been thinking. Her flush ignited.

"I kenned it," Aisla crowed. "Although, I would be doing the same thing if I were married to a tall, handsome fellow, too. Yer man is easy on the eyes. I've seen the way all the kitchen lasses look at him and twitter." She giggled and rolled her eyes. "'Tis the same way they carry on for Patrick and Callan. Though I prefer dark-haired men, myself."

The candid admission made Sorcha arch an eyebrow. At fifteen, Aisla could be considered as being of marriageable age. Not many men were of the same mind as her own father that fifteen was far too young. It was why he'd insisted the betrothal contract with Malvern state she had to be nineteen before any marriage banns could be posted.

Sorcha grinned at Aisla. "Have you a sweetheart, then?"

Now it was the lass's turn to blush, but she skirted the issue by segueing into a monologue about being trapped at Montgomery and not having any chance to meet other suitors. "We never have any visitors, ye ken," she chattered to Sorcha. "Ye've been the first in months. And Papa will no' let me go with him to Inverness." She sighed morosely. "I ken I'll have to marry Dougal Buchanan, the smelly, pock-faced lummox."

She went off on a tirade, pointing out the benefits of bathing and how the entire Buchanan family saw fit to be covered in mud and muck at all times. By the time they had descended to the north end of the training fields en route to the loch, Aisla was red-faced from the exertion and righteous indignation.

"Perhaps your father will let you choose your husband," Sorcha offered.

Aisla shot her a look that suggested she was deranged for even thinking it. "Ye ken? This from the same man who boasted he would marry his own daughter to a dog?"

"I suppose you have a point."

Aisla's brows drew together into a slight frown. "Why do ye no' have a brogue? Ye're Scottish, aren't ye?"

"My mother's English, and insisted on English tutors."

"Why?"

"Because I was to marry Ma—" Sorcha broke off and spat to the ground before continuing, "a disgusting, odious excuse for a man."

"The marquess ye were speaking about at sup last night." She nodded. "Yes."

They stopped at the top of the next small hill, which gave them a full view of the men who were training with swords and bows and arrows. Sorcha's fingers itched for the chance to practice with her bow or even her sword. The only weapons she carried were the dirks lodged in each boot beneath her skirts. She counted about several dozen soldiers on the field and frowned. At Maclaren, they had four times that number.

"Where are the rest of your men?" she asked.

Aisla shrugged. "Most of them left for work in Inverness and Glasgow in the last handful of years, but Montgomery is well protected, if that's what ye're worried about."

Sorcha scanned the surroundings, and once more, marveled at Montgomery's defensible position. No attack from an outside enemy could come without adequate warning. And the pass from which they had entered was well guarded. But it wasn't an outside attack Sorcha was worried about—it was one from inside. She did not trust Rodric. While she enjoyed Aisla's company and would have liked to get to know the duchess better, it was not worth the risk to outstay their welcome.

"Do you train?" she asked Aisla, who was watching the exercises with a wistful look.

Her copper eyes widened. "With the men? Nae, 'tis no' proper."

"Who says?" Sorcha tossed back. "I trained with Maclaren soldiers from the age of three. It's a fact that I can fight better than most of them. How else will you be able to defend yourself?" She eyed the lass. "You can't wait for a man to come to your rescue. If I had, I would have been dead."

"Is that how ye got those?" Aisla asked, her eyes darting to her scars.

"Yes." She raised a self-conscious hand and then dropped it. "I'm sure you've heard the story, and it's true. I fought off a very angry and very hungry mother wolf with two daggers." Sorcha bent to retrieve one from her boot. "Much like this one."

Aisla reached for the dirk and ran her thumb gently along its razor-honed edge. "'Tis sharp."

"I keep them oiled and ready, so that they can pierce through leather and hide," she said. "I used to be able to snare a rabbit at forty paces, though I'm far better with the bow now. I can teach you to throw the dagger, if you like."

Aisla's eyes lit up. "Truly?"

Sorcha faltered, realizing that they would be leaving within the next two days, but she nodded firmly. "Here, why don't we start with your first lesson? See, you grip the blade like this with your thumb and forefinger, nice and tight." She demonstrated, being careful not to touch the edge. "Pull back and then throw. You can also toss from the hilt, but you don't get the same heft." Drawing her arm back, she let the dirk fly a few feet away to sink into the dirt.

She retrieved the dagger and handed it to Aisla. The dagger skidded across the grass on her first few tries, but by the third, it sank blade first into the soil. Sorcha cleaned the dirk on the grass and then gave it a wipe with the hem of her dress. She held it out. "You can keep it."

"But 'tis yers," Aisla stammered, staring at the dagger with a comical combination of longing and restraint. "I cannae possibly accept it."

"I want you to have it." She reached down for the second, matching dirk. "And I'll keep its twin. That way we will always know the other is safe."

Sorcha was unprepared when the girl flung her arms around her neck and nearly didn't get the blades out of the way in time. Though she had two older sisters, they had both married and left Maclaren by the time she'd been old enough to appreciate having female siblings. Embarrassed, Sorcha flushed with pleasure as Aisla pulled away to examine her new gift, holding it up to the light and marveling at the intricately etched designs in its jeweled hilt.

"I promise I will keep it clean and practice every day."

Sorcha smiled. "What we really need is a proper target like the ones down there." She indicated the thatched human-sized targets that some of the men were shooting at with bows, and started down the hill, only to stop when Aisla grabbed her arm.

"We cannae," she blurted out, fear clouding her expression. "'Tis no' allowed."

"What's not allowed?"

"Lasses on the training fields," she said. "'Tis too dangerous."

Sorcha's laughter drew the attention of several soldiers, but she didn't care. It was the most ridiculous thing she'd ever heard. Then again, such a rule did not surprise her from the way the laird treated his own wife and daughter, as if they were nothing but glass pawns to be moved and abused at his whim. She rolled her eyes and shook her head. From what she was seeing happening down on that field, the men could do with a proper lesson.

Excitement coursed through her veins at the thought of getting her hands on a sword, and Sorcha made up her mind. She winked at Aisla. "Come now, surely a wee hellion like you isn't afraid of the puny rules?"

Aisla stuck out her tongue and tucked her dagger into a loop at her waist. "I'm no' afraid to bend the rules, but I am afraid of my father's temper, ye ken?" Her mouth curved into a smile and then widened with unrestrained glee. "Though he left early to visit the southern holdings and is no' due to be back until sup."

"Once we're down there, you can try your hand at the bow as well," Sorcha told her. "I'll wager you'd be a natural." She hesitated, not wanting to invite ugly consequences upon the girl. "Are you certain? I don't wish to force you or cause trouble."

"Aye, Papa'll be mad as piss when he finds out, but by then 'twill be too late."

"You can blame me," Sorcha said with a laugh. "Insist that the Beast of Maclaren coerced you."

"Ye're no' a beast," she replied softly. "And 'twill be just as much my fault as it is yers. I'll face the consequences gladly for a lesson with a bow."

Sorcha was struck speechless by the girl's sense of fairness. She couldn't imagine how someone so innocent and mild-tempered could have been born from the seed of a man such as Rodric. She was lucky that she seemed to favor her mother, in temperament, at least.

As they turned down the path that led toward the fields, Sorcha eyed the lass skipping happily beside her. "Does your father often get angry?"

Aisla slowed her pace, her face conflicted. It was clear that she didn't want to speak ill about her father, but it was also clear from her fearful expression that he was a man of capricious temper. Sorcha suddenly felt sick to her stomach. "He doesn't strike *you*, does he?"

"Once or twice, though I deserved it," she said, ducking her head in shame.

Sorcha stopped so swiftly that Aisla nearly tripped over her own two feet. Rage coursed through her blood in hot violent sweeps that any man—a *father* no less—would beat upon his harmless, innocent daughter. She put her hands on Aisla's shoulders. "Ye dunnae ever deserve it, do ye hear me, Aisla Montgomery?"

The girl's eyes widened. "Yer brogue, 'tis back!"

"Only when I'm angry," she said with a grim smile.

"Dunnae fash, Lady Sorcha." Aisla shrugged with a battle-worn look that was far too old for her tender years. "'Tis only a lash or two. My brothers have faced worse at his hands."

"Are they like him?"

Knotting her fingers in the folds of her skirts, she shook her head. "Callan would no' hurt a fly. Papa used to tell him that he was as soft as a lass's arse, but 'twas Patrick who bore the brunt of it. One time, our father made him stand out in the fields during a storm because he was afraid of thunder. He was a wee five-year-old." She pursed her lips. "And that's no' even counting the whippings and the beatings. They were men, he used to say, they had to toughen up. Callan would weep, but Patrick would never shed a tear. That's why he seems so stoic. He kenned over the years to control his emotions. No' to cry, no' to laugh, no' to be afraid, no' to feel anything at all. 'Tis the safest way." She broke off as if she had said too much, her face coloring with a ruddy mixture of shame, sorrow, and vexation.

"Safest?" Sorcha prodded gently.

The bleakness in Aisla's expression made Sorcha mute. "In Montgomery, if ye care about anything, 'tis taken from ye. That's why Callan never gets to visit the holdings. 'Tis punishment, the laird's way of control." She shrugged again, this time she seemed beaten. "And 'tis the reason I will be betrothed to the Buchanan."

"I am sorry," Sorcha whispered.

Aisla pushed a bright, forced smile to her face and linked arms with her as they crossed the last stretch of ground. "Ye are lucky ye were able to marry for love. 'Tis clear how Mr. Pierce feels about ye every time he looks at ye."

"No, he doesn't..." she trailed off, unsure of what she was going to blurt out, and then said it anyway, "love me."

Aisla threw back her head and chortled. "Are ye daft? The man practically has sheep eyes every time ye open yer gob. To him, when ye walk into a room, the stars fall from the heavens and all the angels weep in yer wake."

With a bark of laughter, Sorcha chucked the cheeky girl

in the arm. "Your head is stuck in the clouds, lassie."

"Shouldn't a lass be allowed to dream? 'Tis the only place we are free, after all. Women are naught but chattel, pieces to be bartered for the sake of the clan. Love is no' and will never be part of that." She wagged a finger at her. "And dunnae think I do no' see your sheep eyes as well, mooning after him."

Sorcha was struck by her perspicacity, but saddened too that a girl of her age would be so cynical. Then again, having a father like Rodric would make a child age quickly. "*Och*, I am *not* moony. Now, come, let us show these lads what real women are made of."

All the men stopped what they were doing as they approached the training grounds. Some of them looked angry, others surprised. Others were slack-jawed, their eyes instantly drawn to her defining scars. Sorcha strode up to the man who appeared to be in charge—a brawny soldier with a shock of tangled brown hair that looked like it hadn't been brushed in weeks.

"I require a sword," she told him in a tone that communicated it was not a request.

His mouth fell open and he laughed. "Lassie, if 'tis a sword ye require, I can most certainly indulge ye. Though the sport I had in mind…'tis of a more pleasurable nature, ye ken?"

Sorcha rolled her eyes, well accustomed to bawdy talk from Maclaren soldiers. Aisla was not, from her wide-eyed expression. "Curb your tongue in front of your lady," Sorcha berated him. "And I'll tell you what, give me a sword. We'll spar, and if you win, we'll leave. If I win, you'll allow us to try our hand at the bows and arrows."

The man frowned as his gaze flicked to Aisla. "The laird willnae like it."

"We won't say a word." Sorcha arched an eyebrow. "Or is

it that you're afraid to be bested by a woman?"

He laughed again, but it had a nervous edge to it. Her scars weren't the only part of her reputation that preceded her. Her skill would have, too. But she wasn't worried that he would refuse, not with his pride on display before all his men. She almost felt sorry for him.

"Someone give the Beast a sword," he growled.

Aisla sidled toward her. "Sorcha, are ye certain this is wise? He's twice yer size, and he's one of the laird's strongest men."

"But I am the infamous Beast of Maclaren," she said with a grin, palming the sword and relishing the weight of it in her callused palms. "Now pay attention."

Diah, she'd missed the feeling of being in a fight. Her blood pulsed hot as she took up position, her sword held high. Her foe stared blankly at the hefted sword before he came slashing forward with a sideways thrust. Sorcha danced out of the way, swinging her sword backward to slap flat-ended on his rump. A spattering of laughter burst through the gathering crowd. She could have cut him, but this wasn't a *real* fight.

Shouting, he rushed her again, only to have the satisfying sound of steel meeting steel echo through the air. Sorcha parried again on the downswing, sparks flying from the force of her strikes. She whirled out of the way of a forward lunge and spun back to deliver an attacking lunge of her own. The tip of the sword cut through leather and wool, scraping along the breastplate her opponent wore.

Sorcha could have continued thrusting and parrying for hours, but they didn't have much time at the fields, and she wanted to show Aisla a thing or two with the bow. With two decisive steps, she caught the man behind the knees and took him to the ground. The point of her sword swiftly followed to rest at his throat.

To her surprise, the crowd broke out into cheers. Pulling the sword away, she reached out her arm to the man, and was surprised once more when he took it to haul himself upright.

"Ye fought well," he said with a grudging half bow. "I suppose the rumors of ye prowess are true." He smiled, and the dimpled effect on his face was startling. "As it turns out, ye also wield yer sword better than I do."

Was that an *apology*? Sorcha's mouth almost fell open in shock. It did fall open when he turned and bowed in Aisla's direction. "My Lady Aisla, apologies fer my careless words before."

"Of course, Geordie."

And suddenly, they were swarmed by the men who wanted to know more about her skills and how the warriors trained at Maclaren. She answered them one after the other and was made to blush when one of the men—a handsome black-haired Scot with the bluest eyes she'd ever seen—remarked that he'd heard she was hideous when she was nothing of the sort. His overt flirtation and blatant interest made her laugh.

"Back off, Fergus, ye clot-heid," Aisla said, shoving him in the shoulder. "She's married."

"*Och*, more's the pity!"

No one but her brothers—and more recently Brandt—had ever complimented Sorcha before. Though she basked in the attention, there was only one man whose notice she craved…and that, sadly, was the man who held the title of husband. And he was set on dropping her off like a sack of potatoes to Brodie lands. She scowled. Perhaps she should be focusing on bonny Scots like Fergus who wanted to pay her compliments.

Handsome Montgomerys aside, she'd promised she would show Aisla how to shoot a bow. They marched over to the archery markers. Several of the men followed, including

Geordie and Fergus. She felt conspicuous as she grasped hold of a bow, testing its tautness and flexibility before drawing an arrow from the nearby quiver. She did not shoot, but handed the bow to Aisla who gaped at her. "This should do."

"Now?" she squeaked.

"No better time than the present." She showed her how to hold the bow and set the arrow, and Aisla mimicked her motions. "Keep your left arm straight and set your sights down the length of the arrow. Now carefully, draw your right arm back until the feathers touch your cheek." She nodded as Aisla did as she was told. "Good, notch the space between your thumb and forefinger under your chin. Release when you're ready. Aim for the first bundle."

Where they stood, there were three bundles tied to stakes in the ground at varying intervals. The first was the closest and would be the least difficult. Sorcha stepped back just as Aisla let the arrow fly with a loud twang. It flew through the air and landed just to the left of the target.

"I missed," she said crestfallen.

"But not by much. Try again." This time she let Aisla do all the steps by herself. "Don't rush it. Time it with your breath. Inhale and release on the exhale."

The arrow lodged scant inches from the target's center, and Aisla looked as pleased as could be. She shot a few more arrows, each of them hitting the bundle at various points before she turned toward Sorcha. "Now, 'tis your turn."

Aisla's command was supported by shouts and whistles, the loudest of which was from Fergus. Sorcha blushed and took the proffered bow. She reached for an arrow, running the stiff fletching through her fingers. As she prepped the bow, the hairs on the back of her neck rose. Somehow, she knew Brandt was watching. She could *feel* the familiar rolling press of his stare. Glancing over her shoulder, she scanned the crowd of soldiers but did not see him. The feeling did not abate. Perhaps he stood at a window at the keep, though it would be hard to see from this distance.

Exhaling, she raised the bow and nocked the arrow. Brandt had seen her skill on the battlefield. She did not need to impress him, though she wanted to more than anything. Aiming the arrow, she released it.

"Ye missed!" Aisla shouted.

"Look again." Sorcha grinned and pointed to the very last thatched bundle, well over a hundred yards away. The arrow was lodged at its dead center.

"'Twas chance," someone called out.

Sorcha raised an eyebrow and lifted the bow again, more confident now. She let the arrow fly, and it knocked the first arrow clean out of the target. The sensation of being watched deepened. She didn't know how it was possible, but she could feel Brandt's pride from wherever he was. It caressed the back of her neck with the lightest of touches.

"What if the target's moving?" Fergus asked, his blue eyes bright with admiration as he slung an arm over her shoulder.

"All the better," she replied, stepping out of the semicircle of Fergus's arm, and swung the quiver to her back. Geordie tossed a small burlap sack into the air as hard as he could. Sorcha grabbed an arrow, following its flight and speed with her eyes before releasing. The arrow smacked into the bag in midair. Loud whoops filled the grounds as Fergus flung another upward to soar into the sky. She took it down with the same effortless ease, and the cheering grew.

Suddenly, loud controlled clapping interrupted the fracas. It was not frenzied with delight. No, this was cold and purposeful. Every head turned to see the scowling laird atop a giant horse with his unsmiling son at his side. A few other mounted soldiers stood in grim silence a few feet away. Most of the men scattered like leaves in a windstorm. Sorcha noticed Patrick's gaze flick to Aisla, concern glimmering for a brief moment, before his features took on the look of stone once more.

"What have we here?" Rodric thundered. Sorcha could feel Aisla quail beside her, and she bristled.

"A bit of sport, Your Grace," Sorcha said, releasing the bow and quiver from her grip. "Nothing more. Lady Aisla agreed to accompany me so I would not get lost."

"Perhaps ye should have remained in the keep where ye belong."

She frowned at his acidic, patronizing tone, but managed to keep her own civil. "At Maclaren, the women train with the men. And it's not unusual for ladies to take the air on occasion."

Rodric's gaze went pointedly to her scars. "And look at where that got ye. Taking the air, and ye got yer face torn off for it." A gruesome smile stretched his lips. "Who kens what kind of predator ye can find out here, aye? Ye'll want to be careful, Lady Pierce, or ye'll again find yerself as prey." The insidious hint of threat left Sorcha cold as his reptilian stare moved to his daughter. "Get ye behind Patrick up to the keep. Yer disobedience will warrant the strap, ye ken."

Sorcha's eyes widened at the open promise of punishment. She wanted to hold Aisla back as she moved to climb up behind Patrick. Her face was pale, though to her credit, she did not show any emotion.

Hell. This was *her* fault. But Sorcha held her tongue, knowing that any response would only make it worse for Aisla. Challenging the laird and his brutality in front of his clansmen would not be a wise course of action. She did not say a word until he wheeled his horse around and rode away.

Patrick did not follow immediately, but trotted his horse toward her. "Up to the keep, Lady Pierce. The laird is right, 'tis dangerous for ye."

Sorcha wasn't sure if it was a warning or a certainty.

"I'm so sorry," she said to Aisla.

"'Twill be all right," Aisla whispered. "Some of it is only bluster."

But not all of it, Sorcha knew. Aisla had confessed as much earlier. Foreboding settled upon her skin as though she'd walked into an unexpected web of spiders. Spiders that spun their sticky threads and waited for spoils. Shivering slightly, she rubbed her arms and began the long trek back to the keep.

Chapter Twenty

It wasn't until later that evening, once the sun had lowered behind the craggy hills that fortified Montgomery land, that Brandt returned to the keep and the room he shared with Sorcha. He'd spent the bulk of the day on foot, walking the undulating terrain around the fortress, visiting the stables for an unnecessarily lengthy visit with Ares and Lockie, and learning the layout of the rooms and corridors inside the keep itself. All in all, he'd made a day of avoiding both his mother and his wife.

Never before had he worked so hard not to think about women. How was it, he mused for the near hundredth time that day, that he had lived a quarter of a century without ever finding himself so frustrated and confused about the female set that he wanted to pull his hair out at the roots, when in less than a fortnight now he'd been subjected to the full spectrum of torture. Both mental and physical.

On the one hand, there was Lady Glenross. His mother. A woman who had never had a face in his imaginings before, and whom now he saw so clearly. All his life, she'd been a nameless person to hate, to be furious with. He'd been so certain that his mother was a cold, uncaring witch of a woman. How wrong he'd been.

Everything was changing now that he knew the truth; everything he thought he'd known had shattered, and ever since breaking his fast that morning, Brandt had been waiting for the pieces to settle into new order. With each step he took as he roamed the keep and lands, he was reminded that he wasn't just a stable master. He wasn't a bastard at all. Every inch of this gorgeous, intimidating land was rightfully *his*. And his mother wanted him to reclaim it.

On the other hand, he had Sorcha. His *wife*. His beautiful, intoxicating, blood-boiling wife. She had been the one who had consumed his mind most of the day. Brandt had left the great hall after his hushed conversation with the duchess, his mind reeling, his pulse unsteady. He'd needed air and distance from the unexpected burden of truth laid down at his feet. At the top of one knoll rolling down toward the training fields, he'd had a clear view of the Montgomery men training there—as well as two slim and skirted ladies. He should have known his mighty Athena would have finagled her way into the center of a training session among Scots warriors.

Brandt had quelled his initial alarm at seeing her among those men when they'd stood back to watch her instruct Aisla with a bow. The young girl was his half sister, he knew, but he hadn't been able to think about that. In that moment, he'd wanted only to watch his wife's strong, trim arms as she helped Aisla nock the arrow and aim. The curve of her neck as she cocked her head and waited patiently for one of her pupil's arrows to drive home.

And when she had taken up the bow herself, even with the distance between them, he'd imagined he could hear the sound of her breathing. He'd felt the steady and calm focus of her aim, as though he were right there at her side. The cheers and whistles the Montgomery men had rained down upon her when she'd proven her skill had given him the oddest burst of pride, too.

When the tall and burly dark-haired Scot had thrown his arm around Sorcha's shoulders, the burst of pride had become something else entirely. Brandt had clenched his fingers into balled fists, wanting only to charge down to the group of men and rip the Scot's arm from its socket. But that would have meant facing Sorcha, and she'd have no doubt seen his troubled expression. He hadn't been ready to speak about any of it yet, and besides…she'd looked so light and happy, showing off her skill. Had the flirtatious Scot tried it again, Brandt wagered Sorcha would have stuck him with her dirk.

Brandt had left then, listening to the cheers in the distance as his wife had done something else spectacular. *Easily done*, he thought to himself as he now entered their bedchamber. She *was* spectacular, and not just with a weapon in hand. As his eyes coasted over the chair in which he'd sat the night before, with Sorcha massaging his muscles so reverently before coming to kneel before him, Brandt thought of several more ways she'd surpassed his expectations.

"There you are," came her voice from the far corner of the room. He closed the door behind him and prepared himself. He had to tell her what he'd learned. And what he'd decided to do about it.

"I've been looking for you all afternoon," Sorcha said as she came out of the shadowy corner. Her arms were crossed over her chest, and she seemed to be holding herself tightly. Awareness prickled up his spine, and Brandt's eyes narrowed in on her.

"What's wrong?" he asked, every last thought and worry of his own fleeing.

Why had she been hiding in the corner?

"We must leave," she said, adding, "as soon as possible."

Brandt crossed the room in a few swift strides and took her by the shoulders. "Tell me what's happened. Are you hurt?"

God damn it all to Hades, what the hell had he been thinking, wandering around the fortress and grounds all day? He should have found her and made certain she was safe and still with Aisla. What kind of fool protector was he, to not keep an eye on his own charge? And here of all places, where Rodric ruled with an iron thumb.

"I'm not hurt, Brandt," she answered, shaking her head.

He'd been so obsessed with everything Lady Glenross had divulged that morning, so torn about whether to stay and stake his claim, or leave and deliver Sorcha to the Brodie as promised, that he hadn't even stopped to *think*.

"Was it that warrior?" he asked, the dark-haired man from the training fields leaping to the forefront of his mind as his grip tightened on her shoulders.

Sorcha frowned. "Which warrior?"

"He put his arm around you," Brandt answered, the hot sparks of a simmering frenzy igniting in his stomach. He'd find him. He'd thrash him to within an inch of his life. He'd break his bloody arms.

Her pinched expression smoothed out, and a smile touched her tense lips. "You *were* watching."

"I left too soon," he replied, grating out the words. "What did the bastard do?"

"Nothing," Sorcha answered, her smile now a full-fledged grin. She even laughed, the husky sound striking him right in the groin. "Not a thing."

Brandt loosened his grasp. "Then why are you so eager to leave?" He took a glance around the room, the deep purple and blue shadows of dusk having crept in. "And why are you hiding in here?"

It would be time to go to the great hall soon, and he'd thought he'd find her getting ready. Her smile faded. The confidence and fire he'd come to expect and admire in her had paled. "It's the duke, Rodric. I don't trust him, Brandt."

He peered at her, a new lance of guilt digging into his chest. "You saw him today."

Brandt had not. He'd been told the laird would be away until sup and had been glad to hear it. Sorcha nodded.

"I angered him by bringing Aisla to the training fields." Her lower lip quivered. "I fear he's punished her."

He released Sorcha's arms to avoid leaving accidental bruises; he wanted to throttle the duke, not her.

"And you," he asked, his voice barely audible. "Did he touch you?"

If he had, Rodric would suffer. On his life, Brandt would see the man dead before nightfall. Sorcha must have noticed the threat glowing in his eyes, too, because she swallowed hard and shook her head again. "No," she answered. "I don't believe he'll harm me that way. It's Malvern…what if Rodric has summoned him? There was something in his eyes today that made me nervous, Brandt. He looked all too pleased with himself."

Brandt nodded slowly as he turned toward the window overlooking the fields. He'd wondered himself if Rodric was allied with Malvern, but the notion that he might have been off summoning him instead of riding out to Montgomery farms had not crossed his mind.

"You're right to be wary of him. He's dangerous," he replied, and nearly laughed. It was an absurd understatement. "The man is a murderer."

Behind him, Sorcha drew in a sharp breath. "Do you speak of the late Duke of Glenross?"

Brandt crossed his arms and turned away from the window, his eyes coming to rest on the inky-haired beauty who had become his unerring compass. All day he'd spent wandering, alone, lost in his own mind. Not ten minutes here with her now, and Brandt felt grounded to the very floor. Rooted to wherever she happened to be standing. He wanted to tell her everything, and so he did.

He unleashed it all—everything Lady Glenross had revealed that morning. All the while, Sorcha stared up at him, her lips parted in awe, her expression shifting with every new confession.

"I should have found you earlier," he finally said, guilt wriggling back into place. "It was selfish of me to stay away, wrapped up in my own troubles."

Her eyes flashed with temper. "Selfish? Don't be an idiot."

She reached for him then, her arms no longer limp with shock at her sides. The reprimand, paired with the gentle grip of her hands curling around his wrists, made him laugh. But Sorcha wasn't in the least bit amused. Her stare remained unyielding.

"You are the true Montgomery laird," she whispered. "The rightful Duke of Glenross."

"Yes."

The expression of fear he'd seen her wearing as he'd come into the bedchamber slammed down into place again.

"*Mo Diah.*" She blinked back sudden tears. "You're going to challenge him."

"He murdered my father," Brandt said. "He would have killed me."

"He still could," she replied, her voice rising. "When he discovers who you are—"

"He already knows," Brandt cut in. "He must know."

And if that were the case, summoning Malvern would only help his situation. The marquess wanted Brandt dead, and so did Rodric. Men became allies when they had a common enemy...in this case, *him*.

"Then what are we waiting for?" Sorcha asked, turning around and rushing toward the bench at the foot of the bed. Their packs were there, their laundered clothes and all of their supplies and weapons. "They think we're heading west, not north. We'll wait until everyone's at sup, and then we'll take Lockie and Ares, and—"

"I'm not leaving, Sorcha."

She dropped the pack she'd just lifted and turned to stare at him in incredulity. "You can't, Brandt. Malvern wouldn't have fought you fair back in Selkirk, and neither will Rodric. Challenging him is unwise."

He went to her, the tension rolling off her in near palpable waves. She was afraid, and that was an emotion he hadn't seen grip her before. His brave, fierce warrior would never let a pathetic thing like fear unsettle her. He cupped her cheek, needing to touch her and calm her. All day, he'd felt upended and astray. But not anymore. Here, with her, he saw his path clearly.

"I'm wounded, wife. Do you think so little of my skill?" he asked, attempting to make her smile.

"Of course not, but I don't think you understand. If he opposes your claim, a challenge for lairdship is a challenge to the death," she said, her voice breaking over that last word. She rubbed her cheek into his palm, as if seeking the comfort he offered. She sighed. "I know you're strong. I know you can fight, but if you lose...if I lose you..."

She didn't finish her thought, and she didn't need to. The worry was written all over her.

"I understand what it would entail," he said, his thumb caressing her skin. "I can't run from this. I won't leave my mother and Aisla to suffer the brunt of Rodric's rule any longer."

They were already living in a prison; his mother's sacrifice so many years before to keep her infant son safe from harm had never fully come to an end. He had to see it through now. Rodric would never forgive her for what she'd done, and she'd pay the price in flesh.

Sorcha closed her eyes, and he could see she understood.

"And if Rodric has summoned Malvern, like you fear, it will be only a matter of time before he tracks us north, to Brodie lands. I will do anything in my power to keep you safe." Brandt's thumb grazed her lower lip. "To protect you."

Her eyes opened, and he was relieved to see a glimmer of her usual stubbornness. "If you die trying to protect me, I'll never forgive you, Brandt Pierce. Or Montgomery, or whatever your bloody name is." He wanted to laugh, but she wouldn't give him the chance. "You've already sacrificed too much for me. If it weren't for my stupidity back in Selkirk, Malvern wouldn't even know you existed. He certainly wouldn't be hunting you."

"We've already gone over this, Sorcha—"

"I should have left. I should have gone back to him and seen the marriage through." Her eyes dropped from his, and she stared into his chest. He could see her mind whirling, her thoughts forming in their deep blue depths. He knew exactly what she was thinking—that she could still appease Malvern, even now, if she returned to him.

"Don't," he gritted out. "Don't even think it, Sorcha. I would only come after you."

And he would.

He'd ride through hell and fight until his last breath before he let her surrender to the bastard. He brought his other hand up and cradled her cheeks, his fingers pressing firmly into her skin. "You will never be his."

Chapter Twenty-One

The second those damning words left Brandt's lips, another deluge arrived, begging to be released. Words he hadn't wanted to think, let alone say. But just as everything he'd believed about his birth mother had been turned over and reordered, so had everything he'd believed about himself and what he wanted.

Brandt had thought he'd wanted his peaceful, orderly life at Worthington Abbey, and the solitude and freedom that came with being a lifelong bachelor. He'd been so damn convinced that he'd be able to leave Sorcha with her sister, say good-bye, and be on his merry way home.

How had he not seen his world crashing in on itself?

"You are mine," he whispered, his breath coming in staccato bursts. His body pulsed as she touched him, the hesitant press of her hands as she skimmed them up his forearms feeling more like a pair of anchors in rough waters. Her eyes were guarded, and she had every right to be. He'd been a boar. "Tonight, right now, you are *my* wife."

"You do not want a wife," she said, her nails scouring

along his skin and stirring up an agonizing heat within him.

"I've changed my mind."

She turned her lips into his palm and kissed him. "Then don't push me away, Brandt."

He couldn't have stopped touching her if the horns blew and bells tolled, signaling an attack on the keep. Brandt angled her chin and kissed her, the brush of his lips gentle but earnest, and when Sorcha answered it, parting her mouth and dragging the tip of her tongue over his lower lip, Brandt let go.

His tongue clashed with hers, twisting and stroking as their kiss evolved into a battle of possession. She pushed against him, her breasts coming flush against his chest and her hands winding into his hair with frenzied tugs. Brandt was the first to relent. He stumbled back a few paces, his wife's trim body surprisingly powerful. Or perhaps she only weakened his resolve. He couldn't resist her, not when she looked at him as though he was her axis or when she kissed him as though someone might yank him from her at any moment. All Brandt wanted to do right then was please her, comfort her, give her every damned thing she'd ever wanted—and what she wanted was him. The thought alone sent a torrent of lust through him.

Brandt filled his palms with her tight curves, starting with her hips and rounding down over both firm buttocks. "God, you feel perfect," he groaned, his lips trailing along the slope of her neck, tasting the salt on her skin. With an instinctive thrust, Sorcha rolled her hips forward, grinding against his burgeoning arousal. He sucked in a breath, the aggressive advance of her body against his doing nothing to quell his desire for her. If anything, it made him even harder, and ready to give her exactly what she wanted.

He laughed into her mouth, their tongues gliding together and apart then joining again. He'd be a damned liar if he tried telling himself this was only for her. Never had he felt so unhinged for a woman. Never had he wanted someone with such blinding desperation.

"Did you just...laugh?" she asked, her voice breathy. Distracted.

Brandt nibbled down her throat and into the hollow of her neck, his fingers climbing up to knead her heavy breasts. He pressed his thumbs over the peak of each one, straining even through her chemise and bodice, and heard her gasp.

"Purely maniacal," he replied, rubbing hard, insistent circles over her nipples. Sorcha threw back her head and arched her back, seeking more pressure. "I'm crazy to have fought this for so long."

She made a murmuring sound of agreement, slivered through with a moan. With a grunt, he hooked his fingers under each shoulder of her bodice and tugged.

Her hands covered his, stalling him. "No, Brandt, wait."

"What is it, love?"

She hesitated for a beat, as if unsure of what to say. "Leave it be."

He recalled her reticence at the river and her insistence on remaining in her shift. Was she self-conscious of her body? Her innocence made him smile. He feathered gentle kisses along her collarbone. "I want to see you."

She huffed a tiny breath. "No, you don't."

Brandt blinked, his eyes focusing on her tremulous blue ones. Fear and self-disgust warred in them, hinting at secrets. "Tell me."

"The scars there," she whispered, unable to hold his gaze. "They're worse than the others." She swallowed hard. "Far worse. I'm afraid you'll be...revolted."

"You are more beautiful than any woman I've ever seen, Sorcha. Scars or no scars. Trust me when I say that whatever lies beneath this gown will make little difference. I would desire you if you had the body of a potato."

Laughter glimmered in her eyes, and after a moment, her hands fell away.

Sorcha closed her eyes, her breathing becoming shallow when Brandt dragged down her bodice and her stays to expose her to his view. His heart climbed into his throat, though he wasn't revolted. Far from it. The fullness of her breasts, tipped by dusky, petal-smooth nipples rushed into his hands. But they weren't equal in appearance. A ragged patchwork of glistening scar tissue traversed the flesh from her shoulder across the entirety of her left breast and across her upper ribs. Shiny pink gouges marred the creamy skin, puckering the flesh in uneven lumps. The wolf had not let her escape unscathed. In fact, the scars on her face were the best of it.

His heart bled. "Oh God, love, what you must have suffered."

"Don't feel sorry for me," she whispered, unwilling to look at him. "Just kiss me, Brandt."

"Sorcha," he said softly as he brushed his thumb along the point of her chin.

She took a shaky breath before lifting her eyes to his. The vulnerability in them speared him. He'd never seen her so uncertain. No words, however reassuring, would be enough. Brandt leaned forward, his lips trailing down the column of her throat before kissing each breast reverently. The salt of her skin was as heady as the finest whiskey. His fingers cupped her mangled flesh, his thumb gently stroking the misshapen welts, before he laid his tongue to each one. She arched into his caresses, seeking more, and he gave it.

"Does this hurt?" he asked, squeezing gently.

Her eyes flicked open. "No…not physically."

Brandt stalled. She meant in other ways. While she distinctly held the scars on her face as a marker of strength, these she viewed as a deficiency. A blemish against her femininity. No wonder she'd sought to remain clothed. Her next words confirmed his thoughts as she turned her face away. "They're hideous."

"Someone has told you this before," he said, understanding striking him like a blow to his midsection.

She closed her eyes, her dark lashes a shroud against what he presumed to be a painful memory. "Just a few boys, when I was younger and didn't know to bathe with my drapes drawn shut."

He wanted to throttle them, these nameless, faceless peeping toms. Though she sounded blithe, Brant sensed effort behind it. "Who were they?"

"Boys from a neighboring clan. I fancied one of them. Or at least I thought I did."

And he'd broken her heart, her spirit, with whatever thoughtless comment he'd made. Brandt wouldn't ask her to repeat it. No, he needed to pull her away from it.

"The sun must have addled your brain today, Your Grace, if you worry I am anything at all like those spying gits."

Her startled stare caught his. "Your Grace?"

"Aye, *my* duchess."

His hot, possessive gaze swept her, his body stirring at her lush, fierce beauty. The terrible scars did little to detract from the svelte perfection of her long limbs, her flat, muscled stomach, and the sweetness he knew lay between her thighs. Instead, they branded her as a fighter. A woman of fury and strength and passion. Brandt was mad for her. *All* of her. He kissed her again deeply, and then met the blazing, sapphire gaze that had captured him from the first.

"Sorcha, you are perfect. Every part of you. Every scar." He kissed her ravaged cheek. "Every freckle." He kissed her nose. "Every lovely unique thing that makes you *you*." He nuzzled the space between her breasts, his hands and tongue finding the taut silk of her nipples once more. "And especially these. You taste like ripe, succulent berries."

She arched against him, her breathing quickening. "You're certain they don't repel you?"

Brandt grinned and directed her palm to the bulging fall of his breeches. "Does it seem like I'm repelled in the least?" He groaned when her fingers closed around him and he gathered her into his arms. "God, I can't believe I waited this long."

"You could have taken me on the river rock," she whispered, her fingers rising to pluck at the hem of his shirt and, mimicking him, scraped her fingers over his nipples. The sensation, paired with her heady, bold talk, awoke the basest of desires inside of him. His erection pulsed and hardened.

"I could have taken you on our wedding night," he rasped, joining in as he continued pushing the top of her dress down farther, the chemise caught in the quickly disappearing fabric. "Tell me the truth, my sweet. You would have given yourself to me, even then, wouldn't you?"

He lowered himself, his tongue and teeth and lips exulting over the newly bared skin. He snagged the waist of her drawers on the way down, and knowing neither of them wanted to move slowly or with caution, took those down as well. His tongue circled Sorcha's navel as he bent onto one knee.

"Tell me," he insisted, wanting to hear his warrior wife's bold words. Needing them. He lifted her foot and set it on his thigh, opening the most private part of her to him. He touched her silky thatch of curls and ran one finger along her heat. "Say it, Sorcha. Tell me what you would have let me do to you."

Her eyes were hazy with want, her cheeks and breasts flush with her longing for him. Paralyzed with desire, she moved her lips wordlessly. Brandt pushed his finger into her wet heat and she moaned, tightening her thighs to grip his hand. But she let out a disappointed cry when he retreated.

"Tell me," he repeated.

"I...I would have let you fill me," she said, her voice weak but clear. "I would have let you touch every part of me, kiss every part, take every part that was yours to take. God, Brandt, your tongue is wicked."

Fill her. That was what he wanted, to pour himself into every part of her body. To breathe with her, feel with her. Make her his. This woman, a stranger less than a fortnight ago, now called him to her with a voice he recognized deep in his heart and soul.

"It is yours." He set his mouth to her, sliding his tongue where she desired it most.

"Brandt!" She gasped and clutched his hair in two fists as he licked and sucked at her dewy flesh. She tasted just as she had before, like a blazing Highland summer sunset, hot and sweet. He clung to her, devouring her with long, needful strokes.

"And I am yours," he heard her say as the blood rushed through his ears, swirled down into his acute arousal, and made him dizzy with need. "I am yours."

...

Sorcha's head fell back on the bed as her limbs turned boneless beneath his hands. Brandt had taken her down this road to pleasure before, but something was different. It wasn't in the way he touched her or the feel of his mouth on her skin. It wasn't in his words, though something had changed... something profound and unqualifiable. It'd been in the tender way he'd kissed her ugly, lacerated flesh, loving her as if she were perfect and unscarred. She'd never imagined willingly baring herself to anyone...but with Brandt, she'd done what she had feared most. She'd trusted him with all of her. The *worst* of her.

He hadn't told her he loved her, but he had said she was his and that she was his wife. The change she saw was in his eyes, in the way he looked at her, as he was now from the juncture of her thighs while his mouth did indecent things. His hands cupped her buttocks, lifting her hips as his lips continued their tender onslaught. Their eyes met and held, and what she saw swirling in their hazel depths made Sorcha's body come apart with the force of a shooting star. Possession. Dominion. *Surrender.*

Pleasure broke through her veins in igneous waves, cresting and swelling, until her entire body felt limp. And still Brandt didn't stop, prolonging the bliss with each decadently punishing stroke of his tongue. The shattering pulses wound through her, making her body arch like a bow even while it felt like her bones had turned into strings of gossamer.

"Brandt," she called out weakly, and only then did he relent.

Her husband inched up her sweat-dampened body, kissing her stomach and each rib, nipping gently at her breasts. She focused on him, on his handsome face, and those glittering eyes that seemed more golden than green. Sorcha never put much faith in Scottish fairy tales, but right now, she would swear that he was indeed part summer fey.

"How did I ever find you?" she whispered.

"With a kiss," he murmured, taking the peak of one breast into his mouth and drawing on it gently. Flickers of sensation spread from the flesh caught in his mouth to her still-trembling core. "With your courage," he said, switching to the other breast. "With your fierce heart."

He turned his head sweetly, as if to listen to the heartbeat that pulsed erratically beneath his ear. Sorcha wound her fingers into Brandt's soft hair, the tenderness of his words wreaking more havoc than his touch. But his words faded as he resumed his efforts, busying himself with teasing her breasts to hard, aching points.

Sorcha took in a breath as she felt the thickened girth of him on her thigh. She was ready. She wanted to take him into her...for him to fill the emptiness inside. Lifting her feet, she ran them along the backs of his and reached down, her hand closing gently around him. He groaned at her touch, his teeth closing over one nipple with more pressure.

"Brandt," she said. "I need you."

He moved higher, to take her lips in a soft sweet kiss, and then surprised her by detaching her slack grip and rising up, onto his knees. "First, I plan to explore every velvet inch of this property of mine."

"Property?" She gaped at the beautifully erect sight of him but wasn't allowed to fully appreciate it, for in the next second, her husband gripped her hips and flipped her onto her stomach.

"Yes." He leaned over and bit her gently on the shoulder. "You belong to me."

"As you belong to me," she breathed, her voice partially muffled by the sheets.

"Yes." It was the only word he said before she felt the hot surfaces of his palms run the length of her back to the indent of her waist, to her buttocks, kneading gently there before resuming their slow return journey. "God, woman, you are exquisitely formed." His voice sounded thick, as though he were having difficulty breathing.

Her voice pulled low with what remained of her concern. "Even with my scars?"

"Especially them. My brave Highland lass." His fingers traced the filigree of welts that curved around her ribs down to the rise of her buttocks, making her shiver. She'd never known that the bloody things were so sensitive, but when

Brandt's mouth replaced his fingers, she almost fell apart in his hands. She made to turn so that she could pleasure him as well, but he held her firmly in place. "No, I want you to enjoy it."

Her wicked lover proceeded to do as he'd promised—exploring every single inch of undiscovered territory with his hands and lips, mapping each and every contour of her. By the time he turned her over, Sorcha was a whimpering mess of aroused frustration. Her entire body tingled and ached with need.

"Brandt, please," she begged, and he acquiesced, settling himself between her parted legs. His face was strained, too, as if his explorations had cost him more than he'd expected. She'd hoped to entice him with a little more grace, but she wanted him with a desire that could not be contained. She clutched wildly at his shoulders. When he positioned himself at the apex of her thighs, Sorcha almost wept aloud at the head of his erection nudging the swollen, wet folds of her entrance. "*Mo gràidh*," she gasped.

Brandt's forearms were corded with muscle as he held himself above her, his hips making small tantalizing circles against her, pressing in more deeply each time. Sorcha tilted her hips upward in a desperate attempt to take in more of him, but Brandt's control was absolute.

"Sorcha," he commanded hoarsely. "Look at me."

She did, and when her eyes connected with his, he pushed into her. She gasped and dug her fingers into the unyielding muscles of his back. They were hard like the rest of him. Like the rock-hard length anchoring her body to his. Sorcha had taken him into her mouth. She knew his size, but still, nothing had prepared her for the breath-stealing thickness of him as he filled her. Completely. Fully.

Struggling to accommodate him, she shifted, feeling her passage adjusting to his girth, and gasped as white-hot sensations streaked through her core.

"Are you in any pain?" he whispered, his voice wrenched tight. "I can stop."

Sorcha blinked, her useless brain catching up to the question. It didn't hurt...not like a blade strike or a tumble off a horse. It felt uncomfortable, more like an odd pressure than any real pain. She shook her head and shifted again, rocking her pelvis into his. More pleasure spiked through her. That felt better, she decided. She wanted more of that. "No, it doesn't hurt, and no...I don't want you to stop. What comes next?"

He chuckled. "My sweet lass, everything comes next."

And then Brandt started to move, retreating almost all the way. Her eyes widened as he slid out of her. The sense of loss was tangible, until he moved forward to fill her again, and ripples of pleasure at the lubricious friction began to gather and build. He watched her carefully, and when he slid his hands down between their bodies to caress the sensitive bud of flesh nestled in her curls, she moaned her approval.

No longer passive, Sorcha felt her body begin to respond to her husband's long, penetrating strokes and his nimble fingers. Again and again he withdrew and filled her, his pace quickening and her own desire mounting. His back felt slick underneath her palms as she arched upward to meet every thrust. Sorcha could see his passion building, too, in the tight clench of his jaw and the dilation of his beautiful eyes, and she was so busy studying him that her release took her by surprise.

Mind-numbing, overwhelming surprise.

"*Oh*," she cried, her legs tightening around his hips as pulse after pulse of pleasure swept through her. Giving in to the drugging bliss that saturated her senses, her inner muscles clenched around him, holding him tight in the warm clasp of her spasming flesh.

"Oh God, Sorcha, you feel so good. I can't..." He was hanging on to his control by a thread.

"Let go, Brandt," she said, touching his cheek. "I won't break."

His voice was a growl. "I don't want to hurt you."

"You'll never hurt me."

Desperately, Brandt pounded into her, intensifying the waves of pleasure cresting within her, until his entire body seized. With a harsh cry, Brandt joined her in bliss, groaning his own release. Neither of them moved for several minutes, their breathing harsh in the silence. He rolled them onto their sides, his body still intimately joined to hers, and cradled her close.

She smiled shyly. "So that's consummation."

"Yes."

"It's not what I expected," she blurted out with a blush.

Brandt's brows drew together slightly as he lifted a damp curl out of her face. "Was it not pleasing?"

"You most certainly pleased me, husband." Sorcha drew a breath, feeling her cheeks heat more, and decided to blurt it out. "It's just that, well, I saw a stallion and a mare...er... consummating at Maclaren once, and well, I guess I expected when you turned me onto my stomach that it would be so..." she trailed off miserably, her face on fire. "Don't you dare laugh," she warned, seeing her husband's twitching lips and the humor twinkling in his eyes.

He bit his lips. "I'm not laughing, I swear."

"You must think me a goose."

"I think you're adorable."

"Adorable is for puppies," she grumbled. "I'm the feared Beast of Maclaren. Trumpets blare and knees quake at my approach."

Brandt drew her close and kissed her nose and then her lips. "Fierce, then. Glorious. Magnificent."

"I do like those."

Laughing, she rewarded him with a kiss, and it didn't take long for their chaste kissing to turn into something else completely. With a shock, Sorcha felt the part of him that was still inside her surge to life, and she met his amused gaze. "Is that normal?" she asked.

"For some men, yes." He nipped at her jaw. "And I'll tell you a secret, my innocent little wife. A man and a woman can…come together the way you saw with those horses as well, though it's not typical for a lass's first time."

Assailed by a barrage of wanton, thoroughly lewd thoughts at such an animalistic coupling, Sorcha blushed as she felt him move within her again, growing and lengthening with every breath. She wondered whether he was thinking of those very same things. Meeting Brandt's eyes, every inch of her warmed at the blatant desire she saw burning in their depths. Apparently, he was.

And as it turned out, the desire was very, *very* mutual.

Her husband liked it when she told him what she wanted, so screwing up her courage, she licked her lips and ran her hand boldly over his tight, bare arse. "Will you show me?"

He gave her a lusty smile. "That will be my pleasure, my lady."

Chapter Twenty-Two

The woman lying beside Brandt snored gently in her sleep. He smiled. She would be mortified and would likely argue that she'd never, not once, snored, but he quite liked the contented little sounds. They were the breaths of someone who was caught in the cradle of a deep, satisfying slumber. And the new Lady Glenross had indeed been satisfied. He'd made sure of it. She slept on her stomach, one arm flung above her head, the other draped loosely over his hip as the morning rays from the rising sun crept over the windowsills.

Glossy curls of thick ebony hair were strewn across the lithe expanse of her back, of which he had kissed every delectable inch. Including the many scars that traversed it in a heartbreaking tapestry. There was no part of her body that he did not now intimately know…the silken skin of her nipples, her lean strong legs, her sweet pliant thighs.

Unsurprisingly, Brandt felt himself growing stiff. If it were up to him, he would keep his wanton wife in bed all day. Last night had been eye-opening in more ways than one. Not only did her lustful passions match his, but Brandt had come to the slow realization that she was his match in every other way as well.

Hell, he didn't know if what he felt was love, but he did know that the thought of being without her left a gaping darkness inside him. Perhaps that was how love felt—like light in a darkened room or that first sliver of sunrise chasing away shadows. Love or not, there was no way he was turning her over to the Brodies. No, Lady Sorcha Montgomery belonged to him. As did this keep and the entire clan. She was a Montgomery now—the wife of a duke, not the wife of a stable master. And Brandt wanted to keep it that way.

He shifted, gently disentangling himself from her sleepy embrace, hoping not to disturb her. But warm fingers drifted over his bare hip bone. His glance slid to meet an awake and curious blue gaze. "Do you always think so heavily when you awaken?" she asked, her voice still husky with sleep. "You have grooves just here." She drew the pad of a fingertip between his brows.

"Were you watching me?" he asked with a smile.

She blushed, her finger inching down his nose to press against his lips. "It's my second favorite thing to do."

"Oh?" He drew the tip of her finger into his mouth and sucked gently. "And what's the first, Lady Glenross?"

Her blue eyes instantly darkened with desire and then widened. "I don't think I'll ever get used to that name. In my heart, I'll always be Lady Pierce. That's who you were when we first met." Brandt bit gently, and her eyes flared in response, her words going breathy. "And now you're a duke, or you will be."

He released her finger from its wet prison. "And you'll be a duchess."

"It never mattered to me, you know," she said. "Who you were. You're everything that I hoped for when I prayed for someone to save me from Malvern."

"*Prayed* for someone?" he teased. "As I recall, my lady, you had a solution well in hand."

The light fled her eyes. "You speak of my trickery."

Brandt lifted her by the arms and draped her body over him. "I speak of your kiss," he whispered, pulling her head down to his, "and the way your sweet little tongue did this." Smiling, he darted his own into her mouth and kissed her soundly. It didn't take much coaxing for her to respond, and by the time their mouths parted, she was straddling his thick erection, her sapphire eyes glazed with desire.

"Are you not too sore?"

Sorcha blushed. "A little, but not enough to...want to stop."

"You are insatiable." He laughed and took her lips again, filling his palms with her breasts and kneading gently.

She wasn't the only one. He, too, couldn't seem to get enough of her. Just when he thought he was satiated, his body rose anew, clamoring for more. Brandt had made love to her twice more over the course of the night, though gently. But now she took charge, undulating her hips in a way that made him blind with lust, and when she finally slid down onto him, he almost lost himself then and there. His devilish wife set a maddeningly slow pace, as if relishing the friction and every voluptuous thrust. She watched him with those intent eyes, already understanding what pleased him and what drove him to distraction. And when their movements grew more frantic and they joined in blissful release, Brandt could only clutch her close, words escaping him yet again.

Words that he should have told her...words he *should* tell her.

But Brandt remained silent, holding her close and letting his body say what his mouth could not.

An hour more passed before they were ready to rise, wash, and dress. Brandt did not want to miss Rodric at breakfast. There were things that had to be said, and truths that had to come to light. It would not come as a surprise if the duke already suspected the truth himself, what with Brandt's uncanny resemblance to his late brother and the fact that he had his wife's eyes. But Brandt knew that Rodric was not a man to be underestimated. He'd been laird for as long as Brandt had been alive and was indubitably cunning.

Sorcha slipped her fingers into his as they walked from their chamber to descend the stone staircase to the breakfasting hall below. It felt good to have her at his side—to know he could depend on her strength and her counsel. He'd told her what he'd planned to do in the wee hours of the morning, after their bodies had been satiated to the point of exhaustion. They'd lain spent in each other's arms, unable to stop touching as they'd spoken about the future.

"You won't be going to the Brodie," he'd told her.

Her heart had been in her eyes. "I won't?"

"No," he said. "And I'm going to challenge Rodric as the rightful heir."

"Is this truly what you want?" she'd asked.

He'd thought it over for a long moment, there in the quiet of the dawn hours with his wife curled against him. Other choices were still open to him—he could go back to Essex to his old life. He would not give Sorcha up, so she would have to return there with him. Archer's influence would protect her from Malvern should he follow. But what kind of life would it be? Brandt was wealthy, and she would want for nothing, but she would still be the wife of a mere stable master and horse breeder.

He was the son of a duke. She was the daughter of one. Sorcha deserved the life she was meant for, and he wanted to give that to her. He wanted to give her *everything*.

"Yes," he'd replied finally. "I want you. And I also want Montgomery."

"Brandt, I would be happy in Essex."

"I know," he'd said and kissed the protest from her lips. "But you belong in Scotland. And so do I."

Now as they stood on the threshold, she squeezed his hand. He kept their palms joined as they made their way to the table. Rodric was there with his family, though today two of his men stood at his back. The big, older one, Feagan, and his lackey, Seamus. Rodric's stare speared Brandt and then fell to their linked hands.

Brandt saw the way his eyes narrowed and turned calculating. The man missed nothing. Patrick lifted his eyes from his plate, but offered no greeting. Callan and Aisla smiled thinly before dropping their own gazes as if to avoid the censure of their father. Brandt glanced to his mother, but did not linger. She seemed drawn, her hands fisted together in her lap. For a moment, Brandt wondered at the conversation before he and Sorcha had arrived. Everyone seemed unnaturally tense.

"A word, laird," Brandt said. "In private?"

Rodric waved a patient hand. "Whatever ye need to say can be said here."

"In front of your men?" he asked. "This is a family matter."

The glare Rodric leveled upon him would have made a lesser man quail. Brandt did not. Bullies did not scare him, especially bullies who were cowards at heart and murdered innocent men for their own gain. The duke's mouth pulled wide in a smile. "Speak then, for they are no' family and neither are ye."

The opening was there. Brandt took it. "Actually, as it turns out, I *am* family. I am your nephew." It grew so quiet in the hall that the sounds of the sparrows chirping in the field were clearly audible. "I'm the son of the man you claim fell to his death so many years ago. The man you called brother."

Rodric's face did not change. In fact, no emotion crossed it whatsoever, which made Brandt suddenly uneasy at the duke's complete lack of empathy. "Go on. Surely ye have a point with yer blabbering of ancient history."

The pain that slashed across his mother's face nearly undid him. His mouth hardened. "Regardless of whether it's ancient history as you say, I am still the son of Robert Montgomery, and I challenge your claim as the rightful Duke of Glenross and laird of Clan Montgomery."

The resulting noise was deafening. Patrick shoved his chair so hard that it smashed to the floor behind him. Aisla clapped her hands to her mouth with a small shriek, and Callan had started laughing. Whether it was from amusement or delirium, Brandt did not know. He felt Sorcha sidle closer. The only two people who hadn't moved were his mother and the laird. The men at his side had drawn their weapons, their faces scowling.

"What the hell is the meaning of this?" Patrick roared. "Ye are no' a Montgomery! Aye, ye have the look of my uncle, but that doesnae give ye the right to come forward with any claim."

"Easy, lad," Rodric soothed and spread his thick arms across the width of the table. "'Tis no' the first time false heirs seeking a fortune have made themselves known. A man must have proof, ye ken." He eyed Brandt. "Have ye any proof of yer extravagant claims?" Rodric's stare was lazy and confident. He did not expect to be contested.

Brandt nodded and reached for his wife's hand. He brought it to his lips and kissed her knuckles, before removing the ring on her finger. She didn't say a word, but her eyes communicated everything he needed to know...her support. Her trust. He took both, gladly.

"I have this. A Montgomery ring, and—"

"Ye could have bought that at any county fair," Patrick

interrupted. "Or stolen it from someone in the keep. It means nothing."

Brandt continued as if his half brother hadn't spoken or accused him of thievery. "And I have my mother."

Patrick scowled, not understanding. "Yer mother? What sort of deception is this? *Who* is yer mother?"

But the laird understood. His furious gaze, promising all sorts of dire punishments, swung toward his wife as she rose from her seat in a slow motion. Not a soul in the hall moved as Lady Glenross lifted her chin regally. They hushed, waiting to hear what she had to say.

"*I* am," she said in a clear, proud voice. "This man was born Brandall Cailean Montgomery five and twenty years ago, and is the only son of Robert Cameron Montgomery, the late Duke of Glenross." Her plaintive gaze swung to her slack-jawed children, but stayed with Patrick, who looked like he'd eaten a toad. "He's yer brother."

The duke's hand snaked across the table like a serpent about to strike. Brandt swung his fist down so hard to intercept it that dishes clattered to the floor.

"Don't. Touch. Her."

Each word was snapped with barely leashed violence. It was all he could do not to slit the man's throat and bathe the stone floors in his traitorous blood. But the light touch of Sorcha's fingers on the small of his back held him in place. Out of the corner of his eye, he saw Callan usher Aisla from the hall after an urgent glance from their mother.

Rodric stormed to his feet, snarling. "Ye dare order me about in my own keep?"

"It's not your keep, it was my father's," Brandt said evenly. "And my claim stands."

As it was, Brandt had the proof he needed to show his legitimacy, including the word of his very alive mother. But Brandt knew Rodric would not give up what he'd stolen without a fight. By any devious means necessary. And Brandt did not plan to be near any dangerous cliffs if he could help it.

"Verra well," Rodric hissed. "A challenge 'twill be. Two days hence."

Brandt's gaze narrowed as Sorcha's fingers dug into the muscles of his back in warning. Two days was enough time for any number of things to happen. Including being murdered in his sleep. "It will be now, unless you are afraid, laird."

"Of *ye*?" the duke scoffed. "A Sassenach runt?"

Brandt smiled. "I assure you, my mother will attest that my blood is as Scottish as yours."

Rodric bared his teeth and nodded to Feagan. "Fetch my sword."

"Father, this is preposterous," Patrick said, his pale eyes flashing. "Let me accept the challenge in yer stead. Let me fight this…usurper."

For a moment, a calculated look flicked across Rodric's face.

"You could if you were laird." The swift, quiet statement came from Sorcha. "It's Highland law. Only the laird must prove himself worthy of rule." She squared her shoulders, her voice carrying far and wide. "As the daughter of the Duke of Dunrannoch, I swear it to be so."

No one said anything for a long moment, before Rodric turned and whirled out of the room, flanked by his men and followed by his glowering son. Brandt also followed, but stopped first to check on his mother. He pressed a kiss to her brow. "I know that must have been hard for you. Thank you for standing up for me."

She lifted a slender palm to cup his jaw. "I should have stood up for ye all those years ago. I shouldnae have let ye go, son." Her voice broke on the last word.

"No," he said quietly. "You did the right thing. He would have found a way to kill us both."

His mother hesitated as if she had more to say. "Dunnae blame Patrick," she said. "He has tried to do the right thing his whole life. He has a great capacity for love, but so much of it has been…buried out of necessity."

Brandt had a keen understanding of that feeling. He'd buried his heart long ago and, until it had been found by Sorcha, he'd almost forgotten its existence. Brandt had grown up with Monty and, though he hadn't been his true father, when compared to being raised under the thumb of a man like Rodric, he couldn't argue that Patrick had likely had the worst of the lot.

"He is my son, as much as ye are," she whispered, and in her glistening eyes, he saw her fear. That her two sons might come to blows as enemies. Brandt hoped they would not, but at the moment, he could concentrate on only one fight.

As he made his way out to the courtyard, he felt the weight of his decisions pressing upon his shoulders. If he failed, his mother would bear the brunt of Rodric's rage. So would Callan and Aisla. He wasn't too worried about Patrick, who seemed to have inherited his father's survival instincts. But they wouldn't be the only casualties. Brandt's gaze flicked to his wife who walked beside him with the carriage of a queen. If he died, she would be sent off to marry Malvern. Brandt couldn't fathom the brutality she would suffer at the man's hands.

No, he *could not* fail.

Just before he walked out into the courtyard, Sorcha pulled him into a narrow alcove before the front doors. "You'll be careful, won't you?" she said, her blue eyes full of concern and no small amount of fear for him.

"Yes." He smiled. "I won't die if that's what you mean."

"That's *not* what I meant," she said with an indignant look. But he kissed her into silence. Deeply. Passionately. She clung to him, her eyes bright and lips rosy and glistening.

"I'll be careful, *mo gràidh*."

Her smile was as bright as the Scottish sun. "Gaelic?"

"I'm a fast learner," he said, kissing her again, this time swiftly before heading for the door. He looked over his shoulder with a mischievous grin at the woman who had made his fledgling heart beat again. "That's one of the two words I know."

"What's the other?"

"*Amadan.*"

The bloom of embarrassed color across her cheeks made him laugh. "That was before I knew you," she called out. "And I only ever called you idiot once. Maybe twice."

"We'll discuss that later. In private."

He was rewarded with another becoming blush that made him want to wrap her in his arms and make a mad dash for the stairs. Brandt didn't think that Rodric would appreciate being kept waiting while he ravished his wife.

Brandt's humor stayed with him until he descended into the crowded courtyard. A path cleared for him to the middle where Rodric stood, sword in hand. Someone handed Brandt a sword, which he examined for nicks and cracks in the steel and hefted for weight. It would do. No sooner had he nodded than Rodric rushed toward him with his own sword leading the charge. Brandt managed to fend off the strike, his blade clashing into Rodric's. The duke was strong and, though fleshy from a life of excess, he still had enough bulk to bolster a heavy swing. They struck and parried, feinted and thrust, each of them trying to find weakness in the other.

Where Brandt was faster, the duke was bigger, and the duel continued as the crowd watched in rapt silence. But Brandt was also younger by a full score of years, which gave him a marginal advantage. After another bone-jarring round, his muscles sore, and a shallow gouge on his forearm seeping blood, he noticed that the duke was beginning to tire. A thin sheen of perspiration coated his brow. Brandt was tiring, too, which made his window of opportunity smaller. He had to end this sooner rather than later. He spun in with his sword, but miscalculated as Rodric leaped aside, his sword coming down hard toward his shoulder.

There was no time to avoid the blow. It was either risk his neck or show his back. He chose the latter. Brandt managed to lurch out of the way, but not before the tip of the sword traced a path of hellish flame down his upper right shoulder and then whipped upward to carve its twin up the side of his ribs. His body was on fire. He could smell blood thicken the air, and dully, from somewhere behind him, he heard a scream.

Rodric grinned. "Dunnae concern yerself about yer lady wife," he said. "Malvern will take good care of her."

They circled each other. Though Brandt was bleeding, Rodric had not escaped unscathed. He was limping and holding one arm close to a few bruised ribs. Brandt knew that Rodric was clever. He wasn't about to do something stupid by not paying attention. He drew a deep breath, ignoring the stinging pain of his separating skin and the burn of open tissue beneath. Sorcha's salve would fix him once he'd thwarted Rodric. Brandt could sense her in the courtyard and, though he couldn't see her, he guessed she would be standing beside Lady Glenross near the steps.

"Mayhap I'll let the men have a turn with her first," Rodric drawled. "Malvern won't mind, ye ken. After all, he lets that animal, Coxley, do what he wants." His grin was ugly. "What do ye think they're going to do to her?"

Brandt set his jaw. "Are you going to fight or blather on like an old woman?"

"Speaking of old women, mayhap I'll even let them have yer worthless mother." Brandt felt a muscle leap to life in his cheek. Sorcha, he knew, would fight tooth and nail to the last, and with her skill and tenacity, she might even be able to escape. But not his mother, and the image of any man attacking her made him sick with rage. The duke pounced upon his weakness like a wolf upon a lame rabbit. "Do ye ken, she came crawling to me like a tavern whore when yer father died? She begged me to take her like the dog she was."

Brandt didn't know where his torrent of strength came from, only that he was propelling forward and then colliding with his uncle. With a howl of rage, he swept the duke's feet out from under him and followed down with the top of his sword. He hovered over the man, grunting with exertion. It would have been so easy to slip the steel through his throat, but Brandt could not kill his uncle in cold blood.

"Do you yield?" he growled.

Rodric's eyes overflowed with humiliated venom, but he nodded, knowing he was beaten. "Aye."

Brandt stayed where he was, poised above his uncle, and exchanged a long look with the quietly waiting Feagan. After several tense moments, Feagan nodded. The battle—and clan loyalty—had been fairly won. "Restrain him and escort him off Montgomery lands," Brandt commanded.

"Yes, laird."

"He is no' yer laird," Rodric hissed. "Do ye want yer laird to be the seed of a weakling who couldnae even fight for his life?" He laughed cruelly, madness glinting in his eyes. "The poor sod would no' lift a hand against me, no' even when he knew he was going to die. Ye remind me of him. Ye have his weakness."

"Empathy is not weakness," Brandt said. "You don't understand it because you have none. Your brother believed in the best of you, and you killed him for it."

"Aye, he was no' fit to be laird."

The admission hung thick and heavy in the courtyard.

And then, a keening wail rent the air. It seemed to come

from the depths of his mother's body even as she shoved through a stunned crowd to slap Rodric in the face. "Ye bloody bastard, I kenned ye killed him!" she screamed.

His answer was calm. "Of course I did. I wanted what he had. Ye and the clan."

"Ye're not fit to call yerself a Montgomery."

She slapped him again, but not before Rodric wrenched free of his captors and wound a tight fist into her blond hair. He brought her up to his face before wrapping his other hand around her throat. "I *am* a Montgomery, ye deceiving bitch. And ye're still my property to do with as I see fit. Death will suffice for yer disloyalty."

As his mother's eyes dilated and her mouth slackened, Brandt prepared to tackle the man, but a blur dashed past him with a roar that shook the hills. He blinked. It was Patrick. With a wild yell, he pushed his mother into Brandt's arms and shoved his father to the ground. Straddling him, Patrick pummeled him with his bare fists, grunts punctuated by growling sobs. No one moved, until the only sound in the courtyard was one of bones meeting wet flesh.

Handing his mother off to Sorcha, who stood nearby, Brandt moved forward, his hand going to his half brother's shoulder. "Patrick, enough." The younger man slowed and obeyed, his face contorted with pain. Brandt knelt beside him. "All will be well, my brother, I promise."

They stood together, and Brandt indicated for Rodric to be restrained once more. "Give him a horse, and take him to our borders." He eyed his uncle, who had one eye swollen shut and a puffy lip. "You are never to return. If you do, you will be killed on sight. Is that clear?"

He and Patrick watched as Feagan led Rodric away, and after a while, his brother turned to face him. Confusion and horror warred over his features, but something else shone there, too. Relief. It was an odd thing to see. Brandt frowned.

Patrick had been groomed his entire life to be chieftain. There was no reason that he would want to willingly give it up. And despite his claims, Brandt was still a stranger.

"Do you wish to challenge me?" Brandt asked softly.

He was wounded and bruised, and any future duel would have to wait until Sorcha's magic salve could do its work. His brother's conflicted eyes met his, and Brandt sucked in a breath. Patrick's gaze flicked from Lady Glenross to Brandt and back again. She held out her hand to him—love, gratitude, and pride shining in her eyes—and he kissed her knuckles.

Finally, Patrick nodded. "If my mother says it to be so, then ye are the true heir by succession. My own father stole that which was no' his, so until ye have an heir of yer own,"— he glanced at Sorcha who stood with his mother—"I will remain yer heir and the next in line." He inclined his head in a somewhat stilted way as if uncomfortable with showing any emotion. "Yer Grace."

Relief shook through him, and his sore limbs were suddenly heavy with exhaustion.

"Good," Brandt said, clasping his brother by the shoulder. "Because I'm going to need your help."

"Ye have it," Patrick said as they walked back toward the keep where Callan and Aisla were waiting. News of Brandt's victory and their father's defeat would have traveled like wildfire through the clan. Brandt wasn't worried his half siblings would be upset over their father's banishment. In fact, he suspected they would show the same relief and approval as Patrick. "Aye. And ye will need my help, as well."

Brandt eyed him, detecting an odd note in his voice. "Why is that?"

"My father sent an invitation to Malvern to fetch his bride two days ago." Patrick's face was grim. "He and his army will be here inside a week."

Chapter Twenty-Three

Sorcha had never sweat so much in her life. As she stood in the courtyard of the Montgomery keep, the noon sun beating down on her and the rest of the men as they skirmished in pairs, she wondered at the unnatural heat of the spring day. It wasn't out of the ordinary to have an early May swelter, but this one had an oppressive edge to it. It made her feel a stone heavier, and it seemed every man and woman in sight was walking and moving a little bit slower, too. It could have been the heat. Or, she reasoned, it could have been the knowledge of an imminent attack on their clan and keep.

Fergus's broadsword came sweeping at Sorcha's head, and she grunted as she blocked it and then struck back before her opponent could take another stab. Her blade came down near his hilt, knocking it from his hand entirely. The Scot stared in wonder at his sword, lying on the muddied ground. He then broke into a wide grin.

"Impressive, Your Grace," he said.

"You won't be smiling like that when it's one of Malvern's men knocking your weapon away," she replied.

He propped one dark brow and nodded, accepting her censure humbly.

"Pick it up," she said, this time a little less brusquely. She'd offered to work with the men, teaching them some of the fighting skills she'd learned at Maclaren, and it had been no small feat that these men had accepted. It wouldn't be wise to shame them for not being entirely up to snuff when it came to battle.

"When an enemy blocks your strike, swivel toward your opponent's sword arm," she said, a bead of sweat rolling off her brow and stinging her eye.

The strikingly handsome Scot she'd been training with the last quarter hour frowned. "*Toward* my opponent's sword?"

"Aye. My brother, Ronan, taught me that. Your enemy will have to turn in order to swing at you again, and you'll gain a moment to prepare."

A few other men had overheard her and mumbled their agreement, and then they started clashing swords again. In the fields, another grouping of men were practicing with bows and arrows, and yet more men were out reinforcing the main gate and setting up hidden watch posts in all directions leading into Montgomery keep. They had a natural defense system in the keep's positioning among the craggy hills, but more defenses would not be unwise.

Sorcha had seen Malvern's men in action before, and they were brutish fighters, a high challenge for even Ronan and his men. There were a handful of vicious warriors here, like Feagan and Seamus, but for the most part, the Montgomerys had never been put to the test. Most of the men had never fought a life or death battle. And now, because of Malvern, they would.

Because of her.

She'd led Malvern here. She was the reason these men

were about to put their lives in danger, and as their new laird's wife, they would never complain or turn away from the fight. But that didn't make her feel any better about the situation. In fact, it made her feel only guiltier.

"Ye should take a break, Yer Grace," came a feminine voice from behind her. Sorcha turned from Fergus to see Brandt's mother sitting in the shade of a yew tree. Its branches were low and long reaching, and many of the men had hung their shirts upon them as they trained. For that reason alone, there were many lasses, both young and old, who'd come outdoors to do their washing and mending. And then there were some shamelessly gaping at the men's sweaty torsos as they swung their swords.

Catriona had a long length of faded plaid in her lap, and she was using a pair of shears to cut out long rectangles of the fabric. Sorcha nodded to Fergus, who bowed his head and went to find another partner.

"What are you doing?" she asked Brandt's mother as she stepped out of the direct sun and into the shade.

"Bandages. They'll be useful for the surgeon, should Dr. Kinnick need them."

A lump plunked down like a stone in her throat. Should Dr. Kinnick need them, it would mean Montgomery men were bleeding. That some might have been killed. It was a bitter pill to swallow...the knowledge that she had brought this upon them. But it was done now. Malvern was coming, and it was the least she could do to help them be prepared.

She looked over to where Aisla was practicing her archery with Patrick and Seamus. They would need every able-bodied fighter if Malvern breached the keep, even the women, and Aisla had shown a natural ability for the bow. She could help from a vantage point of relative safety. Several other Montgomery women had volunteered to learn, and it had floored Sorcha at how loyal they were to the son of their previous, beloved laird. She glanced to Brandt's mother. Their loyalty was largely due to Catriona, she knew.

The lady in question patted the grass beside her. "Sit for a minute," she said.

"I really should help," Sorcha said.

"I'm sure Fergus will appreciate the time to soothe his sore pride," she replied with an arch of an elegant eyebrow. Sorcha peered over her shoulder to where Fergus was demonstrating some of the new moves he'd mastered to a few Montgomery soldiers. Considering he'd spent most of the morning on his arse, he had picked up the techniques well enough. The man was a fast learner, she'd give him that. And he was easy on the eyes, if the sighing of all the Montgomery women around them was any indication.

There was nothing quite like the sight of a man in a kilt, wearing not much else while covered in sweat and swinging a sword. Although Sorcha appreciated that Fergus was a handsome man, he wasn't the one who made her pulse race. No, that would be the man on the *other* side of the training field, also swinging a sword.

Her very virile, very indefatigable husband.

She didn't need to see him without a shirt to have her wits scatter. A secret smile touched her lips—she'd seen more than enough of his beautiful naked body earlier that morning. With that shameless thought, she felt her cheeks burn, along with other unmentionable parts of her.

Unlike the other Scotsmen, he wasn't shirtless. A fact for which she was very grateful. She didn't much like the idea of other women gawking at her husband.

But they did anyway.

Sorcha had to admit Brandt wore a kilt well. When he'd asked that morning for her help to don the Montgomery plaid, she'd understood how momentous an act it was for him. So had his clansmen. Glimpses of his strong thighs were visible above his boots, sinewy and thick with muscle, with each twist of his lithe body. His handsome face was flushed with exertion, his powerful arms swinging his broadsword with deadly grace. He moved like a dancer on the battlefield, with calculated finesse. Much like he did everything else, including lovemaking. Her knees trembled slightly.

"I was in labor with him for three days," Catriona said softly, following her stare.

A rush of heat scoured Sorcha's skin. *Christ tossing a caber.* She'd been caught ogling her own husband by his *mother.* She composed herself, though her face felt like it was on fire. "Was it a difficult birth?"

Catriona patted the grass again, and this time Sorcha sat. The promise of learning anything about Brandt was too good to pass up.

"The delivery was quite easy, but the hours leading up to it were no'." She smiled in memory. "The midwife wanted to force the birth by attempting to turn him, but I told her that the babe would come in his own time when he was ready. And he did." Her fingers shook over the shears. "I held him for only a scant few minutes, but I could already tell what kind of man he would be. He wasnae sleepy, and he didnae wail. As a babe, he was so alert, so focused and quiet, observing everything around him."

"He hasn't changed," Sorcha said smiling. "Stoic to the core."

"I already kenned that one day he would be a great laird." Catriona's voice broke slightly. "I only hoped that by sending him away, I would be giving him a chance. I still dunnae ken if I made the right decision."

Sorcha reached for Catriona's hand and squeezed. "You did. If you hadn't, your son would have met with an end much like that of the late duke's. You *saved* Brandt by letting him go, and now he has returned, as you had hoped."

The duchess smiled sadly. "No' quite as I'd hoped. I didnae expect that Rodric would force me to remarry so quickly, and to him." She glanced apologetically to Sorcha. "Forgive me, I am sure ye dunnae want to hear such things."

"No, I do," Sorcha said, guessing that Catriona had never spoken to anyone of what had happened. She'd kept it all inside for so many years, harboring the secret silent hope that one day the son she'd given up would return. "Did he give you a choice?"

"Yes," Catriona said. "To stay as his duchess or leave. Though it wasnae a choice, no' really. I could have gone back to my father's clan in the south, but if Brandall returned to Montgomery, how would I have ever kenned? In setting him free, I had closed my own cage." Her agony was a tangible thing. "So I married Rodric, even though my heart would always belong to another."

"I'm sorry."

"'Twas the bed I made," she said. "I hoped and prayed for Brandall to return. I love my children, ye ken, but Rodric was no' the man he pretended to be. Even I didnae ken how deep his hatred of his brother had run all those years. He wanted to erase the memory of him from Montgomery."

"Brandt told me about the portrait in the gallery. The covered one."

Catriona nodded. "'Twas all he left of him, though he ordered it draped. I suppose he wanted to appear as if he mourned. But Rodric broke clan alliances and dismantled everything Robert had built. Montgomery became an isolated fortress, and he was its sovereign." She swallowed. "We were forbidden to speak Robert's name, to even reminisce of him. Those who did were punished."

"Punished?"

She shrugged. "Whipped, beaten, humiliated. I was the worst transgressor, of course. But the pain was worth it. I couldnae let my husband's memory be erased from history. My children ken their brave, kind uncle."

Sorcha felt a pulse of rage course through her veins. Any man who beat defenseless women deserved a special chamber in hell. But not everyone thought that way, she knew. There were still many clans who believed it was a man's right to do as he wished with his wife. Including the marquess to whom she had been betrothed. "I truly wish Brandt had not let him go, for it would give me great pleasure to smash my fist into his cowardly face."

She had not agreed with her husband's decision to release Rodric. He was too dangerous of a man to be on the loose with an axe to grind. And he would no doubt run to Malvern, if indeed they were allies. But perhaps that was what Brandt hoped for—he wanted a chance to face him on the battlefield, should Rodric return.

"I cannae regret my choices. My son has returned, and I've been blessed with Patrick, Callan, and Aisla."

Sorcha wanted to chase the sadness from her eyes. Marriage to a man like Rodric could not have been easy to bear. Montgomery had not only become Catriona's prison, the duke had become her warden. She wanted to turn the duchess's thoughts to happier times.

"What was Brandt's father like? Is he much like him?"

"Robert?" Her eyes brightened, and Sorcha nodded. "I see a lot of Robert in him. I see his strength and his patience. I also see his dry sense of humor."

"Dry would be a kind way to put it." Sorcha laughed. "What about horses? Did the duke like those? Brandt seems to have a way with them that I've never seen before."

The duchess's smile overtook her entire face, making the eyes that were so like her son's sparkle. "*Och*, that he gets from me. My father raised Scottish racehorses, and I learned to ride before I could walk. Everyone used to say that we had a mystical hand with them—the fairy's touch. 'Twas my father, his father before him, me. And now Brandt. Callan has a bit of it as well, though he lacks the patience."

Sorcha nodded. When people had special gifts in the Highlands, it was often said that they'd been blessed with them from the fey folk. Brandt did seem to have a magical touch with Ares, and Lockie as well.

Catriona's eyes fell to the ring on Sorcha's hand, her eyes misting. "Robert gave me that ring the day we wed. It fills my heart to see it on yer finger. He would have liked ye." She put down the plaid in her lap and reached across for Sorcha's hand. "Ye're a good match for Bran. I ken it in the way he looks at ye"—she broke off with a knowing smile—"and the way ye look at him. 'Twas like that between Robert and me."

Sorcha couldn't help the usual stab of guilt. Though Brandt had made her his wife in every way and seemed to care for her, their beginning had not been based on trust. It weighed heavily on her. Yes, she was halfway to falling in love with Brandt, and he had found his family, but at what cost? Malvern was not a forgiving man, and these innocent people would all pay the price in blood. Because of *her*.

"Yer Grace," Catriona began to say.

"Please, none of that. You must call me Sorcha."

Brandt's mother nodded, her fingers plucking at the plaid. "Yer clan…do they approve of my son? Or are they angry ye've broken the contract with Malvern?"

Sorcha ran a palm over the grass, the blades tickling her skin, as she considered how to answer. The truth was, she didn't know how most of them had reacted. Finlay and Evan had been furious at first, as had Ronan. But her eldest brother had almost seemed to warm to the idea of Brandt as a brother-in-law. After all, following the attack on their camp, Ronan had placed his trust in him to take her to safety. That had to count for something…if he were still alive.

"Sorcha? What is it?" Catriona asked.

"My brother, Ronan, and his men held off Malvern's attackers, giving Brandt and me a chance to escape." She paused, remembering the last image she had of her brother, fighting Coxley. Only one of them would have walked away, and Sorcha's pulse skipped and throbbed with dread not knowing who it had been.

"So they do support ye?" Catriona presumed.

She nodded. They had, albeit reluctantly. Once her father and the rest of the Maclaren people learned her husband was the rightful Montgomery laird and the new Duke of Glenross, their anger at her impetuous marriage might be somewhat appeased. It all depended on how successful Malvern would be in his retaliation. But she knew no matter what, she was a Maclaren, and Maclarens never abandoned one another. It was their family code of honor, and it was the sole reason she'd done what she did—she'd learned early on that it was easier to ask for forgiveness than for permission.

"I only wish we had enough time to send for them," Brandt's mother sighed. "The Maclarens are famous for their warriors."

They would have rushed to the Montgomerys' aid without hesitation. But then, Lord knew what had happened to them over the last handful of weeks. What if Malvern had already taken his anger out on them? Sorcha closed her eyes against the flashing memory of Niall, his arm pinned to the slab of stone Coxley had used as a chopping block.

The sensation of delicate fingers touching down on Sorcha's head and sweeping through the tresses at her temple opened her eyes. Catriona looked at her with tenderness. "I shouldnae have worried ye. Our men are strong, as well, and they'll defend ye with their lives."

"I don't want any man giving up his life for me, or for the choices I made," she blurted out.

"Ye weren't alone when ye married Bran, were ye? He stood up beside ye and said his vows. Ye made yer choices together, and as his family, we'll stand by ye as well."

For the price of a horse for stud, Sorcha wanted to reply.

Their marriage had started on all-too-shaky ground, and recent developments, though pleasant, did not erase that. Nor did it eclipse *how* she had come to marry Catriona's son in the first place. She'd employed the scheming tactic used by many an English lady seeking to catch a fortune or a title, only the prize had been freedom.

What had been meant as soothing reassurance only crushed Sorcha's heart more. If Catriona knew the truth, every last drop of compassion she now saw in the woman's eyes would evaporate. She would instead see the same cold hardness that gripped her chest and stomach whenever Sorcha thought upon her own deceit.

She stood, suddenly longing for another skirmish with Fergus. Or better yet, someone with more skill. Someone who could knock her down a peg or two.

Catriona caught her hand before she could move away, though, her eyes drawn into a frown, as if she had somehow heard a piece of Sorcha's thoughts.

"We all have our demons, and heaven kens 'tis easier to fight the ones on the outside than the ones that live within us." She released Sorcha's hand, leaving it at that. She couldn't manage more than a small grin at Brandt's mother before taking up her sword and turning to go back into the broiling heat of the sun.

She did have her demons; she'd brought them to life when she'd made the split-second choice to trap a stranger into ruining her reputation and then suffering through a forced marriage. Had that choice been a mistake, though? Brandt had brought her more pleasure than she'd ever considered possible. He'd made her feel whole for the first time in years.

Sorcha expelled a harsh breath. She wasn't halfway to falling in love with Brandt…she was already hopelessly, irretrievably in love with him.

One thing was certain—they would weather the coming storm together. What was not certain was whether either of them would survive it.

Chapter Twenty-Four

He'd made a mistake in letting Rodric go.

Sparing his life had marked Brandt as a merciful laird, and after having lived under the rule of one as stringent and cruel as Rodric, the clansmen and women had seemed awestruck by such action. What Brandt didn't yet know was whether or not they also thought him a fool for it.

Brandt had spent the last two days and nights with the writhing suspicion that the ousted laird would return one day, a force of warriors at his back, and attempt to reclaim his seat as laird and duke by laying waste to all and sundry who opposed him. Every time Brandt closed his eyes, he saw the tip of his sword at Rodric's throat. One thrust and it would have extinguished his life, as well as any chance of an unwanted homecoming.

He took the well-worn path from the loch to the stables, the cool hand of evening pressing against the back of his neck. He'd taken a quick swim to wash off the grime and sweat from being in the fields all afternoon and was heading back to the keep to check on Ares. It had been another scorcher of a day, the sun in its cloudless blue sky unrelenting as the Montgomery men and women had trained. Their skills had improved, remarkably so, over the last few days, and Brandt had been relieved to see more clashing steel than swords being knocked out of hands, more arrows flying true than falling short or wide of the hay bales dressed as targets. While he'd been training with them from time to time, he knew he had little to do with their drastic advances. He'd been overseeing fortifications along the keep's outer walls, preparing traps in the hills and woods surrounding the loch and keep, and organizing the different waves of defense the clansmen and women who could not hold a sword or bow or axe could take to avert the enemy. Things like tossing powder explosives, stones, and hot coals from the ramparts.

No, the Montgomerys' improved swordsmanship and archery skills were due to Sorcha's hand in the training. His wife had been tireless, dedicating all hours of every day to the task, barely stopping to eat or drink or sleep. Brandt had bid her to rest once or twice, but after a biting retort that she'd rest after they'd fended off Malvern's attack and lived to tell about it, he'd left her alone. The weight of unbearable responsibility had been bright in her eyes. They were so transparent, those twin blue depths. He could practically see every thought, every emotion, in them, and he wondered if she could read him as well as he could her. He feared she could. Perhaps that was why she'd been quietly on edge.

Malvern would stop at nothing to see Brandt dead and to reclaim what he believed was rightfully his. It reeked of irony...hadn't Brandt just fought Rodric for the same reason? For his rightful seat as laird? And he'd won. He'd taken back what was his, and Malvern likely had no doubt he could do the same.

As Brandt entered the stables, he felt a physical yearning for his wife, one that had only grown in intensity since he'd taken his place as laird. The need to be with her, touch her, make her his in every possible way. It was how they'd spent the last two nights. No words, just giving. Taking. Coming together and relishing in each other's bodies. Simply being with her was enough. Or at least it had been.

Right then, as he reached Ares's stall, he felt a pang of loneliness. He missed her voice. Her smile. He missed listening to her unleash her temper and her opinions. Sorcha had met him with matching ferocity in their bed the last two nights, but now Brandt suspected part of that had been only to ward off conversation. Something was on her mind, and he wanted to know what it was before Malvern showed his ugly face on Montgomery lands.

Ares came to the stall door and whickered hello. Brandt rubbed his hand up and down the stallion's snout and scratched his chin. "Your leg's finally healed, you old brute."

Thanks to Sorcha. Even during the last busy days, he'd seen her darting off to the stables to check on Ares. It touched him that she cared enough to check on his horse's wound, and it made him doubly awed to then see her pick up a sword and show grown Scotsmen how to properly wield it. She was such a contradiction, and yet so perfectly balanced. She would be an exceptional duchess. The people here already loved her.

Brandt ignored the stitch in his heart and took the carrot he'd been carrying in his trousers pocket. He held it up, and Ares's lips closed around the top, gingerly accepting the offering. "Your manners have improved as well."

It was entirely possible his wife was the reason for that, too.

"He's magnificent."

Brandt turned to see Callan exiting another stall. His half brother, he reminded himself. The fact that Callan had their mother's coloring instead of Rodric's made it easier to look him in the eyes without feeling the need to pick up something to defend himself with. Brandt still felt a bit tense around Patrick. Strange, he knew, considering even *he* looked like Rodric.

"I've never seen his equal," Brandt admitted.

Callan approached the stall, his eyes hinged on the beast currently mashing the carrot to pulp. "He doesnae ken how big he is," he said, a smile forming.

Brandt cocked his head. "What do you mean?"

Callan crossed his arms and leaned against the stall door, watching Ares still. "He's a gentle giant. I suspect he still feels like a foal, despite his size."

Brandt was quiet. He'd thought the same thing more than once. Other men looked upon Ares with trepidation, but Brandt knew the animal was more loyal and steadfast than he was truly intimidating.

"You have an affinity for horses," he guessed.

Callan nodded, meeting Brandt's stare. "Our mother does as well."

That didn't surprise him, though he hadn't known. There had been little time to sit and get to know her. Like he and Sorcha and the rest of them, Catriona had been busying herself with tasks of preparation. He hoped for the opportunity to learn more about her, and his brothers and sister, when the threat of attack had passed. He still couldn't quite believe that he had a family. Monty had been his only family for so long, and even though Brandt now knew the truth, it didn't change how he felt for the old man. Monty had raised him, kept him safe, taught him everything he knew. Brandt admired him more than before, if possible.

"Is it odd," Brandt asked, "knowing you have another brother?"

Callan laughed. "'Tisn't odd. 'Tis a relief. Do ye ken how many times Patrick lorded it over me that he was eldest? Now he kens what it is to be a younger sibling."

Brandt didn't join in Callan's amusement. "I can't imagine he likes that very much."

"Truthfully? I think he's just as relieved as I am. As we all are." Callan straightened up and turned serious. "I'm sure ye ken what it must've been like, living with a man such as my father. He left Aisla and me alone most of the time, but Patrick was never allowed an inch of space to breathe. The laird kept him close. Close enough to let him see how horribly he treated our mother, and all the while Patrick couldnae do a thing about it. It tore him apart. The evil things he did tore us all apart."

Though Brandt had known of the abuse, powerless fury simmered in the pit of his stomach at the thought of his gentle mother at the mercy of his uncle's brutality. "What kind of things?" he heard himself ask in the casual tone of a stranger.

Callan met his eyes, mirrored pain blooming in them. "No' counting the use of his fists, he humiliated her at every turn, flaunted countless mistresses, and he burned her with a brand."

"*Burned?*"

"With a hot iron. Marks for every time she spoke about yer father. Her backside's covered with them, Aisla told us."

Black dots swam in Brandt's vision, and sweat peppered his forehead. He felt sick at the depth of his uncle's cruel perversions. "Could you not get help?" he asked, his voice raw. "From a vicar, anyone?"

Callan shrugged and shook his head. "Who would go against such a ruthless laird? There was a time, once, when Patrick tried to defend her. He was about ten at the time, and he suffered for it." Callan's eyes darkened at the memory. "Rodric strung him up in the courtyard yew by his ankles and left him to weather the entirety of a lightning storm."

"He could have been killed," Brandt said, repulsed but also confused. Why had Rodric risked his heir's life?

"Aye," Callan said. "But he had a spare, ye ken? From that point on, Patrick knew he meant no' a thing to our father. That he'd no' hesitate to hurt him, or anyone else, should he defy him."

He truly had been mad with power. Brandt wished, yet again, that he'd been able to see the challenge for lairdship through to the death, as he knew Rodric would have.

"Nae, 'tis better now ye're here," Callan went on. "And the timing was good fortune, too. Lately, Rodric had started to question whether or no' Patrick would be best suited as heir."

Ares nudged Brandt in the shoulder, seeking another carrot, but Brandt just scrubbed his chin. "Why wouldn't he be?"

Callan checked around the stables, though they seemed to be the only ones present. The rest of the men and women would be gathering in the keep for sup soon.

"Patrick doesnae spend time with the lasses. He takes notice of them, aye, but he's never taken to one in particular. I suspect 'tis only because he didnae wish to submit any lass to the same scrutiny and danger as our mother had been made to suffer."

Brandt understood then. "And Rodric thought Patrick might prefer men to women."

Callan murmured his agreement. "He may have the look of Rodric, but he's no' his man. Nae, he's more like ye, Sassenach." His brother grinned. "Or should I call ye, Yer Grace?"

"You should call me Brandt," he replied, clapping his younger brother on the shoulder. "We should go up to the keep. I don't think they'll begin sup without me."

"Yer their laird. 'Twould be disrespectful to eat before ye were seated."

Brandt gave Ares a last pat on his neck. "It'll take some

time getting used to that."

He was laird to an entire clan. The Duke of Glenross. Leader of hundreds of people. Keeper of hundreds of acres of Highland land. *Wait until Archer hears the news*, he thought with a creeping grin as he and Callan strode up to the great hall.

Sorcha was seated beside him, his mother to her left. Patrick kept his chair at Brandt's right, though Aisla now sat beside Patrick, and Callan had taken the seat to their mother's left. And instead of solemn silence in the great hall, there was a contented roar of many conversations, and even some bursts of laughter.

He and Sorcha said little to each other throughout sup; again, he felt her withholding something from him. Using her exhaustion as a shield. He let her be; nothing he wanted to say could be said in the presence of others. After a time and plenty of drink, a handful of older men began to stand and recount past battles. Fights they had won and at what cost. The younger men listened with rapt attention, and Brandt could tell the stories were mostly for them. To fill them with pride and hope that when it came their time to battle, they would live to tell the tales as well.

When Catriona, Aisla, and Sorcha stood to leave the great hall, and leave the men to their tales, Brandt itched to stand and follow his wife. But it would have been in bad form, and it would not have gone unnoticed. So he stayed seated, listening to the banter and joining in the cheers at every retold victory. It had been a long time, though, since Montgomery had waged battle. Their reclusive state over the past quarter century had turned those past warriors into old men. By the time the men had settled down and Brandt stood to withdraw, he felt even more uneasy. The physical yearning for his wife had returned, and he was sorely tempted to enter their shared bedchamber—still the guest room, as the thought of sleeping in Rodric's bed in the laird's chamber made Brandt ill—and lose himself in her once again.

Someone cleared his throat, and Brandt realized that Patrick had asked him a question. Callan snorted with a knowing smile, following his stare to where Sorcha had climbed the stairs not a half an hour before, his memory still hinged on his wife's tempting derriere. "What is it?"

Surprisingly, amusement also glinted in Patrick's eyes, which was unusual for him. "I asked whether ye were satisfied with the preparations on the loch side. I'm no' too worried about an army breaching the north shore. 'Tis much too difficult to pass through the quarry, and we need the men on the front side."

"Agree," Brandt said. "But we cannot leave it unguarded, either."

"I've ordered a dozen men along the battlements." He nodded to Feagan, who sat at the next table and was listening intently. "Feagan says Seamus will cover that end."

Brandt gestured to the seats his mother, his wife, and sister had vacated, and waved Feagan and his men forward. He pushed some of the trenchers to the middle and lined up a few of the empty dishes. "If this is the keep, and here's the loch, what of this area leading into the pass? And this open area here at the foothills?"

The men all followed his finger on the table, nodding in unison.

Feagan answered. "We have men on either side of it as well as in the hills. Some of our best archers will be here." He jabbed a hand toward each of the front sides of Brandt's makeshift outline. "Our best offense will be for it to seem that most of our men are on the plains here in front of the villages."

"Good," Brandt said. "I think you should set extra men here and here." He pointed to where the hills on either side of the loch would be.

Patrick frowned. "Ye suspect an attack from there?"

"I've heard of Malvern on the battlefield, and he is clever. It wouldn't surprise me if he sent Coxley to approach from the rear."

If Coxley was still alive. Brandt hoped to God he wasn't.

"The quarry around the loch is impassable this time of year," Seamus piped up.

"Let's not leave it to chance." Brandt stood and surveyed his brothers and his clansmen. "Get some sleep. If luck favors us, we will have one more day to prepare, but if she doesn't, we will need to be battle ready."

"Yes, Yer Grace."

After the men left the dais and departed the hall, Brandt turned to leave, but a hand at his shoulder halted his departure. "A word," Patrick asked quietly.

"Of course."

Patrick looked uncomfortable. "I wanted to thank ye for what ye did for my mother—*our* mother—and our sister." His voice lowered and shook. In fact, his entire body shook with the force of his choked emotion. "Ye have my sword and my fealty, Laird."

Brandt did not hesitate; he pulled his brother into his arms. He met Callan's anguished gaze over Patrick's shoulder and felt his own eyes mist at what the admission must have cost his brother, who had been severely castigated for any sign of weakness, any show of emotion.

"He'll never hurt any of you again," Brandt said fervently, looking into his brother's pale blue eyes. Oddly, the color did not make him think of Rodric. Perhaps because they weren't inhumanly glacial. No, Patrick's eyes were all too human and all too vulnerable. "I swear it."

"Are ye no' afraid that he'll return?" Callan asked.

Brandt lifted cold, determined eyes to his youngest

brother and reached out to clasp his arm as well. "Afraid? No. Hopeful, yes. I want him to return, so one of us can kill him." Brandt grinned. "Though, if he does, I wager it will be young Aisla who will put an arrow through him. She's gifted with the bow."

Patrick nodded. "Yer wife has been a good influence on her."

"They've been good for each other."

That reminded Brandt of Sorcha and his earlier inclinations. Callan burst into laughter at the besotted look on his face, but Brandt did not have the grace or will to look ashamed. He would not be faulted for desiring—or loving—his wife.

"I don't blame ye," Callan chortled. "Yer duchess is quite a lass."

With a grin, Brandt chucked his brother in the shoulder. "Go find your own."

He took the stairs two at a time, stopping to catch his breath at the door to his bedchamber before opening it. He was glad that he had, because the sight that greeted him snatched the air from his lungs. Sorcha had just finished her bath and was rising from the water like a river nymph, her skin rosy and glistening. His greedy eyes followed the droplets sluicing from her breasts to her stomach to the sable triangle between her legs. Brandt felt his mouth go dry with a sudden desperate thirst, one he could slake only with her inimitable body.

Even with fresh bruises from training discoloring her limbs and hips in darkened swatches, she was stunning. A warrior goddess in the flesh. And she belonged to him. He watched the play of muscles on her strong, lean thighs as she stepped out of the wooden tub onto the length of toweling that Morag must have placed there. Brandt could hear the maid moving behind the privacy screen, but he was too busy ogling as Sorcha dried herself, her fingers drifting over her breasts and her thighs. Morag's presence was the only thing keeping him from crossing the room, picking up his wife, and tossing her onto the bed.

Sorcha's eyes met his and held them as Brandt looked his fill in silence. A visceral current shot between them, hot and bright. Carnal lust shone boldly in those luminous blue eyes and struck him straight in the groin. He could never get enough of how sensuous his wife was—with those limber legs, mouth-watering curves, and exceedingly passionate nature, she was a hedonist's dream. He was already painfully erect. When she lifted a slender leg to the edge of the tub to chase the droplets with the toweling, he couldn't help the growl that broke from his throat.

With a squawk, Morag hurried from the room. His beautiful wife stepped toward him, but before the door closed, Brandt already had her in his arms, with his mouth on hers. He groaned at her taste. She was sweetness and honey, light and laughter. She was water to his thirst. And he wanted it all…every drop of it. When he finally lifted his head, Sorcha's lips glistened, and her eyes had darkened. The secrets she harbored were still there, but for the moment, they'd been eclipsed by the desire sweeping through her.

"Husband," she said. His minx of a wife smiled at him and dropped the toweling to the floor. Lust poured through him. She reached for the hem of his kilt and shot him a naughty grin. "My favorite part about kilts is the easy access."

When she grabbed gentle hold of his erection through his smallclothes, Brandt almost spent himself then and there. He wanted her with a longing that made his brain shrink to the size of a pea, while other parts of him grew larger still. His wife's fingers left him to undo the ties of his smalls. She made quick work of his shirt, and a few galloping heartbeats later, he wore only his kilt. He arched an eyebrow at the fact that he was still partially clothed, but she only smiled.

Brandt gathered her warm, naked body in his arms, holding her to him. The yielding softness of her breasts pillowed into the hardness of his chest. His thick arousal pressed up through the folds of his plaid into the firm planes of her stomach. She was muscled, too, his Sorcha, though everything about her was all woman—the beautiful peaks of her satiny nipples, her slim waist, her firm, rounded arse. Groaning softly, he took her mouth in another kiss, though this was different from the first. There was nothing gentle in this kiss. It plundered. It ravaged. It *took*.

Sorcha dug her nails into his shoulders and dragged her lips from his. "Take me here, now, where we stand," she said, her breathing clipped as she bit her bottom lip. "I couldn't stop staring at you in the fields today and imagining you… with me."

"How did it make you feel?"

"Wet."

Brandt didn't need to hear any more. If he didn't bury himself into her, he was going to burst. Reaching down to grasp her buttocks, he hefted her upward and shoved his plaid to the side. Without being prompted, Sorcha hooked her legs around his hips and sank her body onto his shaft. She was, indeed, quite damp. Soft and wet and slick. Their movements were limited, their muscles working frantically as she ground herself down into him using her thighs while he guided her with his hands. It was a ragged, desperate coupling, one with its culmination looming hot and fast.

"Sorcha—"

Brandt wanted her to find her pleasure first, but he'd lost all control. So had she. There was nothing but lust and feeling and carnal heat bursting between them. Her eyes were closed, her mouth parted in cresting bliss as her hips slammed into his. And then her body was rippling around his in molten undulations, coaxing forth his own furious release. He swallowed the sounds of her passion with his mouth as he spilled his seed into her and tumbled backward to the bed, whereupon he collapsed.

Sorcha sprawled on top of him and gave him a satisfied grin. "Well, that was different."

For the second time since he entered the chamber, he caught his breath. "To say the least. I should wear a kilt more often."

Sorcha rolled off him to the side and trailed a hand down his coarsely furred thigh. "That you should, my laird. I like the look of your knees."

"Only my knees?" he teased.

"And other things."

Brandt laughed and tucked her into his side, drawing the blankets over their legs. He didn't want to ruin the moment, but he knew that they were both only stalling. He'd wanted to make love to her, but he also wanted to know what was in her head. He grazed one of the fresh bruises on her ribs with the backs of his knuckles.

"Why are you pushing yourself so hard?" he asked.

For a moment, he thought she wasn't going to answer him, that she was going to shove her feelings down to where she didn't have to deal with them. But then her head tipped up, her eyes shadowed. "I owe it to them," she whispered. "To you."

"You don't owe me anything."

Pain flicked over her face. "I *do*. I've brought this on everyone. My family, your family." She broke off with a pained gasp, her eyes falling away. "Watching all those children learning to fight today gutted me. They shouldn't have to defend their lives because of what I've brought upon them." A sob shook her frame. "They don't even know the truth—that the Maclarens forced you into marriage."

"Actually, I did it for a horse." He tapped her hip. "A very valuable horse. Which I still have to collect, by the way. Not that I'm complaining about the other very pleasurable benefits to marriage thus far."

She scowled up at him. "*Brandt*, they're fighting for a *lie*."

"Sorcha," he said gently, grasping her chin. "Look at me." Damp, agonized eyes met his, and Brandt drew his thumb across one tear-tracked cheek. "I love you."

Her pupils sharpened, her lips parting on a silent gasp. "You *love* me?"

"More than life. Regardless of where we started, we are here together. I'm here because I want to be. With *you*. I've found my family because of you. I was able to save my mother, my brothers, and my sister from a tyrant because of *you*." He kissed her softly. "If you won't hear me in English, I'll say it in Gaelic until I'm blue in the face."

A watery smile tugged at her lips. "All that?"

"Well, maybe not all," he said, gathering the love of his life close. "Maybe just I love you, then—*tha gaol agam ort.*"

Sorcha's eyes pooled with tears again, but her grin was luminous. "Well done, though your pronunciation needs some work. Your tongue needs to roll the vowels." She reached up to cup his jaw, her tongue darting wickedly into his mouth. "Like so."

Brandt pursed his lips, thoughtfully. "I may be in need of more lessons."

"Happy to oblige," his wife replied saucily. And as he scooped her into his arms, the last thing Brandt was thinking about when her sweet tongue took his to task was Gaelic.

Chapter Twenty-Five

Everyone had been wrong as to when Malvern would arrive.

Feagan sounded the horns as dawn broke across the skies. They did not have an extra day to prepare. They did not even have the morning. Malvern's army was spotted crossing Buchanan lands to the south, at least a thousand men, most of them Scots. Sorcha cursed her countrymen but understood their betrayal in the same breath. Many of their families were starving, banished from land and home, and Malvern would have offered them more coin than they knew what to do with. The scouts had reported that the army flew the marquess's colors, but Malvern himself had not been spotted.

Dressing quickly, Sorcha wondered whether he would even show his face. He was not known for braving the front lines with any of his infantry during a battle. No, he stayed in the rear, in relative safety like the gutless coward he was. Brandt hurried back into the room, his face tight. He wore the Montgomery kilt again and looked every inch the laird of his clan. His eyes snapped to hers, opening in surprise. She had worn Montgomery colors, too, a sash made from his plaid draped over her shirt and belted over her breeches.

He drew her into a swift kiss. "You'll need to stay here with the women and children. They will need you to defend them." Brandt's eyes met hers, his heart in them. "You're the only one I trust with my mother and Aisla."

Sorcha nodded. She wanted to be on the front lines with him at his side, but she understood his fear—he had only just found his family. She grabbed her husband's shirt by the fistfuls and dragged him to her for another hard kiss. "Don't die."

He shot her a wicked grin as they descended the staircase. "I won't. I plan on thoroughly seducing my Gaelic teacher. I've a feeling she finds me bonny."

Which would explain why she was smiling when they reached the bottom of the stairs. Her amusement faded quickly. The great hall was filled with pale-faced women and children. Aisla and Catriona were at the middle of it, giving instructions and calming those who were crying. There were a lot of tears, and for good reason. Montgomery was about to be under attack, and just days after it had been freed from the bleak rule of a madman. Sorcha hurried to where Aisla was waiting and stopped, stock-still, as the girl turned to face her.

She was dressed in a blue shirt, men's breeches—Callan's, Sorcha presumed—and boots. But that wasn't what shocked the words from Sorcha's mouth and made her heart constrict painfully. Three lines of green pigment slashed one half of her face from brow to cheek, much like Sorcha's own scars.

"Ye're the bravest lass I know," Aisla said. "I wanted some of yer courage."

Sorcha was struck speechless. All she could do was take Aisla's shoulders in her hands and squeeze, tears stinging at the corners of her eyes. It was unimaginable that another person would look upon her scars as a symbol of bravery, and yet here this lass stood, her war paint mimicking the scars

Sorcha had always been made to feel ashamed of.

Never again.

"We'll take courage from each other," she told Aisla, and meeting Catriona's gaze, then several other women standing around them, she added, "We are not helpless women. We stand together, protecting the wee ones and fighting as warriors *here*, should any of Malvern's men make it through. We are Montgomerys, and we defend what is ours!"

Heads nodded, grim but resolute expressions transforming many of the panicked faces she saw. Sorcha felt her husband's hand on her waist, and she turned to him, sinking into his embrace. She breathed in his scent, the one her body had already memorized, and ran her palms over his broad shoulders. It was tempting to hold on to him, to cling to him and command that he come through the battle unscathed. But the other women were watching her, and as their lady and laird's wife, she had to display the same courage she'd just demanded of them. She had to be worthy of the painted scars on Aisla's cheek and brow.

"Say it again," she whispered.

Brandt's lips moved against her forehead. "Say what?"

"That you love me," she answered. He'd said the words a handful of times before, and they'd caressed her body and soul as well as any part of his body could. She needed to hear them again, and in the privacy of her own mind, she admitted why: because it might be the last time.

"I love you, Sorcha," he said, kissing her temple, then her brow. "And I'll tell you as much every day for the rest of our lives. Our very long lives, in case you were thinking any different."

She smiled, not surprised in the least that he'd read her mind.

"And I love you, husband," she said, and after raising her chin to take his mouth in a fast kiss, she pushed him away.

"Now go, and think only of the fight. I'll take care of things here."

She watched Brandt draw in a long breath, as if drinking in her face to carry with him into battle, and then with a short nod, turned to exit the great hall. As soon as he was out of sight, the sounds around her came into focus. The women had begun to plan their own positioning within the cavernous hall. Aisla was pointing out the alcoves on either side of the room where the children could crouch and hide for the duration of the battle. Catriona had gathered a group of women to prepare a corner of the hall into a makeshift infirmary, and Sorcha realized the wounded would be brought here as well.

"These tables and benches," Sorcha said, seeing the places where the clansmen sat while taking their meals in a new light, "can be turned on their sides and put to use as barricades."

The women were not weaponless. More than half of them carried bows and dirks, a few had crossbows, and even the children had baskets of stones. The room was a commotion of activity over the next several minutes as tables were upended and dragged across the stone floors. Outside the walls of the hall and beyond, Sorcha could hear the firing of rifles and the muted crash of swords, along with the muffled shouts of men. As the women positioned themselves behind the tables, and more used the hearth to boil water for cleaning future wounds, she tried to shut her ears to the sounds of battle. But try as she did, they seemed to grow only closer.

Sorcha found Aisla instructing two wide-eyed women on the bow and pulled her aside. "Is there somewhere else to send the children, should the fight reach this hall?"

Already the youngest of the boys and girls were taking shelter in the alcoves, but Sorcha needed another place to send them. A safer place, should they require it.

With a pinched brow, Aisla nodded. "Aye, there is,

though it may be a bit tricky—and a risk. 'Tis a number of tunnels leading out to the southern walls of the keep, to the quarry. Callan and I used to play in them during dry seasons, though they're usually half filled with mud and water during the spring. They could be bogged down right now, for all I ken."

Sorcha's relief swelled at the idea of the tunnels leading out. The southern end of the keep would be facing the craggy hills, and in the opposite direction of the current battle unfolding at the north and northwestern sides of the fortress.

"Send two women to the nearest tunnel to see if it's passable," she said as a rapid volley of musket fire sounded, much closer than before. It did not escape her attention that the tunnels could be a way *in* as well, but Malvern's men would likely not know of them.

Aisla nodded and started to turn away when she suddenly jerked to a stop, the flush of purpose and vigor draining from her face. Her eyes had gone wide as saucers, her pupils to pinpricks. A hush clamped down over the rest of the hall, and the small hairs on the back of Sorcha's neck stood on end, even before she turned to see what it was the women were reacting to. She had not yet turned fully when already her instincts knew.

And they were dead on.

Standing within the side entrance to the great hall, in the doorway that led directly to the kitchens, were a handful of men dressed in breastplate armor, another scattered handful in leather and plaid. Two of the men stepped forward, and their faces drove the breath straight from Sorcha's lungs.

"Lord Malvern," she whispered, a shock of nausea slamming into her. The marquess's upper lip pulled into a smug sneer.

To his right, his man, Coxley, grinned viciously. "Miss me?" he drawled.

"Sod off, Coxley," she hissed, even as her heart cinched tight. *Ronan*. What had become of her brother? She ordered the tears threatening her vision to retreat, and to her relief, they obeyed.

A third leather-and-breastplate-clad man came forward, and Sorcha's pulse quaked. It was Rodric, his pale blue eyes fixed like bait hooks on Catriona.

"Ye traitor," he seethed.

"*I?*" Brandt's mother returned, holding out an arm to stay Aisla as the girl started for her side. "Ye're the betrayer, Rodric, no' I. Ye've led these men against yer own kin!"

The man tossed back his head and thundered laughter into the high ceilings. Beside him, Malvern and Coxley stood, emotionless, their somber glares reserved only for Sorcha. They'd used Rodric, she knew, and the ex-laird had willingly allowed it for his own benefit. The half-dozen enemy warriors were unbloodied, though they were not unstained. From their knees down, each man's legs were coated in a dripping layer of mud. They had taken the tunnels Aisla had just spoken of, Sorcha realized. Rodric had known of them and had led the way. Malvern would not have breached the keep without his help.

"Ye are my wife," Rodric said. "I own ye, Catriona, and ye'll pay for standing up against me."

With a twitch of Malvern's wrist, his men surged forward. Screams erupted in the hall, echoing off the ceiling and bouncing off the walls as the women rushed to arm themselves. Sorcha's entire body went cold. She held no weapon; nothing but the single dirk at her hip. She'd leaned her sword and bow against one upended table while she worked with the other women to build their barricades.

She palmed the hilt of her dirk and readied her grip, slicing at the first Scottish traitor who came at her. Her blade met its mark, carving into his jaw before she whirled to the side and slid the blade along the back of his ribs as well. The leather he wore parted easily and she heard his cry of pain and fury. Finished with him, Sorcha darted away, sticking her blade into the back of another man's thigh as he was herding two of the Montgomery women toward the alcove where the children huddled and wailed. He growled and swiped behind him but Sorcha had already whirled out of reach.

As she moved, she saw Coxley's mammoth form lumbering toward her. She couldn't see Malvern and she didn't care; at that moment, it was Coxley she needed to defend herself against. The man who had bested her own brother. Had he *killed* Ronan? She ground her teeth and let out a scream of rage as she gripped her dirk and prepared to meet him, head on, his sword at his side. He wasn't planning to harm her—not mortally, at least. But before he could reach Sorcha, a small figure whipped in between them, a bow in her hands, one slim elbow pulled back as she nocked her arrow.

"Aisla!" Sorcha shouted, though her voice was more of a rasping and breathless cry. "Behind you. Coxley, no!"

Her warning came too late. Brandt's sister screamed as Coxley's immense arm slammed into her bow, knocking the weapon to the side and out of her hands. The arrow loosed without force and skidded along the stone floor.

A body slammed into Sorcha's back and took her to the ground, her knees cracking painfully as she landed, her dirk knocked from her hand and spinning out of reach. She heard Aisla scream again and from the corner of her eye, she saw Coxley shoving Brandt's sister against the laird's table, one hand closing around her throat, his knees pressing her into a caged position. A pair of hands grabbed Sorcha's arms from behind, restraining her as she was jerked from the floor and dragged forward.

Around her, all was screaming and chaos, and for the briefest of moments, her faceless captor was knocked off-kilter, his hands loosening around her arms. She twisted to make a lunge for Aisla and stopped short at a startling sight.

Her sister-in-law held the twin dirk Sorcha had given her days before, the blade buried to the hilt in Coxley's side. The man's body had arched away from her, a guttural cry ripping from his throat. Aisla stared in horror at Coxley's face and screamed as she withdrew the dirk, only to plunge it in again, this time higher, in the unprotected gap in his breastplate armor, just below his left arm. From its angle, Sorcha guessed, the tip of it would have lodged right into his vile, black heart. She felt a moment of triumph, and no small amount of relief that Aisla had saved herself from such a monster.

It was then Sorcha's captor returned, wrenching her arm and spinning her around. She lashed out with her leg, trying to kick his feet out from under him, but he intercepted her powerful kick, jamming his knee into her inner thigh. Bright pain flared, and she crumpled, her captor's hands clutching at her as she writhed for freedom.

"You've avoided your fate for too long, Lady Maclaren." Her limbs went numb with recognition.

She snapped her gaze up and came eye to eye with the Marquess of Malvern. "My name is Montgomery."

"A trifling matter that will be dealt with." He jerked her closer to him and, with a growl, tugged her forward. Her feet stumbled, tripping over each other as he dragged her toward the kitchen stairwell entrance. She thought she heard her name being shouted, and as she twisted in Malvern's cruel grip, one of his hands readjusting to wind his fingers into her hair like a barbarian, she caught sight of Aisla's dark blue shirt dashing through the melee, toward the great hall's main entrance.

Sorcha prayed the girl got away to alert the men, but as Malvern slammed her into the walls of the kitchen stairwell, her feet sliding down the steps, his brutish grip on her brought tears of pain to her eyes.

"Let me go, ye bastard!" she screamed, anger boiling just beneath her fear.

"You worthless witch," he replied, his voice unnaturally calm and collected. "Did you truly believe I would allow some dirt-heeled nobody to take a piece of my own property from me? Make me look like a blundering fool?"

The stairs leveled out, and she felt the heat of the kitchens, could smell yeasty breads and burning meat. His grip on her hair wouldn't let her so much as look around for any nearby weapon, though she knew there had to be knives about. She swung her free arm in futile lashes, reaching for something—anything. But Malvern only laughed and slammed her hips purposefully into the edge of a table.

"You are mine," he hissed.

A sharp ache dug into her hip as Sorcha scratched at his face, her nails gouging into his skin. "I am wife to the Montgomery and will never be yers!"

Malvern growled and unknotted his fingers from her hair in order to clasp both of her arms together at her back. "Oh, you will be. My men will make you a widow, and then they'll watch as I take what's mine. By the time I've finished with you, you will beg for my mercy, you savage little hellcat."

He shoved her through a slim opening between two walls and then yanked her again to the side, the crown of her head slamming into a low ceilinged tunnel as the floor sloped down. It hurt less than his promise to make her a widow; the threat coiled like barbed wire around her heart as her feet skidded downward and landed in a cold murk that went up to her shins. A musty odor overtook the kitchen's scents, and a ball of panic billowed in her chest. This was the tunnel they'd used to sneak inside, and now, he was taking her from the keep. Taking her away from Brandt.

Her shoulders smarted with pain at the vicious hold

he kept, shoving her forward through the black tunnel, her senses overloaded with the smell of rot and mud now rising to her knees, the muted sounds of their heavy breathing, and the taste of blood in her mouth.

She felt the tunnel closing in around her, her hope sinking, drowning in the rising mud. She could not allow this man, this crazed, power-hungry devil, to win—but how could she stop him? With no weapon, no way to defend herself? And with her husband busy battling the hundreds of warriors Malvern had sent in order to see his reputation repaired and upheld.

A spot of sunlight flashed up ahead. They were approaching the tunnel's exit, and what lay beyond it was anyone's guess. More of Malvern's men? What would he do, throw her down and attack her then and there? Panic threatened to consume her wits as the half circle opening drew closer. Through it, she saw reeds and marsh and low scrubby brush. An idea took hold—a desperate, likely impossible idea—but it was all she had. If she could get on top of him somehow...if she could pin him under the swampy mess and hold him there until he drew the muck into his lungs...

At the head of the tunnel, Sorcha heard the shouts of men just outside. Malvern's men? She came to a stubborn halt at the tunnel entrance, jamming her back into Malvern's front. He grunted and moved to push her forward, but Sorcha surprised him by dropping as far down onto her knees as his grip on her arms would allow. She wrenched her shoulders in the process, but her intent proved effective—Malvern stumbled forward, bashing his head on the low ceiling as he went. He yanked her forward, but his grip had unintentionally loosened. Sorcha landed on her side in the marsh, and with every ounce of strength she had left, broke free of his hands and rolled on top of him.

More shouting reached her ears, but she ignored it, her

hands jamming down against Malvern's chest and thrusting him beneath the thick, marshy surface. Water and mud closed over his face, and Sorcha screamed with the effort it took to keep him there, his big body thrashing underneath hers. She was strong, but not strong enough. Malvern bucked her off and the next thing she knew, he was on top of her, shoving her down into marshland. Water filled her ears, the cold sting of it rushing up her nose and into her eyes. She clamped her lips, her breath tight in her lungs as Malvern's fingers throttled her throat, holding her down, squeezing. He wouldn't kill her, she knew. But that didn't mean he would be merciful, either.

Bright spots mixed and popped with black bursts of dots before her closed eyes, and Sorcha knew she had but seconds before her mouth opened on instinct and gulped in water. In that moment, she thought of Brandt. Heard his whispered promise to tell her he loved her every day for the rest of their lives. A last pulse of fury shivered through her, and Sorcha bucked, one of her knees miraculously free to move. She slammed it up, connecting with soft tissue, and Malvern grunted and groaned.

In the next moment, all of his weight was lifted from her. Sorcha jolted up, out of the water, hacking for air. She blinked and saw a tumult of men clomping through the marsh around her sodden body, her chest heaving to fill her lungs.

Malvern was on his back, his arms up in surrender as the points of two broadswords pressed into his neck and chest.

"Move, and ye die, ye worthless piece of English scum."

The voice came through Sorcha's waterlogged ears and struck her with a sobering clarity.

"Ronan!" she choked, her eyes landing on the broad back and muscled arms of her brother. He was alive! And he wasn't alone. Beside him, her younger brother, Niall stood with his broadsword gripped menacingly in his right hand, the tip drawing blood from Malvern's neck.

"Let me kill him, brother," Niall breathed as Sorcha stumbled to her feet. Behind her, more men on foot, and wearing Maclaren plaid, were taking care of the last of Malvern's men who had remained behind to stand guard. And cleaving one of the men in half was the Duke of Dunrannoch. Her head was still swimming, her vision blurred, and her throat ached from where she'd been strangled, and yet Sorcha wanted to sob in relief and joy that her father and brothers, and more of the Maclaren warriors, had somehow converged upon Montgomery keep in the height of battle.

"As much as I'd like to see ye do just that, 'twould bring us only more trouble from the Crown," Ronan answered Niall, his hand coming to rest on Niall's shoulder. "We deliver the marquess alive."

Deliver him? Sorcha didn't understand. Deliver him to whom? Niall grunted as he lowered his sword, leaving a shallow wound seeping blood in its wake. "On yer feet," he ordered.

A few more Maclarens surrounded them in the marsh, including her brother, Finlay. He took Sorcha by the arm, his fingers too hard on her bruised flesh. But she didn't mind—this grip was one of support and worry, not cruelty.

"Are ye well, sister? Did the bloody bastard hurt ye?"

She shook her head, her vision still wobbly. "I'm well," she said, breathless. "Why are you here? How did you know to come to the Montgomery? Or this path through the quarry?"

Niall came to her side as Ronan and Finlay led Malvern away at the ends of their swords. More men kept their muskets trained on him as they splashed through the marsh. The water had drenched her boots and trousers, and she started to shiver.

"Sorcha," Niall said, his arm coming around her waist as he threw a plaid over her shoulders. "We'll explain later. 'Tis still a fight at the north wall of the keep and in the hills. Our men are surrounding Malvern's, but we need to help secure the main gate and beat them back. We left our horses at the top of the quarry."

She nodded, knowing the time for answers would have to wait. All that mattered was that they were here, now—and that Brandt and his clansmen would have the brawn of the Maclaren warriors at their sides.

A distant scream tore her from encroaching relief. It had come from within the keep.

"The women and children…they're in the great hall—" she started to say.

Her father strode up to her, his forehead bloodied, though it only made him look even more fierce. He was a warrior through and through, and had not softened with age.

"Go to them," he said, tossing her a bow and a quiver of arrows from his own back, "and protect them. Ye're better with a bow than all of our archers combined. Niall, go with her."

She felt Niall go rigid at her side, knowing her brother felt the order as a dismissal.

"No," she said, pushing her brother's arm from her waist. "I can go alone. You need all your warriors with you, Papa, and naught but a few men are back in the great hall to contend with. Go!"

She trudged through the marsh, back toward the dark tunnel, thinking only of Catriona and Rodric. Of Aisla and the children huddling in the alcoves. By then, the women and children might have scattered throughout the keep in escape. Sorcha's only hope was that she'd find Brandt's mother still alive. She gripped her father's bow, nocking one arrow as she plunged back into the tunnel.

Chapter Twenty-Six

Brandt plowed through the half-dozen ragtag Scotsmen surrounding him with nonlethal strikes. He did not wish to murder his countrymen because they'd fallen for Malvern's gilded promises. Still, he recognized that they were mercenaries, hired to fight for coin. Malvern's men, who were hardened killers, were a different story. They did not deserve one iota of mercy. Neither did their leader. Though there was no sign of him. Or Coxley. Or Rodric, who Brandt had expected would have returned to Montgomery swaggering at the marquess's side. A grim feeling of foreboding filled him.

One that was suddenly compounded by his sister, racing down the hill in a billowing blue shirt and screaming his name.

What the devil was she doing out of the hall? And where was Sorcha?

His eyes scanned the courtyard behind Aisla, but there was no sign of his wife. Swamped with a coldness that dug into his bones, he rushed to meet her, leaving bodies strewn in his wake. He was so focused on getting to his sister that he almost lifted his sword against his brother and halted just in time.

"Where are ye going?" Patrick asked, kicking a Scot in the stomach and plunging his sword into one of Malvern's soldiers. He, Feagan, and Callan were single-handedly fending off the small portion of Malvern's army that had managed to breach the pass and the men defending on the front fields. They were the last line of defense before the keep.

"It's Aisla," Brandt said, not breaking his stride. "She's not in the keep, which means something has happened."

"We'll take care of the rest of these," his brother said. "Ye go and make sure they're safe."

Nodding, Brandt sprinted up the hill behind his brothers, knocking Aisla to the ground just as a rogue arrow whizzed past where she'd been standing. Belatedly, Brandt noticed that Aisla's clothing was damp, and it suddenly registered that the dark fabric was drenched in blood.

"What's this? Are you hurt?" His heart shrunk, even as his eyes searched her for signs of injury. Sorcha would have protected Aisla and Catriona with her life, and the understanding made his breath hitch painfully in his lungs.

"'Tis no' mine," she gasped, fighting to catch her breath from the tumble they'd both taken to avoid the arrow. "'Tis the blood of a man named Coxley. Shoved my dagger between his ribs just like yer wife showed me."

Brandt grabbed his sister by the arms and drew her upward. "Sorcha, is she alive?"

"Aye, I think so," Aisla said, her eyes widening. "But she was fighting a tall man with pale blond hair and a cruel face when I ran to find you."

Malvern. The very thought of his wife in that sadist's clutches made every hair on his body vibrate in rage. This time, he vowed, when Brandt saw the man he would not hesitate to put him down like the dog he was—if his wife hadn't already finished him off. He did not doubt Sorcha's skill to defend herself, but she was on her own, and Malvern was a seasoned man of war.

"Is he alone? The marquess?" Brandt asked, belatedly grasping that Coxley was no longer a threat. Because of his sister. The small lass he was interrogating had taken down one of the most repugnant men Brandt had ever met. How the hell had he gotten so close to her?

"He's with Rodric and some other soldiers," Aisla said. "They came through the tunnels."

"Tunnels?" Brandt asked with a frown, pulling her toward him before he decided to make a wild dash for the keep.

"The ones that lead to the loch. Usually, they're filled with marsh water this time of year, but somehow, they managed to crawl through."

Malvern and his men must have killed the men Brandt had ordered to be placed on watch and had found some way down the quarry to use the tunnels Aisla spoke of. No wonder they hadn't been at the front leading the army—they'd been sneaking in from the rear. And with Rodric's help, they had managed to brave the keep. If they held the women and children hostage there, the battle would be over. The men would not risk the lives of their families. Nor would he, for that matter. Sorcha and Catriona were still in there.

A part of him raged that he hadn't been told of the bloody tunnels in the first place, but like Aisla had, Patrick and Feagan would have likely assumed them to be blocked and impenetrable. He dimly recalled Seamus saying as much. A scream from the keep had him bolting toward it. Aisla kept pace with him.

"Go to the stables," he shouted over his shoulder. "You'll be safe there."

She shook her head. "I want to help."

"Aisla," he began, slowing to face her.

She cut him off with a resolute scowl. "I killed Coxley, ye ken."

Brandt faltered. She did have a point. He couldn't fathom that his slight baby sister had felled a man who was notoriously hard to kill. Then again, it wouldn't be the first time a man had underestimated a woman and paid the price for it. She'd done Sorcha's marks proud.

Grudgingly, he nodded and handed her a dirk from his boot. "Stay behind me."

Brandt crept up the stairs to the keep entrance with his sister on his heels. He glanced over his shoulder and was surprised to see his dirk held in her confident grip, a fierce look on her face. He almost smiled at the effect of what was certainly Sorcha's influence. He hoped to God that she was still alive, or Malvern would pay with his last drop of blood. Quelling his roiling emotions, Brandt placed a finger to his lips and eased the door open.

Light as a wraith, Aisla followed. They inched through the shadows until they were near the rounded arches that led into the great hall. The push of voices reached them, wrapped in the soft sobs of children and louder jeers. Peering around the edge, he scanned the hall. There was no sign of Malvern. Or Sorcha.

Children and women sat against the walls, their faces wreathed in terror. But pride swept through him as he took in that they hadn't gone down without a fight. A few soldiers lay prone on the floor, groaning and holding injured limbs. Brandt risked another quick look. Rodric stood upon the dais with Catriona. Brandt counted seven men with him. Two standing over the women and children, and the other five at his uncle's back.

"How many?" Aisla asked in a low tone, handing him back his dirk. She had retrieved a fallen crossbow and now held that along with two bolts in her grip.

"Seven," he whispered. "Eight counting your father."

"He's no kin of mine," she hissed.

"And he has Catriona."

Brandt grasped his sword and bent his head over the hilt. The odds were not terrible. He had taken on a dozen men and lived to tell the tale. But he'd never fought while someone he loved was so exposed, and Brandt had no doubt that Rodric would use Catriona, and the rest of the women and children, however he saw fit to gain the upper hand. He thought of the way Rodric had branded her and felt fury envelop him. It didn't matter if he had to take down a hundred men, he would do what needed to be done. Exhaling slowly, he turned to where Aisla squatted beside him to tell her to go for help. But she wasn't there.

All he saw was the back of her blue shirt and the flick of Montgomery plaid as she rounded the corner, into the hall.

Bloody hell.

"Father, happy to see me?" he heard her say in a loud clear voice, and then the unmistakable twang of the crossbow. That was his cue. He lurched to his feet and flung the dagger Aisla had returned to him, sending it straight into the neck of the man on the other side of the room. A second dirk from his belt lodged itself into the chest of the man on the right. The man Aisla had shot crumpled, and she'd loaded the extra bolt and taken out a second man before the other two at the dais rushed her.

Brandt leaped in front of her, his sword raised.

"Stop!" Rodric's barked command echoed throughout the hall, and the two soldiers charging him and Aisla skidded to a halt. Rodric got to his feet, hefting Catriona up with him. The lazy, insouciant motion of it clawed down Brandt's spine like a warning. A glint of something in the overthrown laird's hand confirmed the premonition. Rodric gripped a wickedly curved knife, the blade of which was pressed into Catriona's side. Brandt lowered his sword.

"If anyone is going to kill this interloper, 'tis going to be me," Rodric said, to which Brandt's mother protested with an attempt to pull away and kick at her husband. She whimpered and winced as the tip of the dirk pressed deeper into her flesh.

"Is this what you think a powerful duke and laird is, Rodric?" Brandt asked, his breathing coming short at the sight of that dirk and his mother's pain. She was masking half of it, he knew. The stain of blood blooming through her dress proved it, and the sight made Brandt's heart stutter. "A man who turns traitor on his own clan? Holds women and children hostage? Funny. I thought the word for those things was 'coward.'"

Rodric gnashed his teeth and pushed on a false smile at the same time. The effect was blood-chilling, but Brandt wasn't about to let him know that. He kept his eyes steady, his grip on his sword's hilt firm.

"I'm simply flushing the vermin from my home and lands, Mr. Pierce," he replied. "With the help of some like-minded men, ye ken. Lord Malvern is already seeing to yer widow."

He had Sorcha, then. Where Malvern had taken her, and what he was currently doing to her, nearly rendered him blind with rage and fear.

"Release my mother," Aisla grit out from where she stood just behind Brandt's right arm. He prayed she didn't do anything brash again, like raise her crossbow and shoot. He didn't know how true her aim was, but Rodric would not hesitate to use Catriona as a human shield should he see a deadly bolt flying at his head.

"With pleasure," Rodric said smoothly, another macabre grin splitting his mouth. "Though first, I'll have this man surrender his title as duke and laird to me, or I'll carve her open from hip to breast."

Despite his chilling words, Brandt was the one to let out a mirthless laugh this time. "Too afraid to challenge me for it, Rodric?" The man's ice-flecked eyes snapped, and Brandt realized he'd touched a nerve. He pushed on. "You haven't had enough time to recover from the wounds I left you with, I wager. Maybe you should have one of your men here champion you. I'd suggest Malvern's best soldier, Coxley, but it seems your daughter already killed him."

Rodric's lips were tight with rage, his knuckles white from his savage grip on Catriona's arm and the dirk with which he'd already drawn her blood. The suggestion that he required another man to fight in his stead, and that his own daughter was more effective in a fight than he, had caused him to shake off his smooth, foreboding exterior and wear his true one: callous and cruel and utterly incensed that his dead brother's son had stolen his title from him.

"I willnae just kill ye," Rodric said, flinging Catriona to the side so harshly that she landed on the dais, knocking over a chair as she fell. He sheathed his dirk and drew out his broadsword. "I'm going to gut ye and hang yer innards over the ramparts. Then I'm going to do the same to my conniving wife. I should have killed her while she still had ye in her womb."

"You like to talk," Brandt said, only pretending that the man's crazed words hadn't made him sick. "I wonder if that's because talking is the only thing you're good at."

Rodric charged at him, his sword raised and a guttural cry ripping from his throat. His two soldiers had scattered, and Brandt spared only one moment to be sure Aisla had backed away before meeting Rodric's sword with his own. The initial blow shivered through his arms and bones, straight to his spine, but he kept his grip, thrusting Rodric's sword away and slicing into his leather breastplate with the same stroke.

Brandt parried Rodric's sword as he attempted to flay

Brandt's thigh, then warded off a second blow as his enemy's broadsword jabbed at his gut. Rodric clenched his teeth, lunging and slicing at Brandt as if he were possessed by the devil himself. Unhinged. That was the word to describe him, and as their swords clashed, again and again, their circle of battle widening out, Brandt began to wonder if he'd misjudged Rodric this time. If perhaps he was crazed enough not to tire as he had during their earlier battle in the courtyard. Madness sometimes gave men impossible strength.

They spun toward the alcove where the children and women were huddled, Brandt's shoulders and back beginning to burn from the stalwart bite of Rodric's blade. The children and women screamed and fled in all directions, the commotion distracting Brandt, especially as one young child ran within striking distance of Brandt's swinging sword. He eased the momentum just enough to let the boy pass, unharmed—but as he did, a searing pressure in his calf sent his leg collapsing beneath him.

"No!" He recognized his mother's anguished scream as he reached for his calf and felt the long shaft of an arrow.

Someone had shot him from behind. One of Rodric's men, no doubt, though Brandt didn't have time to see who. He'd expected Rodric to fight dishonorably, though he had not expected to be shot from the back. He raised his sword to fend off a downward blow from Rodric and tried to stand up, when a second glaring pain tore into the back of his shoulder. This time, the shooter was knocked down in a barrage of pots, pans, and garden tools as the women in the hall fought back, but it was too late. The damage had been done—Brandt crumpled to his knees. His weapon clattered to the stone floor and, though he managed to duck and swerve out of the path of Rodric's sword, in that moment, he knew the turning point in their battle had come.

And he was not on the winning side.

"I dunnae ken what I'll like more," Rodric said, as Brandt pushed up onto one knee, gripping his calf and unable to reach the shaft of the arrow lodged in his shoulder. "To hear ye beg for yer worthless hide, or to watch ye bleed out when my sword sinks into yer gut."

"I'd sooner die than beg you for anything." Brandt spat at his uncle's boots before breaking off the feathered end of the arrow lodged in his leg. He fought through the agony as he pulled the arrow from his flesh. "But if I'm going to die, I'd rather take you with me like my father should have done."

With a burst of inhuman strength, he rose and lunged toward his uncle with the bloody arrow in hand. Rodric didn't have time to leap back as Brandt raised one arm to deflect his sword and stabbed his right fist forward. He'd meant to bury the arrow into Rodric's side, but his injured leg buckled, limiting the force of his strike. Slippery with blood, the arrow slipped and lodged into his uncle's thigh instead.

Rodric howled and lifted his sword, his face contorted with rage, and Brandt braced himself for the oncoming stroke. His body was on fire with agony, but he wasn't dead yet. If he could time it just right, he could roll his body into Rodric's legs and throw him off-balance. It was a long shot, but he would fight to his last gasping breath.

Time slowed as he counted down the seconds. He'd been close to death before, many times. But no other time had he seen his life and those who had filled it with such stunning clarity—Sorcha, Monty, Archer, Catriona, Aisla, Patrick, Callan—his family. His world. And his *wife*, his beautiful fearless wife. God, it had taken him so long to find her, but it had been worth it. She had saved him in so many ways. If there were anything he wished for, it would be to see her face…to know she was safe.

And then he felt it. Nothing more than a whisper of sensation across the back of his neck, but every bone in his body knew her presence. *Sorcha.* Out of the corner of his eye, he sensed motion, heard something hiss through the air, and then a shaft caught Rodric squarely in the chest. Brandt didn't care if his uncle's falling sword sheared his arm from his body. Greedily, he turned to see a mud-covered apparition at the entrance of a corridor holding a bow.

He blinked. Perhaps he'd lost far too much blood. It *felt* like her. His wife. But perhaps he'd only imagined it.

"Brandt," a voice said. It sounded like her, too.

He blinked again as the voice's owner knelt over him. "*Diah*, he's bleeding heavily." Gentle hands cradled his head. "*Mo gràidh*," she whispered.

It *was* his wife, Brandt realized dully. She was covered in muck and sludge, but he could never not know those deep blue eyes that filled him with so much hope and love and joy. "You're alive," he murmured, touching her dirt-caked cheek.

Sorcha smiled through her tears as she bent her lips close to his ear. "Of course I am. I believe you mentioned something about thoroughly seducing your Gaelic teacher. Wild horses could not have dragged me to Hades."

"You're insatiable," he whispered.

"For you, always."

A loud groan broke the moment between them, and Brandt looked up to see Rodric lying on his side. His glance also took in the forms of his sister and his mother standing close by before it fell back to his uncle. The wound Sorcha had inflicted had not been fatal. It would be, if left untended. His wife was an exceptional shot, which meant she had done it on purpose. Her eyes held his and she nodded. "His life is yours to take."

But before Brandt could move, his mother sank to her knees beside her blubbering husband. She grasped the arrow, and for a moment, Brandt thought she was going to break it and pull it out as he'd done with his leg. Rodric deserved to die, but if she wanted him to live, he would leave it to her. She was the one who had suffered at his hands for so many years. Rodric's life wasn't his; it was hers.

Hazel eyes—twin to his own—met his. And then Brandt knew.

Rodric would not live.

With an anguished cry, ripped from the depths of her soul, his mother twisted the arrow and shoved it toward her husband's heart. "'Tis for Robert," she said. Blood gurgled from Rodric's mouth as he fought the press of her hands, but she held steadfast, leaning over him with all her strength. "And for yer children. And for *me*."

A commotion arose from the end of the hall as Rodric's head dropped back onto the stone floor and his gurgles ceased. Catriona released the arrow, her hands bloodied, and Brandt reached for her. The rising clamor seemed to envelope them as his mother took his hand and let him pull her into an embrace. She was breathing heavily, but her sobs had stopped.

"It's over," Brandt said to her. He felt a hand on his shoulder—the one with the arrow in it—and sucked back a groan of pain as the arrow was ripped from his flesh.

"Didnae think yer expecting the pain would make it any better," Callan said. Brandt opened his eyes, practically seeing stars, and twisted to see his brother crouched behind him, the arrow in his hand. More men wearing Montgomery plaid, including Patrick, had filled the great hall, as well. Most were bloodied and dirty, and as they gathered around Rodric's body, Brandt saw somber looks on every last weary face.

"Malvern's men are scattering," Callan said, rising to his feet and tossing the arrow down as he looked upon his father's corpse. Aisla inched her way forward, gripping the back of Callan's arm. Brandt wanted to flop back onto the stone floor in relief. They'd done it. They had won.

"Patrick, Callan," their mother said, dabbing at her eyes as she rose to her feet. "Aisla." She took them each into an embrace, as she had with Brandt. And, though they didn't speak any words, Brandt knew what was being said. This was their new beginning—a life finally out of the shadow of Rodric's tyranny.

Brandt winced as Sorcha prodded at the rapidly swelling tissue of his lower leg. She tore a strip from the end of her plaid and bound it about his calf before tending to the inflamed gouge in his shoulder.

"It wasn't too deep," she told him, pressing the heel of her palm to it over another strip of plaid that she deftly wrapped over his shoulder and under his arm. "But both will need my mother's salve. You'll live, my brave laird."

Sorcha helped Brandt stand, his calf and shoulder hot points of throbbing misery, but his wife's fingers as she clung to him helped to dull it. He took her chin in his hand and angled her face, wiping it clean with a corner of his own plaid. New bruises and welts marred her forehead, including several others around her throat that had the unmistakable look of fingerprints. His incisors bit the inside of his cheek. "Where is Malvern?"

The man had strangled his wife. If he wasn't already a corpse, Brandt would see it done in short order. But Sorcha only shook her head.

"He is no longer our concern," she said.

"What does that mean? Is he dead?"

"The Maclarens have arrived," Patrick put in, and Brandt's eyes jumped from his bruised, yet beautiful, wife to his brother. "They're helping us to drive out the last of Malvern's army."

Brandt tested his leg and tried to stand on his own. If he was to meet the Maclarens, he wanted to do so without looking like he was ready to faint dead away.

"And Malvern?" he asked again.

"My father and brothers have him," Sorcha answered.

"They *had* him," one of the Montgomery men said from behind Patrick. The dark-haired one named Fergus. The one who'd put his arm across Sorcha's shoulders and flirted with her during training. Those weren't the only reasons Brandt scowled at him now.

"What the hell do you mean, they *had* him?" He limped to where his sword lay and stooped to pick it up. A newfound purpose gave him strength, and that was to see Malvern in irons or dead.

Fergus frowned. "He's a slippery snake, that one. One minute he was there at the edge of the woods, and the next he wasnae. He cannae have gone far on foot. We'll find him."

"Stay with our mother and sister," Brandt said to his brothers. "There are women here who were wounded by Rodric's men. I'll deal with the marquess." He eyed the tall Scot who had spoken. "Fergus, you and your men, with me." He glanced over his shoulder to his wife. "Stay with your family."

Brandt's scowl deepened as he limped to the bailey as best as he was able. Wounded or not, he'd find the bounder himself and run him through. He pushed open the doors and came to a dead stop. Montgomerys and Maclarens alike thronged the courtyard. Several of Malvern's soldiers were clad in irons at the center, including his very own target—the marquess was moaning on the ground beside his father-in-law. Though Brandt had never met the laird, he could see where Sorcha got her eyes and her fierce demeanor, and where Ronan, who stood at his side, got his brawn.

"Wee bastard tried to flee," the Duke of Dunrannoch boomed. "My boy, Ronan, caught up to him right quick."

"He broke my bloody leg," Malvern whined.

Ronan shrugged his big shoulders, mouth twitching. "He tripped."

"He's lucky he broke his leg instead of his worthless neck," Brandt snarled as he made his way down the stairs. Sorcha appeared behind him, and he hesitated. "What are you doing here? I told you to stay back with your family."

"Ye're my family, ye oaf," she hissed. Brandt only laughed. God, he loved her temper; even her insults felt like passionate promises whispered in his ear.

"Just so," he said, reaching back to grab hold of her fingers as they came to the bottom where her father and brother were standing. Ronan smiled but waited out of respect for his father to speak.

"I led my men here expecting to find my daughter married to a Sassenach stableboy," Sorcha's father drawled, a pair of assessing blue eyes measuring him from head to toe.

"Stable *master*, Your Grace," Brandt corrected.

Sorcha's fingers tightened around his in chastisement, but he could still somehow sense the smile she held in check.

"Though now I've kenned ye're the Duke of Glenross, Laird Montgomery," the old Scot went on, his eyes falling to their joined hands. Something hopeful flashed in them. "I cannae say 'tis not a vast improvement of circumstances, Yer Grace. Even if ye did steal my daughter from beneath my nose."

"She was worth stealing," Brandt said, breathing easier now that her father's fierce glare held a bit of levity. "As far as the former, I couldn't agree more." He made a clipped bow. "Duke of Dunrannoch, Laird Maclaren, I welcome you to Montgomery, and thank you for your timely assistance."

"Call me William," the duke said, clasping Brandt by his uninjured shoulder. "And no thanks needed. We always love a bit o' sport, dunnae we, lads?"

A victorious cheer went up from the Maclarens that was

immediately taken up by the Montgomerys. The relief Brandt felt was palpable. His family was safe from Rodric. And Sorcha was safe, at last, from the despicable man sniveling at her father's feet. "Escort the marquess to the dungeons until we can decide what's to be done with him."

The last of Malvern's army was rounded up, and shortly after, the sound of hoofbeats reached them, the horn once again sounding. In the distance, a huge regiment of horses was cantering up the road through the training fields, followed by several carriages. Men around him reached for arms but paused when Brandt raised one hand. He felt his heart expand as he recognized the flag and the noble face of the man riding at the helm of the contingent.

"Who is that?" Sorcha asked.

"That, my love, is the Duke of Bradburne." He laughed at the sight of the beautiful woman riding beside him. "Along with his wife, the duchess, if I'm not mistaken."

The men in the courtyard cleared to make room for the new arrivals as they rode up. Archer dismounted, his proud face scanning the men and falling to Malvern, who kept his head downcast, his shoulders quaking. He had every right to tremble—the Duke of Bradburne was a powerful peer and one who had the influence to strip Malvern of everything he held dear.

Archer assisted his wife to the ground and they approached together. Quick introductions were made to the Maclaren laird and his son, who stepped back to give them some privacy.

"I daresay Brynn and I missed all the fun," Archer said, clasping Brandt by the arm. Brandt groaned as the embrace pulled his weight onto his injured leg. The duke gave him a cursory glance, quicksilver eyes pausing at his bloody shoulder and narrowing. "Glad to see you're relatively in one piece, my brother."

"Honestly, Brandt," the Duchess of Bradburne, Lady Briannon Croft, admonished with a smile as he kissed her knuckles. "Are you ever *not* injured?"

"I like to keep things exciting."

Briannon smirked as her eyes jumped to Sorcha, still wildly mud-splattered from her fight in the tunnels. "I see that."

Brandt tightened his fingers on his wife's, drawing her forward. "Allow me to present my wife, Lady Sorcha Montgomery, the Duchess of Glenross." He turned to her, allowing the depth of his esteem for his unequaled, battle-weary wife to ooze out of every pore. Brandt didn't care if he looked infatuated. He wanted the whole world to know she was his. "This is His Grace, the Duke of Bradburne, and Her Grace, the Duchess of Bradburne, my dearest friends."

Sorcha curtsied to the duke and duchess, looking every inch the warrior goddess she was, her face held high. "It's an honor, Your Graces."

"A pleasure," the duchess said, her smile growing warm. If she'd taken notice of Sorcha's scars, she gave no indication of it. "Please call me Briannon."

"And you must call me Sorcha."

The duchess linked arms with his wife, uncaring of the mud caking her clothing, and they walked back into the keep together. Sorcha shot him a perplexed look as they went, but Brandt could only smile. Archer shrugged, seeing the exchange. "You know Brynn," he said with a resigned shake of his head.

Brandt did. The duchess was stronghearted and stubborn. She and Sorcha would get along well…or pummel each other to pieces. He had a feeling that it was going to be the former. He hoped.

"So did I hear you say your wife is Lady Glenross?" Archer asked, the question of the last name clear as they turned to follow their wives. "And a duchess? What have you gotten yourself mixed up in this time?"

"Alas, no diverting fake identities, I'm afraid," Brandt said after a moment. "Apparently, I'm laird here and rightful heir to a dukedom. As it so happens, Monty wasn't my father, after all. It's a long story. I'll tell it to you over a pint, shall I?"

Archer had never looked so utterly confounded. "Are you telling me you're a bloody *duke*?"

"Ah-ah, don't forget '*Your Grace*,'" Brandt said, wagging a finger. "It's only proper."

Archer vaulted an amused brow. "Don't get cocky."

"I learned from the best." He grinned at the man who'd been like a brother to him his entire life. "Not bad for a stableboy from Essex, eh?"

"You were never just a stableboy, Brandt," Archer said quietly, his teasing turning serious. "You were always a Croft to me, a true brother. When your messenger reached me in London telling of your troubles with Malvern, I dropped everything and mounted a company immediately. Brynn insisted on coming to your aid as well, despite her recent confinement and my foot being well and truly down."

Brandt's voice was choked with emotion. "Thank you."

"You would have done the same for me. You *have* done the same for me. You saved my neck too many times to count, Brandt." They both knew he was speaking of his risky exploits as the Masked Marauder before he married Briannon. Archer shrugged. "You led us a merry chase, but we managed to track you all over Scotland. Though as it turns out, you had everything well in hand." His eyes flicked to Malvern, who was being led away in irons toward the dungeons. "The marquess is wanted for extorting hundreds of thousands of pounds from the Crown in false land and tenant fees. I've been tasked with seeing him back to London to be tried for his crimes, if that's well and good by you. He'll likely be hanged."

"I'll be happy to see the last of him." Brandt suspected Sorcha and her family would as well. He would do everything in his power to make sure that Tarben Castle and its holdings would be returned to the Maclaren.

Archer paused at the top of the stairs, his gray eyes twinkling. "Despite your wounds, it pleases me to see you well and content." The duke's tone grew grave. "When I learned who you'd taken to wife, I'll admit I had my doubts. She has somewhat of a…reputation across Scotland. It has a lot to do with how we tracked you so easily, in fact. The Beast of Maclaren is quite a moniker. But you are, aren't you? Happy?"

There was no malice in his friend's tone, and the truth was, Sorcha wore the nickname proudly. Beast or not, he wouldn't change one hair on her head, or even a single scar. Brandt heard his wife's low laughter echo through the open doors of the keep, and he smiled. Happy seemed too mediocre a word to describe what he felt, but even he couldn't find another that could do his feelings justice. There was no simple word to describe Sorcha and their relationship, or to encompass the enormity of what he felt for her.

With a nod, he looked his best friend in the eye. "She's the best thing that ever happened to me."

Chapter Twenty-Seven

The Montgomerys had been starved of boisterous celebration for so long that when they began to rejoice a few days after their victory, no one seemed able to stop. Even the death of the previous laird did not curtail the festivities; a murderer would not be mourned.

One feast led into another, one song to dozens more; the great hall was overrun with dancing and singing and booming orations by men who, by the end of each spirited account, had been the very warrior to chase off the enemy and single-handedly save Montgomery keep, along with the women and bairns and all the unborn babies that would no doubt make their debut in nine months' time.

Sorcha had never smiled or laughed so much in all her life. The clanspeople here had been starved of merriment, just as she had been, and like her new family, she could not seem to satiate herself. She and Brandt had welcomed the Duke and Duchess of Bradburne, as well as their caravans of servants and soldiers, along with her own father and brothers, and every last Maclaren who had trekked to Montgomery lands. Ronan, she discovered, had won his fight with Coxley that day in the field, slicing the English brute across the back. Coxley had gone down, and Ronan, presuming the man dead, rejoined his men who were still fending off the attack. After Malvern's men had withdrawn, he'd returned for the body, but he'd found naught but a patch of grass, spattered with blood.

Ronan and what remained of his men had turned back toward Maclaren to seek reinforcements. And, though Sorcha had told him she and Brandt were heading north toward the Brodie, the fortified Maclaren army had the luck of passing by the monastery, where Abbot Lewis informed them of Sorcha and Brandt's change in destination.

Sorcha's heart filled at the memory of her brother's words in the hall after the battle…that every last Maclaren warrior has always been, and would always be, willing to die to defend and protect their own. The Maclaren soldiers who had given their lives hadn't just been defending *her*—they'd been defending other Maclarens who would suffer the brutality of Malvern.

"*You* were the one to set our freedom into motion," Ronan had told her. "Because of you, sister, Maclaren is free, and none of the men who stood up died in vain."

The release from the guilt that had plagued her had been almost immediate.

She had spent the last handful of days trying not to think on what might have happened had her clansmen not tracked them to Montgomery. If they had not been there at the marsh when Malvern had dragged her out of the tunnel. And Brandt, every time he saw her expression darkening, would take her hand and kiss the ridge of her knuckles, threatening to distract her if she didn't stop worrying.

"Is that a promise?" she'd whispered once.

"I take my duties as laird quite seriously, Sorcha

Montgomery," Brandt replied, a flare of mischief sparking in his fey-bright eyes. "And it is my duty to make my duchess smile more than she frowns."

"I've been smiling for days," she shot back, and feigning exhaustion, added, "I don't know how much more pleasure I can endure."

Brandt had leaned closer to her ear, his breath hot on her skin. "Come up to our bedchamber with me and I'll show you how much more."

And he had. Her husband's lips and hands had proven time and again that she had a rapacious appetite for pleasure. For *him*. Even now, as Sorcha sat on a blanket spread under the courtyard yew, with Briannon and Catriona deep in conversation at her side, she watched Brandt with longing. He and Archer, along with some of the Maclaren and Montgomery men, were taking a reprieve from the festivities as they repaired the arch over the water well, damaged during the siege. Though the spring weather had returned to a more expected crispness, shirts had been discarded, and bare chests were shining with sweaty exertion.

Brandt still wore a bandage over his left shoulder and one around his calf, but her mother's salve was doing its job. Neither dressing, nor the fast-healing wounds he'd received along his shoulder and ribs during his first battle with Rodric, took away from his air of strength and masculinity. They seemed only to enhance it. Sorcha knew the contours of her husband's chest and stomach and back by heart, and she imagined running her fingers over the dips and swells of his muscles with mounting desire.

Sorcha let her attention drift toward Lord Bradburne, who had clapped his arm around Brandt's shoulders. "Your duke and Brandt get along so well," she said to Briannon.

Catriona entered the conversation then. "'Tis true. I cannae tell ye how glad I am my Brandall had a brother in yer husband, Lady Bradburne."

"And now he has more brothers than he knows what to do with!" Briannon said, the strong Scottish ale she'd been sipping making her voice loud and merry. Catriona and Sorcha laughed, causing Brandt and Archer to look over at them, but they only grinned before turning back to their task.

Yes, her husband's family had grown exponentially. In the corner of the courtyard, two of his new family members—Ronan and Patrick—were sparring with their hefty broadswords. The competition was friendly enough, but there was no mistaking the pride each man was bringing to the exhibition. She glanced to where her youngest brother Niall lounged against the stone wall of the keep, waiting for his turn to show off his sparring skills. Callan stood at his left, his mouth moving, and every now and again, Niall would break into laughter.

Aisla had seated herself on a ledge jutting out from the keep's wall to Niall's right, and more often than not, Sorcha noticed her brother's eyes traveling furtively over her legs, which she'd crossed at the ankles and swung playfully. The lass wasn't oblivious to his glances, either, Sorcha noticed, especially when Aisla shifted her seat to slyly raise the hem of her skirt an inch.

A breeze rustled the new leaves on the yew, bringing the scents of roasting meat and vegetables from the kitchens into the courtyard. Sorcha felt as if she'd glutted herself for days on a banquet of food, and that evening she would do so again. The carousing would continue in the form of a wedding celebration. Her mother, the Duchess of Dunrannoch, was due to arrive with yet more Maclarens by that evening, and Catriona had insisted on a proper reception. She had insisted the water well be repaired and in full use before then, too.

Sorcha wasn't the only one ogling her husband as the men worked—Briannon couldn't seem to keep her eyes off her duke. It was obvious they were very much in love. They made a handsome couple. Sorcha wondered what their daughters looked like and made a mental note to ask Briannon later if she had any portraits of them.

A whimsical sensation fluttered in the pit of her stomach at the thought of bairns, and her gaze swept to her husband. Brandt had never mentioned them, though he had never taken any precautions during their lovemaking *not* to conceive. In truth, Sorcha had never seen herself as a mother. Or perhaps she had never allowed herself to imagine it because of to whom she'd been betrothed.

Though now, with Brandt, envisioning her own family—with bairns who inherited his beautiful fey eyes—suddenly seemed like heaven.

...

Brandt leaned back in his chair on the dais watching the dancing unfold. Nearly a week of feasting had gone by and yet, no one showed any signs of slowing down. Sorcha's mother had arrived the day before, which had necessitated a new round of festivities and marriage celebrations.

Though his wife favored her father in coloring, Brandt could see where she had inherited her backbone of steel. Lady Dunrannoch was a slight woman with chestnut-colored hair. Her eyes were also blue, though not the same vibrant shade as her daughter's. And she was English, hailing from Cumbria, which meant that she and the Duchess of Bradburne had a few acquaintances in common. They sat together at the table, heads bent and smiles on their lips, their husbands engaged in similar conversation. Archer had promised to do what he could to have Tarben Castle and its holdings returned to the duke once Malvern's properties were seized.

Sipping some excellent whiskey that Archer had brought

from the Earl of Langlevit's Dumfries estate, his glance drifted to the throng of dancers. He'd narrowly escaped being dragged to the middle of the hall due to his healing leg, but the truth was, he'd rather watch.

Brandt's gaze sought out Sorcha, who was dancing with Ronan. He would never tire of watching her...whether she was swinging a sword, dancing a Scotch reel, or riding him while caught in the throes of pleasure. She lived life with so much passion, it astounded him. Even now, dressed in a sapphire gown befitting a duchess, she exuded a vitality that made his blood simmer. Her dark hair was pinned in glossy ringlets away from her face, her scars in prominent and proud view. She had never looked more beautiful.

"Ye get that look on yer face every time yer thinking of yer wife," Callan said, plunking down on one side of him. Patrick sat down on the other. "'Twas the same look that young bounder had with our Aisla."

Brandt's eyes narrowed as Niall escorted Aisla back to one of the lower tables for some ale. The two had been getting too close for his comfort as well.

"I could give him a wee thrashing," Callan suggested with a hopeful look, but Brandt shook his head.

With the amount of testosterone in the hall, any scuffle would turn into a big bloody brawl without much provocation. Sorcha's middle brother, Evan, was spoiling for a fight, since he had missed out on the battle, and Brandt would rather not indulge him.

"Aisla can handle herself," he said. "What of you two? No lasses to tempt your palates?"

Patrick shot him a rare smile, his eyes brimming with amusement as a group of young ladies sighed and stared despondently toward where they sat. "There're so many of them that Callan doesnae ken what to do with himself."

His brother puffed his chest and winked. "'Tis no' my

fault the lasses find me bonny."

But Brandt noticed it wasn't only Callan getting attention. A few of the women had their eyes on Patrick. Brandt suspected it would take his brother some time to loosen up, without the specter of Rodric hanging over his shoulder every minute.

Patrick leaned in as Callan took his leave once more to dance with a buxom blonde. "I've been thinking that I'll head south with Lord Bradburne when he leaves. Travel for a bit. See London and surrounds. He offered to introduce me to London society." He trailed off uncomfortably. "Now that ye are laird, I mean. Before my place was here, but now..."

The decision did not surprise him. Brandt expected it was twofold. Patrick did not want to hover as the new laird found his feet, and he also wanted to be free of the ghost of his father, who had chained him to his duty from birth. At least for a time. Brandt understood the inclination.

"Go where you must, but know that your place is here, brother," Brandt told him. "This is your home, and it always will be."

"Thank ye," Patrick said. "Ye'll look after Mother, won't ye? And the wee lass, too, though I expect that'll no' be easy. I dunnae ken what's gotten into Aisla."

"With my life." Brandt grinned, knowing exactly what—or *who*—had gotten into their sister. "Have you told Callan? I daresay his head might just explode."

Patrick laughed, the uninhibited sound drawing a startled glance from their mother. "I'll send for him for a visit once I'm settled." He stood. "In the meantime, I spot a beautiful lass who needs rescuing from an over-ardent Maclaren."

Brant watched the carousing for a few moments longer and stretched out his leg, wincing at the twinge. It wasn't hurting him but tended to stiffen after a while. He kneaded the cramping muscle with the heel of one palm.

"Is it paining you?" a worried voice asked.

He looked up into the gleaming blue eyes of his love, who stood beside his chair. Sorcha's cheeks were bright with flushed color, and Brandt couldn't help himself. He reached for her arm and drew her down into his lap.

"Brandt," she gasped.

"No one's watching," he said with a low laugh. "They're all dancing."

"*Everyone's* watching. Including your mother, and mine."

He kissed her neck, breathing in the fragrant scent of her. "Actually, they look like they're plotting how many heirs they should expect."

Guarded eyes the exact shade of her glittering dress met his. She swallowed and gathered her lower lip between her teeth. "Heirs?"

"We should probably start thinking of that, don't you think?"

"Now?" she said on a breathless gasp.

Brandt grinned at her one-word answers. "I love throwing you off-balance and making you speechless. Though I much prefer doing it with my tongue in your mouth."

"Brandt!" But her color had heightened, and he could feel the clench of her thighs on top of his. He was sure that she could also feel the thickened shape of his arousal, a constant affliction, it seemed, whenever she was near.

"I want you," he told her in a rasping whisper, his knuckles skimming down between their bodies to her trim waist. "I want to put bairns in this flat stomach of yours. I want to see you become round and luscious and beautiful. I want part of me to grow inside of you."

Her mouth went soft and her eyes grew dark at his words. Words he never imagined he'd utter, but everything had changed. *He* had changed. And it was all because of the radiant woman cradled in his arms.

She crawled out of his lap and stood as if he hadn't said

a thing, her beautiful face reserved and expressionless. Then she bent and licked his ear, making aching parts of him throb. "Meet me upstairs in fifteen minutes and dunnae be late, ye ken."

Her hoarse brogue was a seductive promise that nearly unmanned him. It took Brandt more than the allotted fifteen minutes to calm his raging erection enough to stand and not invite ridicule, and another forty-five to take his leave. By the time he climbed the stairs to his bedchamber, his body was almost bursting with anticipation. No doubt her punishment for his tardiness would be dire. Brandt opened the door and closed it, his eyes feasting on the sight that awaited him on the bed.

His gorgeous wife was naked.

And asleep.

With a low chuckle, Brandt undressed, climbed into bed, and then proceeded to wake her in the most delicious way possible. He made love to her with exquisite slowness, bringing her to ecstasy with his hungry tongue and hands before allowing himself his own shuddering release. And afterward, when they lay in each other's arms, spent and satiated, Sorcha looked at him with all the love in her eyes, her hands pressed to her belly. "I hope you succeeded."

"Me, too."

"What do you think he or she will be like?" she whispered as he pulled the blankets over them and drew her back into his chest. Brandt curled his body around hers in a protective embrace, one arm tucked beneath her breasts. He kissed her bare shoulder.

"Strong. Brave. Fierce."

"With your eyes," she said.

He drew his fingers through her long glossy locks that felt like satin in his fingers. "And your hair."

"Your quiet reserve," Sorcha added. "And your humility."

"Your love for life. Your courage."

She tilted her chin toward him, and Brandt took her lips in a soft, sweet kiss. "They'll be loved, won't they? Any children of ours?"

"Without a single doubt. And even if we didn't have this tremendous extended family of ours placing wagers on my manly prowess as we speak, any child would be cherished and adored by the two of us." She laughed, and he stroked her cheek. "I love you, Sorcha, and I will treasure any child made out of that love."

"I love you, too."

Brandt held her close as sounds of the revelry from belowstairs drifted up to them. But there was no other place he preferred to be. Montgomery was a place. Worthington Abbey had been a place. The circle of his wife's arms would always be his home, he knew that now. And for the first time in all his five and twenty years, Brandt's sense of restlessness eased.

Sorcha shifted in his arms, turning to face him. "I forgot to tell you about my dowry. My father brought the documents turning the land over to you."

"I don't need any land."

"You'll want this one," she said. "It's rich in a vein of cairngorm crystals, remember? Scottish topaz. It was why Malvern wanted his hands on it so badly."

It could have been chock full of diamonds for all Brandt cared. Mesmerized by the feel of her velvet skin, he stroked his fingers along her arm, dipping to the curve of her waist and the sensual rise of her hip. "I already have the most precious gem of Maclaren lands in my possession, albeit it's one in the rough."

Sorcha poked him in the shoulder with a mock scowl, but her voice was small when she spoke. "It's true I am rough around the edges. I'll never be like Lady Bradburne. She's so refined and elegant. I feel like a fumbling lummox beside her. Are you sure this…I'm…what you want?"

"Too late to change your mind now, Your Grace," he said with a wolfish grin. "And only a true Highland lass will do. Ye and yer horse."

She pouted prettily. "Ah, I see. This is about Lockie. I should have known."

"Aye, he's mine." His grin widened. "And ye're mine, ye ken?"

"I ken," she said smiling at his play.

"And I happen to *like* your edges." To make his point, he dragged a slow finger up over her hip bone. "These and these," he said, moving to the point of her elbow and up each rib before filling his palm with her scarred breast. Her nipple tautened to a tight peak between his thumb and forefinger. "And especially these."

"Brandt—" Her voice was a breathy moan.

"The real question is," he said, "whether you're willing to be *my* lady."

She threw one limber thigh over his and dragged her fingernails lightly over his chest. "What does that entail?"

"A certain amount of compliance."

Sorcha licked at her lips. "You mean submission?"

"More like surrender." Brandt shifted to crawl over his wife's body. Lifting his weight upon his elbows, he hovered over her, his hips poised over hers. He circled lightly, eliciting a delicious sound from her lips as his unyielding hardness met her pliant softness. "Of the most pleasurable kind."

His wife grinned and wrapped her long, strong legs around him before thrusting her hips upward and over to flip him on his back. "I'll surrender to anything as long as you're here by my side." Her wicked laughter filled the room—and his heart. "Or beneath me as the case may be."

They'd been her words the first time they'd made love, but now they were his.

"I am yours."

Epilogue

Three years later, September 1822
Worthington Abbey, Essex

Screams of bloody murder filled the gardens at Worthington Abbey, making every last hair on Brandt's body stand on end. Good Lord, half a dozen children could make a bloody racket. The Duke of Bradburne's estate grounds had been awash with chaos the last week, ever since the house party had gotten under way. Five days, to be exact. Five long, strained days. Brandt sat back in his chair in the gardens and rubbed his temple, a snifter of whiskey gripped in his other hand as he caught sight of his son, Rabbie, and the Bradburne heir, Brandon—Brandt's godson and namesake—toddling along on matching chubby legs while being chased by their hapless nannies.

It wasn't that he was not overjoyed to be in Essex again. It was only his second time returning to his childhood home since he'd become the Montgomery laird and Duke of Glenross. The first had been to arrange for the transfer of his stables. Lockie, as he'd imagined, had made a fine addition, taking well to Rosefire, the mare he'd had in mind for breeding. He and Sorcha were well on their way with a third foal...a colt who had the makings of a champion.

His precious horses aside, he'd also had much to oversee the last few years in the Highlands, helping to turn the settlements and farms Rodric had long neglected into profitable livelihoods again and earning the respect and trust of his clansmen. Despite his true Scottish roots, he was still a Sassenach to many—mostly because of his clipped English accent—but he hadn't made an enemy yet, and Sorcha assured him it would take only another decade or two before they started to admit they liked him.

It also wasn't as though Briannon's guest list had been filled with names he did not recognize. No, this wasn't like the ostentatious *ton* house parties that the old Duke of Bradburne had been accustomed to holding when Brandt and Archer were lads. This was a reunion, with he and Sorcha, along with the Viscount and Viscountess Northridge, and the Earl and Countess Langlevit all in attendance for the next fortnight. People Brandt truly liked and cared for, and not one of them someone with whom Brandt felt the need to make hollow, pleasant talk.

His discomfort over the last five days had nothing at all to do with his surroundings and everything to do with his wife.

From his seat, he watched Sorcha and Lana, Lady Northridge, strolling through the arbor, one of his wife's hands pressed against the curve of her lower back while another pushed a pram. Lana guided a second pram as they walked an idle pace. The cut of the dress Sorcha wore attempted to conceal the swell of her stomach, but the heavy afternoon breezes were not only rustling the rose shrubs and shaking the trellis, they were also gusting against the yellow fabric, shaping it around the full expanse of her rounded, very pregnant abdomen.

The doctor in Montgomery had been certain by his count that the babe would not come for another month or two at least, and so Sorcha had insisted on attending the reunion to celebrate the Duke of Bradburne's birthday. Briannon had been planning it for so long, she'd argued, and who knew the next time all of them would be able to converge at the same time? He'd relented, unable to deny his lovely wife anything she wanted so desperately that she'd promise not to sit a horse or lift a bow or tax herself in any way.

But they had barely arrived in Essex when Brandt saw the faint frown etching her brow, and the heavy, shadowed look in her eyes. It had been a little over two years since she'd last entered labor, hours later delivering a dark-haired, hazel-eyed boy that Brandt had instantly fallen head over heels in love with. They'd named him Robert William—Rabbie for short—after both grandfathers, and since then he and Sorcha's lives had revolved around him. But two years had not been long enough for Brandt to forget the way his wife had looked a day before she'd gripped her stomach and announced it was time. The frown etching her brow, the shadowed look in her eyes.

And now five days had passed, and every day she grew more reserved. Quieter.

"Just keep drinking," came the advice of the earl sitting beside him. Langlevit smirked into his own snifter of whiskey. "I was in your very shoes months ago."

Considering the earl's twin sons—John and Gregory—currently nestled inside the prams Lana and Sorcha were pushing, were six months old, Brandt figured his concern was as transparent as water.

Langlevit's wife, Irina—enjoying a well-needed respite in the chair beside her husband as her sister, Lana, took her nephews for a quick turn about the garden—chucked the earl lightly on the arm. "Nonsense, Henry. Lady Glenross will have an easy time of it when her babe decides to arrive. Don't worry His Grace unnecessarily."

The countess's labor had been long and difficult, Brandt knew, and from what Sorcha had imparted in whispered confidence just the other night, Langlevit had admitted to Irina that he'd been afraid he'd lose her. But she had come through, and their infants had been hale and hearty. Though Brandt thought he saw a remnant of worry ghost across the earl's eyes as he gazed at his wife.

Birthing was no easy or assured thing. Healthy in body and mind, Sorcha had done well with Rabbie, and Brandt couldn't stand to consider any alternative with this second babe. Still, she looked exhausted. And ready. But it wasn't time…and that was what scared him most of all. Because if the babe came early, it portended complications. Foretelling due dates wasn't an exact science. Even Rabbie had come a few weeks after he'd been due, which had been another of Sorcha's arguments to travel to Essex.

"I wonder only if we should have stayed put in Montgomery with her being so close to her time," Brandt replied as a new burst of screeches erupted from the dogwood trees directly behind him.

"Your wife is healthy," Gray, Viscount Northridge, said, catching his soft comment as he resumed his seat across from them and reached for his refilled snifter. He'd disappeared a quarter of an hour earlier to check on his youngest, eight-month-old Thomas, who was sleeping inside while his wife walked with Sorcha and the Radcliffe twins. Gray was followed by Archer and Briannon. "And the fresh air and walking will do her good."

Langlevit snorted. "Is that your professional opinion, Doctor North?"

North was Gray's nickname, just as Archer was known

to his friends as Hawk, courtesy of one of his lesser titles, the Marquess of Hawksfield.

Gray grinned. "With four children of my own, I'm clearly the most virile of you lot, so yes, it is indeed my expert opinion."

His sister Briannon's eyebrows shot up into her hairline. "Gray! Such talk is entirely inappropriate. What will the servants think?"

"What they've always thought, Brynn dear," he replied with a long draught from his glass. "That we're shocking *ton*."

"Speak for yourself," Archer put in, sitting with a relaxed sigh and stretching his legs out in front of him. "I am the epitome of blue-blooded English decorum."

Brandt couldn't suppress his snort.

Archer had disdained those aristocratic roots of his... until Briannon. Each of the men here, in fact, had been changed in some integral way by the women they'd married. And Sorcha. God, she had changed him the most of all. He'd been rootless, wandering, and adrift in his own head until she had grounded him. Tethered him. He'd found peace because of her...peace in who he was as a son, father, brother, husband. He glanced at Archer, his oldest mate. Brandt had even become a worthier friend for it.

In a word, Sorcha made him *better*.

He was torn from his thoughts by a volley of delighted squealing as Rabbie and Brandon ran at full tilt toward the table looking for sweets left over from the afternoon tea they'd all enjoyed in the garden.

"Papa," his son squealed and climbed up into his lap. "*Pòg.*"

Brandt smiled at the demand for a kiss. Catriona had been teaching him Gaelic and the boy was a quick study. Brandt looked into eyes that were mirrors of his own and kissed his son's pudgy, dirt-smudged cheek with a loud smack, making

Rabbie giggle. The young English nanny hovered, clearly rattled that her young charge had disturbed the adults, which was frowned upon in most aristocratic households. Brandt did not mind. In Scotland, Rabbie had the run of the keep and drove his doting grandmother, along with everyone else, to madness with his antics.

"Getting into trouble, are we, lad?" he said. "Best we listen, aye?"

"I ken, Papa," Rabbie said.

Brandt would never get used to the feeling of wonder that overtook him whenever he looked at the miracle that he and Sorcha had created. Rabbie yawned and rubbed his eyes, clearly in need of an afternoon rest after all the excitement. Brandt kissed him again before handing him off to the waiting nanny.

"It's time for your nap, too," Briannon said to Brandon who had immediately gone to his mother. She kissed him, watching as the nannies took them back to the manse. "They grow up so fast," she murmured. "Don't they?" The duchess's hand fluttered over her midriff and a secret smile crossed her face, one that Brandt was not the only one to notice.

"Brynn," Irina shrieked, her mouth falling open. "You're not…"

Briannon nodded, blushing, her hands grasping her husband's. "Yes, though not very far along."

"What wonderful news," Langlevit said and lifted his glass. "Congratulations, both."

Gray smirked at his sister's announcement. "See? The Findlays are virile. Fertile, I mean." He laughed, narrowly escaping one of Brandon's wooden soldiers that Briannon launched at his head. "It seems that more celebrations are in order!" Grinning at Archer, he clapped his brother-in-law on the back. "If you need any advice, Hawk, on how not to lose your sanity with four children, you know where to find me."

As if on cue, Gray and Lana's nearly four-year-old son, Oliver, and his two-and-a-half-year-old sister, Kate, darted in front of the group, each of them screaming and laughing. A moment later, the reason why came roaring out of the dogwoods behind them. Their older sister, Sofia, now eight, had donned one of the masks her cousins had brought down from the Worthington Abbey attics in order to act out a play during tea that afternoon. The hairy beast mask was a ghoulish-looking thing, and she was clearly enjoying scaring the wits out of her younger siblings. Archer and Briannon's daughters, Clara and Philippa, nearing four and five, followed on her heels, clearly frightened but determined to imitate their daring older cousin.

"Come now, girls, take pity on the young ones," Briannon called out.

"Sofia!" Lana called from where she and Sorcha had stopped strolling. "You'll give them nightmares for a week!"

"Have you heard the news?" Irina asked excitedly as her sister approached to hand over the sleeping twins to the unobtrusively waiting maids. She went to check on the babies, cooing over them gently. "Brynn's expecting."

"How lovely," Lana said, taking Sorcha's arm to help her into the chair beside Brandt.

"Lovely news indeed," Sorcha said with a slightly discomfited smile. "Though I wish for the sake of all mothers that pregnancy was less…everything."

The women laughed and nodded. Brandt wouldn't know. He didn't think he, or any man for that matter, had the strength to withstand such an ordeal. Archer, North, and Langlevit seemed to be of the same opinion as well. Anyone who said that women were the weaker sex was sadly misinformed.

"Less long, less painful, less swollen," Irina said.

"Less hungry," Lana added. "Less thirsty."

Briannon grinned. "Less grumpy, less messy."

Brandt leaned over to stroke his wife's hand, threading her fingers through his. Tired blue eyes met his, and, though a reassuring smile touched her lips, he saw a quick spark of pain. Her teeth sunk into her lower lip as her hand gripped his with terrible force.

"*Oh*," Sorcha breathed, her eyes going wide. Her expression alternated between agony and mortification. "Speaking of less messy," she whispered, "it seems the latest Montgomery has decided to make an appearance."

Everyone jumped into motion at once, and a flurry of servants appeared at Briannon's decidedly unladylike shout. Discussion broke out as to the best way to get Sorcha back to the abbey and whether she should remain in the chair. Someone else gave an order in an authoritative voice to fetch Dr. Hargrove, the longtime physician who had already been summoned to Worthington Abbey by the duke in advance of their arrival as a precaution. He had delivered nearly all of the children in residence, with the exception of Sofia.

"But it's not time," Brandt heard someone say, and realized that it was his own baffled voice.

"Time or not, Your Grace," Irina told him, her violet eyes sparkling, "your *bairn*—that is the proper Scottish term, is it not?—is coming. Now are you going to sit there all day or get up and do something?"

Brandt snapped out of his shock and stood. He leaned over and scooped his pale wife into his arms. He met the shocked gazes of the servants who had been about to lift the chair and the impressed stares of the other men. "I'm stronger than I look."

Even fully pregnant, Sorcha weighed nothing in his arms. He would walk to the ends of the earth this way if he had to. By the time they reached the house, an airy room on the first floor had already been prepared. He deposited her into the wide bed, kissed her clammy forehead, and was instantly shooed from the room.

Bewildered, he stopped a rumpled-looking Dr. Hargrove on his way into the suite. "It's too early, isn't it? For the babe to come?"

"It will be fine, Your Grace," the doctor said, but Brandt thought he detected an odd note of worry in his voice.

Brandt clutched the man's arm, his nostrils flaring. "Don't let...please, don't let..." He trailed off, the awful words clogging his throat. There was no way he could articulate his fears. No way he *wanted* to. But the onset of Sorcha's labor was way too early. "Please do whatever you can," he finally said in a hoarse whisper.

Dr. Hargrove nodded. "Of course."

Brandt sank to his knees on the plush rug and remained there long after the door closed. After a while, he felt strong hands helping him up and leading him down the corridor to a study. Archer's study. A glass was placed into his hand, his body pushed into a chair. He sipped through the unnatural lethargy that had taken hold of his limbs. Felt the burn of whiskey sear a path to his roiling stomach.

"She's in good hands, Brandt." Archer's voice, he registered dimly.

"The best," Langlevit agreed.

"It's too early," Brandt whispered, staring into his drink for answers that weren't there. He set the glass on the table. "I have to be with her."

A firm but gentle hand rested on his shoulder. "Sit."

Brandt looked up into the eyes of his most trusted friend. A friend who he wouldn't hesitate to smash to bits if he kept restraining him.

"You won't do anyone any good going in there," Archer said. "She'll be in labor a while yet."

Brandt shook his head. Rabbie had come right away once the pains had started. Chances were this one would as well...

if there were no complications. His heart lurched. "She's my wife." He swallowed convulsively, his eyes stinging. "You don't understand, I can't lose her."

The hand on his shoulder squeezed. "I do understand. We all do. We've all been there. She'll come through it, Brandt, she *and* your babe. I had every confidence in Dr. Hargrove with Brynn and her weak lungs through three deliveries. He delivered Langlevit's twins and most of North's brood. He is the best doctor in England, do you understand? Nod if you do."

With a shuddering breath, Brandt nodded.

Archer released him, but pulled an armchair close and sat. "Now drink up and tell me about your sister Aisla's wedding."

Brandt blinked, his desperate mind grasping at the suggestion with the ferocity of a starving pauper given a crust of bread.

Aisla had recently married Sorcha's youngest brother Niall. The two eighteen-year-olds had eloped. Though the pair had clearly been interested in each other over the last handful of years, the union had come as a surprise. Mostly due to Aisla becoming pregnant out of wedlock. Niall had escaped from being thrashed to within an inch of his worthless life by Sorcha, who had also been four months pregnant at the time. And then Niall had disappeared, taking Aisla with him. They'd gone to Inverness whereupon they'd gotten married.

And all hell had broken loose.

Especially after the rushed nuptials that no family member on either side had witnessed. Both his and Sorcha's mother had been devastated to learn of the wedding after the fact. Niall had copped a well-deserved thrashing off his own older brother, Ronan, for getting Aisla with child in the first place. And Aisla had not escaped scot-free. The tongue-lashing she'd received from Catriona had echoed all over the Highlands and would be remembered for years. A proper wedding celebration had been planned at Maclaren on Brandt and Sorcha's way back to Montgomery from this visit to Essex.

By the time Brandt had finished recounting that tale, plus a few more about Sorcha's brothers and his own half brothers, Callan and Patrick, his mind had calmed somewhat. To his surprise, more than a couple hours had passed. And he felt pleasantly numb. Though he suspected that that had to do with the bottomless glass of whiskey resting in his fingers.

"Aisla is headstrong," he said, swirling the amber liquid. "But she'll make a good mother. And Niall will make her a good husband if he can get his head out of his arse." He sat back and chuckled. "I don't remember any of us being so stupid at his age."

Archer laughed. "You have a selective memory."

They were all laughing when a knock came at the open door. Brandt leaped to his feet. "Beggin' yer pardon, milords," a maid said with a curtsy. "But Dr. Hargrove sent me to summon the duke."

"Which one?" North joked, but Brandt was already off and running.

Brandt took the fact that the maid was smiling as a good sign, but he still ran pell-mell down the hallway. He pushed open the door and stood on the threshold. His glorious, beautiful warrior of a wife sat propped against a mound of pillows in the bed. The room had been cleared to give them some privacy. Sorcha's face was glowing, and she held a small bundle in her arms.

"Come meet your wee daughter, *leannan*," she told him.

His heart exploded in his chest when he approached and kissed his wife. A *daughter*. A tuft of bronze hair covered her crown, and her face was perfect, though she was indeed wee. He frowned. "Is she supposed to be that small?"

"For her claymore, yes," his wife said with a smile. "But she'll grow. Would you like to hold her?"

Sitting beside her on the edge of the bed, he took his daughter gingerly, her fragile body tiny in his big palms. Her eyes fluttered open, and they were a brilliant blue…just like her mother's. She studied him so alertly, so *fiercely*, that Brandt couldn't breathe. A laugh bubbled up in his throat. He shouldn't be so shocked—after all, warrior goddesses gave birth to only miniature warrior goddesses. She settled in his arms as if determining him to be of no threat she couldn't handle and went back to sleep.

A shriek cut through the moment as Rabbie burst into the room like a whirlwind. "*Piuthar*," he shouted. "Papa, *piuthar*."

Brandt smiled at the Gaelic for "sister" Catriona must have taught him. "Aye, *mo gràidh*, your sister has arrived."

Rabbie climbed up onto the bed and snuggled into Sorcha's side, his hazel eyes wide at the infant cradled in his father's arms. Brandt felt his wife's hand fall upon his arm. He glanced at her holding his son, so much happiness brimming in her beautiful blue eyes that it made him speechless. Brandt felt full. He was surrounded by love and laughter, and so much hope for the future. He had no words, only action. He leaned over to take Sorcha's lips in an achingly tender kiss.

"*Pòg, pòg*," Rabbie chanted, leaning in to plant his own wet kisses on their cheeks. Laughing, Brandt nuzzled Rabbie's neck to his son's chortling delight, and his heart swelled impossibly as his son placed the gentlest of kisses on his baby sister's head. Brandt gathered his family close, kissing both his children, and then his wife again, slowly, sweetly. He had an endless supply of *pògan,* it seemed, enough to last for forever.

"I adore you, my fierce Highland lass," he whispered.

Sorcha grinned. "Not as much as I adore you, my handsome, stalwart Scot."

Authors' Note

Dear Reader,

We absolutely loved writing this final installment of the Lords of Essex series for you! If you enjoyed reading about Brandt and Sorcha in *My Scot, My Surrender*, be sure to check out the other books in the series: *My Rogue, My Ruin* (book one), *My Darling, My Disaster* (book two), and *My Hellion, My Heart* (book three).

We are huge fans of brawny Highlanders with lots of heart (who isn't?) and if you are, too, you will be excited to hear about our upcoming new series, Tartans & Titans, which will feature Aisla's and Niall's story as well as Ronan's story.

We are so grateful to our wonderful editor, Alethea Spiridon, and our brilliant publisher, Liz Pelletier. Thank you to the entire production, design, and publicity teams at Entangled, with special thanks to Crystal Havens, Curtis Svehlak, Holly Bryant-Simpson, Riki Cleveland, Heather Riccio, Melanie Smith, Anita Orr, and Erin Dameron-Hill. To our loyal readers, thank you for reading our books. Lastly, to our amazing families, we love you.

Be sure to check out EntangledPublishing.com for many more awesome reads in the meantime. And again, thank you so much for being such great supporters and advocates of great books! Happy reading!

Fondly,
Amalie and Angie

About the Authors

Amalie Howard's love of romance developed after she started pilfering her grandmother's novels in high school when she should have been studying. She has no regrets. A #1 Amazon bestseller and a national IPPY silver medalist, she is the coauthor of the Lords of Essex historical romance series, as well as several award-winning young adult novels critically acclaimed by Kirkus, Publishers Weekly, VOYA, School Library Journal, and Booklist, including *Waterfell*, *The Almost Girl*, and *Alpha Goddess*, a Kid's IndieNext pick. She currently resides in Colorado with her husband and three children. Visit her at www.amaliehoward.com.

Angie Morgan lives in New Hampshire with her husband, their three daughters, a menagerie of pets, and an extensive collection of paperback romance novels. She's the coauthor of the Lords of Essex historical romance series, as well as several young adult books, including The Dispossessed series written under the name Page Morgan. Critically acclaimed by Booklist, Publisher's Weekly, Kirkus, School Library

Journal, VOYA, and The Bulletin, Angie's novels have been an *IndieNext* selection, a *Seventeen Magazine* Summer Book Club Read, and a #1 Amazon bestseller. Visit her at www.AngieMorganBooks.com.

Discover the **Lords of Essex** *series...*

MY ROGUE, MY RUIN

MY DARLING, MY DISASTER

MY HELLION, MY HEART

Discover more Amara titles…

THE BITTERSWEET BRIDE
an *Advertisements of Love* novel by Vanessa Riley

Widow Theodosia Cecil needs a husband to help protect her son. Placing an ad in the newspaper, no one is more surprised than she when her first love, the man she thought dead, reappears. Ewan Fitzwilliam has been at war for six years. Now he's back but Theo will not consider marrying him. They must overcome bitter lies from the past and Theo must reveal her deepest secret in order to reclaim the love that has long been denied.

LADY EVELYN'S HIGHLAND PROTECTOR
a *Highland Hearts* novel by Tara Kingston

Playing bodyguard is not in Gerard MacMasters's plan but Lady Evelyn Hunt is in danger, and it's up to him to keep her alive. After a crushing betrayal at the altar, Evelyn wants nothing to do with love. Kissing a gorgeous rogue is one thing, but surrendering her heart is another. When she stumbles upon a mysterious crime, nothing prepares her for the dashing Highlander who may be her hero—or her undoing.

THE MAIDEN'S DEFENDER
a *Ladies of Scotland* novel by E. Elizabeth Watson

Madeline Crawford is a daughter of the disgraced Sheriff of Ayr. Fierce Highlander Teàrlach MacGregor was her father's head guardsman. They dream of a future together. Those dreams come to naught when Madeline is betrothed to the son of her warden. Madeline and Teàrlach's love is forbidden but Teàrlach vows to fight, even the king, to make her his.

TYING THE SCOT
a *Highlanders of Balforss* novel by Jennifer Trethewey

At first, Alex Sinclair, the future Laird of Balforss, has difficulty convincing Lucy FitzHarris to go through with their arranged marriage. Once Lucy arrives, she cannot resist the allure of her handsome Highland fiancé. But when Alex betrays Lucy, she is tricked into running away. Alex must rein in his temper to rescue his lady from unforeseen danger and Lucy must swallow her pride if she hopes to wed the Highlander she has come to love.

Printed in Great Britain
by Amazon